I0611964

SAMURAI SQUADRON II

SPINWARD FRINGE BROADCAST 19

RANDOLPH LALONDE

ALSO BY RANDOLPH LALONDE

FANTASY

Highshield

Brightwill

NEM: Awakening

NEM: Crimson Shores

SCIENCE FICTION

THE SPINWARD FRINGE SERIES

Spinward Fringe Broadcast 0: Origins

Spinward Fringe Broadcast 1 and 2: Resurrection and Awakening

Spinward Fringe Broadcast 3: Triton

Spinward Fringe Broadcast 4: Frontline

Spinward Fringe Broadcast 5: Fracture

Spinward Fringe Broadcast 6: Fragments

The Expendable Few: A Spinward Fringe Novel

Spinward Fringe Broadcast 7: Framework

Spinward Fringe Broadcast 8: Renegades

Spinward Fringe Broadcast 9: Warpath

Spinward Fringe Broadcast 10: Freeground

Spinward Fringe Broadcast 10.5: Carnie's Tale

Spinward Fringe Broadcast 11: Revenge

Spinward Fringe Broadcast 12: Invasion

Spinward Fringe Broadcast 13: Warriors

Spinward Fringe Broadcast 14: Rebel

Spinward Fringe Broadcast 15: Pursuit

Spinward Fringe Broadcast 16: Hunters

Spinward Fringe Broadcast 17: Clash

Spinward Fringe Broadcast 18: Samurai Squadron

Spinward Fringe Broadcast 19: Samurai Squadron II

Spinward Fringe Broadcast 20: Samurai Squadron III (2024)

OTHER SCIENCE FICTION TITLES

Psycho Electric - A Spinward Fringe Novel

The Last of the Bullet Chasers - A Spinward Fringe Short Novella

Rogue: Assembly

THE CHAOS CORE SERIES

Trapped

Cool Pursuit

Savage Stars

HORROR

Dark Arts

AUDIOBOOKS

Spinward Fringe Broadcast 0: Origins
Spinward Fringe Broadcast 1: Resurrection
Psycho Electric - A Spinward Fringe Novel

Other Audiobooks are available on the Google Play Store as
Auto-Narrated performances.

www.RandolphLalonde.com

Samurai Squadron II: Spinward Fringe Broadcast 19

This is a work of fiction. Names, characters, places and incidents either are the product of the author's imagination or are used fictitiously. Any resemblance to actual persons, living or dead, events or locales is entirely coincidental.

All rights reserved.
Copyright 2023 Randolph Lalonde
EBook ISBN: 978-1-988175-60-7
Print Edition ISBN: 978-1-988175-59-1
Cover by Randolph Lalonde with images provided by Adobe Stock

Thank you for purchasing this book.

If you would like to purchase, preview other books by Randolph Lalonde or contact the author for any reason please visit my website.
www.RandolphLalonde.com

ONE

On Her Feet

THERE WERE MORE ships in orbit than the last time they visited, and Minh-Chu started to see that it was already becoming a busy port. The halls leading to the Bitter End's Lobby had been cleaned, but it wasn't easy to tell. The problem was that, unless you were one of the Rebel Captains, with your own slip on the station, it would take over twenty hours to land and visit.

Shamus Frost had set a hard cap of fifteen thousand people on the station at a time, and the station was at that capacity. Minh-Chu wasn't accustomed to seeing people in the broad hallways. There were dozens of them along the way to the Lobby, many of them camped out, some on a blanket where they laid out random knick nacks and small space-farer essentials that they were trying to sell. Leon, the officer in charge of the Privateering Initiative for Haven Fleet, was walking beside them. "Why are there so many people in the port hallways?"

"We're working to restore the accommodations as fast as we can, but there are only so many repair drones. They stay here because it's warm, and there's air," Leon replied apologetically.

"Where did they come from?" Minh-Chu asked as he and Easy followed Alice and Iruuk down the hall.

"The station has become a dumping ground for unwanted crewmembers and passengers," Leon replied. "Frost hasn't had the people to provide any kind of port control or security, so he's turned his focus inward, let the next mayor try to figure it out. On the brighter side, Carnie's property in the station is looking better than ever, and the security there is tight. I bet he's enjoying the tour."

Minh-Chu knew two things about their visit to the Bitter End. They were there to pick up new crewmembers, including a few pilots and that it would be a brief stop. Alice had Iruuk on her left and Theodore on her right. The Clever Dream was nearly empty. Dame and Nigel remained aboard to monitor things from there and to keep the ship ready.

Minh-Chu didn't know much about what Alice wanted to do on the station but he was pretty sure she wasn't just there to pick people up. He was told to come armed, and everyone in their small party was. Minh-Chu and Easy had their heavy armour, but they were retracted into the shape of a black bomber jacket and combat boots. Alice's suit was similar, but instead of being black, her vacsuit was powder blue, a colour she'd become known for, and her long coat was glossy black with a new design that had it split up the middle like long suit tails. There were slits down the sides of the coat too and it was shorter in the front. He had no idea where the design came from, but it and the higher collar made her look otherworldly in a way, and certainly a little regal.

Her confidence was good to see, but Minh-Chu's frustration was growing as he considered how little he knew. "Wait, stop, I can't do this again."

She did, and Iruuk, who was in armour that conformed to his fur, making him look like he'd been dipped in silver with the exception of his cocking head, regarded him, wide-eyed. Alice turned towards Minh-Chu and asked; "What's up?"

"Jake did this three days ago, and now he's hanging out in a luxury suite on Gold Haf, waiting for... who knows what?"

"Did what?" Iruuk asked.

"Took me and a few of my pilots into a situation after only telling me half of what was going on, or what could happen. You know, he only told me about the first half of the plan, not the second, where he jumped out of a perfectly good fighter and flew back to Gold Haf in nothing but stealth armour." Minh-Chu didn't know how irritated he really was until he was saying it out loud.

Before Alice or anyone else could reply, a young man sitting against the wall to their left held a pair of slender tubes up. "Gobber sticks? Watermelon and Citrus."

Minh-Chu gave him a ten-pip chip, taking the opportunity to cool down. "Sure. One of each. Wait, how old are they?"

He nodded and gave him one of each. A bad deal for candy that should have cost a single pip for four. "Fresh as you'll get unless you can fab them yourself. Big flavour. I have gum, too."

"Thanks," Minh-Chu said, slipping the candy into an inner

pocket of his jacket. His command and control unit chirped, signalling that it was safe foodstuff.

Iruuk gave him a five platinum coin for a citrus stick and they started walking down the corridor again. "Turning an audio scrambler on. No one will hear us unless they come within five metres."

"All right, now we can talk," Alice said.

So, Minh-Chu calmly started over, more calmly. "I'm impressed that you've gotten on your feet, and have some kind of plan after being back for three days."

"But you need to know more about why we're here?" Alice asked.

"Wait, is that why you're not letting me in on everything you're planning for this trip? Telepathy?" Minh-Chu asked. "I mean, I get it, if you already checked with my brain and it told you I'd be fine with everything that'll be going on, then why fill me in, I guess."

"That's not exactly how telepathy works, besides, I've turned that so far down that it's just a little extra sense, barely anything. I'm not taking any risks. No, I've just been doing a lot of thinking and I'm not really looking forward to what I might have to do."

"Which is? I mean, Jake just surprised me because I didn't know half of what he did. If you want my help here, let me in. I know things, I've seen stuff."

"Okay, sorry," Alice replied, her cool expression cracking with a smile. "I guess some of my Dad's habit of planning until the last second and carrying most of the weight on his shoulders is rubbing off."

"It's not always what it's cracked up to be, that habit," Easy said under his breath. "Just sayin'."

"He's right. So, we're picking our people up and..." Minh-Chu waited expectantly.

"I want to see how many ships I can get on their way to the Rose system in one hour. I know Yawen and Sel are with us, as usual, so we'll be going back with two destroyers at least. Leon's signed several corvette captains up as Privateers, so I want them along too. Haven Fleet has extended kill bounties for Order ships, so they don't even have to capture anything."

"Just help us blow the enemy out of the sky," Minh-Chu added. It was encouraging, and he would have discovered that too, but managing Samurai Squadron took up most of his time, so it would have been a while before he got around to reading the Privateering Initiative Update.

"Aside from that, word got out that I was off my feet, so I need to show everyone that I'm fine," Alice said.

"So, are you okay?" Minh-Chu asked.

"My head has never been clearer," she replied. "I mean, it feels like a good thing, but I'm looking forward to having a second opinion. For all I know, my brain is as smooth as an egg and my thinking seems clearer because I have the thought capacity of a rim weasel."

"Um, the scans show good, dense brain features," Iruuk corrected.

"I know, I was just kidding." Alice was leading the way again as they approached the armoured double doors leading to the Lobby proper. They were textured to look like old, heavily varnished wood, but Minh-Chu knew they had a thick metal core. He'd taken a few minutes to have Frost's update speed read to him while he was flying between the Triton and the surface. The private manufacturing centre was already up and running, and security throughout the active parts of the station had been shored up. The problems they faced outside of the large section claimed by Carnie resembled those of a small town, and Minh-Chu didn't envy the acting mayor.

Four security androids, their faces shaped like bare metal human skulls, regarded them, then opened the Lobby doors. It was nearly at capacity. Every table, booth and stool was occupied, with everyone else standing in groups.

Yawen was surrounded by crewmembers from her ship, the Renegade. Sel Marda wasn't far off, accompanied by crew from his ship, the Hammer. Minh-Chu saw that it was the custom. He saw ship names on jackets, vacsuits, and vests. Most of them were new: The Loose Debtor, Overcharge, Merchant Call, Marra, and Dread Shot. Some of these newer crewmembers were casually mixing with people from other ships, but not all. At a glance, the atmosphere seemed casual, but they were waiting for something.

Heads turned towards Alice and silence passed over the room like a slow wave. It was during that growing silence that Minh-Chu spotted two short, stocky Nafalli who were definitely descended from the burrower tribes: Faloo and Noro. Woone, a Nafalli who looked like she could be from a heritage that mixed with Tree and Burrower Tribes was there as well, and they approached eagerly.

They weren't alone. Quan, a group of six marines in black vacsuits, but lacking their more complex heavy armour, and a crowd of other people in vacsuits that had been reshaped into more casual styles were coming over as well. Then, as Minh-

Chu stood beside Alice, he noticed that she was starting to grin, and following the direction of her gaze, he saw why.

Captain Sel Marda had his arm around a younger man who Minh-Chu recognized from the pilot rosters of Haven Fleet. Harry Marda, who was more well known by his callsign; Ram, was a good pilot who was always uptraining, with less of an eye on competition in the sims. What was more important at that moment was that both the brothers were beaming. They came forward almost as quickly as the Nafalli. Captain Marda called out; "Look who's come to join your Squadron, Ronin! My own brother."

"I'll put a Samurai Squadron jacket on his shoulders the moment we get to the Squad Room. That is, if you can live up to your record," Minh-Chu said, shaking Ram's hand. The brothers were elated.

"Not so fast, Commander," Captain Marda said with a wink. "I'm offering him a turn at the helm of the Hammer. A starfighter might not be enough for him after that."

"I'll only be on the Hammer for a few days, I need to catch up with my brother, the Captain. Think you could hold on to that jacket for a tick?" Ram asked.

"Since it's family, sure, but I'll be sending some viewing material your way," Minh-Chu replied.

Meanwhile, Alice was enveloped in more than one furry Nafalli embrace, and Woone spent some extra time with Iruuk as they clung to each other for a time. Yawen got into the mix, and took her turn, taking Alice into her arms and kissing her on the cheek. "Don't do that, okay? No more point blank explosions for you."

"I'll do my best," Alice replied. "I've been meaning to ask, where'd you get the new armour?"

"Oh," Yawen replied, looking down at the transparent red layer of hardened pieces over her yellow vacsuit. It covered her vital areas and had a slightly different shape this time. "I ran into some people from Grace, and they offered it as a trade for one of our small shuttles. The stuff is a combination of nanobots and a new kind of transparesteel. It works with the vacsuit's reactive program, so it can move, stretch and flex. I'd give you one if I had a spare, but you'll have to settle for the tech specs."

"Sure," Alice replied. As they spoke, Minh-Chu noticed that there was a kind of metal backpack inside the gel-like armour on the rear side of the suit.

Instead of being intrusive and scanning that himself, he decided to ask for the technical specifications of Yawen's new armour later. Quan approached Alice then, a fake-looking smile frozen on his face. Alice's cheer visibly shrank away as she made eye contact with him. "It's good to see you again, Alice. You seem well."

She leaned in and gave him a hug. "Thank you for coming out here for me."

"I'm happy I did," he replied, worry in his eyes. If Minh-Chu was standing practically anywhere else, he was sure he would have missed what he said next; "There are very bad people here. Murderers."

"I know, not all of our allies are going to be..." Alice started.

She stopped as he shook his head slowly. "I understand, but even without a direct read, which I do not do unless I have permission or am under threat, I can tell people like Sel, Ethan, and most of the others are good at heart, and want the right things, but there is one here who revels in cruelty. They have done something unthinkable."

All levity was gone from her as Alice asked; "Who?"

Yawen, Sel and many of the others there heard her simple question. There was no way the humans there could have overheard what Quan told her, so Minh-Chu knew that everyone was aware that someone on the station had done something that they knew she wouldn't approve of. It was Sel Marda who stepped up. "Kiri Cruise, Captain of the Overcharge. She brought a load of high-tech scanning, science gear and supplies in this morning."

"She's been bragging about hitting a Science Ship," Yawen added. "I asked if it was an Order affiliate, and she told me to mind my business. I was going to corner and press a couple of her crew, but thought I'd wait until you came in."

"We thought it would be better," Captain Marda said.

"She just applied to the Privateering program day before last," Leon said, bringing her record up. "The Overcharge checks out, but I haven't done an interview with her or her first officer."

"She's looking to join the Rebel Captains, seems pretty sure she'll get in," Sel said.

"Where is she?" Alice asked.

Before anyone could answer with words, they were looking at a small group of crewmembers wearing fresh white and green uniforms. They all had a logo on their shoulders - a tree on white with curling branches. "That's the Nebula Scout insignia," she said as she started for them at a march, her hands loose at her sides. The posture was one Minh-Chu had seen more times than he could ever count in the military. She was ready to draw and fire or move at an instant's notice.

Iruuk, Theodore, Minh-Chu, Easy, Yawen and a small crowd of marines who hadn't officially joined the crew of the Triton yet followed her. Faloo, Noro and Woone caught up. They were the last to realize that a confrontation was about to happen.

"I knew I should have handled this before you got here," Yawen said apologetically. "I know exactly what you'd do."

"Maybe," Alice replied as the half dozen crewmembers of the Overcharge who were there turned. Some of them were still cheerful after seeing how serious Alice was. It seemed like a silent jeer, and Minh-Chu wondered if she would take it as an insult, a sign that these people already weren't taking her seriously. In a clear, loud voice that was earned in her short time in the Apex Officer Training Program, she asked; "I'm looking for the Captain of the Overcharge."

"Right here," Captain Cruise said as two crewmembers moved out of the way. She was wearing a suit with extra armour that looked like it was made to withstand intense interstellar radiation. The white and green colour scheme and logos matched the simpler gear her crew wore.

Captain Cruise was still in a celebratory mood; "Captain Valent? I've been looking forward to meeting you. I'm thinking of joining your group here. The Rebel Captains. I mean, the name isn't great, but we can work on that once I decide where me and my crew fit in. Oh, and I picked something up for you," she said, offering a small oval device. "These are pretty expensive, a high-gain scanner and recorder that..."

"You put these on your shoulder or helmet," Alice said,

accepting it and turning it over in her hand. "You stole this from a science ship along with those uniforms." It was a statement.

Captain Cruise's expression fell into one of worry, but Minh-Chu doubted her sincerity as she replied; "Was I not supposed to? No one aboard said she knew you or anyone here in the Shattered End."

"Did you destroy it?" Alice asked, her expression and tone devoid of emotion.

This was a dangerous moment, judging from Minh-Chu's experience with Jake. If she was still similar enough to him, then she was focusing on the moment, standing ready, perched on the edge of making a decision that would lead to a drastic chain of events. "No, we were going to take it, but after we got their food, fuel and most of their gear, the crew put some kind of field up around their bridge and charged the deck throughout the rest of the ship. I lost two guys, so we left. Well, for now. We'll get back to it when their power reserves are gone."

"Were you starving? Out of water or food?" Alice asked.

"No. It was a good haul," Captain Cruise replied with a shrug, her worried facade fading quickly. "What? Every captain here has done the same."

"No, we haven't," Sel Marda said through his teeth.

Yawen regarded him and shook her head slightly as if to tell him to keep out of it.

"Where'd you leave them? What are their last known coordinates?" Alice asked.

"Why would I tell you? You'll just take the ship for yourself and screw me out of the prize," Captain Cruise replied.

"Restrain her crew," Alice ordered calmly. Iruuk, Noro and the marines that came in with Quan got to work right away.

Captain Cruise started reaching for her sidearm. Alice shook her head. "You don't want to do that. There's a greasy spot in the far corner from the last guy who tried something here."

"You can't intimidate us," Captain Cruise said. Alice caught the woman's collar with a snap as she drew her pistol and placed the broad muzzle of it against Cruise's forehead. It happened so quickly that Minh-Chu could only watch.

Iruuk and the marines had the rest of her crew on their knees, their hands bound behind their backs with strips in seconds. Captain Cruise was trying to look unfazed, but the colour was draining from her face, and she glanced around, looking for a way out before staring into Alice's eyes. "You're not going to shoot me. You'd never get the coordinates."

"I'll shoot you, then I'll get the information out of him," Alice said, pointing her sidearm at the crewmember to her left. "Or her. Or him. I'll send boarding teams to your ship and check the logs. Then it'll be mine. We need ships more than people now."

"What if I give you the coordinates?" Captain Cruise asked.

"Then I'll send a rescue team out there," Alice replied, still calm.

"No, what will happen to me?" Captain Cruise asked.

Alice's lip curled into the merest hint of a sneer. "Whatever happened to that explorer crew will happen to you."

"Dodd, send her the details on the Frekse," Captain Cruise said.

A moment later, the location data on the exploration ship was sent to every communicator in the area. Alice turned to Minh-Chu and said; "I'm going to send the Clever Dream out, it's the fastest thing we have. Do you have someone who can lead a rescue?"

"I'm your man. I'll scramble a few more fighters and dock them to the Dream so they have cover and extra hands if they need them," Minh-Chu said.

"They may be out of air or power already. We took all their reactor fuel before they pushed us off the ship with that trick," Captain Cruise said.

"Right, we're running back to the hangar," Minh-Chu said.

"I'm going with you," Iruuk said, and every Nafalli there nodded their heads.

"All right, we're running faster then," Minh-Chu said with a chuckle, turning and leading the way until Iruuk leapt over him and took off on all fours.

The last thing he heard Alice say was; "Captain Vega. Target the Overcharge and lock weapons onto it. Destroy it if it tries to leave, and slag anything coming or going."

TWO

A Small Jump

IT TOOK LONGER than Minh-Chu liked for his pilots to return to their Archangel fighters and latch onto the Clever Dream. "Come on, Breaker, we've got to go," he said over their secure channel.

"Got it, latched, locked," Breaker replied.

"We're off. Make sure all your dampeners are running and synced," Dame said from the controls of the Clever Dream as it lifted off. The ship's rise was so rapid that the hangar doors above barely had enough time to open like an iris. As soon as they were a quarter kilometre away from the port, the main engines throttled up to maximum. The inertial dampeners in Minh-Chu's fighter whined for a moment as they adjusted to the gravitational forces.

He looked through his cockpit window to the trail of broken

stone running behind the shattered planet as they left its gravitational pull. There was no atmosphere, making the view so clear that it almost seemed artificial. It was difficult to judge distance and scale with the naked eye without the haze of an atmosphere. "Everyone do another systems check. This could be a trap."

"I'm glad I'm not the only one thinking it," Easy replied over comms. "I mean, I don't really think it's a trap, but, you know, there's always a chance. I don't know these people, right?"

The Clever Dream turned away from the trail of asteroids, meteors and dust. The space in front of the Clever Dream split, revealing another dimension where eerie blue light fitfully danced in auras and hot streaks. The ship slipped through the portal and his instruments told him they were barely in the new space. The forces around them were trying to push Clever Dream and the fighters attached to it back into their home dimension. It was that same energy along with a protective wormhole that let them travel many orders of speed faster than normal. Space didn't have the same meaning there either. According to Minh-Chu's understanding, pointing your wormhole through different kinds of energy and certain areas changed how much distance you could cover as much as your rate of acceleration. The mechanisms and software within their Quad Drives made sense of it and plotted courses for pilots, and he was thankful for that.

Minh-Chu's system check finished with green marks across the board There were several instruments that he couldn't test while they were outside of normal space, but they'd been looked over four times that day, so he was confident that they were fine. "Auto-check passed."

"I'm all good here," Pixie announced.

"My bird checks out," Breaker said.

"All systems normal," Easy replied. "Again."

"The Clever Dream is perfect," Dame announced, surprising Minh-Chu, who wasn't actually asking that she run through her checklist manually or with the onboard artificial intelligence's help. Lewis probably finished the diagnostics of the whole ship in ten seconds or less.

"How's the rescue team? Anyone have real experience with boarding operations or assistance?" Minh-Chu asked.

"According to the records, Iruuk has limited experience as a volunteer and the required officer training but he's not the most qualified here. The rest are not prepared to lead this mission," Lewis replied on a private channel with Minh-Chu. "I recommend you do it."

He hesitated for a moment then replied; "I'm in a fighter," Minh-Chu said.

"The likelihood of encountering resistance after we've determined that this isn't a trap is extremely low, if that makes you feel better. You leading the mission makes me feel better. You have a history of evading difficulty and have shown that you handle the worst circumstances well," Lewis insisted.

"All right, you've got it," Minh-Chu said. He looked at the location of the Frekse again and spoke on the encoded mission channel. "I'm taking the lead. Anyone else notice that the coordinates and trajectory of the Frekse put it on course for the Shattered End? It's like it was on approach, or trying to study it from a distance."

"I know," Breaker replied. "Looks like they found it somehow, maybe tracked it down from its old spot? You know, before the big explosion that sent it away from its home system."

"Curiosity can get you into trouble," Easy grumbled.

That ended the discussion on a sour note, so Minh-Chu got back to business. "Lewis, do you have any defence androids aboard?"

"Only four. Alice wanted to make as much space in the Clever Dream as possible for new crewmembers. She didn't want to use shuttles to transport them to the Triton," the AI replied.

"So much for that," Minh-Chu said. "All right. We might need them, depending on how much damage there is aboard the explorer ship. How are the volunteers?"

"They know how to prepare for this and are trained on the gear we had in storage," Lewis replied.

"Good, because we're about to come out," Minh-Chu said as he watched the transit timer count down to zero. The Clever Dream left the bright space behind, and it took a moment for his eyes to adjust to the starry void beyond. He looked at his instruments first. They were where they expected to be, millions of kilometres behind the Shattered End. The tactical map in his head showed one ship, and he used visual scanners to zoom in on it.

"Shodan Yards Fifteen-Sixty," Easy said appreciatively. "Looks like the explorer model, all right. They've got the enhanced arrays."

"That thing's taken a beating," Pixie said.

It was true. The once long, sleek semi-oval ship sported scorch marks and bent sections of the hull. It was a design that Minh-Chu saw before, a corvette class model that many people and small companies enjoyed repurposing. The rearmost hangar was open. There wouldn't be enough room for the Clever Dream, but there was plenty of space for his fighter. "Everyone actively scan. I want to see if this is bait. I'll contact whoever's on board." Minh-Chu sent the standard hailing ping on every channel, and even activated the encrypted calling system that people used for more private communications.

A second later it felt like his heart dropped into his stomach as a red graphic appeared on his communications display. "I'm getting a Standard Distress Response that's telling me life support has already failed, there is no fuel and they have less than one percent of their power reserves left. I'm landing in the rear hold."

Dame was calm and clear as she replied; "Iruuk is ready with the marines. We cannot scan through several sections of the ship. Be careful."

Minh-Chu let the more detailed schematic slip into his mind and his mental image of the tactical map became muddy. If it were Ashley in his place, he was sure she could hold both in her awareness at the same time, but he didn't force it. There were other things to concentrate on, like his approach on the small hangar. He manually increased the shield recharge rate and set his thrusters to fine control so he could manoeuvre in the confined space. As he entered through the ripped metal doors he flipped a switch that activated the emissive properties of his hull. His Archangel fighter glowed bright white, and the whole landing bay was bathed in the eerily clear luminance.

"This place has been scraped. I see landing spots for three small shuttles, open excursion bins, and equipment racks. It looks like the crew of the Overcharge took everything in the hold at least," he said. "The deck plates show scorching, my sensors say it's from arcing electricity, but there's no power now." His scanners picked up several bodies down the hall. "Forwarding my scan results, try to figure out what happened here, please."

Lewis replied a few seconds later. "You are right. There is no power running through the deck plating. Four humans were electrocuted. Three were shot. I don't see any evidence of functional traps inside the ship, but there are still some relatively small compartments that are resisting scans."

"I see them on the map, thanks Lewis," Minh-Chu said, deactivating his shields and bringing his fighter down to the deck. "Come on in, Iruuk. Bring three of your best. Make sure there's a complete seal on all suits. I don't want any of us to get fried. Pixie, Easy, Breaker, you're on overwatch."

"Starting a patrol," Breaker replied.

The tactical display inside his cockpit showed Iruuk and three marines flying from the rear of the Clever Dream to the hangar. The barrier thrusters built into their heavy armour made it look like they were dressed in horizontal bands of light as they thrust towards their destination, flipped around, and then decelerated.

Old instincts were taking hold as Minh-Chu activated his heavy armour. It spread from his thick bomber jacket and boots as horizontal slats covered him and affixed to the base of his helmet. An icon in the bottom left of his visor display showed that he had a full seal. If he made contact with a charged surface or cable the electricity would pass over the outer layer of his suit. He opened the compartment built into the back of his seat and took the survival package out. It affixed to the back of his suit like a backpack, adding to his armour. He regarded the rifle beside it then decided to leave it there and closed the compartment. Instead, he checked his sidearm, pulled a hand scanner from the bottom of his pack and activated it.

"We're ready, Sir," Iruuk said over their proximity radio. The three marines with him were in brand new heavy armour from the hold of the Clever Dream. The soles of their boots gripped the hull using a dynamic adhesive layer that clung and released on a microscopic level as they walked.

Minh-Chu climbed down from his fighter and led the way into the ship. The hand scanner was giving him more detail, but he still wasn't getting through the three compartments they couldn't see through. "We're going to sweep the open corridors on our way to the compartment I'm marking as 'C9.' It's a room just off the main hallway. This ship has one corridor running right up the middle. I don't want to branch off that unless we have to."

"Sir, shouldn't we head straight for the bridge? There may be security footage or internal sensors that can show us the location of survivors," a Marine suggested.

"Not yet. Follow me," Minh-Chu replied. It wasn't time to explain why, but he'd be happy to sit down with the marine later. There were scorch marks from pulse weapons and an armoured door that had been cut through.

"The crew put up a fight," Iruuk said mournfully. "I can't imagine being on an exploration ship, probably just curious like Easy said. They shouldn't have run into trouble. I hate pirates."

"It happened suddenly. I think the Overcharge came in at high speed, firing a couple of missiles ahead to get through the hangar doors. They've done this before." There was an efficiency in how the emergency doors were cut and where the crew of the Frekse were when they were killed. To the left and right there were laboratories with botanical and biological samples of every kind, and several scientists who were killed while they were at work. The looting must have taken hours after the ship was taken. Minh-Chu didn't know exactly what the hanging hoses and cables were attached to in the labs, but he was pretty sure the crew of the Overcharge made off with canisters and devices. The plants were dead, exposed to vacuum. Biological samples, including several animals, were drifting in their enclosures, and transparent tanks with submerged samples had frozen.

"Those two support cabinets have Edxi samples in them," Iruuk said. "Not large enough to be complete organisms, and they're not eggs either."

"Stay focused, if there are survivors they'll be here," Minh-Chu stopped at a secure storage door. It was like a vault, over a metre thick. "This chamber is meant to shield everything inside from heavy radiation and impacts. It's very old tech, but it works without power."

"There was probably something like this on the First Light, right?" Iruuk asked.

"The inner hull of the ship," Minh-Chu replied with a nod. "It was thicker, actually. Made to withstand combat before energy shielding was common in that part of the galaxy." As he spoke he plugged into a data port that was built into the door. "I'm hoping that at least some of the crew were able to hide in here with an air supply. Maybe a heater."

"Should we check the other vaults?" Iruuk asked.

"No. None of them is large enough for a person. They look

like specimen drawers and cabinets, judging from the shapes of unscannable parts of the ship," Minh-Chu replied.

The door panel lit up, drawing power from his command and control unit. He sent a rescue signal through, identifying himself as an independent crew from the Clever Dream out of the Haven System. He added a personal message; "The pirates are gone and we've established a defensive perimeter around your ship. We are here to assist." He set his comm-con unit to start translating his message into a long list of languages. "Dame, forward everything we're recording to the Triton and Alice. Add an exception for the Sciences department. We're here to record a crime, not to steal research."

"That is admirable. Communications are sending everything on as you ordered," Dame replied.

"This is horrible. Do you think anyone survived?" Iruuk asked.

Minh-Chu felt the floor shudder and the vault door started to open outward. He moved out of the way and was relieved to see three people in emergency vacuum suits. "They're hypoxic. Connect to their suits, refresh their oxygen and power supplies." He moved in and turned the nearest survivor around so he could connect a line to the small support pack on his back. Once it was connected he turned him back around and looked through his face visor. He had a short, neat beard and a trustworthy face. His eyes opened, he looked around the compartment and began speaking in a foreign language that seemed flowery despite his desperation. "This one's good," announced a marine as a female survivor roused.

"Three out of three," Iruuk announced as the survivor he

was assisting looked at him and froze. "It's all right. My fur looks like metal because of my armour. I'm a normal Nafalli beneath."

"I was barely conscious," the bearded man said to Minh-Chu through the translator program. "We had an hour left at best, our air re-oxygenators were almost finished and the reserves are gone. Are you really here to help?"

"We are. I'm Minh-Chu, I'm from the Triton, a Privateering Carrier out of the Haven System. We're former Haven military. I can take you to our ship for treatment."

"No, we can't leave our research behind. We survived the Fall, the Overtake, and have accumulated a great deal of knowledge. We won't leave it behind. My people sacrificed too much." A tear rolled down his cheek, he started to breathe heavily.

"Try to relax. We'll repressurize a compartment, starting with the bridge. Are any of you in need of medication?"

"Nothing urgent, no," he replied. "I'm Kowen. This is a research trade ship. The Frekse out of Nalport on Grace. We were tracking the location of a new kind of communication repeater and found a planetary remnant travelling at a high relative speed away from the galactic plane."

"Then the pirates attacked," Minh-Chu said calmly. "The Overcharge. We're here because we found their captain and tracked you down. We don't agree with what they did here. Can we transport you and your ship to the Triton? It's a large carrier. We can perform repairs."

"What cost? They took our platinum reserves, we don't have..."

"Maybe you can share your research in exchange?" Minh-Chu requested. "We're very interested in anything you have on the Edxi, or how you were able to track down one of those communication nodes. There's a whole science department aboard our carrier who will want to talk to you."

"For repairs? You'll trade data for repairs?" the fellow who was getting to his feet with Iruuk's help asked.

"We'll fix you up either way, you have my word," Minh-Chu said. "I'm Minh-Chu. A Captain in command of the Samurai Squadron fighter wing."

"From a ship called the Triton. A warship with a science department?" Kowen asked.

"The Triton is a lot more than a warship," Minh-Chu said. "You'll see."

"We will," Kowen replied.

"How can we trust them after what we've been through?" the other man asked, pushing Iruuk's hand away.

"We have to trust someone, we have nothing," the woman said. "I'm Olana, the Supervising Officer aboard. Thank you, Minh-Chu. I'm wondering, are you affiliated with any major corporation or government?"

"That's a long story, but we're funded by Jacob Valent," Minh-Chu replied.

"The war criminal?" shouted the fellow beside Iruuk.

"We need help! The life support system has been gutted, we have no fuel," Konak retorted.

They both looked to Olana who was pensive. "What are you doing out here?"

"Rescuing you at the moment. We heard the Overcharge attacked you and we're here to help. That's a crime where we come from. Our main mission is to fight the Order of Eden and its allies. We're privateers under the Haven Alliance which includes the British, Lorander and others."

"Thank you for your help. I don't want you to transport this ship, but we'll take any help you can offer. In exchange for repairs and a full restock of our supplies, we'll give you all our data."

"What? That's..." objected the man beside Iruuk.

"Shut up, Tuss," Olana hissed. "Can you do that for us?" she asked Minh-Chu more calmly.

"We can. We have the Captain of the Overcharge in custody. Hopefully, most of your equipment and supplies are on that ship. We'll fill in the rest from our stores."

"Thank you. We have dead to see to, so if you can leave us with a support system for now, we'll get to work."

Minh-Chu encountered commanders like Olana several times when he was in the Freeground Military. She seemed practical and even through the translator her intentions were crystal clear. He would make sure that everything she said would be monitored through the new vacsuits he'd deliver from the Clever Dream in a few minutes. There was no room for error. If they were the enemy in disguise, then he had to make sure they wouldn't find turning on them easy. If not, he'd apologize if he had to. It was how Jake would handle it. "We'll set you up with enough survival gear to get you through until the Triton can get here."

THREE

The Headless Giant

REMMY SANDS WAS FOCUSED on the timer as it counted down. Nine, eight, seven, the numbers flashed on the Nutri Master food fabricator. Agameg was taking one last look at the holographic data stream that they'd been examining for three days. He didn't take breaks, even stretching while reviewing, delving into the public and Order of Eden local networks. "I don't understand how some of you hazard new foods practically wherever you go. I have had some near gastronomical disasters with some of my experimentations. I've given that up."

"Well, I don't blame you, but some of us like to explore more than others," Remmy replied as the device dinged and the transparent dome lifted. "Besides, this is the highest-rated recipe in the station's database. The Rustic Five Bean Cheese burrito."

"It's probably Forma," Agameg said.

"Why are you so negative today? I mean, we're finally leaving," Remmy replied as he carefully picked up the warm burrito. The flatbread wrapping was perfect, making it a neat, hefty package.

Something about it drew Agameg's attention and he crossed the room to get a better look. "Well, I don't like that we'll be going out as ourselves. I realize we'll be well-armed with cloaked rifles and hidden armour, but this is beyond human daring."

"It's not our decision, so why stress about it?" Remmy said with a shrug. "Besides, we're going straight to the other end of the station, where there's practically no Order folks around. From there we catch a ride."

"He hasn't said who we'll be travelling with, only that it won't be a normal transit," Agameg said, looking at the burrito in Remmy's hand. "It's a neat food. Tidy. I still don't know, though. You can't see what's inside. I smell dairy solids. Don't trust it."

"That's cheese. A delicacy," Remmy replied, taking a big bite out of one end. It was hot with a texture that was at times slightly coarse but then creamy. He enjoyed the intact beans and guessed that it wasn't forma at all, especially when he tasted what must have been cheese, which had a dark, tangy flavour. He nodded. "Worth it. I've never had anything like this." He took another bite and after chewing a little he discovered a flavour that was completely unknown to him along with a burning sensation that had nothing to do with temperature. Sweat erupted on his upper lip, palms and forehead. It was surprising but not in a bad way. "Damn, that's hot!" he laughed, pushing a button on the drink dispenser to the left of the fabricator. "It burns!"

"Do you need medical assistance?" Agameg asked, his solid-coloured green eyes going circular with concern as he started scanning.

"No, it's okay, I've seen ancient entertainment with this. I think it's hot sauce or salsa. It's normal," he finished with a wheeze.

A cup with a straw in it was pushed onto the counter from a compartment and he drew on it deeply. Grape slush filled his mouth and interacted with the spicy flavours strangely, but he enjoyed it. "Perhaps you should dispose of the rest of..." Agameg was silenced as Remmy took another big bite. "...what is wrong with you?"

"It's exciting, I think I like it," Remmy said around a bite before flooding his mouth with more grape slush.

"How's the burrito?" Jake asked as he emerged from the suite's bedroom. His armour was retracted into his boots and long coat, but the military vacsuit along with his muscular form made him look even more intimidating.

"Good, you should try it," Remmy said, pointing at the food fabricator.

"He is having a mild physiological reaction that I find alarming," Agameg said, still scanning.

"I don't try new foods during missions unless I have to, thanks though," Jake said. "We should get out there. The station tram will be around in five minutes."

"I'm ready," Agameg said. His armour was retracted into a dark blue main piece that covered him from hip to neck. It looked like a life support suit, which made perfect sense because he had relaxed into one of his native Issyrian forms. Fine strands hung where a human's cheeks normally were, and

more flowed back from his forehead like hair. They were strong
fibres with plenty of nerves that could smell, feel changes in the
air, gravity and come together to assist in shapechanging. His
mouth was a slit, and he was missing a nose entirely, but
Remmy liked his eyes most. They were large, expressive, sensitive ovals that were solid green from edge to edge.

"I'm good, experiment's over," Remmy said, shoving the last
of the burrito into his mouth and biting through it. A spurt of
hot sauce flowed forth and he cringed, a tear forming as he
stomped his foot. He chewed faster and swallowed, which
didn't seem to help.

Jake chuckled and asked; "Are you all right?"

"Hot sauce. I can walk and deal with it," Remmy said
around the last of it. "So good though. It's a powerful food."

Jake led the way out of the apartment, his stride long and
quick. They were still right in the middle of the section of Gold
Haf Station that was filled with Order of Eden recruits and
personnel. Remmy didn't look as dangerous as Jake, who still
gave the impression of being a former member of the military.

He'd switched his vacsuit to beige and brown colours with
his armour collapsed into the shoulders of a cape that was knee
length and high boots. It was a tribute to late twentieth-century
science fiction shows that he enjoyed, but couldn't get most
people into. He finished his grape slush and chucked it into a
recycler as they passed through the lobby. "So, how's Ayan
doing?" he asked.

Most other people didn't ask Jake personal questions often,
if ever. It was something Remmy didn't really understand. How
could you become friends with someone if it never got personal?
Jake replied with a little smile. "She wishes she was here. She

keeps calling this a data heist, and I keep telling her it's the most boring mission I've ever been on."

Remmy agreed. It was a heist of sorts. The access codes and biometric data Minh-Chu, Ashley and Tammy collected made it possible to tap into the Order of Eden's local intranet and there was so much sensitive information coming in that they couldn't count the breakthroughs. The codes were being replaced, however, and their access was closing up. The Order Cultists may have been downright stupid when they rolled the new Order of Eden walled Internet out, but that wasn't going to last. It turned out that they weren't the only people who used the code leak to get information.

Even still, it was time to go. Someone from the station would eventually notice the small hole in the hull that Agameg, Remmy and Jake used as an improvised airlock to get in. Remmy regretted that they didn't have a chance at getting close to Bion or any Order officers while they were there. It was too risky. The chances that someone had a scanner made to detect someone in a cloak suit were extremely high, especially after Minh-Chu stunned a recruiter. The little scanners the Order put up all over their section looked like three tiny spikes attached at the base that was small enough to fit in his hand. They were everywhere in the Order's section of the station according to the data they stole. There were no blind corners anymore, and that put a major kink in any kidnapping or assassination plans.

Jake went on about Ayan as they got into a station tramway car. "I wish she was here too, but she's taking this pregnancy seriously. The way she sees it, she'd be endangering a lot more than herself. Laura's started crawling and trying to talk too, so she wants to be around her constantly. Other than that she's busy, making sure Haven Sciences gets on its feet properly."

A young Order of Eden officer in a crisp dark green uniform came from a forward car with a soldier behind him. Jake noticed them but finished what he was saying. "I had no idea scientists could be so competitive, even combative, but she's a good diplomat and a better officer. It'll turn out."

"Jacob Valent." the young officer said. It was a statement, not a question.

He stood up, squaring his shoulders. Jake's hand came to rest on his sidearm and Remmy moved into place beside him, doing the same. He was very conscious of the scan-shielded, cloaked weaponry and equipment hidden between his back and his cape. Agameg stood behind them and whispered; "We are well outside of the part of the station under the Order's influence, but they may have soldiers on their way to another platform ahead of us."

"You found me," Jake said to the officer, nodding at Agameg's statement without taking his focus away from the Order of Eden officer. "Now, the question is: should you do anything about it, Cadet?"

"I am an Officer," he replied.

"With a Cadet emblem on your shoulder," Jake said. "Pretend you didn't see us." The tram stopped, its doors opened, and Jake stepped out casually.

Remmy followed him and stopped when he did. The young Officer and his soldier drew their weapons. They were low-powered. Exactly the top tier that was allowed on the station. A headshot would result in a brutal stun, but anything else wouldn't do a thing. "Halt! Security has been alerted!"

"Remmy?" Jake asked.

He knew what that meant, and Remmy quickly checked the station's alert board. There was no advisory for the area they were in. "Nope, nothing happening."

Jake shook his head at the Officer. "Station security doesn't care or won't get involved. You're on your own, kid. You think you know everything, I was your age once. I was about the same age when I graduated from Freeground Fleet Academy. If I could tell my younger self anything, it would be; 'you're so green that you don't know what you don't know, so take your time.'"

There was a flash of doubt on the Officer's face, and, to Remmy's astonishment, Jake turned his back on him and started walking away. Remmy followed, trying to look as nonchalant as Jake, and Agameg did the same without missing a beat. "I hate it when you do that. Those young humans are angry, confused and terrified. Anything could happen."

They made it out of the small tram station and Jake strode much faster. "Last call for boarding: Centis Transit Charter Seven-Zero-Zero-Three-Three-Eight. Ticket holders only," a voice said over the sound system.

"That's our ride," Jake said.

A sight that surprised Remmy to the core greeted them as they rounded the corner. It was Captain Ruby Sima, a leader who was formerly under Jake's command and once master of The Redstone, a Heavy Haven Fleet Destroyer. Her hair was arranged in five red tails that stuck up from her head like fins. Her vacsuit was glossy red with black embellishments including tall boots, a cape, shoulder pieces and long gloves. "Ready to go?" she asked.

"Absolutely," Jake said. "How's the headless giant?"

"Better than I thought. Nothing fell off when we used the Quad Drives," she replied. "Are my passengers getting off here?"

"No," Jake said, glancing at the neatly dressed port representative, who was watching and listening to everything. There were two hospitality androids beside him with skin that looked a little too rubbery to trick anyone into thinking they were human. He was wearing a non-descript pastel yellow uniform, holding a flimsy interface screen. The rest of Jake's response was casual but quick. "The station doesn't deserve the havoc your passengers would bring aboard."

"We have two casinos and many affordable accommodations," the port representative said invitingly. "The nightlife is particularly exciting this week."

"Oh, can we stay?" Remmy teased, aware that Ruby was looking him up and down. They looked like they could have come out of the same old-time-y space opera serial.

"I don't think so, Junior. We should move on." There was an edge to his tone that warned that it wasn't time to joke around.

"So, three ticket holders? I don't have identification on you," the station representative said, looking at his display. He swiped up and down, left and right.

"We're in a hurry," Jake said, following Ruby back into the airlock. They wouldn't find any record of them boarding the station, and Remmy wondered what kind of trouble that could cause if they stuck around.

"Wait! There's a debarkation process!" shouted one of the hospitality droids.

Ruby tapped the control that started the large airlock

cycling. Four soldiers in red vacsuits were waiting there, definitely part of her crew. "So, headless giant?" Remmy asked as he looked back the way they came. The station representative was leaning in, regarding them quizically. He waved back at him with an awkward grin.

"It's slang for taking over an automated transport," Ruby said as the airlock finished closing. "There's a cockpit on this thing, but no one used it until we came along."

Remmy checked the station's advisory data to make sure that security hadn't been alerted. There was a note regarding their section that read; Suspicious activity. Notice sent to administration for urgent review. "Well, the admins don't like us leaving without following procedure. There's a five thousand credit fine for unregistered guests."

"Oh, is that all?" Ruby asked, rolling her eyes. "Let me guess: they sell people to the mines down there to work it off if you can't pay."

Remmy checked and nodded. "You're one hundred percent right. There's even an administration fee for the sale, but it doesn't say what it is."

The inner airlock doors opened, revealing a short accordion-style connecting corridor between the large transit ship and the station. "Run for it," Jake said. "I don't think we'll be back here."

The corridor was short, and they were in the captured starliner's airlock in seconds. Ruby tapped her command and control unit, activating a secure channel. "Get us out of here. Rip free if you have to."

The debarkation corridor detached from the station and began to retract as the ship's thrusters pushed them away. The lumbering ship rolled, as though whoever was at the controls was more used to flying a starfighter and was trying to make the ship behave the same way. The ship rocked underfoot as it accelerated and the dampeners fought to keep up. "I guess this thing isn't made for fancy flying," Remmy said.

"Our pilot likes to go heavy on the throttle. I shouldn't encourage it, I know, but who doesn't like a little speed?" Ruby replied. The inner airlock doors opened and they came out into a section of the ship that looked more like a fancy foyer, but it was old, with dented walls and missing pieces of filigree around the doors. "Welcome to our ride. The ship is courtesy of Daxon Two's junk drift, and the shields are thanks to half a dozen portable generators from the Redstone."

"I saw that you pulled a lot of gear out of that ship," Jake muttered. "Fleet sent me the bill."

"We put it to good use," Ruby said. "Especially the Quad Drives. Loan me a Clever Class Corvette or something bigger and I'll give 'em back."

"You'd better, along with the rest of the gear. I've got a list," Jake said. It seemed like he was having fun with the situation.

"Don't worry, everything worth anything will get checked in when we load onto the Triton," Ruby replied.

The bridge was behind a heavy pair of doors, but that was as much security as Remmy could see. The nerve centre only had four seats, and two of them were stools. It definitely looked like the kind of thing that was meant to be automated. "So, is this ship joining the privateering fleet?" Remmy asked.

Ruby snickered and stroked his cheek. "Oh, you're cute. No, we're not going to try to hot rod this thing into a fighting ship. I plan on abandoning it as soon as the crew transfers."

"Well, uh," Remmy stammered.

"So," Ruby said to Jake as they watched the small tactical monitor on the control panel beside them. There was no sign that the Order of Eden Heavy Cruiser Locon was about to give pursuit. The station's Navnet system was showing that their starliner was following a clear course out of the solar system. "Why show your face on Gold Haf?" she asked Jake.

"I like to be chased," Jake replied.

"No, seriously," Ruby said, shaking her head.

"I needed to see what their response was like, especially with new recruits. This place will be overwhelmed by Order ships in a few hours if they're any good. I'm hoping that lasts at least a few days."

"A distraction," Ruby said, nodding. "I like a good distraction, but what do you want to distract them from?"

"We just want as much attention here for now. There are so many Order targets in the Rose System that..."

Ruby finished his thought; "...some other spot will get caught with their pants down. My guys are ready. If you have the dropships..."

"Captain, there's a group of Order fighters changing course. They'll be on us in about two minutes," said the copilot.

Ruby spoke into her command and control unit then; "Cargo: dump the luggage."

"Yes, Ma'am," came the response through her command and control unit.

Remmy looked at the Navnet panel, wondering if she was dumping mines, or drones, or... then he saw it. There were thirty transponders that were pretending to be Centis Transit Seven-Zero-Zero-Three-Three-Eight, copies of their ship. They were splitting off, slowly moving in every direction.

"Deactivating transponder," the copilot announced. "Ready to increase shield recharge rate."

"Activating emergency thrusters, time to get the hell outta here," the pilot said.

Several indicators on the Inertial Dampener panel turned yellow as the ship accelerated. Remmy had qualified as a pilot for several classes of ship, so he knew what was going on. The thrusters they were using were made to break the ship out of a dangerous gravity well, but they were the closest thing to afterburners that anyone could find on a starliner. "Nice. You really do like a good distraction."

"You can find all kinds of parts in a junk drift. You should see it out there in Daxon. People are starting to fight over the wrecks, and some of them are worth fighting for. This heap was barely worth the trouble. We took everything we needed to make a minefield, including a couple dozen transponders that we programmed to look like this ship. There are even a few holoprojectors and mass multipliers out there. Those fighters are in big trouble," Ruby said.

"Aren't you worried about the legacy of those mines?" Agameg asked.

"We used Targonax explosives. They won't blow up before they're armed and once you do that the compound starts eating itself so it'll just be inert gel after about twenty hours. The only thing we've left behind is a minor collision hazard that'll be pretty easy to clean up."

It was the kind of strategy that Remmy had seen in the Freeground and Haven military manuals. Both organizations frowned on leaving munitions and explosive mines behind.

"So, the Daxon System was worth it." Jake said.

"Absolutely. We saved about a hundred-fifty people who needed to get out of there and recruited three hundred or so rebels from military orgs that were crushed by the Order. A few of these guys were screwed over by Vindyne, too. My crew can't wait to get aboard the Triton, though. This starliner is falling apart," Ruby said.

The fighters split up to investigate the fake ships. "We're at minimum safe jump distance," the pilot said.

"Good, get us out of here," Ruby ordered. "Good work."

FOUR

Looming Shadows

CAPTAIN VOLLIS MIKAN looked through the thick transparesteel window at the front of the Officer's Lounge at the blue-green-grey surface of Rodus. The low murmur of the ship's leaders behind him as they ate breakfast was a comfort. Most trained Citadel Assassins preferred the quiet, but Vollis had enough of that. The buzz of a bridge, mixed conversation of a crowd that was mostly ignoring him made Vollis feel like he was a part of a living galaxy. A place that hadn't just suffered a trillion human fatalities. That was an action he would have never condoned, even if it did delay the Edxi invasion by several years.

Executive Jagat Ozov approached from behind with Moxa, a Samantha model fabricant who was bonding with him as an aide. Vollis didn't have to look at their reflection in the window to know it was them. Their gaits were just as good as seeing them. Jagat's was loping and even. Moxa's was almost exactly like every other Samantha model - regimented and relaxed but hers was a little shorter, quicker. It may have developed because she was performing as the Executive's aide over the last three days. Vollis expected a relationship where Jagat took advantage of the new fabricant, but he saw no such thing. Instead, he challenged Moxa with meaningful work, and there was nothing wrong with that, especially since she was thriving.

The thought of putting another pair of fabricants under the Executive's direct command when they were ready crossed Vollis' mind. He decided to put the instructions in the system as soon as he was finished in the Officer's Lounge.

"Captain, a scout ship is returning from Tabrus," Moxa announced. "They've sent a report in advance."

"Only one?" Vollis asked. "Tell me." He listened closely and watched the holographic images as he traced the lines of the ritual scars beneath the tattoos on his chin.

"The scoutship's drives were damaged because they pushed their ship too hard in the escape, so their message comes late. All other personnel on Tabrus were killed, despite their attempt to defend in the air and hold their ground on the surface. The primary drop team, led by another Samantha model named Eyria, had discovered a small abandoned base of operations. She believed it was the hiding place of the android Alice Valent used as a decoy on Rodus."

"She was an assassination android. Regardless of her sophistication, her type is outlawed on hundreds of civilized worlds, including Earth and Mars. We should have no desire to pretend she was anything else. Please, go on," Vollis said, watching her make the modification in her report.

"They found ruggedized data drives on the premises and were loading them onto their dropship when they came under attack. Eyria's auto-log shows that she may have killed Alice Valent before her team was wiped out. They were not prepared to meet someone with her tactical skills," she went on.

"No embellishments, please," Vollis said. It was easier to take the bad news while he was concentrating on critiquing her report style. He guarded against any enthusiasm at the thought of one of his fabricants defeating Alice Valent. If it was true, he'd be able to retire from combat and work on developing improved versions of soldiers full-time.

With a nod, Moxa moved on to the next part of the report. "One of the perimeter sensors confirms that Alice and the material our drop ship was there to collect, the drives, were taken aboard the Clever Dream and removed from the planet. By all appearances, they've moved on, leaving a Haven Node behind. New Zero was given access to it, and they've closed us off."

"New Zero?" Vollis asked, doubting that Alice was dead. They wouldn't leave the body, but her people's medical technology was at least as good as Citadel's.

"New Zero is a megacity that the Siren Corporation is reviving a few blocks at a time. We don't know exactly how they're blocking us from using the Haven Node. It's taking a long time to determine that without a relay system of our own between Rodus and..."

"Thank you, I understand how micro-wormhole communication relays work. Is there more?"

"The casualty list," Moxa said, bringing it up between them. "I am sorry, Sir. It would take less time to tell you who survived."

"Three survivors," he said, looking at the trio. "Have them report to assessment then give them whatever leisure time is recommended plus a day. What else?" he asked, hoping for news of Bion and the Locon. There was more than one problem there.

"A sighting on Gold Haf. It was Jacob Valent. A hidden DNA sensor confirms it," Executive Ozov said, straightening his tailored jacket. "The Junior Officer who saw him didn't pursue or attempt to subdue him or his companions when they were in range."

"Why isn't the Officer here, in front of me now?" Vollis asked, making an effort to shed his rising frustration as he felt his blood pressure start to rise.

"Bion is taking command of the new recruits and a core group of officers," Jagat said with a shrug. "From the rumours I'm hearing, he's got a hell of an ego on him, so I'm guessing he's having a conversation with the Junior Officer."

"Where is Valent now? Do we know?" Vollis asked.

"He and two companions boarded a starliner that was last reported in the Doxan System. The Locon's scan results indicate that there are six hundred forty-four souls aboard along with a large scan-shielded cargo bay that could contain contraband."

"Who met him in the port?" Vollis asked.

"We can't tell. She was using an illegal DNA, voice and visual scanner. We think it's built into her armour," Moxa replied, showing him a hologram of a red blur about two metres wide and three tall. "We can't even pull a shape."

"This was five minutes ago?" Vollis said, looking at the time stamp on the edge of the image.

"Yes, they've used a Quad Drive to leave the system, Sir," Moxa reported.

"Engage our entire scanner network. If there's any sign of them as they leave the system, I want to see it," Vollis ordered, and the instructions were passed onto the bridge automatically. "Just because we think they used a Quad Drive, doesn't mean they have. There must be ways to fake a trans-dimensional entry wake, and since that starliner was never designed for the technology, they may be trying to trick us into thinking that they've gotten away into some near-dimension."

"Yes, Sir," Moxa replied at the same time as Jagat. They were both learning something

It may not be true, and there may not be any way to fake a dimensional departure, but Vollis wasn't willing to risk it. His subdermal communications system buzzed, indicating that there was a priority transmission coming in. It was Captain Luda Kutty, master of the Locon. He put the call through the unit tattooed across the back of his hand and regarded her image when it came up. Her head was shaved and the green jacket she wore was more squarely cut than was standard for Order of Eden uniforms with broader shoulders. "Why isn't the Vice-Admiral contacting me?" Vollis asked her.

"He has been discharged by Bion. I am the commander of the Locon now," she replied haughtily.

It was an issue he decided to take up with Eve when she arrived. "Are you contacting me to report that Jacob Valent has slipped away on an unarmed starcruiser?"

"Yes, but more importantly, Bion is no longer going to be transmitting neural or biometric tracking data. He has given me the honour of informing you that the experiment is concluded.

You will destroy all research records and samples now. These are the orders of Bion," she said.

Vollis scoffed and silently admonished himself for allowing himself to do so. "You can pass my response on to him then: No. I helped design his pre-programming as requested by the Over-lord, but I didn't authorize his birth. I believe we're three to six iterations from a ready model. If you were able to contact my counterpart, you'd see that he agrees with me. Bion will report to the Rixe within the hour, or I'll go there and assess him myself."

"I'll relay your request to him," she replied. "Bion doesn't have specific instructions for you at the moment, but he orders that you keep the Rixe ready." The communication ended.

The hologram disappeared and Vollis was left staring at Executive Jagat, who regarded him with a quizzical expression. "Who is Bion? Did you cook him up here?"

"That one's body was made on another ship that is several steps behind in neural research. They used a DNA pattern from the old Vindyne records to create him. There are vast modifications, of course, but in general, they wanted to create a body using the seed from a respected enemy. He's a relic from a previous era, but made modern using memories that my team and I modified using very specific engram programming."

"Memory patterns from who?" Jagat asked.

Vollis nodded at Moxa and pointed at a seat several meters away before turning an obscuration field on. No one would be able to see, hear or record them. "Do you recall the early days of the Order? When the religion was being built on the Miracle Child?"

"Yes," Executive Ozov replied. It looked like he may have

heard a rumour about it, and wasn't looking forward to its confirmation.

"Bion is the evolution of that idea. The effort to revive Hampon. This version was not supposed to be activated outside of containment, but I fear that my counterpart has done so because Scanlon's virus has destroyed all the data we had on Bion's neural development."

"Vice Admiral Saman Fizal. Your counterpart on the Jano," Jagat said. "So, he decanted Bion to test him on Gold Haf?"

"As a recruiter, I assume, but this has gone wrong already," Vollis said. "I expect he killed the master of the Locon so he could appoint his own commander. The Jano is cloaked, performing deep scans of the outer belt in the system. I'll have to send a message and wait for her Captain to decide whether or not to break his silence. If he does not, then I'll have to..." Vollis was interrupted as another priority message came in from the bridge. "Yes?"

"Captain, we are detecting an inter-dimensional emergence near Rodus orbital space. It is a close match to the sensor data collected near Gold Haf," an Aspen model reported from the command seat.

"Launch all our training fighters immediately. Send our patrolling units to intercept. Warn local Navnet that we are in pursuit of a pirated ship," Vollis ordered. "Disable the transport's engines the moment it emerges into normal space and get boarding crews ready. I want everyone aboard in custody or dead by the end of the watch. I'm on my way to the bridge."

"Yes, Sir," came the response.

Vollis deactivated his obscuring field and shouted; "Combat stations! Now!" the alert alarm whooped the instant he finished giving the order to the dozen officers in the room. That was easily a third of the command staff, and they surged to their feet.

"Permission to join the lead boarding crew, Captain?" Executive Ozov asked as he kept up behind him.

"Granted. Go, get the best soldiers you can find onto a dropship, and bring me Valent or the next best target. I wish I could join you," Vollis said over his shoulder.

FIVE

A Lumbering, Stumbling Giant

THE FIRST CLASS cabin's main room was large enough for six or seven people to lounge around in. There was iron filigree that was once perfectly black around the doors. It wasn't flat against the bulkhead anymore, showing how much the ship had twisted and flexed over time. The furnishings looked new, and that was a relief. There was nothing like kicking his feet up after feeling like he didn't even belong in his own body.

"So, you look different than I expected," Ruby said to him as she returned to the room with a bottle of amber-coloured liquid. "Lorossa Nectar. We found it in the first-class bar."

"I'll pass, thank you," Jake said, He was still fully armoured as well. "How well connected to the ship's systems is your bridge?"

Ruby rolled her eyes and sat down in an armchair upholstered with yellow and green flowers. "We installed what was missing. Don't worry," she replied. "I get it. After the Triton, it must feel like this is a giant paper zeppelin," Ruby said, turning towards Remmy. "What do you think of first class?"

Her Irish accent was interesting, he was still getting used to it. "It's nice. I could go for a nap. So, is there a chance that there isn't a full set of controls in the cockpit?"

Then there was a message for her, the audio came through. "This is Parsons. The Quad Drives aren't holding up. Same problem as before but worse now that we've dumped all that ballast. Our mass is too off balance."

"How long have we been accelerating?" Ruby asked.

"Just shy of six minutes, we're going to have to come out near Rodus," Parsons replied.

"Hold it together until we're out of the system, at least," Ruby said, getting to her feet.

"We have to stop accelerating, we will be tossed out, we can't balance the mass out again," Parsons replied. "I'll make sure we don't fall apart when we transition to normal space and you figure out what we do after that."

"Is this ship that off balance? Are there chunks missing?" Remmy asked.

"Yes, and yes. The ship got a little churned up in the junk drift. Some things were easier to cut off than they were to repair," Ruby replied in a rush. "This ship was made to travel through wormholes using a dampening system that burned out when the crew were killed a couple of years before we found it. The dampening system we replaced it with isn't exactly as robust as the original and it weighs about one-eighth as much."

"So, we could break up?" Remmy asked, sealing his helmet.

The provisioning system built in tucked a dense, vanilla-flavoured cube into the corner of his mouth.

"We should get closer to the outer hull," she replied.

"Paper zeppelin," Jake sighed. "How is the gear set up?"

"In guided dropping bells. We're good to leave this boat at a moment's notice. The only worry is the new recruits. They have to take lifeboats," Ruby said as she led the way out of the room. She reached back and picked up the bottle at the last moment then deployed her armour. The horizontal slats covered her body in less than a second. A pocket formed for her to stash the bottle into along the front of her thigh.

"I saw that you kept all four hundred twenty suits of armour," Jake said.

"You really read the whole invoice from the Redstone, didn't ya?" Ruby asked as she rushed towards the small bridge.

"Every successful privateer is part businessman," Jake replied.

"I'm surprised you had to pay anything. Aren't you mates with the Defence Minister?" Ruby asked.

"We are, that's why I wasn't executed a little while ago. I made a deal that got me here," Jake replied, glancing around.

Ruby tapped her left command and control unit a few times, looked up and around, then did it again. "God dammit, I can't sound the brace alarm."

The bridge door opened and the copilot replied; "Wireless is down. They're already jamming us."

"What?" Ruby asked, looking a the tactical display near the door. It was a thin screen that someone hung there. She pressed a pair of icons - Brace Alert, and Ship Wide.

A voice that Remmy thought was inappropriately passive

announced; "Brace for emergency manoeuvres. If you are not near a seat or bulkhead, lower yourself to the deck and spread yourself out."

"Those are terrible instructions," Remmy said, earning a nod and a sideways smile from Jake. "Anyone who can't get a grip to anything bolted down would get tossed all over the place."

"I think it's more of a sense of security thing. You know, giving the poor sods in steerage something to do so they're not pondering immediate doom," Ruby replied.

"Twenty-four fighters coming in," the copilot announced. "Message from Citadel ship Rixe."

"Put it through," Jake and Ruby said at the same time.

"It's your zeppelin," Jake said.

"This is Captain Vollis Mikan," came the perfectly enunciated words of the commander of the Rixe. "Your ship has been flagged as having the subject of a Watch And Report Notice aboard. Jacob Valent is also a wanted war criminal who we will be taking into custody. Shut down your engines and prepare to be boarded. Teams are on their way. Any attempt to resist will be answered with lethal force."

"Rixe Actual, you must have us confused with someone else. We did take three passengers on at Gold Haf station, but they are innocent travellers," Ruby replied, muting the receiver and shrugging at Jake. "Do you have those spray-on disguises?"

"No, I could make one, but what's the plan there? I don't think they'll give us the time we need to..."

"Torpedo launch from the Rixe, medium range, no radiological or antimatter alarms," the copilot announced.

"Countermeasures?" Jake asked.

"Yeah, right," Ruby scoffed. "We haven't had a chance to get more decoys ready."

"It's going to hit us on the lower aft quarter," Parsons said as she struggled with the controls. The nose was coming around to point at the night side of Rodus.

The ship rumbled as the torpedo struck. "Breach, couldn't tell you where," the copilot announced.

"This is Garrety, we're open one compartment deep. Aft. Frame thirty-two. Missed engines and everything really important. Didn't lose anyone," came the damage report.

"That will be your last warning. Your shielding is ineffective against our torpedoes," Captain Mikan said.

"What do you want to do here?" Jake asked.

Remmy glanced at the tactical monitor. They were about to be surrounded by fighters. The transport was moving into a stable orbit around Rodus. "That's City Thirty-Five. Panda. I read the reports on it while I was stuck in the infirmary getting poked and probed."

Ruby fixed him with a look of curious concern.

"I'm much better now, don't worry. But we could disappear there."

"Over five hundred of us?" she asked.

"He's right, thousands could go to ground there," Jake said.

"So we need time," Ruby said.

"Then let me get you some," Jake said, activating the receiver. "This is Jacob Valent. I boarded this vessel using fake credentials. To save the crew and passengers, I'm willing to give myself up but I need to know the exact terms and I'd like some assurances."

"I can't believe the voice pattern checks, Admiral," Captain Mikan said.

While they were having their conversation, Ruby was instructing her pilot to fake a loss of control leading to orbital destabilization. Remmy regarded the Captain with a shocked expression. "Are there enough escape pods?"

Ruby shook her head and flicked one of her armour's horizontal plates. "You're trained for flight, right?" she mouthed.

Remmy nodded impatiently. "But, your whole crew?"

She nodded, indicating that they were trained. Meanwhile, Captain Mikan was saying; "...position to have a say in the conditions of your surrender. We will destroy the ship and kill everyone aboard."

"Mayday," announced the pilot as she increased the thrust on their portside aft thruster well beyond tolerances. She was about to fake some kind of damage, and Remmy realized that they really were about to abandon ship sometime in the next two to three minutes. Parsons continued making her announcement on all emergency channels. "Damage from a torpedo fired by the Rixe has caused a control failure in one of our main thrusters. Our new trajectory is taking us towards the planet. I repeat, mayday. We are about to lose an engine and suffer critical damage."

The fighters moved away, and Remmy looked at the scratchy video feed from one of the orbital Navnet satellites. One of their largest thrusters was sending a white tail, its cowling was almost the same colour along the edge. The ship shuddered as there as it exploded, sending debris towards the other main thruster beside it then went out. "We're having technical issues, please hold," Jake said, muting the receiver.

"I will order my fighters to fire if my teams cannot board the ship, Admiral," Captain Mikan warned.

"Okay, so we're on course to crash into the planet," Jake said. "What's the plan for the Quad Drives? You have four aboard, right?"

"Right. They'll be taking care of the ship," Ruby said. "They're set to explode - but in a controlled explosion so they don't damage the atmosphere - and the ship will disintegrate, so there won't be any fatalities below."

"And no one gets the Quad Drives," Remmy said aloud.

"Then you organize a rescue," Ruby said to Jake.

"I'm forwarding all this to the Triton," Jake said. "How long until we're in the atmosphere?"

"One minute, eighteen seconds," replied Parsons. She and her copilot were unstrapping and picking up their emergency bags.

"Admiral, Admiral, Valent!" Captain Mikan was shouting through the communicator.

Jake unmuted the communicator. "I'm sorry, we're abandoning ship. I suggest your people get to a safe distance. You'll have to pick me up on the ground. Oh, by the way, I've already been on trial for all the crap you're accusing me of - well, not all, but most - and I've paid for my crimes. You should have been there, I'm pretty sure you would have had a good time. Oh, and call me Jake. We're going to get to know each other, Captain."

Everyone left the bridge and rushed to the nearest airlock, which was only a couple of short corridors away. The friction of the atmosphere was already turning the ship red. "Are we going to make it?" Remmy asked.

"Yes, but it's going to be complicated. There's a storm right under us and the sun just set for the area we're dropping on," Parsons replied. "You could have chosen a better spot."

"It was a choice of convenience," Remmy replied.

"The storm will help us," Jake said. "Unless you get hit by lightning. That could burn your shields out."

"What? Electricity would flow across the energy field, right?"

"Not if your shielding is pushing through thick rain," Ruby replied.

"Actually, no one's tested that outside of a sim," Jake added as he checked Remmy's gear.

Agameg came running and checked Jake's gear. "This is not going well."

"No, it isn't," Remmy replied.

"Are you having cramps because of the burrito? It had dairy. You're most likely intolerant. Your record shows you've never had real cheese," Agameg said as he checked Remmy's equipment with deft hands.

"Cramps? Dairy? You checked my records? This isn't the time!" Remmy shouted.

"So, no cramps then, interesting," Agameg replied. Remmy turned and checked his gear.

"What's a burrito?" Parsons asked.

Ruby was listening, watching the interaction while she made sure that her crew was getting ready to jump. "We're coming down faster than we thought, but we're all right. Send the Bell Droppers out of the cargo bay, and launch all escape craft the moment we're clear." The display on her command and control units lit up with acknowledgements. "My people are well trained. I bet we lose half the recruits though."

"The Triton's been alerted. I'm transmitting everything live," Jake said.

"How?"

"I have a Haven Node in my pack," he replied.

"They make them that small?" Ruby asked.

"The internals are about the length of my arm, so, yeah. We have a direct line to every node out there. Remmy, can you give the Locon an order?"

"Will do, but we'll probably only get to do this once," Remmy replied. "They'll plug this hole in the network the moment I use it."

"As long as it saves our butts. Send all their drones and long-range torpedoes out after the Rixe. Make sure that they deactivate communications so they can't be aborted or called back," Jake said.

"I have a script for that," Remmy said, making a few quick modifications and running it.

"Now that's an advantage," Ruby said. "I knew I'd enjoy this trip. How long will it take for the Locon to get those instructions?"

"They already have. There's a Haven Node in orbit near Gold Haf Station, so there's practically no latency. I knew our intelligence mission would pay off."

"No, you didn't. You complained often," Agameg corrected.

"Okay, fine, but I'm happy I was wrong," Remmy laughed as he watched the Locon's launcher status. Every torpedo and missile launcher sent a single round of munitions out before anyone did anything, and twenty attack drones started a trip to Rodus and the Rixe. "It's going to take about an hour for most of that trouble to find its way to the Rixe, but I bet they'll call their fighters back to play defence."

Jake hit the emergency button on the airlock. Before he had a chance to think about it, Remmy, Agameg, Parsons and her copilot rushed through as the outer door opened. A dark sea of clouds stretched out below them for as far as the eye could see. "This is definitely better than sitting around downloading sensitive information."

"You are a crazy person, Remmy Sands," Agameg said over their proximity radio. "But I think I'm starting to enjoy your company. Please don't die again."

SIX

A Less Than Ideal Landing

THICK CLOUDS, rain and the darkness of night made the tumble down impossible to control at first. Remmy could barely hear the storm through the thick protection of his heavy armour until a triple hammer of thunder shook the sky. In the light of the next strike, the shadows of dozens of soldiers were revealed. I'm going down back first, Remmy realized.

Haven Ranger training kicked in. He activated the thrusters hidden under the horizontal armour slats of his outer suit. It wasn't like flying a ship. In the Haven Heavy Armour Suit, you are wrapped in strips of emitters covered by flexible metal that could turn into barrier thrusters that were like shields, but made to push you around. It felt like you were the thruster, not like you were being propelled from behind. He looked at the instrument display in his visor and saw the artificial horizon, altitude, speed, direction and the other environmental readouts. "Fast down, fast down. I'm marking the landing zone," Jake announced over the general communications channel.

At a glance, Remmy confirmed that the signal was encrypted and it was rebroadcasted over laser link. All other forms of communication were being jammed from orbit by the Rixe, including Navnet. He signalled that he'd received the message and set a course for the landing zone. There would be no clearance or directions given from City Thirty-Five.

His suit slowed his spin automatically, and he smiled at the sensation of being pushed through the air. The feeling of flying in the suit terrified some people, but he was from the other crowd. He loved it, even though he was far from the best suit pilot. That's why the order; 'Fast down,' made him nervous.

That infantry term was invented specifically for getting to the ground as fast as possible without killing yourself. Remmy wasn't good at it. He came around, nearly collided with another soldier, and then pointed his suit towards the ground. A dropping bell was below him, accelerating towards the ground. The name came from the armoured, self-guided equipment container's shape. He was just starting to manoeuvre past it when a strike from the Rixe, high in orbit, sent the bell spinning out of control. He collided with it and was sent to his right.

His shields, which were down to seventeen percent, and dampeners took the damage. Remmy engaged his autopilot again and let it reorient him properly so he could continue flying down. A red flash on his tactical display informed him that the dropping bell was blasted to pieces. Others were being targeted by the Rixe. They were relatively slow, even though they were travelling faster than terminal velocity under thrust.

They flew in straight lines, while the soldiers were a little more creative and much smaller.

Remmy silently cursed his luck as he tried to make something out in the darkness below. The chances of a collision were so low at the moment that it shouldn't have been a concern. The near collision was a fluke, but he knew that the risk of that would grow as he got closer to the landing zone, so he watched the space nearby as he turned his acceleration all the way up.

The sound of the wind whistling around him was only secondary to the whining of over a hundred barrier thrusters in his suit straining. The other soldiers he could see looked like men and women made of light as they pushed down through the lowest level of cloud cover and then into the rain-filled air beneath. I am moving faster than the drops, Remmy thought to himself as he kept one eye on the altimeter. He tried to stop himself from glancing at the icon that would activate the suit's cloaking systems. They wouldn't work while he was in flight, not in that atmosphere.

The soldier nearest to him was from the Redstone flight crew, and he moved ahead, eager to get to the ground. His body jerked, then flew off to the left. Something, rounds from a ship above them, not the Rixe, sent him off course. His nerves kicked in, and his palms started sweating.

"...are clear. I repeat, all passengers and personnel from the starliner are clear!" shouted one of Ruby's officers.

Then, for a moment night was turned to day and he got a clear look at the sprawling ruins beneath him. City Thirty-Five was to the right. Its polished metal walls and pristine towers stood in defiance of the greater city around it that hadn't been rebuilt since The Fall. That's where they were headed, and he still felt like he was about to hit at such a great speed that there would be nothing left but his over-built boots, helmet and a broad spatter.

It was time for Remmy to begin decelerating, so he let his suit's movement automation flip him end over end in a move that made his stomach lurch. The taste of the spicy burrito returned and he swallowed hard. The flexible horizontal plates flared again as the thrusters pushed hard to slow his fall. A building was coming into focus beneath. It was a domed, curved structure with a transparent roof. I am moving way too fast, he thought, sucking air in through his teeth, and bracing himself.

In the second surge of brilliant light, he saw someone who really was destined for that fate he feared as they passed him so quickly that Remmy wasn't sure what he was seeing at first. They flailed, thrusters trying to adjust as they realized that there wasn't enough time to decelerate. When they struck the ground a second later, they penetrated the roof of the building like a bullet, then struck the floor beneath with such force that it collapsed a section to the left of Remmy's landing spot. He adjusted, doing his best to shift his trajectory to the right without taking away from the thrust focused on the ground so he wouldn't have a similar end.

Remmy looked up and ahead of him in time to see the third flash of light as the ruined, twisted, red-hot remains of the starliner broke through the clouds. His faceplate blocked out enough light so he wouldn't go blind as he watched the last of the Quad Drives explode, reducing the ship to next to nothing but harmless specks of white-hot matter. The drives could have done much more damage, but whoever set their destruct sequence was careful to control the explosions. The tiny shards that remained were made of the most resilient inert metals and would land in the ocean, too small to harm anyone.

The voice Remmy had assigned to the program that ran his armour announced; "Touchdown in five!" It sounded like an ancient radio announcer, a choice he questioned as it counted; "Four!"

Remmy cast his gaze downward and saw that he was about to land at about the same time as Agameg and another pair of soldiers he didn't know. "Three!" it said in his ear as though a new year was about to start. It looked like he was down to a speed that he could survive.

"Two!" The approach was still a little rapid for his taste, but Remmy was sure that his suit would protect him from any damage. He questioned the integrity of the roof, however.

"One!" It said, mirroring his jubilation at making a firm touchdown on the rooftop, which was thankfully made of transparesteel and not glass.

Agameg was already on his feet and regarded him, his face frozen in an exaggerated glad expression. "We didn't die!" he proclaimed.

"That was a hell of a rush!" shouted the next soldier to land.

Remmy spotted him just in time to see that he was about to hop. "No, wait! Don't!"

He jumped a full metre, landed on his feet and shrugged. "It's transparesteel, don't worry, buddy."

It was then that Remmy saw what he'd feared. The transparent part of the roof wasn't the problem. It was the bracing that held those heavy metal plates in place. They creaked under the strain, it didn't look like anyone had done any maintenance in a long time. To prove his point, the soldier who told him everything was fine hopped up and down.

"Do not do that," was all Agameg had to say before the roof collapsed under the soldier and for several metres in every direction.

Remmy activated his thrusters in time to control the fall so he landed safely on his feet. A transparesteel panel came down on his head, clashing with his shields before it clattered to the garden cobblestones. "Are you all right?" Agameg asked after neatly sidestepping a panel.

"I'm good," Remmy replied as he watched the soldier who made the mess land awkwardly and then hurried to his feet.

"This isn't a great spot," Remmy said as he looked up. There were hundreds of blue lights, each one a soldier decelerating towards the ground, and a few shadows that his computer marked as escape pods and small shuttles. A red blip appeared on his tactical scanner. It disappeared and reappeared until someone confirmed that it was an enemy ship. Remmy pulled his rifle from where it was affixed to his back and shouted; "Everyone in range, I've spotted a bogey." He zoomed in and let his suit confirm that it was an Order of Eden dropship. "Marking it."

"Spotted, two more," Jake said from somewhere above.

The dropship Remmy spotted wasn't flying down. Instead one of its turrets fired at an escape pod. "Switching to guided rounds, firing at DS-1," Remmy said, letting his suit assist his aim, locking onto the ship, then touching his trigger. The lock held and he squeezed it. The recoil was so hard that his rifle's dampening system hissed and the stock collapsed. As it reset,

Remmy started running. "They'll know where that came from," he announced to everyone on the top floor.

It was like running through a jungle. The top floor of the building was a greenhouse and it looked like only two or three species had survived, reaching out with vines and thin branches from their planters. Agameg finished firing his anti-air guided round and caught up. "Get clear! They'll be shooting back," Remmy ordered.

"Nice shoo...g, ...emmy, Aga..., n.. ...et out... there," Jake said through a spotty connection.

"There! We jump there!" Agameg said as he led the way to a wide crack in the wall ahead with enough room to get through. The sound of something striking the roof rapidly behind them drowned out the rain and high-pitched chorus of thrusters above. Remmy brought up a rear-view window in his faceplate and saw warped transparesteel panels and bracing falling as a dropship hovered overhead.

In a second his sensors captured a list of statistics. Only a few caught his attention. Its shields were low, there were four double turrets firing in all directions, and the aft door was opening. "On me! We're taking that thing down!"

Remmy made it through the crack in the side of the building first. It felt like time slowed down as he started to fall again. The street was far below, but he knew where the dropship was, and had an idea. "I'll distract them. You and Agameg take care of the rest."

Jake, his suit's barrier thrusters making him look like a yellow-red fireball as it burned through the rain, strafed the bottom of the ship. He was barely ahead of the turret gunner's aim, who would probably hit him soon if Jake stayed within his arc.

Remmy activated his thrusters and turned, lining himself up with the cockpit. He increased his shield charge to maximum, cranked the throttle and in under two seconds rammed it so hard that he heard the g-force dampener in his equipment pack whine. He managed to hit his mark and was affixed to the cockpit canopy like a tree frog. The mental image made him chuckle briefly.

"You are very creative, Remmy," Agameg said as he flew by, strafing the side of the dropship with his heavy rifle. He was so close and quick that the gunner missed him entirely, the barrels of his pulse turret impotently sweeping from front to back.

"Hi!" Remmy shouted as he looked through the canopy at the pilot and copilot. "Come outside, it's a beautiful day!"

It wasn't the way he usually went about things, to be upfront and brutal. Remmy had always been one of the smaller recruits in Freeground Fleet, then Haven Rangers, and finally Haven Fleet. Then his body was rebuilt with new physical augmentation. The only thing it didn't improve much was his height, but he was still changing and was still getting used to his new physique. He'd never tried using it for violence outside of re-training, which limited his interactions to dummies and practice robots. Even then, he hadn't had much time to play with his new body.

The knees of his heavy armour remained affixed to the canopy as he rose up, cocked his fist, then, with the assistance of artificial muscle built into his suit, punched the middle of the canopy. It felt better than he expected, especially when he heard the sound - like a hammer and anvil only lower pitched -

and saw a dent. "Looks like another quality Vindyne starship," Remmy said as he watched the pilot panic and the copilot quickly unbuckle his restraints.

"Keep it up!" Jake said as he flew past the ship again.

Remmy punched the centre transparesteel panel of the cockpit window and his visor highlighted it in red. He checked his tactical overlay and saw that Agameg and Jake were both hovering behind the ship, firing. As Remmy popped the warped panel inwards, he could hear the panic of the soldiers inside.

The copilot opened the hatch leading into the main cabin of the ship, started at the massacre he saw there thanks to Remmy's friends, and then closed it. Remmy's laughter was cut short as the pilot drew a pistol and fired. The shot deflected off Remmy's armour. He reached in, ripped the pilot's restraints away, nearly pulling the seat free of the deck, and threw the pilot out next. Jake had come in through the cockpit door in time to see the pilot's final flight. He turned towards the cockpit, and yelling above the din of the storm, said; "You're switching sides right now, or my friend is going to teach you to fly without a ship."

The copilot lunged for the control panel, and Remmy pushed him back before he could touch anything. His suit warned him that, in his quick response, he'd misjudged things and broken the man's neck. "Crap, sorry!" he shouted. "This thing's going down."

"Everyone aboard DS-1 has been defeated," Agameg announced over the laser link that connected every allied soldier there like a giant communication mesh.

There were several cheers as Remmy pushed off and activated his flight systems. "We need to get to the ground and cloak," Jake said, retreating from the cockpit using the hatch at the back.

The surviving soldiers from Ruby's crew had finished their descent. The streets of the ruined outer city were littered with them. Within moments they all disappeared as cloaking systems that they couldn't use as they landed under thrust were activated. Many who had been shot and killed in the air were left behind. "Tell me this wasn't the plan," Remmy said to himself as he, Agameg and Jake touched down.

"It wasn't," Parsons, Ruby's lead pilot, replied over the general channel.

"We'll talk about this later. Get under cover for now," Ruby replied sternly.

SEVEN

Emergency

MINH-CHU WAS STARTLED by how quickly the Triton
arrived in the Frekse's area. He was on the bridge of the Frekse,
putting the First Mate's body into a bag. He'd been shot through
the head, probably with a blade pistol, judging from the ragged
holes in his neck and face. Olana, the interim Supervising
Officer of the exploration expedition was closing the bag with
her captain's body inside.

Tuss, one of the other surviving crewmembers, was at a
terminal looking at a list, cursing in his own language as he
assessed the damage to his botanical research instead. It was
extensive. As far as Minh-Chu could determine from the
complaining he overheard, all but a few moss samples were
completely lost.

Before he was ready, Minh-Chu heard Ashley in his ear

saying; "We're about to send mooring cables out to the Frekse. The Captain isn't waiting to clear it with the commander of the ship. What's going on over there, Ronin?"

It was a private call, but she was following Haven Fleet's procedure by using his callsign. "Nothing, everything's going pretty much as planned. We're helping them wrap their dead. Did Sciences get the upload from Tuss? Olana said they decided to send it early as a sign of good faith."

"Yes, two people from Sciences have already come to the bridge. They tried to ask the Captain all kinds of questions, and she told them she was too busy for that stuff and sent them back to their corner. There's something wrong. She wasn't direct, she was rude."

"One minute, my tactical system shows you're in position to launch cables," Minh-Chu said, muting his end of the call. He looked to Olana. "The Triton is here, and they're firing lines. You're about to get pulled into position for boarding."

"That was fast, your ship was hiding somewhere nearby?" she asked.

"It has a fast jump drive," Minh-Chu replied. The deck shuddered slightly several times. "That's the lines connecting to hard points on your hull. They're using them to hold your ship steady so they can pull you into a bay or attach you to a mooring point."

Alice opened a holographic channel on his command and control unit and an image of her appeared on the bridge life-sized. Her vacsuit had turned black, and she was wearing all but the headpiece of her heavy armour. Minh-Chu was taken aback at her cold expression. "Officer Olana, I wish I could meet with you in person, but something has come up and we don't have time. I appreciate your grief and your hardship. We were able to find nine crewmembers from the Overcharge, including their captain. In a moment they will all be in stasis. I have put a KOS bounty on the remaining five crewmen who are at large on your behalf. I don't condone the piracy of innocent ships."

"What is a KOS bounty?" Olana asked.

Alice took a moment to tune her translator before nodding and, with a full absence of emotion on her face replied; "It means; 'kill on sight,' and since they are still on the station and many of the armed inhabitants have done bounty hunting before, I'm sure they'll be taken care of soon. I've verified that they were responsible for the act of piracy, so there's no doubt of their guilt."

"That's not how we do things," Olana said.

"I understand. You're probably from a civilized nation where hunting predators down and killing people before they are tried for crimes isn't a moral act. I'm from a similar culture. We are far from our nations and their laws now. Those five crewmembers were logged by their own ship as boarding and killing, or attempting to kill members of your crew so they could steal from you. I can't allow that and don't have time for a more measured punishment. I don't have time for this conversation either."

"I don't care if..." Olana started, but she was cut off as Alice held her hand up.

Her holographic image stepped towards her and stared into her eyes. "You've stumbled into a war, Officer. Take what I'm about to offer and run back home as fast as you can. My people have captured and unlocked all of the Overcharge's systems. Most of what they took from you is still aboard and there is more than enough room for your crew. The Captain, First Officer and seven of her people are in a makeshift brig aboard that ship. As I said, they are in stasis. Do whatever you want with them, just don't release them back into the wild. I can't have a pirate ship originating from the same port of call as the Privateering initiative we're running, it will put too large a black mark on the whole effort. The Triton has pulled you into position and a temporary crew is manoeuvring the Overcharge so it will dock with you. The helm and all control systems are unlocked, so you can take possession of the ship that attacked you immediately. Do you have a pilot who can get you home?"

Tuss stood up and said; "I'm a capable pilot. This is acceptable."

Olana stared at him, scowling, but didn't have time to say anything else before Alice went on. "Good. Like I said, most of the stolen goods are still there, and all of the Overcharge's supplies are intact, so you have more than you need to go home. You could keep exploring, but considering how close you're getting to contested systems, I suggest you at least pick another direction."

"What about repairs? Your Officer promised..." Olana asked as Kowen stepped into the hallway having overheard Alice. He was already agog.

"That promise was made under a very different set of circumstances. Good luck," Alice's hologram said before it disappeared.

Minh-Chu's command and control units both flashed red and he saw that an Emergency Recall notice had been given. A chill ran down his spine. "I'm sorry, I have to return to the Triton."

Going back to the earliest days of his Freeground Fleet training, every member of the organization was taught that there was only one thing to do when you got an Emergency Recall notice. You dropped whatever you were doing, even in mid-sentence or during triage, and returned to your muster point. For Minh-Chu that meant one of three places: The hangar of the Triton first, the Squad Room second, or the Tactical Centre beneath the bridge as the third option. His orders were specific. Make sure the fighter pilots who were out on patrol were recovered as quickly as possible, then report to the Tactical Centre.

Iruuk and the marines were already running to the aft section of the ship. Minh-Chu took up the rear and dropped into his fighter. He lifted off and was turning towards the open doors at the back before his canopy finished sliding closed. "Ronin to Green Group, make emergency landings in the Triton. Hangar Three has been marked for us and is already open."

As affirmative signals came from each of his fighters, Easy asked; "What's up?"

"Are we being recalled to Haven?" asked Pixie.

"No, just the Triton. We need to finish recovery so the entire ship and squadron can respond to an emergency," Minh-Chu replied, hoping that would hold more questions back. He switched to Ashley's call, still listening to his squad. "I'm on my way back with the rest of the squadron and the Clever Dream. What's going on up there?"

"I don't know, but every department is going nuts, even communications," Ashley replied in a whisper. "We're setting course for the Rose System and they're plugging in extra Quad Drives. All the backups, the reserve, everything."

It must be Jake, Minh-Chu thought to himself, immediately punching his canopy in frustration. That was the kind of thought that shouldn't be allowed to pass through his mind while he was moving as fast as he could towards an emergency landing. "One minute," he said, switching back to the Squad Channel. The Triton loomed larger every second as his thrusters flipped so he could begin deceleration. The rest of his group was ahead, closing on the port side hangar built into the underside of the great ship. "We've practised this. By the numbers, we're retro thrusting all the way in."

"Aye, I'm first," Breaker said as his fighter lined up with the hangar, most of its thrusters firing forward as hard as they could to slow him down. To Minh-Chu's satisfaction, he cut power the moment his ship's small, mostly recessed wheels touched the deck and then he rolled out of the way, to one of the small ship elevators built into the deck.

Easy came in faster and bounced three times before his fighter turned, took out a railing and stopped. "Son of a bitch!" he cried. Pixie came in perfectly and was completely still as soon as her landing gear touched the deck. Minh-Chu's fighter touched the deck a few centimetres in from the lip of the deck, he felt the bump of the inner door seal as he crossed it. As soon as his fighter came to a halt, he saw the Clever Dream come in above them all. For a moment it was like standing next to the sun, as it decelerated backwards, its main thrusters forcing it to slow. It came down onto the deck hard enough to make it vibrate and Minh-Chu checked the status of all the ships that were on missions. There was one small shuttle on its way. It was coming from the Overcharge.

He checked the details and saw that it was flown by Sass, a

pilot he'd assigned to shuttle and utility flying. Alice sent a team out to secure the Overcharge, and Slick assigned Sass as the pilot. He'd done well enough getting the shuttle to the Overcharge, then mooring the ship with the Triton. He'd even flown the Overcharge from there to the Frekse, where it docked again. This was the last portion of Sass's mission and Minh-Chu cringed as he watched the shuttle come down too fast and too steeply. The front starboard side of the passenger shuttle smashed into the unyielding deck before it righted itself and skidded into one of the rear struts of the Clever Dream's landing gear. Minh-Chu put a notice in for Sass to report to him as soon as the emergency was over. He didn't look forward to seeing him.

The hangar door closed, and his Com-Con unit informed him that it was safe to get out of his craft. He was out and running across the deck. "All pilots, report to the Squad Room. We are on alert status. I'll be in the Tactical Centre." he got to the heavy doors leading into the rest of the ship as a deck crew was emerging, and they parted for him. "Thank you," he told them, his proximity radio passing the message on.

The run from there to the nearest lift with command centre access was a blur. Most of the crew were rushing to their emergency stations, and they made room for him as he rushed in the other direction. He stepped out of the elevator, nodded at eight security officers in heavy armour as he passed between them, and then marched into the large Tactical Centre. The lettering on the doors still read COMMAND AND CONTROL CENTRE from its early service for the Sol System, when it was a ship of exploration. Minh-Chu's alarm only grew as he saw that Captain Stephanie Vega, Alice, Slick, holograms of Ayan

Anderson and Defence Minister Terry Ozark McPatrick were all in attendance, standing around a long oval table. At the far end was Jake, who was running in full armour.

"Ronin, you're just in time. We're putting the details together right now," Oz said.

He was more alarmed than ever. If the situation was big enough to involve Haven Fleet, then it had to be world-shattering. "Wouldn't miss it, what's up?" His gaze focused on Jake, who was ducking under a thick girder.

"We're going underground. The Rixe has deployed scan drones that can see through cloaking. We took out the first wave, and lost some people, but thanks to Alice's last trip here and her intelligence, we're headed to the lower levels of old City Thirty-Five. We might be able to set up there and put a plan together for a counter-offensive."

"So, things didn't go well on Gold-Haf?" Minh-Chu asked.

"It was boring, but it went really well. We got away with a full status report on the Order Fleet, their corporate support map, and tactical analysis of every ship in their arsenal. There's another one point four zettabytes of data we weren't able to get through, so have fun with that. Oh, and we got some scans on Citadel ships, you might want to start there. The Rixe is the latest Zhan-Class carrier and it's leading the hunt on us. We expect the Locon to get here soon, so the manpower on the ground will probably triple in the next couple hours." Debris fell around him and he redoubled his pace. "That's all I can offer now, I'll listen in."

Alice picked up the thread of the conversation as soon as he finished his last syllable. "Ruby Sima, the former Captain of the Redstone, put a plan together to use a starliner they found in one of the Doxan junk belts to travel to the Rose System. They were already en route when Jake contacted them and asked for a ride. The pickup went perfectly, and it looked like they were going to make it all the way here, but a shift in mass aboard the starliner forced them out of transit space near Rodus orbit. They were attacked by the Rixe and had to abandon ship. Now there are two hundred eighty-seven soldiers and new recruits heading underground. I'll be working with Captain Vega to put a rescue plan together."

Engineering Chief Finn stepped up to the table and brought a wireframe diagram of the Triton up. "We're already underway, but with our current systems we won't get there for about thirty-nine hours. We're connecting all our spare Quad Drives, and auxiliary power systems and re-tasking external emitters to enhance our space compression. With the help of the entire sciences and engineering departments, we think we can cut our transit time by two-thirds. This is temporary. We're going to burn a few drives out. I never want to do this again." He looked around the room while he pointed at a red spot near the Triton's chain of fusion reactors. "Just making sure you hear me. This kind of thing will get us there fast, but we're going to be burning out a few hundred million platinum worth of tech. We're also repurposing our gravitational shielding in a very new and exciting way that'll probably lead to my first few grey hairs."

"We can try to hold up," Jake said as he slowed. Debris had stopped falling around his hologram. "You might have more time if we can find a spot they can't scan through. There are a few of them nearby."

"We're on our way, Lad," Frost said from his seat behind Captain Vega.

"The assault comes next. If we're lucky and smart, we'll get there before Eve's Base Ship, the Messenger and its escort arrives." With a gesture, a hologram of the massive tear-shaped Base Ship appeared with nine destroyers and two dreadnaught class carriers. She pointed at two white shapes flanking the group. "These represent two more Citadel ships that could come in for support. The Hammer and the Renegade will be arriving in the Rose System in a little under two days at their best speed, so we can't expect help here. We'll have to plan the perfect mission if we want to save our people."

"We have our work cut out for us," Iruuk commented from where he sat behind her.

"We're at our best when the odds are not in our favour," Minh-Chu said.

"That's not the worst news, at least not in the long term," Alice said, looking at her mother.

Ayan straightened the top of her white vacsuit and nodded, her expression grave. "You've had some good luck, running into the Frekse when you did. Everyone who thinks twice about the Haven Nodes has been wondering if there is a way to track them, to find them from afar. According to the research that was being conducted by the Frekse, there is. Fleet Sciences has reviewed their data and can confirm that they were using an Edxi device to find a Haven Node, and one hidden Edxi scout ship. We don't know where the scientists aboard the Frekse obtained the device yet, only that it's some kind of living organ that can be used to find any kind of active dimension breaching technology. They were following the signal given off by the Haven Node in the Shattered End when they were attacked by the Overcharge."

"So, can we tell how many of these the Edxi have?" Minh-Chu asked, breaking into a cold sweat.

Ayan nodded at the Defence Minister. "From what we can tell, there are thousands. Our scans of Edxi wrecks in the Haven System show the presence of several of these organs in every jump-capable ship we've found. It's part of their navigation system as far as we can tell." Oz took a deep breath, looked around and went on. "There is a possibility that they know where every Haven Node is, and that will lead them to the heavily populated solar systems we sent the nodes to."

"We drew them a map so they can plan their next hunt, or invasion," Slick said.

"If Citadel or any part of the Order has an understanding of the same technology, then they'd have advance warning of our ships' arrivals and locations in normal space whenever a Quad Drive is in operation," Oz went on. "We're hoping that isn't the case, but there's no way to know."

Ayan nodded and continued as she looked through a holographic document on her end that no one could make out. "There is a way to determine what's visible to them. We have to find a way to turn things around and use our Nodes, our Quad Drives and other technology to read their network. That way we can reduce our vulnerabilities and perhaps operate our technology safely. It is possible. Until then, we'll have to do something difficult."

"Turn all the Haven Nodes off," Jake said as he caught his breath and took a sip of water.

"Exactly," Oz said. "All the Quad Drives on loan will have to be recalled. Haven Nodes will be shut down and cloaked until a reactivation signal can be sent."

"I'm shutting mine down. I don't want to, trust me, but they could be using the signal to track us underground," Jake said.

"Leave it on silent standby," Ayan said. "We'll be able to reactivate it using a quad drive or another node when it's in range. I love you, Jake."

"Love you too, see you soon," he replied. Jacob Valent's hologram disappeared.

There was silence around the table until Minh-Chu cleared his throat and said; "So he had a nice long weekend in a luxury suite and now he needs us to pick him up. Let's go get him."

EIGHT

Tunnels

JAKE HAD FOUND them the perfect landing location in the ruined outer regions of City Thirty-Five. They were right beside a crevasse that gave them access to several entrances that would take them to the old underground, where they could put over a hundred metres of matter between themselves and the sky.

The soldiers followed their training, doing their best to make sure that the officers and specialists from Ruby's crew kept up as they moved down into broken sections of the old city along with them and started moving east through damaged tunnels. Remmy was right there with them, helping people into the entrance to one of the narrower but more well-preserved walkways. As time wore on, a knot of nerves tightened in his chest with the awareness that it was taking way too long.

The rain had become a drizzle and the fire of thrusters sweeping by overhead kept everyone moving. Jake did his best to lead a small group with hand rockets and heavy rifles in making random strikes at them. It wasn't enough. They'd chosen the best option, to run, as far as Remmy was concerned.

Before they could get half of the Redstone crew inside, the strike from above hit.

There was someone in command of the Order forces who knew well enough to activate high-powered energy bursts so their sensors could detect anyone who was cloaked. Anyone who wasn't in a tunnel was revealed as though they were standing in the middle of a field at midday. Jake and the small contingent of soldiers with him rushed into the tunnels.

The Rixe along with fifteen fighters and several dropships fired down on them. Even from orbit, the Rixe's smaller weapons were accurate enough to obliterate two large groups of Ruby's crewmembers, making them disappear in an explosion that took out the side of an abandoned skyscraper.

The ground shook, and Remmy was forced further into the tunnel by Jake and Agameg, as it collapsed behind them. The last time Remmy saw the sky, it was filled with drop pods.

THAT WAS the beginning of a run through the underground as his tactical display showed that the enemy was already finding ways to give chase from behind. The way ahead was complex, and even with sensors mapping as they went, they found that they were momentarily lost several times.

Jake was no help for several minutes as he spent more time communicating with someone. Everyone who noticed hoped that he was talking to someone who could offer immediate help, but when he finished he looked grim. No one asked why.

Remmy was busy learning a lesson all over again. The reports from months ago when Dame, Easy, Alice and the crew of the Clever Dream visited the underground areas of Old City Thirty-Five were severely outdated. The data they had indicated that there should be underground pockets of life. Villages, even town-sized gatherings of scavengers, scrap crafters, workers, civilians and criminals. That was completely wrong. It was a relief to Remmy, but other people expected some kind of private security from the restored city centre to sweep in and push the Order of Eden back. He knew better. Panda, the wealthy portion of City Thirty-Five, had tall walls and energy shields for a good reason.

As for what happened to the outer residents in the underground, well, there had been a mass exodus from Rodus. It was a government program that was subsidized by the Order of Eden made to clog the interplanetary transportation and Haven System immigration systems, but it backfired. Haven Nation turned immigration into an industry, and while it did struggle in some places, the solar system was starting to thrive.

That didn't change one question that Remmy should have asked himself before they rushed into the labyrinth of tunnels and caverns beneath the ruins of old City Thirty-Five. Where did the Rodus Government get all the volunteer emigrants to fill the fleet of starliners that took them away from the solar system?

The confirmation that the underground was a ghost city started to grow in Remmy well before they came to the first major cavern. Security and flood doors were wide open, their guards long gone. Small pockets of ramshackle homes had been left in complete darkness, and he spotted a few small collapses that made it clear that the spaces they rushed through were giving in to neglect. "Where are we going, Jake?" Remmy asked as he dropped back to the middle of the pack of soldiers.

"There's a vault up ahead. Scans are bouncing off it, but the notes from Captain Marda say that he was looking into it as another site for a base before his crew left the planet for good. It should be a good place to hold up. It's several levels down from the surface with as much protection as we could find on this side of the city centre wall. He said there were rumours that there was a secret way out of it too."

The soldiers that chased them were starting to catch up. "We've got to get some distance before we go into hiding," Remmy said, looking at the scans of the tunnels ahead as they moved into another narrow passage where they could barely fit two abreast.

"I know, but it's all choke points and no advantage so far," Jake said as they continued running.

"We've got soldiers trying to get around us using tunnels to our right and left," Remmy said, thinking aloud.

"Then there are the ones behind us," Jake added.

"Wait, I'm seeing two-dimensional thinking," Remmy realised as he looked at his tactical map.

"Okay, that's something," Jake said. "Are they really coming at us on the same level? They're not trying for a vertical advantage?"

"They might be afraid to. The only open tunnels are below us, so they might be afraid that if they get ahead of us and try firing up that we'll collapse them onto them even if we block our way forward," Remmy said.

"Not really a bad thought, but I've passed more than one hole in these tunnels," Jake said. "They could rush ahead and set something up for us. That's actually a good idea."

"You're thinking we should start trapping them?" Remmy asked, checking his inventory. "I've got one Light Spider, five shaped charges and ten grenades with built-in sensors."

"Holy crap," Jake laughed. "What were you expecting on Gold Haf?"

"I thought we might throw a party for the Order, so I brought some fireworks," Remmy replied. "You went light?"

"No, but I didn't think you were going heavy too. I expected you to carry a lot of extra infiltration gear," Jake replied.

"He brought that as well. His pack is quite efficiently set up," Agameg said as he fell back with them.

"How's our flank movement?" Jake asked him.

"We're moving through eleven parts of the tunnel system, just ahead of our pursuers," he replied. "I would say most of us are moving too slowly. We've avoided casualties in the tunnels so far, but won't for much longer."

"Traditional tactics say we should find the smallest choke point possible, block everything else and put two heavily armed soldiers there, rotating as their shields deplete," one of Ruby's officers, Clay, suggested.

"We don't know how many soldiers they have. They could send drop ships filled with frameworks all night," Jake replied.

"So, thousands," Clay said.

"Tens of thousands. Tonight," Agameg replied. "The capacity of one Zhan Class carrier could provide for that and there are other Order ships in the area."

"All right, what's the plan?" Clay pressed, breathing heavily.

Jake ignored him. "There's an opening coming up."

"First area with pillar buildings. It's a town. I'm not reading any humanoid-sized life," Remmy said, seeing it on his tactical map.

"We'll start setting traps up now. Order everyone at the rear of the pack to make twenty metres of the tunnels a complete no man's land. Use the Fleet Handbook, if they aren't trained, they shouldn't be part of the action," Jake said. He sent the order to everyone who was qualified and was at the rear of their group.

Everyone got it within. Agameg, Jake and Remmy found niches in the side of the tunnel to fit in so they could let the rear half of the soldiers in their line pass and then they started setting up traps. It was easier for him to assume that framework soldiers with minimal autonomy would fall victim to them.

"You have one minute!" Jake ordered. "If you finish early, you have time to drop an extra grenade, but don't finish late!"

In every tunnel their people were moving through, the rear-most qualified soldiers stopped and did the same thing Jake, Agameg, Remmy and Clay did. Jake and Remmy set up a pair of mini-drones from Agameg's pack that would fire small shield-taxing beam weapons. Clay and Agameg drilled a pair of short-range electromagnetic pulse grenades into the floor and covered them with a ripped carpet. As a final touch, Jake set hand rockets up to launch at the first person they detected as they approached the next corner. Jake placed two in a utility panel while Remmy's were further down the tunnel affixed to the side of a hole in the floor so whoever jumped over it would have a nasty surprise.

"Time's up!" Jake announced, and only one of their tunnel groups had to quit early because the enemy was catching up. "We're moving to this point and mustering there."

It was a relief, being able to run full tilt for about thirty metres, then they caught up to the pack and were slowed down to what Remmy considered a light jog. Some of the soldiers from Ruby's crew were struggling to keep any running pace, even with their armour augmenting their movements. It wasn't a big surprise. At least half of them were from communications, flight, intelligence, engineering and other departments that didn't require them to stay in marine shape.

Jake's voice filled their encrypted frequency. "Get in there and get ready to fight!"

"Hurry! Twenty-five more metres to the cavern! Go! Go! Go!" Ruby shouted.

As he emerged into a dark underground city with pillar buildings that were fifteen storeys tall or less, depending on how large they had to be to touch the ceiling and floor, he saw what he was afraid of. Dozens of soldiers from Ruby's crew kept running away from the tunnel openings. Instead of turning around and getting ready to fight, they looked for cover. Thuds and cracks sounded from inside the tunnels behind them as traps went off.

Remmy checked his rifle, shields and armour status as the visor display showed him that all the traps that Jake's group set up had gone off. The enemy soldiers rushed into that hallway so quickly that they activated everything. The movement there had stopped. "Knights. The only thing that could get through that is Order Knights," Clay said to no one in particular. "We've gotta keep running."

Remmy saw that there was no motion in the tunnel he, Jake, Agameg and Clay trapped. There were several collapses. Dust and debris burst through several tunnel doors, especially the makeshift ones, as the rest of the traps went off. "They'll clear that pretty quickly or find ways around it," Jake said. "These aren't Knights though. I see a few regeneration patterns that match basic framework soldiers."

"We run right now," Parsons said. "This is a ghost town. We can use the buildings and all the other crap these people left behind for cover."

"First, we make a mess," Ruby said, pulling a hand rocket from her pack. "My last one."

Jake did the same, nodding at Remmy as Agameg brandished his final anti-ship rocket. "Close the tunnels."

"Clear! I'm marking targets and we're launching HR-Thirty-Threes!" Ruby ordered.

Several soldiers stepped in line to either side of Jake, Remmy, Agameg and Ruby. Clay was nowhere to be found, even though his inventory said he had four rockets on him. Remmy held his rocket up and locked onto the pair of heavy metal doors that had been marked for him. "Fire!" Jake ordered a few seconds later and Remmy had the satisfaction of watching his and four other rockets strike a broad tunnel opening with four lanes for hover and wheeled vehicles.

The rest of the passages on that massive wall collapsed as well, and their supply of anti-ship weaponry was almost completely depleted. "All right, so that was three times the fire-power we needed to accomplish the task," Ruby said with a chuckle.

"Re-check your numbers, please," Agameg said. "It was

barely enough for some of the entrances. Exaggeration won't help our situation."

"Watch it. I'm still your superior," Ruby snapped.

Out of nowhere, Parsons stepped in and asked. "Should you be?"

"Get back in line," Ruby snapped back.

"No! I told you there were great big holes in your plan, and you ignored me!" Parsons shot back with so much venom that she must have been holding it in for days.

"The starliner was almost ready to go when we found it, and we couldn't keep the Redstone. It was the fastest turnaround we could have hoped for," Ruby shot back. "If you calculated the mass balance for the Quad Drives properly, we'd be..."

"No, that's not my fault. I calculated everything in advance, but your knuckle draggers couldn't follow the plan, so we were screwed the moment you dumped your makeshift space mines. If we just jumped back home on the Redstone instead of running half a dozen missions in the Doxan System, we would already be on the Triton right now. Not here, waiting for these Order assholes to catch up to us underground!"

Ruby took a deep breath and replied with a much calmer tone. "You know how it works. We took a risk and the plan went out the window, blaming me or anyone else..."

"Ah forget it!" Parsons dismissed all of it with a broad gesture that looked violent thanks to her heavy armour suit. "I'm off your crew! Your creative thinking has paid off over and over, but now you've got us directly in the worst kind of shit this time. I knew it would happen eventually. We're trapping ourselves underground, hoping that the Triton can come to the rescue, but it's two days away. I did the math. We'll probably not get out of this one, but if we do, I'm going to find a squadron that has a fighter I can fly. I've had enough time at the helm for an egotistical, adventuring captain! I hope you get a little shuttle with a bunch of cheap androids, and I still wouldn't envy your pilot, even if it's a narrow-function AI!" Parsons stared at Ruby for a moment, and when her former Captain didn't offer a reply, she unslung her rifle and walked right up to Jake, where she saluted and asked; "Where do you need me?"

"We're retreating, moving through the town to the east. Fall in behind Remmy," Jake replied.

There was wisdom there. Parsons had no red flags or disciplinary marks on her record and she's flown most of the ship types in the fleet. Remmy hadn't taken a look past the first page, but that's what it said. Sure, soldiers of any kind didn't have the right to choose their commanders, but they weren't in the Fleet anymore. This was a volunteer effort, and Remmy thought it was a good move for her to offer her services to a higher power, at least for the time being.

He hoped she was joining the Triton crew, especially when he saw her qualification scores. She was a great pilot and understood logistics better than most. An interesting combination. He nodded at her as she came to stand beside him, still calming down. He wondered if she'd offer apologies to Ruby later, but was happy she'd decompressed either way.

"All right, we shut down one side of this place, so they can't come in from the west and that'll give us some time," Jake said. "That leaves about fifteen entrances to the north and south. We don't have the firepower to close all of them, and we don't have the manpower to hold this place, so we're moving on. Watch for citizens or anyone else who could be squatting here. Form up behind your commanders. We're headed east."

When Clay came back to fall in behind Ruby, she threw him to the ground, opened his pack and took every grenade, battery and hand rocket he had on him. "If you're not going to fight, you damn well don't need this." After checking his armour, she put him back on his feet and said; "Keep pace and shoot wherever the soldier unlucky enough to stand beside you tells you to."

The quick but careful journey through the darkness of the abandoned pillar town was nearly silent. They moved from building to building, rushing through open areas just in case there was something they couldn't detect waiting to take a shot at them from above.

NINE

The Sword Is Drawn

AYAN COULD SAY without a doubt that she hadn't seen Jake as she did while he was transmitting from somewhere underground on Rodus. Even still, she didn't tell anyone that the very edge of fright was in his words and expression. She was sure few other people would have been able to tell. What surprised her about the footage he sent was that Remmy could function at all. He'd been buried alive once, it nearly killed him, but he was keeping up with everyone, even helping Jake lead the way. That was encouraging, but knowing that Jake and so many members of his former division, the Special Operations Combat Unit, were barely keeping ahead of disaster, wrenched her heart in a way that she hadn't experienced in a long time.

Within minutes of Jake signing off, Ayan sent all of his combat data to her allies. The Nafalli Tribes, British Alliance,

Lorander, the Mergillians and some of the new merchant groups that were forming in the Haven Solar System. There were omissions, but she knew they couldn't help. Terry Ozark McPatrick, the Defence Minister and friend woke every Admiral in Haven Fleet up right away to argue Jake's case. He doubted he could get any support, but he had to try. She'd take her turn at trying to convince them to help too.

Desperation was usually a weak stance to take in negotiations. Ayan planned to use it as an advantage. Perhaps seeing that she'd all but lost her stiff upper lip but found a driving resolve could push people to help.

Making her home on Haven Shore, the first island that she settled with her people on Tamber, turned out to be a boon. The military base there was the unofficial headquarters for the entire fleet. Her home was half an hour away from it by transit. There were influential people she could visit in person if it came down to it.

Daisy was taking care of Little Laura in the nursery. The android was a true gift. At first, she volunteered to help with her adopted daughter, even taking her on an adventure to keep her safe aboard a ship filled with children that had to go into hiding for a time, Daisy had become Ayan's full-time assistant since then. She slipped into the role seamlessly, taking over for Leon. If it weren't for her, Ayan wouldn't have been able to focus on the meetings.

The first communication was with the Mergillians, who connected with her using an audio-only call and turned her request down in the first two minutes. They were still bitter after being turned down for a grant of ships and supplies. Their people were still training as officers and crew, so the refusal was reasonable, especially since the Mergillians only kept three small fighting ships in the Haven System to help with patrolling. Giving them modern vessels that only a few hundred of them would know how to use when they required tens of thousands of trained people would have been a disaster.

They didn't say that was the reason for their quick refusal when Ayan asked for their help in the Rose System, but that's what it came down to, she was sure. They had hundreds of older military ships that could have assisted there.

The Nafalli were making her wait. It wasn't like them, but they'd delayed the meeting one hour four times. That was one group that she expected support from, especially since they'd told Ashley that they were putting crews together and preparing their ships for weeks.

As a coded fleet call came in, Ayan braced herself and tried to put her meeting with the Mergillians out of her mind. Ayan tugged at her loose black overcoat and looked at her white Haven Sciences vacsuit. Everything seemed to be in order, only she was using the thin coat to cover all her fleet insignia. It looked more like a large shawl, a new design that wouldn't become a part of a regulation uniform, but that was why she was wearing it. People might assume that she wasn't speaking as an Admiral so she didn't have to explain it to them.

With a flick of her finger, she let the call in and watched as a hologram of Commodore Lamonthe appeared. Standing tall with a shaved head and a cold expression he said; "I just received a message from the Operations Officer of Kambis Production Facility Three. He indicated that someone was sending supplies there so they could start up five fabrication lines today. I'm lucky there's a law on the record that obliges him to tell the Fleet when a major facility begins operation, otherwise, I'm sure I wouldn't have had any indication."

"You're dancing around the question," Ayan replied. "What you mean to ask me is; 'are you responsible, and what are you going to be making?'"

"Well?" Lamonthe asked.

"It's my facility. I'll probably build some important ship components," Ayan replied. "I don't know exactly what yet, but Sciences just finished half a million simulated tests on the Mark Five Quantum Drive, so I'll probably start with that."

"That's military," Lamonthe said.

"The military hasn't seen it yet, and I paid for the research. Everyone is very happy with their bonuses. If you want to classify it as military technology, you can go ahead and begin navigating your way through the red tape. You should get started on the Windspite, too."

"What is the..." Lamonthe started, then shook his head as though he was trying to free a drop of water from his ear canal. "Wait, I know you're going to make classifying this technology a nightmare, you probably already set up a maze of bureaucracy that'll take my people three days to navigate before we get to see the plans, but tell me: what were the results of the Mark Five Trial? At least tell me if it's worth it."

"The Mark Five is a fifth the size, has over ninety percent of the same power output, and there were no interactions with negative effects in all but the most negligible percentage of travel."

"So, it's small enough to install in and power a starfighter in place of its reactor? You did it?"

"My team did it, but it's privately owned technology. Mine.

It wasn't designed on Fleet Sciences time or using their equipment." When she started redeveloping the Quad Drive using her own small, private company, it wasn't so she'd have leverage over the military. It was so she could own the technology once it was ready to be sold to the general public. The same could be said for the Windspite and several other projects that only existed digitally as a small staff refined them with the help of advanced software. "A range of Mark Five prototypes are being fabricated today."

"Wait, they're ready for that? How many system failures have you had in simulation?" Lamonthe asked, his eyes widening.

"None. Every simulation ended in a recoverable ship, even in interrupted transit," Ayan replied.

"You're going to keep the prototypes away from the military?" Lamonthe asked.

"Why not? The Fleet barely goes anywhere other than the Cefa System these days," Ayan replied. This was why Oz let Lamonthe do his job by questioning the creation of the new Quad Drives. As Defence Minister, Oz could have shut her whole operation down regardless of the red tape, skipping legal loopholes, but Lamonthe had to navigate the maze. It was part of his job.

Ayan couldn't resist making her point about the Fleet's purely defensive stance while she had his attention. "What do you need with something that slips part way into a near dimension with physics that would break the rules here?"

"How much faster is the Mark Five range of drives?" Lamonthe asked.

"That's not the important part. The research that went into

the Mark Five resulted in another software update for all other drives that will make them all safe. User error is the only risk now. We've also been able to create at least ten different versions of the Mark Five Quad Drive that will suit every kind of wormhole jump capable ship, some of which come with wormhole generators."

"So, some of these can make a ship capable of interstellar travel? That's not something Haven Fleet needs. That's a design made for the market. It's too soon."

"Or you could install the technology into small scout ships or jump fighters." His interest was more than piqued. Lamonthe was practically drooling at the prospect. "This new wave of technology can be used to fix so many other problems too." She would have to do a little more work to make it the revelation she needed for leverage but he was ready to hear her pitch. Lamonthe was brilliant, but sometimes he had to be led to a topic the right way. "Too bad the technology is shelved. All Quad Drives and the related technology are about to be put away, possibly for good once they're returned."

Lamonthe nodded gravely. "We can't have something that any Edxi ship can detect just calling out their..."

"What if I told you there's another solution?" Ayan asked. He was right where she wanted him, thinking about the shutdown as a problem, not the solution to one.

"You've figured out how to shield them from detection?" Lamonthe asked. There was no spite in the man, she knew he didn't hate her, but his resting expression came with a scowl, and he had a tendency to miss almost any attempt at humour. That, along with his dislike for Jake made him more of a nuisance than she thought he should be.

Ayan made him wait as she sat down in the middle of a large, thickly cushioned sofa. "If there are hundreds of thousands of Haven Nodes and just as many Quad Drives in use, then the data becomes less useful. We could give Lorander all the Mark Ones we have in storage. They've offered a good price and are willing to trade us navigational data on the entire Iron Nebula and every territory adjacent to our Stellar Cluster."

"Nine hundred drives?" Lamonthe asked.

"Updated. Tamper proof. The technology would still belong to us, and the best explorers we know would be able to sell us whatever they learn. It's a direction Fleet Sciences must move in. Then we give every ship passing through the area the new Comm Node module for free. I'll sell them for cost."

"New Comm Node?" Lamonthe asked, his eyes widening.

"A Haven Node that fits in your hand. The power source is external, so is the computing power, but everything else is in there. I'm sure every Captain would want one for thirty-five hundred platinum."

"That's one-one hundredth the cost of a full Haven Node. How many can you make?" Lamonthe asked.

"Only twelve hundred, and it will take a month. The manufacturing systems we have would strain, and the materials we need are in short supply," Ayan replied. "Well, I'm only referring to what I have in storage. The military reserve would be able to produce another ten thousand, but that would be needed for Quad Drives too. If we want to update every civilized world we know of, and extend our H-Node communication network on a broad scale, we'll have to start moving into the Doxan System and further out. I know of at least one abandoned mine that we can use, but it was attacked by the Raiders a long time ago. Military support will be needed."

"Maybe you could use your AI cluster and researchers to advance energy to matter fabrication so we wouldn't have to..."

"Go back to school or stop commenting on science you don't understand, Commodore. There are limits. Maybe they're temporary, but we're not past them yet. What I need is help. Today. Ships with trained crews, fighter squadrons and marines that are willing to fight the Order in the Rose System right now."

Lamonthe's expression hardened again. "The Fleet can't be seen rescuing a war criminal. You have my sympathy, Ayan, but..."

"Then I don't have time for this conversation," Ayan said. "I'll pay for the creation of a resource-gathering company of my own, or buy one. Maybe I'll go down the list of vendors for my little company and buy one of them so they can collect for me exclusively. I'll have to create my own security firm too, but I think enough people with military training will go private for me, so I should have something up and running within a week. That should be enough time for me to properly resign from Fleet Sciences. I wonder if Lorander would be interested in a partnership? I'm developing several technologies that they'd be interested in, not just the Quad Drive."

"You wouldn't leave Fleet Sciences to go private," Lamonthe replied. "Not even for this."

"Especially for this! Never forget that I own roughly one-seventh of the solar system, and most of my property claims haven't been settled yet. I could take an entire planet and a few moons. Forget the Quad Drives, I might start a nation of my own if there's no goodwill left between me and the nation I founded. Perhaps I'll call it Allegiance. I wonder how many allies Haven will have if I start producing and sharing the technology they're after? I'd have to establish a new government as well, and that would come with a military, but I don't think I'd have to start from scratch on that last point. How many ships will leave Haven Fleet and join me? What will you and the bureaucrats have left once the owners of the Haven System form a new government?"

"Are you threatening a civil war? Dictatorship? Over a convicted war criminal?" Lamonthe asked, boggling.

Ayan realized she wasn't calming down. As she made threats, not all of them empty, she was only becoming more irate, so she ended the call. Lamonthe would wag his tongue at anyone who would listen. One or two members of the Admiralty wouldn't bother listening to him, assuming that Ayan's threats were empty, only a way of trying to force his cooperation. A few Admirals would take her seriously and start raising alarms. The rest would probably offer their support in whatever she planned to do. Some of their pledges would come in secret, others would be made loudly.

Ayan silently cursed at herself for going too far. She never considered splitting a piece of the Haven System off for herself and her friends when she formed Gazer. Her company was meant to bring some of the technology she developed back under her control so she could support Jake after he was separated from the military. Lorander already wanted to start talking about creating a trade partnership, and she would be talking to them about it if Jake wasn't in trouble.

Creating a new government, claiming a planet, and most of

the other threats she brandished against Lamonthe weren't part of her plan. There was one threat that stuck in her mind, though. Leaving Fleet Sciences, taking everyone she could with her to work in her company had a good ring to it. While she, Alice and Jake were in the Fleet together she didn't notice that Haven took ownership of everything she helped develop. After Alice was given the bill for the Clever Dream, and she had to fight for the Triton to keep its Quad Drives and several other technologies behind Jake's back, it started to feel like she wasn't really part of the Fleet family. If Oz didn't help her keep Jake and his ship equipped, she was sure she would have left altogether. A sinking feeling began to overwhelm her as she started to think that creating a large science department right in the middle of a military organization was a bad idea.

The double doors across the room slipped open almost silently. Oz, out of uniform, with a rucksack and a large backpack entered. "Lamonthe just tried to tell me that you're about to fund a corporate rebellion," he said, grinning.

Ayan ran over to him and embraced one of her oldest friends. "Or near equivalent. I couldn't make him budge on getting help from the fleet, so I thought I'd start a panic. What's this all about? Have you left your post?" she asked after enjoying a brief, comforting squeeze.

"My Deputy is taking care of things for now. Arguing with the Triumvirate wasn't getting me anywhere. Take a look outside," he said, glancing at the window seat across the room.

Ayan ordered the window to become transparent by pointing at it and raising her finger. The walkway outside was filled with heavily armed marines. There were two Clever Class Corvettes hovering above from that angle, and combat shuttles on her home's private landing pad. There wasn't a single insignia in sight. "You brought friends, and I didn't hear a thing."

"I didn't want to wake the baby, Daisy said it was naptime," Oz replied with a shrug.

"They let you take half the Fleet?" Ayan teased.

"I ordered the maximum protection staff allowed for my vacation. There are three more Corvettes patrolling overhead, fully crewed. Most of these people are from the old Freeground Fleet," Oz explained. "You know, volunteers, our people who want to make sure nothing happens to me while I'm on vacation."

"Well, I hope you have a fine time," Ayan replied, grinning.

Her command and control unit buzzed, and the screen showed that British Alliance Rear Admiral Atwell was waiting. Only she wasn't calling, she was being shown in by Daisy through the hangar entrance. "Oh, you might have to hide," she told Oz. "I don't think the Defence Minister should be..."

"Who is it?" he asked.

"Atwell."

"Oh, shit," he said, looking around. "Where does this go?" he asked, pointing at a broad pair of doors.

"Closet," Ayan said, leading him in the other direction. "This way to the kitchen."

He rushed through the door and made sure it closed behind him. "Mind if I listen in?"

"I'd rather you did," she replied.

Rear Admiral Atwell entered. Her uniform was crisp, navy blue, and shaped into a smart-looking jacket and trousers.

"Admiral Anderson. Soon to be Valent, as I've heard. Congratulations."

"Thank you, Rear Admiral," Ayan replied, sitting down and gesturing for her guest to do the same. "Please call me Ayan."

"You've assembled quite the force outside. I recognized one of them from that documentary about the First Light crew. I've watched it three times."

Ayan was curious as to who it could be but put the thought aside for the moment. "It's a long documentary. I've barely watched it twice."

"I've stood on the simulated bridge behind Jonas through one viewing, I confess to being an admirer of the whole original crew," Atwell said. "Perhaps that's one of the reasons why I've come here. I'm happy to inform you that I've been given command of the Twenty-First British Alliance Battle Group, and I intend to take it to the Rose System. The Order has shown an interest, and the British Alliance would like to show them that we're fully invested in this war."

"It sounds like you should be announcing this at a news conference, or sitting down with Gavin Hale to talk about it," Ayan replied.

"Well, that's the sticky bit. You've always been a personal ally to the British Alliance, and your lineage tracks back to the New British Colonies. You're practically one of us. Before the Haven Nodes were shut down, my leadership was rather keen to highlight the relationship that's inferred between you and the British Alliance. That's a long winded way of saying that you are becoming more popular back home. Even the story of you and your mother has been dramatized. It's all coming up in your favour, and I couldn't be happier, if I'm being honest."

"I didn't know. I'm sorry, I've been busy," Ayan said, not sure of what else she could say.

"No reason to apologize, I'm only telling you that the Military has had difficulty explaining to the average citizen that they have good reasons for being here. Now you've made it much easier. I'm not in a position to allow you to direct the course of the Battle Group, but the intelligence we have, thanks to your people, leads us to believe that there is a current Order presence around and on Planet Rodus. You happen to have the technology required to get us there faster than any of our other allies, so, now I'm asking for your help."

"I can't outright give you Quad Drives from the defence reserve, the Admiralty would eject me from the Fleet. I couldn't install one of the new ones my company is making either." As much as she liked threatening to with Lamonthe, Ayan knew that Haven Fleet would stop her right away. Her facility was definitely being watched.

"What if your people did everything? The Quad Drives could be guarded, operated, and you could even navigate our ships whenever they're in use. They would never be our property, and you could remove them at the appropriate time?" Rear Admiral Atwell proposed.

The phrase that made it all legal was; 'They would never be our property," and Ayan grinned. "How many capital ships are in your battlegroup?"

"Fifteen," she replied. "We are ready, Admiral."

"It'll take at least four hours to set the drives up," Ayan said, hoping that Oz could help her find the crewmembers they needed.

"I'll have my staff facilitate. I will return to the flagship.

Please send us whatever tactical information you have regarding the City Thirty-Five hot zone," Atwell said as she stood. "I wish I could stay and visit."

"Some other time," Ayan said, wishing she could hug the woman, but the Rear Admiral was already on her way out of the room.

As soon as the door closed behind her, Oz came in from the kitchen. "I'm already getting transportation and security set up. We're going to use the last Quad Drives from the refit inventory. The Mark Threes."

"All right, I'll line up an engineering officer for each," Ayan said as she was about to activate a holographic interface. Then a hologram appeared of a white-furred Nafalli wrapped in a warrior's robe. It looked like thick dark red bands that were artfully woven across her tall, powerful-looking furred body. "I am Lawrren, Master of the Argool. We have begun travelling to Rodus and the Quad Drives that were installed during our refit are working perfectly."

Ayan's jaw dropped and she froze for a moment, looking up at the hologram of the Nafalli with the ghost-white eyes. If she was appearing life-sized, she was nearly three metres tall. That was far from the most surprising thing. Ayan was expecting to be contacted by someone representing the Nafalli in the military alliance. The last thing she foresaw was that they'd simply act, especially with a mother ship like the Argool, a fighting ship with over ten thousand warriors aboard. It took three months for the War Forge to refit the ship and the crew critical to her operation trained in simulations for the entire time, multiplying the days they spent taking courses, doing drills and qualifying as experts by three. To hear that they were already en route was shocking and moving. "Is the Argool fully crewed?" It wasn't the right thing to say, but it was the first thing to come to mind.

"Yes, and we have several smaller updated vessels with hundreds of volunteers aboard that are affixed to our hull. They are representing all of the tribes in the Haven System," Lawrren replied.

"Thank you. Please tell the tribe leaders that I'll forever be in your debt," Ayan said.

"Then we are family," Lawrren said, her expression relaxing. "As we became forever indebted to you and your family when you offered to share Tamber with us. You are truly a leader amongst your people." The rest came through in a growling Tree-Tribe Nafalli language. The translator presented it as; "I will howl your name every time I slay an enemy on the first day of battle."

"Thank you," Ayan replied, "I'm honoured. I'll make sure you're linked to all our allies on their way to the Rose System."

The hologram faded out and Oz put an arm across her shoulders. "Now it feels like we're in the fight."

"What ship are you taking there?" Ayan asked.

"I'm taking the Merciless out. Her Captain just got reassigned, but the new crew is still in place so I'm taking the chair," he replied.

It was an updated ship, equal to the Merciless, a powerful carrier. "How would you like to test the latest Quad Drive?"

TEN

The Underground

"THIS IS LOCKED DOWN TIGHT," Remmy said as he looked at the monolithic door. It was the only entry that their scans could find to the heavily fortified location they'd crossed the pillar town to reach. They could see it as they moved at Jacob Valent's driving pace. Its smooth metallic surface caught the scant light, adding its slight blue tint to it before it was reflected on the floor and ceiling of the massive space.

The worst thing about not finding so much as a switch to open it for Remmy was that over a hundred surviving soldiers were looking to him and Jake to find a way in. Ruby set her scanners on high and pointed both her hands at the door's surface. The command and control units that were issued to the Special Operations Combat Unit members came as a pair, and both of the bracers on her wrists had high-powered emitters and receivers. The data came back and she read it as Remmy searched for a hidden panel. "This door has been enhanced with Sotorium, I've never seen it before."

"We don't know how to make that anymore," Clay said as he looked at the results again. "But these doors look new. Who poured them? They had to be made in place. We're five kilometres from the surface."

"The underground freeway we came in would be big enough to move them in," Ruby said, shaking her head. "This is a relic. A two-metre thick door that may as well be five times thicker and pure ergranian."

"Sotorium? Refresh me?" Jake asked as he scanned the floor at the foot of the entryway, quickly looking for anything that could be an access point.

"Oh," Clay said, delighting at the opportunity. "It was a reactive material a bit like Ergranium, but it actively spread any kind of energy across its interior material. So, if you shoot it, you won't see the damage because the energy you exerted would be transferred incredibly quickly. Something this size could survive anything we have. Oh, and if we do manage to break some of the material it'll burst at the site, creating a kind of ablative filler that's almost as resilient. It might take years to get through with the right cutting equipment. Sorry, I never get to talk about these ancient materials. My speciality is in starship repair, but I'm sort of an obscure engineering nerd too."

"Everyone scan around this thing, we've gotta find an access panel." Remmy turned to Ruby as he continued to look along the foot of the door. "Can you pass your results on? I don't want to risk burning my sensors out."

Every soldier started scanning the area, even as some of

them were fighting to catch their breath after the long run. Jake led a group out from the doorway so they fanned out, looking for an access panel in the rocky surface of the massive cavern and the walls of the pillar buildings that flanked the portal.

Ruby sent her results and watched as he brought them up as a large hologram. "What are you looking for?"

"If this door's been here for long enough, moss or something could have found its way into a crack, or seam that'll show me the shape of a sally port or panel or something," Remmy said, glancing at the soldiers who were wandering off a little, focusing on the screens on their command and control units or the displays within their visors.

"Oh, I was hoping you were looking for something I didn't," Ruby said with a little snicker. "I mean, you were one of the best digital intrusion experts in the fleet."

Most people knew one thing above all other details about him; that he'd collected a massive database of ancient entertainment, and more recent news and created a program that was particularly good at catering it all to the viewer's tastes. He'd only met a handful of people who bothered to read about him and what brought him to the Haven System. It was a compliment, and he didn't know what to say, so he countered with a little information about her. Maybe she'd take it the same way. "You're probably better at reading a scan than I am since you spent three years with Crean Exploration. You were part of the crew who found Bounty."

There was a long pause before Ruby replied; "Then you know that's why I joined the Resistance. We celebrated that discovery, and Regent Galactic moved in for a harvest as soon as someone leaked the location and basic details about the system.

We thought we would be selling data, settling rights and charting safe routes through to the planets like Lorander. Then Regent Galactic got there faster than anyone could imagine, kicked us out and started ripping up everything worth a pip."

"I'm sorry, sounds like that's still an open wound. Didn't mean to poke at it, but I tend to find the wrong thing to say within a few hours of meeting people. Sometimes it takes a minute or less," Remmy apologized.

"No worries, it's just been a while since I thought of it. I stood on Bounty Three, Four and Five before we made the announcement. It was incredible, we never thought we'd find that many places in one system that Class I bios could settle on without terraforming."

Class I was an old reference to beings that were well suited to Earth. Remmy hadn't heard the term since he was in the Fleet Academy learning about some of the more adventurous, early explorers. "What was that like?" Remmy asked as he got back to his own scanning.

"Here! Gaddon's alive! He's got people with him," shouted a soldier from the north side of the wall.

Looking up from his work, Remmy saw several dozen soldiers coming in, most of them carrying equipment and weaponry. "They took a detour, thank Haven." The last part of that statement drew a momentary glance from Ruby. It was the first time he'd said; 'thank Haven,' but he hoped it would catch on.

"We went north a bit, got lost when there was too much rock and metal for our transmissions to get through, then followed a tracker to a couple of drop bells. We got everything. I'm thinking of opening a store," he and Ruby came together in a welcoming embrace that looked much more familiar than friendship.

"I've got it! This is it!" called a soldier from the wall of a pillar building fifteen metres away from the door. He was pointing at a door to a cybernetic parts shop with a window display featuring a toppled mannequin with missing arms. Remmy ran towards it and gave the shop a quick scan.

To the left of the entrance was a door leading to a security room that wasn't a part of the store. There were thick cables leading from it into the ground and then to some point past the large gates. "Good catch," Remmy said as he confirmed that there were no traps or other devices in the control room. The security door between him and the controls would have stopped most intruders. Jake was in his ear then, asking; "How does it look?"

"It's a control room. There might be others around. There's power, I'm just about to break in. Doing one more sweep for alarms," Remmy said as a pair of soldiers tried to do the same thing from behind him. One stepped forward with his sidearm out, pointing at the lock.

Before he could pull the trigger, Remmy batted the weapon away. "If you trigger an alarm we could be stuck out here when the Order floods this place with every troop they've got."

"I've gotten into more complicated..." the crewman started to counter.

"Get back and follow orders," Remmy said, pushing him back into the store behind them. He started scanning around the door as he spoke more calmly. "Listen, I'm sure whatever ship, storehouse or bedroom you snuck into once was guarded by some kind of security system, but that doesn't mean you have any business even looking at something that everyone here thinks is pretty important. I haven't looked your records up, but this isn't the time for a job interview, so I'll take a look at your qualifications when..." A tiny detector three millimetres wide on the wall opposite the door came up on his scanner as a known security device. He moved to it, stepping around a fallen shelf with several cheap cybernetic hands that had been left behind and took a closer look. "Well, hello there. This is what I mean. It's calibrated to set an alarm off if it detects the specific vibration of the door opening without receiving a specific signal first."

"What happens if the alarm goes off?" the other crewman asked from the entrance.

Remmy started a program that tried the known frequencies that the device might expect and watched the results as he replied; "I don't know. There could be a lockdown or worse." Explaining what was going on helped with his growing impatience. As he waited for his digital tool to find the right frequency he was increasingly aware that Order of Eden forces could start moving in on their position at any moment.

Gaddon rushed into the shop and looked at Remmy, who was climbing up on a shelf under the detector. "Hey, I've got six or seven tons of gear here. Need anything?" he asked with an Irish accent that matched Ruby's.

"The hero of the moment," Remmy said. "Thanks for grabbing all that stuff. I'm good, this detector will be blind in a sec. Did you see any Order guys on your way here?"

"No, sure we lost them and got well ahead of whoever they're sending here using the long way, if they're coming at all," he replied.

"Oh, they're coming. We're not lucky enough for them to lose interest," Remmy said as he found the frequency that would communicate with the detector, found its model number, and then verified that it was actually a cheap one. He pointed his right command and control bracer at it, pulled the nozzle out of the end, and used his micro fabricator to cover it with a tiny amount of foam that would dampen any vibrations. "And Bob's your uncle."

"Bob?" asked the crewman who was about to shoot the door earlier.

"It's something from ancient television, probably with cultural roots so deep that we'd have to do real research to find out who Bob is," Remmy said as he crossed the room back to the security door. His audience just stared at him. "Nevermind. The sensor won't detect a thing."

"How are we doing? There's motion in the southern tunnels," Jake said over the local command channel.

Remmy plugged into the data port beside the door, activated his intruder program, and the door popped open a moment later. "I love it when people use whole words as passwords. One minute, Admiral." He paused a moment, realising his mistake. "Sorry, habit. Don't worry, it won't happen again. I can be taught."

"Are we getting in there today, or should I start setting up for a siege?" Jake asked.

Remmy looked at the panel, and found a very obvious layout of buttons with a simple control screen. "I can't believe it." He looked again, then flipped a switch that sent power to the door. He pushed a simple button marked with a piece of tape that said; 'OPEN' next and a shudder underfoot made it obvious that something was happening. "I think I got it."

"You got it!" Ruby said over the command channel. "Checking it out, keep everyone outside."

Remmy was about to rush out of the room, but stopped and grabbed the crewman who nearly shot the door. "Okay, what's your name."

"Dubin, like Dublin but without the 'l,'" he replied.

"Okay, without the 'l,'" Remmy said, moving him in front of the board. "This controls that big door outside. As far as I can tell, every switch and button is labelled and that screen has a bunch of obvious status stuff on it. Looks like reading the board explains the board."

"Oh, right, this is all flat fancy," Dubin said, nodding.

"Okay, does that mean it looks complicated or simple?" Remmy asked.

"Oh, flat fancy's just the way we say the opposite of fancy where I come from. It's this little moon in orbit around..."

"Okay, so this is simple to you. This button opens the door, this one closes it, and there's a safety switch for both," Remmy said, pointing the few features of the panel out.

"I get it, right. Simple. What's this do? These sliders under the covers here?" he asked.

Remmy looked at it for a moment, looked at the schematic on the inside of the cover and nodded. "That's a backup battery system, don't touch it. I'll leave a few guys here with you so you don't get lonely."

"Wait, you're leaving me here?" Dubin asked.

"Yeah, you just got a promotion, or a demotion depending on what you were doing for Ruby, I guess," Remmy replied. He left the building, tapping four soldiers on the shoulder and pointing at the store. "Make sure Dubin, our button man, is safe."

"Aye," replied one as the four of them took positions beside the outer door and the security room.

Ruby, Gaddon, and Agameg were at the threshold of the giant doors, stopping anyone from going inside. Unlike the cavern behind him, there was no bare rock. No one had moved into the space. Heavy cables, spokes that were two metres wide and closed compartments spread out from a central pillar that was over a hundred metres thick. Green, white, blue and yellow lights that blinked and shone up and down its length, along with the compartments on every other surface lit the entire space enough for them to see that it was over a kilometre long and more than half as wide. "Anyone know what this is?"

"It's a giant computer," Clay breathed.

Gaddon slapped him on the shoulder. "He's asking if anyone's seen something like this before. This in particular."

"This looks old, and some of that tech has the covers off. We may have to figure out what to avoid before we get in there," Jake said. "Quickly."

The awe the place inspired was already wearing off for Remmy. He could take a closer look later, but hearing Jake's question brought everything back into focus. This was supposed to be where they held out until help could come. "Any chance you could give Captain Marda a call? Ask him about this spot?"

"Not an option at the moment," Jake replied.

As he examined the area closest to the door, Remmy saw that a lot of the cables and several of the modules had been pried apart, their innards stolen. "It looks like whoever lived here was harvesting the tech. My scanner's not matching anything to modern parts lists."

"It's ancient, that's why," Clay ventured.

"You're right. Some of the technology resembles old Issyrian inventions, from the Second Wave human advancement era," Agameg said. "I'm not an expert, but I would say the underground settlers were stealing components and materials. The town behind us may have grown on the industry of salvage. I suppose we'll be taking advantage of this place as well when we use its doors," Agameg said. "Not that I'm objecting."

Remmy continued to scan the area right in front of him, but he found himself smiling a little as he noticed Ruby scanning the centre column. She walked forward slowly, as if she was drawn to the collection of unknown advanced technology. "There's a door and a lift inside that pillar. It's a big one. We might have a way out of here. A hidden way."

"All right, we don't have time to make sure," Jake said. "Dubin, you just became the most important guy here. You're going to make sure that the door closes behind us and then run through it. Got that?"

The door was still opening, so Remmy guessed that Dubin would have plenty of time. "Okay," the man replied uncertainly. "Wait, wouldn't anyone be able to open the doors using those controls once I'm gone?"

"Don't worry, that room won't be there anymore," Jake replied.

"Nice. No time to investigate our find. Haul all our gear inside," Ruby ordered, tearing herself away from her scans for a moment.

ELEVEN

Test Work

WE NEED THIS. *If it won't work, then we're going to lose half the squadron,* was the thought going through Minh-Chu's head as his Archangel Heavy fighter materialized around him. His opponents were three of the best fighter pilots in the squadron. They were flying simulated Regent Galactic Firestrike light fighters with shielding they would never have in real life. Other details like armaments, dampeners and missile load outs were up to them too, so he had no idea what they had in store for him.

The simulation was perfect. Minh-Chu's body believed that he was in his cockpit, not the lounge section of the Pilot's Den. He detached from his drop ship, a Clever Class Corvette, and took off. The trio in the simulation with him played the role of patrolling Order of Eden pilots who were watching over the Locon. In order to strip Minh-Chu of a key advantage, they knew what his mission was. The Locon was undergoing a resupply mission and was affixed to Celine Station. One Archangel fighter with the Fury loadout could take it out of action, but only if it could get a clear line of sight on the target.

To Minh-Chu, the problems with the Fury setup were numerous and he tried not to think about them again. His wingman, Sass, fell into formation behind and to his port side. "I'm ready, Ronin."

"All right, the Locon is right where we expected. No sign that we've been detected. That's about to change. Time to make some noise. Follow me. Afterburner safety disengage." Minh-Chu said over their scrambled laser link.

"Disengaged," Sass replied.

"Set your Navnet software to receive only. Check your trajectory against it, adjust, and lock your course," Minh-Chu said, watching a trio of fast cargo delivery ships pass overhead. A blinking light on his communications panel told him that someone from Navnet control was trying to communicate with him, but he ignored it.

"Done. Rechecking... yup, that's done," Sass said.

"Verify that our target is docked to the station," Minh-Chu said as he did so and he saw that the last of the mooring rods were being affixed to the large ship. They were meant to keep the vessel steady while supplies were being moved to the Locon using long extendable boarding corridors. "I see it."

"They are, checking my angle," Sass said. "I'll be able to hit Engineering Control and the Atmosphere Processing Centre once I'm in position. I have a question, though; why didn't we drop in closer?"

"It wouldn't be a good test," Minh-Chu replied. "We also

can't risk a whole Clever Class Corvette at that range. The Locon has close-range interdiction capabilities, so it could trap the Three C and take it out."

"Ah, right," Sass replied.

"Final check," Minh-Chu said, looking the status of his fighter over. "Ready."

"Ready," Sass said.

The night side of Planet Rodus was far below, the glittering lights of the cities shining through a mostly clear sky. "Engage full thrust in three, two, mark," Minh-Chu said and he enjoyed the thrill of every thruster that he could point aft going off at once. "Now every navigation tracker and tactical system on this side of the planet can see us. Power everything up and get your capacitors nice and full."

"Aye, Ronin." Sass sounded more nervous than excited. It wasn't a good sign, especially since it was only a simulation. "Forward shields up, geometry set in a long leading spike."

"Perfect. Just get there and fire then fly past. That's all you have to do," Minh-Chu said reassuringly. He activated all his power systems and made sure that his capacitor banks were charging up. Everything checked out, and he opened all four of his gun ports. The Slayer Seven Railgun forks extended to the left and right of his cockpit and locked into position.

The hum of the power plants behind his seat was loud enough to trigger the audio-dampening system in his helmet. The normal AC-30 Micro Fusion reactor had been replaced with two XR-90's, which were the largest, highest-powered power plants that the new Archangel could use.

"Ronin," Sass started, sounding even more nervous. "These fighters weren't made for this, were they?"

"This exact configuration, no," he replied, pausing as they passed within three hundred metres of a long cargo ship's train of containers. "The Archangel was made to operate at this power level and to account for the instability these guns would cause though, so we're not pushing them past the limit."

"Enemy contact. Three up," Sass announced. "Firestrikes. Two with heavy missile loads and one with four extra gun pods."

"That's the ace, she's in the lead. I'm marking her as Dame," Minh-Chu said. "Guessing, but I'm marking the other two as Carnie and Breaker."

"I am so dead," Sass muttered under his breath.

"Activating digital and scanner noise countermeasures," Minh-Chu announced as he activated the high-powered transmitters that were added to the left and right sides of his craft's fuselage. They looked like short spikes, not so much like antennae, adding a touch of savagery to the profile of his fighter. "They're manoeuvring into our path, accelerating so they can match speed and get in behind us, you see that?"

"Yes, Sir," Sass replied.

"What do we do?"

"Well, we can't avoid a head-to-head, so we'll have to make sure they want to avoid one," Sass replied.

"Lining up on Dame," Minh-Chu said as he let his guns gimbal nine degrees to starboard. They could only turn fourteen degrees in any direction, so he was lucky she was flying into his firing arc. There was no way he could make the shot at that range unless he got very lucky. Striking his target was secondary, however. He checked his aim and then announced; "Firing guns, following it with a Biggie." With a squeeze of the trigger, he sent several hundred high-speed rounds towards Dame, Carnie and Breaker. As soon as he finished Ronin launched one of his Big Surprise Mark Fifteen torpedoes. It cloaked immediately, disappearing in front of his eyes as it slid into open space. That was something that was available for missions, but no one had bothered to load one onto their fighter, not even in sims.

"Long-range missile launches!" Sass said, launching Smart Chaff. The three sparking, spinning decoy shards were flicked out of the underside of his ship. It was too soon, the enemy fighters were over a hundred thousand kilometres away.

"Our jamming should take care of the missiles. Set your Smart Chaff to auto-launch," Minh-Chu instructed.

"Yes, Sir," Sass replied.

"Dame's wingmen are trying to distract us so we can't get another shot on them," Minh-Chu said as a warning tone that told him that two of the dozen long-range missiles that were launched were steadily locked onto him, regardless of their guidance jamming signals. "Firing one decoy drone," he said as he tapped a button on his left flight stick twice. A small drone the size of his hand launched from the top of his ship, began to emit a weak gravity field, a holographic shell, and an energy profile that made it look like his fighter only without the thin stealth coating.

It was a louder, more obvious target, and the missiles veered off to chase it. "Thank you, Lorander. I'm going to put an order in for a case of that coating to make sure I never run out," Minh-Chu said as he watched the drone try to fly away from the missiles and fail.

"I overhead Carnie saying those drones cost fifteen thousand platinum each," Sass said.

The Big Surprise went off for the first time, revealing itself. To the naked eye, nothing happened, but a five kilometre wide bloom of energy pulsed on his tactical display, showing that Carnie had been caught in it. His shields were probably reduced to zero. It didn't get a chance to go off again, and Breaker's fighter spun then ripped it to shreds with his guns. "Figures. A retired Bullet Chaser would have reflexes for that," Ronin muttered. "All right, launch all your Biggies at the Locon now. We might not get another chance. We need to see if they can manoeuvre to the target and then damage its shields." He armed and launched his second and last Big Surprise Fifteen.

Minh-Chu was back to trying to use his onboard tactical system to line a shot up on Dame, who was weaving just enough to keep her and her wingmen from being hit at such a long range while they waited for Ronin and Sass to close in. He had to make a threat, to scare them right off for at least an instant. Making a solid hit would help. "We're closing to seventy thousand kilometres to the Locon. Power down to normal high thrust," Minh-Chu said, reducing his power until his afterburners disengaged.

Four fighters launched from the Locon's forward fighter bay. "New contacts," Sass shouted.

"All right, just watch for missiles. Don't be afraid to fire those drones off, I'll pay the bill if it comes up," Minh-Chu said.

Minh-Chu saw a shot at Dame and her wingmen as they flew in formation and pulled his trigger without hesitation. The low ripping sound of his guns as they vibrated on their mounts surrounded him. Carnie and Dame were unscathed, but Breaker's shields failed to entirely stop the heavy railgun rounds and his main port thruster was ripped to shreds. He turned his fighter towards Sass immediately. "Oh, God, he's got a missile lock!" Sass shouted.

Breaker fired six missiles in quick succession, flipped his ship end over end then started decelerating with his remaining thrusters. It would take him much longer with one of them gone. "Launch a decoy drone, evade," Minh-Chu said calmly.

Sass's fighter automatically sent a burst of three Intelligent Chaff shards out, then another, and another as he ejected a drone decoy and tried to manoeuvre. "Sorry, Ronin!"

"We're entering manoeuvring range with Dame's group," Minh-Chu said as he watched Carnie open up with guns as the nose of his fighter turned to point at him. A few minor hits registered against his forward shields, and Minh-Chu manually shunted more power to the coverage around his ship. "Carnie thinks he's got me here."

Three of Breaker's missiles lost their way thanks to guidance jamming. One went after the Intelligent Chaff instead, and two managed to destroy a decoy drone. That left Sass in the clear. "Holy crapola! That worked!" he cheered.

"Watch it, Dame's..." Minh-Chu said as her fighter moved in a quick arc, keeping its six pulse cannons pointed at him. She opened fire, punishing his port side shielding with a barrage of deadly light.

Minh-Chu was just about to turn his guns on Carnie, who was weaving behind him as he took shots at his aft shields, which were starting to suffer. The pulse cannons on the Firestrike were some of the most powerful energy weapons in use by the Order of Eden. and it showed. Minh-Chu shunted power from the capacitors for two of his railguns to his shields, watched them regenerate to full coverage immediately, and then set it back. "It is good to have power," he said to himself as he cut his thrusters, flipped end-over-end, lined his guns up with Carnie and opened fire. One pair of railguns punished his shields at first, then the capacitors for guns three and four finished recharging and joined in. Carnie's shields were down in the first second, then heavy metal rounds ripped holes through the port side of his ship, passing through forward armour, the magazine, fuel tank, upper manoeuvring thruster then his aft armour. Carnie attempted to break his attack off, using his starboard thrusters to push him out of Minh-Chu's line of fire, then blasting with his remaining main engine.

Minh-Chu spun his fighter around and pointed in Dame's general direction as Sass shouted; "Help!"

Minh-Chu opened fire at vacuum where Dame was an instant ago. It was too late, she'd already burned his shields down and done too much damage to the hull on one side of his ship. It wouldn't be able to emit a stable protective field on his starboard side. An alarm sounded in Minh-Chu's helmet. There was a hail of missiles on their way from the Locon, several fighters in the distance, and a pair of corvettes that had come along to assist while their mothership tried to decouple so it could manoeuvre away from the station. Minh-Chu launched all but one of his decoy drones, sending five into the void. He was coming up on the supply ships and their armed escort. Relative to him and Sass, they may as well have been standing still in space, but it would give them an opportunity. "We can shake Dame off if we use these guys as cover," Ronin said.

As Minh-Chu took his first shot at Dame, who was using

Sass for cover against him, he spotted Carnie, who was moving in from the other side. He adjusted his position in time to avoid a double missile launch. The jamming signal should have sent the munitions off in random directions, but they launched perfectly straight instead, missing Minh-Chu only to impact Sass' fighter, sending him into an uncontrolled spin. "You dumb-fired them at close range? And they call me crazy," Minh-Chu said, wishing Carnie could hear him.

"I'm out, sorry," Sass said as his fighter collided with the edge of a freighter, then self-destructed a few seconds later.

Dame, Carnie and he all had to make some fancy manoeuvres as they drifted at incredible relative speeds through the outer gathering of security and supply ships around the Locon. Irritation rose in Ronin at what Sass just did. It wasn't that he was defeated in the simulation, it was what he did right before he was knocked out. "If he had time to apologize, if he had time to activate his destruct system, then he had five seconds to keep fighting," he said through clenched teeth.

An Order Corvette had its blunt nose pointed at him. The lights from its upper turret illuminated his view as Minh-Chu took a deep breath and evaded, nearly skipping himself off the hull of another as he streaked past it. As he exhaled, Minh-Chu let go of his frustration, breathing; "Not all of us find our calling in our first passion." By the time he finished exhaling, he knew what he'd do with Sass, and the issue was out of his mind.

A small pip sound informed him that his shields had taken a minor hit from behind. It was Dame, she was following him through the maze of ships gathered around the Locon. With a quick flick of manual switches, the push of a few buttons, he deactivated all his jamming systems, redirected the power to sensors, sent a scan pulse out ahead of him in a broad cone, and then directed all the energy he freed up to shields. "Yes, yes, there it is," Minh-Chu said as he spotted what he was looking for and Dame raked his aft shields with her pulse cannons. "Follow me, follow me," he said as he manually shunted more power to his forward shields. "You don't see it yet, or you think I'm bluffing if you do."

A group of shipping containers that read as empty loomed ahead and he pointed his nose right into the middle of them. The momentum of his ship was taking him in the right direction, and he could see the Locon was just past it. "Oh, this could be the end of the sim and the beginning of a whole new chapter of rightful razzing," he said to himself. His aft shields were nearly down, but Dame had stopped firing, seeing what was about to happen. "I'm not bluffing."

A collision alarm sounded, then his ship passed through several layers of thin metal and he came through the other side shouting; "Like wet tissue! I believe in physics! The beauty of the universe, and the glory of antigravity kinetic shielding!"

All three of their Big Surprise torpedoes went off right next to the Locon's shields. Thanks to the scanner jamming signals that they sent ahead, the torpedoes went unnoticed. Sure, given enough time, the Locon's scanners and the crews manning them could have sorted out the mess of random signals and noise, but intelligence said that it would take them at least five minutes and twenty seconds with a trained crew and the right software. He hoped that would prove correct, because the shield charge in the middle of the long ship had been reduced to nearly nothing.

At long last he was close enough to his main target, the Locon, and he had a moment to line it up and open fire. The rip-roar of his guns vibrating around him, the whine of power systems dumping energy into them, and the low pinging sound his tactical computer made to indicate that he was hitting the sweet spot of the Locon made for an exciting combination. There was a place where the energy shielding was thick but the armour beneath was thin - a ninety-degree hull join at the base of the squat bridge tower - and he watched as the shields failed in that section. As the shield strength dropped the last five percent, the high-speed, dense railguns rounds that were made to conduct energy around them started making it through the ship's armour plates. Minh-Chu watched as his scanners used his own jamming signals to detect what was going on with the capitol ship and was delighted as his rounds dug through the hull armour, and several decks, then penetrated the fuel reserve. He adjusted his angle slightly and sent rounds towards the main reactor. The point wasn't to penetrate it, there was little possibility of that, but to bounce high-speed shrapnel throughout the power control systems inside the ship. It worked. The reactor housing was impenetrable, at least for the moment, and deflected rounds were sent in many directions, passing through several decks.

The countermeasures from the Locon and the station were aiming at him, and Minh-Chu redirected power from two of his guns to his shields, rebalanced them to protect his ship equally in all directions, and started to line a shot up on Dame, who was charging at him again, pulse weapons firing.

Streaks of anti-starfighter fire lit up the sky around him as Minh-Chu spun his Archangel around. Supply ships, the Locon and the station passed beneath him as his momentum carried him along. If he could make it out of the station's immediate defence torpedo system, he would be rescued by a Clever Class Corvette. He only had to stay alive.

Dame hammered at his shields with her guns, costing him eighty percent with a steady barrage as she followed his manoeuvres manually. She was too close, too locked in, and he fired back in bursts, coming close but missing every shot until he finally caught her forward shields, raking them. Missile warnings and countermeasure gun alerts filled Minh-Chu's ears and he launched his final drone. "This can't be the end of our dashing hero!" he shouted.

Dame knocked his forward shields down to five percent as she tried to slide out of his sights, but Minh-Chu foresaw the move, and raked her with his guns as she passed, putting rounds through the nose of her fighter. It drifted away.

Then, like a bolt out of a black sky, Carnie's fighter rushed him. It closed so quickly that he must have thrust ahead and turned around. He cut his afterburners and started firing one missile after another, all straight at him without using guidance.

Minh-Chu dodged, feigned, caught one on his port side and watched his shields drop by a third, turned, and then noticed a notification that his drone was destroyed by one of the base's anti-fighter guns. The Clever Class Corvette appeared in a brief bloom as its wormhole opened and closed. It was still sixty-thousand kilometres away.

As Minh-Chu spun the nose of his fighter in Carnie's direction, his ears were filled with a warning tone. There was an uncountable number of missiles coming in his direction. The station had fired recklessly, ignoring the civilians in the area. Many of the ships waiting to land in the station's smaller bays would be caught in the crossfire but they didn't seem to care anymore. He activated his countermeasure launcher and was rewarded with several hollow clicks. As Carnie evaded a burst of fire from his guns, Minh-Chu's fighter was struck by several of the larger, high-speed anti-fighter missiles and he was back in the Pilot's Den.

TWELVE

Everybody's Simming

MINH-CHU DIDN'T FEEL SO MUCH as a hint of nausea or disorientation that he'd come to expect after disconnecting from simulated space. It was thanks to a team that was assembled by Ayan and Jake before he was dishonourably discharged from Haven Fleet. They completed several phases of the next generation of technology, where someone could experience several days' worth of experience in one as though they were there. That kind of full immersion required a special support pod for the person's real body.

The type that Minh-Chu and his squadron were finally given access to couldn't change the passage of time as much as a full pod, or egg as Jake called them. Its maximum compression was by a factor of three, so in the real world, he, Dame, Carnie,

Breaker and Sass were only in the simulation for a little under four minutes.

A member of the Triton Science Team stood beside his lounger and watched him anxiously. "How are you feeling?"

"Good, Marco. Other than the violent death I just had in the sim, coming back to reality was nice and smooth," Minh-Chu replied.

"Oh, good, the team will be happy," he said. "You're using a prototype that's being prepared for the general market."

"So, Fleet will be selling these?" Minh-Chu said as he pulled the node affixed to the back of his neck off and put it back on the holder beside the lounger for cleaning.

"Oh, no," he replied. "We'll be selling them to the fleet and then everyone else, from the sounds of it. I don't know exactly how that works, but the tech belongs to Jake, or Ayan, or a bunch of Haven System shareholders. Hey, aren't you one of them?"

"Yeah, but I won't let it change me. I mean, I only ordered one platinum-plated toilet in the private station I'm having built in orbit around Unity."

Marco stared at him for a moment, looking a little stunned.

After a little snicker, Minh-Chu shook his head. "I'm just kidding. I own a share, but I'm too busy out here to do anything with it. Good work on the brain bud."

"Thank you, I'll pass that on to the team. So, how was your, er, flight?"

"Felt like I was really there," Minh-Chu said as Carnie and Dame slipped out of their loungers and put their brain buds into their holders. "You set me up," he said to her with a grin, and then he pointed at Carnie. "You took me down."

"Sure did. Can't say it was easy though," Carnie said with a big smile.

The blue-yellow light of transit space shone through the large windows behind him, painting the room in swirling hues. The room was filled with pilots who looked like they were napping peacefully, but his entire squadron was actually in the same simulation.

"Are you certain that the jamming systems in the simulation were set up right? We were highly effective. Most of the countermeasures and tracking systems the Order was using weren't locking or tracking us at all. Less than twenty percent overall, by my estimation," Dame asked.

"If our intelligence is right, and we're pretty sure it is, our jamming setup should be even more effective, especially against the capital ship point defence systems. There's nothing we can really do about the new power levels they've tuned their shields to, though. Ever since we took the Haven System back, they've been increasing their power levels. We need pulse missiles on some of our ships so we can bring them down faster."

"Loadout Three then?" David asked as he approached with an old-school input screen. It was as thin as an old piece of paper, and a lot of people were using them because of the tactile experience.

"Right. Let's skip straight to the Blockade Simulation with every ship we're expecting," Minh-Chu replied. "Good to see you, by the way. How are things with the deck crew?"

David was once a technician aboard a slave ship Jake liberated and a member of the resistance on Tamber during the occupation. He and his wife were two of the first people to transfer out of their positions aboard the Merciless to the Triton. "We've been drilling so much I was kicked out of bed the other night for going through it in my sleep," he replied. "We're all glad to be part of the fight, and these Archangels are the easiest thing to work on. They're classics in the making with teeth. Speaking of which, I've gotta get down there. Everyone probably thinks I'm laying about with a drink in my hand."

"Thank the crew for me. We'll know what we're bringing sometime in the next hour so you can start setting our fighters up," Minh-Chu said, shaking his hand.

"Sure thing," David said before tucking the touchpad under his arm and walking off.

"God dammit!" Slick laughed as he took his brain bud off, got out of his lounger and tossed the brain bud onto it.

"Mission success. The guns did the trick, the heavy Archangel loadout is still manoeuvrable enough to take lighter fighters on, and I made it all the way through," Pixie announced. "Even with him dogging me the whole way," she pointed at Slick.

"Oh, I'll get you next time," he replied, still cooling down.

"So you didn't find the Archangel sluggish?" Minh-Chu asked her.

"Well, it doesn't spin and burn like our usual medium or light load outs, but it's more than fast enough. I was down to thirty percent on Xetima G though. I don't know how good it would be under barrier thrusters only," she replied.

"All right, half-hour break so we can let everyone else finish up and clear their heads. We're doing the Blockade Simulation next," Minh-Chu said.

"You're buying me a drink," Pixie told Slick with a toothy grin.

The darker side of Minh-Chu's experience, Sass, approached, making sure that he was finished talking to everyone. "There's a conversation coming, Captain. I'd rather get it out of the way."

Minh-Chu led him across the lounge to a sofa that was against the bulkhead beside the deck-to-ceiling window. "That was an advanced mission," he started, watching the young man nod. It was best to get to the point. "You won't be going with us on this mission. Your chances of making it back aren't good."

"I know," he sighed, dropping his face into his hands. After a moment he straightened and, with tears in his eyes, looked directly at Minh-Chu. "Ronin, Captain, I don't think I'll ever be ready to be a member of Samurai Squadron. I don't think I should even be a pilot."

"You're here because your technical skill and instrument awareness are way above normal. Maybe you don't have the touch for flying, but there's a spot for you on the ship. A place where you can play an important role."

"You're not disagreeing with me, though," Sass replied, wiping a tear away.

"No. If you want to fly, spend a few hundred more hours in simulations on your own time practising the fundamentals. But it'll be a long time before you'll have a chance to volunteer for the Squadron. On the other hand, Samurai Squadron needs support, and the Triton needs people who can handle the tech around here. We need you." Minh-Chu knew Sass was doing everything he could to hold himself together. The people who he hoped would be his squad mates were still around, even if they'd left the lounge after leaving the full-dive simulation. The young crewman didn't want to break down in front of them, and he was doing everything he could to hold himself together. Minh-Chu wanted to keep the dismissal as quick as possible, and balancing that with kindness was the real challenge. "Call me if you need anything, any time."

"I understand," Sass said, looking past Minh-Chu.

He was looking at Slick, who had approached quietly. "I need people on the Flight Deck, and Sciences is always short on instrumentation people. There are other spots, I'm sure, but I'd take you as a staff member any day. How about taking a seat at a Tactical Scanner Station? You've got the training and the hours."

Sass stood and saluted. "I'm your man, Sir."

Minh-Chu's heart was lighter at the sight, and he caught himself sighing. Minh-Chu got to his feet and shook the young man's hand. "You are relieved, Sass. Good luck in the next chapter in your career."

"Thank you for everything, Captain. Good hunting tomorrow," Sass replied.

"Go relax for a few. You're going to be flying with me as an Order pilot in the next sim," Slick told Sass. "Maybe you can take a shot at your old boss before the night's over."

"Yes, Sir," Sass said before hesitating for a moment before he left.

"Tell me you really need him," Minh-Chu said, keeping his voice low.

"Oh yeah, I do. The Sciences Department have sucked up almost everyone who has any idea what they're doing at a scanning terminal. I've seen his record, he has a memory like a steel trap, works well with all the analyst software and can stay tactically aware better than most. Glad he's not your wingman tomorrow, though."

"That's the next problem," Minh-Chu said. "Who is my wingman tomorrow?"

"Good luck with that one. I'm going to go buy Pixie a drink before the next sim starts," he replied, patting him on the shoulder. "She'd be a good choice, by the way."

"I know," Minh-Chu replied. Everyone who was finished with the simulation was on the other side of the Pilot's Den, the bar. All but a few pilots from the squadron were there along with over two dozen volunteers who scored high in simulations. Some of them had no interest in flying in real combat, and still more weren't ready but they could all stand in as Order or Citadel pilots well enough. The vast majority of enemy fighter pilots didn't have real combat experience. Even fewer had over five hundred simulated hours, while the average player in the upcoming simulation had at least five times that many.

He took a moment to look across The Pilot's Den from the archway dividing it from the Lounge at the front of the ship. It hadn't been that busy since they launched from the Haven System. The excitement of the exercises brought the eyes of hundreds of spectators. The promise of real action sometime in the following twenty hours further bolstered morale. "I hear Dame and Carnie got ya," Ashley said as she joined him, her dark eyes still watering from being under. It was the only side effect she and her sister suffered while they used Brain Buds.

"Yeah, those two are starting to work almost too well together," Minh-Chu said, putting his arm around her waist and squeezing her to him for a moment. "How'd you do?"

"It's like Gren and Garma share a brain. I was able to slow

Gren down early on, but she worked with Garma so she could keep targeting me from a distance. I only got to send one torpedo at the Locon. Maid got a clear shot that took out its main avionics and caused a fuel leak that led all the way out of its hull. I wouldn't say it was disabled, but there was a good start. Switching to railguns was a good idea."

"You gave it to me," Minh-Chu said.

"Huh? When?" she asked.

"I was looking through the tactical info on the Locon and the Rixe when I said something about closing the distance faster. Then you said something like; 'distance doesn't matter much if...'"

"...you're using the right weapon," Ashley finished, nodding, then adding; "You're welcome."

"I'm going to thank my Dad when we finally get a node out his way, too," Minh-Chu said. "When I started noticing girls in school, he gave me the only advice that's been any good about them. About people in general."

"What's that?" Ashley asked.

"Listen."

"One of my favourite things about you, sugar. I think you're the first person I've been with that does that. That listens to me," Ashley said, but she looked away at the end and seemed concerned.

Before he had a chance to ask her about it, he looked to the main entrance. Alice, Iruuk, and Theodore were coming in. She was still in black, sidearm in its holster on one thigh, a pocket balancing it on the other, and her expression was as stony as she did earlier. Before they drew too much notice, the trio started heading to one of the largest booths. "I'm surprised to see them here right now." When he last saw that trio, they were busy in the Strategic Centre. He was sure they would be there for hours.

Ashley nodded, adding; "Something is definitely up with her."

THIRTEEN

The Message

MINH-CHU FOLLOWED Ashley's lead as they joined Alice in the oversized booth made to accommodate some of the larger known intelligent species in the galaxy. He almost missed something that he would never forget about Alice. She looked towards Noah "Carnie" Lucas, her boyfriend and her expression was still stony at first.

Then the lines of her face softened and a tear emerged as sadness emerged followed by something else. Just like something Minh-Chu had seen happen with her mother, her skin turned red, more than a blush, this was pure tension and anger. He saw it once when Ayan didn't think he was looking after they left Freeground. To most people, it was a place she left behind gracefully, but seeing her old life denied from her by law bit her deeply, and he was one of the few people who knew about it.

When Alice pounded her fist on the table and shouted; "What was he thinking?" everyone jumped. She closed her eyes and let her breath out slowly.

Concern followed shock, especially in Iruuk's big, young eyes. "I'll be fine, Fur Face. Quan warned me about this before he went to bed a few minutes ago."

"Are sure you're okay?" Ashley asked.

Alice nodded. "Still pissed off, but I'm getting a grip. When I heard Jake was trapped I shut every piece of my empathy down. Not just the gift, but everything. I was able to think clearly, all right, but Quan told me it would all come back at once."

Theodore was nodding. "Worse, I'd imagine. Suppression is even less healthy the longer it goes on."

"I know now. I mean, if I thought it through, I'm sure..." Alice looked towards Ashley, then Iruuk and groaned. "I'm not dying, guys. I'll be fine."

"Sorry, can't help that I love ya," Ashley said, taking Alice's hand, which was still only half unclenched. "Don't do that anymore, 'kay?"

Iruuks long muzzle bobbed as he nodded emphatically. "I got an alert about your vitals. Your stress levels went right up for a minute."

"Don't worry, I won't be shutting all my feels behind a door again," Alice replied. Her gaze met Minh-Chu's then.

He held it, looking into her dual blues as he guessed that it was only half of what she wanted to say. It was something she'd do again if she had to, and she probably worried that he'd call her out right there, judging from a hint of guilt that was starting to show on her face. He knew her mother too well, reading her was just as easy. It wasn't his way to drag the notion that she'd resort to forcing her mind to clear again out of her. There was an opportunity to reinforce her trust in him instead, so he changed the topic; "So, I'm guessing you'll be drinking something relaxing?"

"I'll get you something. Don't worry, it has Tamber bananas in it," Ashley said, excited.

"I'll have..." Iruuk started, but he stopped as Ashley leaned over and put her finger across his lips and nose.

"I'll guess," she said.

"Don't worry, she's usually really good at this," Minh-Chu said, watching Noah nod his agreement.

"Usually?" Iruuk asked, uncertain.

"I heard that," Ashley said as she continued on to the bar.

"I should go help her carry, and make sure that whatever she chooses is appropriate to Nafalli physiology," Theodore said. "And that she doesn't bother getting me anything with fresh fruit. It would be wasted on an android."

Alice, who seemed much more like herself, put a privacy tab in the middle of the table and an obscuring field surrounded them. It was smaller than Minh-Chu had seen before, the size of her fingernail. "That's nifty," he picked it up, felt a slight electric charge then put it back down. "New?"

"A design from my mother, I just fabricated it," Alice said as she turned it, brought up a small holographic interface, set it to self-tune, and watched as the blurry field seemed to disappear. "You can't tell that this one's even on unless you try to listen in or scan us."

"Or listen?" Iruuk asked.

"Oh, if you try to listen to us you'll hear us talking about an ancient animated program called That Time I Got Reincarnated as a Slime. Don't ask, it was his suggestion," Alice replied.

Iruuk nodded. "I asked the Remmybase for something that was strange, funny and that no one in the Haven System had watched yet. It's pretty good. Humans got really creative in ancient times. I'm surprised it was made without help from an artificial intelligence."

"Huh, all right, I'll have to check it out with Ash. The ancient anime I've seen was a little more dragged out."

"I don't get this," Noah said, waving at the laid-back bar crowd. "How can we sit around, talking about cartoons and having drinks while there are hundreds of people in trouble?"

Sometimes Minh-Chu forgot how young Noah was, still a teenager when he was picked up near Haven Shore after crashing in an Order shuttle. That wasn't as long ago as it seemed. "Well, we could form a weeping circle and recite wallowing poetry, I think that's one of Iruuks' old traditions."

"Uh, only in times of great helplessness and tragedy," Iruuk said softly. "It's not something my family ever did."

"Well, we should be with his Dad, planning or something, right?" Noah asked.

"My father's sleeping. He sleeps as much as he can before an involved hunt," Iruuk explained.

"Oh," Noah said awkwardly. The steam in his outrage was already cooling.

"The next simulation set is almost finished, there's just a little more data to drop in and we'll be ready to test our plans. I don't think there's anything else we can do," Alice said.

"Besides, I used to blow off steam whenever trouble was coming. I think it's a good idea, actually. I don't know why I stopped." She stared at him for a moment then asked; "What's up?" He paused a moment and she added; "I'm not in your head, don't worry. My telepathy's on a break."

"The one time I wish it wasn't," he sighed. "I wish I knew what it was. I guess I have a bad feeling about this one. I've been in big fights before, but I've seen the tactical read on this and I guess... I mean even after the guns were proven out, I didn't feel better, you know?"

"Everyone gets the jitters eventually," Minh-Chu said. "It's the safest way to test your resolve."

"What do you do when you get the jitters?" Iruuk asked meekly.

"I tell them; 'Hey! Jitters! You're making me crazy! Go bother a gardener or someone else who isn't in real danger!'" When that failed to elicit so much as a chuckle from anyone at the table, he cleared her throat and answered seriously. "An untested sword is not a true weapon. I don't know where I heard that, it was a long time ago. I think some of us are tested several times before we even see an enemy. I remind myself that I've trained, been in danger before, and concentrate on the job. The details make me forget about my nerves, and the more I know about my situation - how my fighter is set up, what I learned during preparation, the systems that are running, life-saving technology, and what I'm there to do - the more I've put between me and the jitters. I know I'm ready for tomorrow, so I can have a drink and take a break before we use a simulation to get ready to save my friend and all the people who are trapped with him."

"I think it's important to remember that they're together, too," Alice said. "They're armed, and I'm sure they're not making it easy for the Order to dig them out. I wish I was there, that we were already helping, but I can't focus on that. I'll play my part in the planning instead."

"Yeah, thanks, I guess I started getting used to working on a base, and the routines I got into. It tricks you into feeling safe, you know?" Noah said, asking no one in particular but getting several nods in return.

"So why are we in a secrecy bubble?" Minh-Chu asked Alice.

"Can I add some data to your next simulation about Citadel ships? They're gathering in the Rodus System. I know there are three in the area now, and there are two more on the way," she replied.

"Sure. Now that we know the new railgun loadout can do some damage to a capital ship and handle itself against other fighters, we should test the worst-case scenario," Minh-Chu replied.

"As long as it helps us get ready for this mission. I mean, you're not going to just throw everything in the solar system at us for another test, right? I mean, it would be fun, but..." Noah trailed off.

"You're right, I'm tempted to make the challenge level ridiculous. Like climbing a mountain with a pinky finger while rim weasels are fighting in your pants. Sadly, we have to be practical. Everyone from Intelligence has worked on the scenario we'll be running next," Minh-Chu replied. "Don't worry. We're going to be running at three times the speed in the sim, so I hope that we can get five or so runs out of it. Are you joining us?" he asked Alice.

"Definitely. I'll be leading my real team off the Clever Dream, so you'd better get us a nice landing spot on Rodus," she replied.

"I'm looking forward to it," Iruuk added.

Theodore and Ashley returned with the drinks and put them down. A creamy, white glass with a straw and a tiny bunch of bananas hanging off the rim found its way to Alice, who tried it and nodded. "That's really good. I don't want to get too screwed up before the sim though."

"Oh, it's a very light relaxer," Ashley said. "Mostly real fruit from Tamber and water."

Alice drew on the straw again, took her time to enjoy the texture and flavour, then sighed and said; "Thank you. I should let you pick whatever I'm drinking from now on."

"You're welcome," Ashley replied before taking a sip of her Licorice Doll, an old favourite of hers. "I'm guessing we're about to talk about something serious, since there's a weird barrier up. I swear you were talking about a smart slime guy as we got close to the table."

"The new barrier tech. We'll be able to add it to our comm-cons soon," Alice replied. "It fakes a conversation outside of the bubble so no one can tell what we're really talking about it."

"As long as the fake conversation isn't more interesting than the real one, I guess," Ashley said with a shrug.

Minh-Chu tried his drink and found what he expected, cold black tea, probably from one of the new farms on Tamber. He enjoyed it because it was strong and not too sugary. It wasn't what he would have ordered, but it was a good choice.

With everyone settled in, Alice took one more draw on her straw, then a moment to enjoy it, and got down to business. "Rogue's message was packed with new information. She's been talking to artificial intelligences that use the Stellarnet to find out what's happening in the physical world, and since the Haven Nodes spread all the way to New Udalpur, near Earth, she's been hearing more about Citadel. More about Sol Defence."

"I don't think I like where this is going," Ashley said before Minh-Chu could say the same.

"No one does. Citadel helped the winning side in the most recent civil war, and now Sol Defence has taken them back into the fold. The good news is that Rogue was able to get more current information about their ships and what might be coming. They've stopped making the classic style of Sol Defence ship, so the Zhan carriers and the rest of the line have been discontinued. The Sol System Civil War destroyed several of them. She wasn't able to get all the data about what remains of the current force, but there's a lot that'll help us guess what we're up against. New power output readings, expected crew complements, and what kind of equipment people were able to see on the outside. I hope it helps."

"Where are they getting their new ships?" Iruuk asked.

"They're negotiating a contract with Regent Galactic," Alice replied. "Some of the early designs have already leaked. They don't have space for Geists anymore. That's the first sign that they're changing how their fleet is going to work in the near future."

"So, the only ships that have telepathic assistance are the ones that are in service now?" Noah asked.

"I wish," Alice said. "Rogue had more to say about that. She's been talking to a few interesting artificial intelligences and one of them, a follower of the Iron Mind named Assessor, found out about a drug called Perso. They said that a little protects humans from telepathy, shielding them. A full dose can give some of us full telepathy. The Iron Mind and his followers are worried about it because they think that human intelligence could surpass artificial intelligence again. I'm worried because it could make existing Order and Citadel commanders into something like a Geist. One that can just disappear into a crowd if they have to. Rogue and I are pretty sure that the drug, which has leaked onto Udalpur's black market and is spreading, came from the Sol System. It's got to be military, they've probably been developing this for decades at least. Sol Defence has been obsessed with telepathy for hundreds of years."

"Oh, that just sucks," Ashley said. "At least a Geist takes a lot of space and resources. They don't exactly blend in with a crowd since they look more like a pale whale than anything on two legs."

"Right," Minh-Chu said. "If they replace them with humans hopped up on this, well..."

"Rogue is doing her best to keep in touch with the Iron Mind's followers. They're trying to find out everything they can about this drug. Until then, there's still a ship, a Citadel ship that's breeding Geists. Not all of Citadel's leaders like the new direction their organization is going in now that it's legitimized. They're completely ignoring what's going on in the Sol System and doubling down on the new alliance with the Order. That's very good for us. Rogue says that the ship breeding new Geists is on its way to the Rodus System. There's something else: every

Zhan Class Carrier and larger is responsible for some kind of project. The Rixe is making better framework soldiers, for example. That one got to the Rose System recently. Rogue's worried about it. Baking reliable intelligence into the frameworks has been a problem for the Order, one we don't want them to fix."

"Wait, so the framework soldiers we've seen were the dumb ones?" Noah asked.

"Well, yes. Wiped or refabricated before they could grow a personality or grasp the concept of independence. The Knights and volunteers are different, but I mean, we all know that," Alice said. "A few of the frameworks that were quick fabricated, you know, fleshed out as fabricants, have even escaped after being on for too long. There are ways to block incoming signals that force them to break down, or regenerate so they don't have time to ponder their own existence."

"What? So a few of the Order's framework skeletons became real boys and girls, then kept going instead of breaking down when they were supposed to?" Noah asked, as amused as he was shocked.

Alice laughed and replied; "Apparently. Rogue knows one. She didn't say much about them, but it was supposed to regenerate with a full brain wipe months ago, but it got some kind of back alley implant that stopped it from happening. The framework tech has been out too long, people are figuring it out."

"Well, that's a bright side," Minh-Chu said. "Did Rogue say anything else?"

"A few personal things," Alice replied. "But nothing that'll help with the simulation right now. Oh, this probably won't come up, but no one is supposed to touch the Envoy if we see it.

She installed a program aboard it that's running it through several automated tasks as it makes several jumps around the local systems in the Ninety-Eight. Rogue said she'd tell me more about it later. I think she's using it as some kind of decoy, maybe gathering data along the way. The Order is definitely after her."

"Do you know where she is?" Ashley asked.

"No idea. There wasn't much about what she would be doing next, but I know whose side she's on. Ours. Meaning the Freeground originals and everyone we love. The difference is, she doesn't want to come home. It's complicated, but I think she'd rather do things for us as some kind of tribute from afar. I think it's sad, but I'll be telling her that she's welcome to join us whenever she wants."

"Yeah, I think I understand," Iruuk said. "Like an exile who wants to earn their way back. We have legends about people like that."

"I suppose the difference is that Rogue didn't do anything wrong," Theodore added. "I would enjoy meeting her, I think."

Minh-Chu checked the time and nodded to himself. "Can you add that new data to the simulation so the ships can be updated? It's just about time."

"Sure," Alice replied, looking at Noah. "Can I borrow him for a minute before things start up?"

"Just a minute," Minh-Chu said, watching the pair look into each other's eyes. There was something sweet about them that wasn't there before, and he hoped it was because of some new understanding, or that they were settling into a less superficial phase of their relationship. He took a deep breath and looked at Ashley, who didn't notice him staring at first. When she did, he said; "Time to rally the troops."

"Have fun. I'll see you in the sim," she replied.

Minh-Chu slipped out of the booth and quietly made his way across the Pilot's Den to the bar. A hush fell over the room as more people noticed him. Then, cursing his short stature under his breath, he climbed up onto the bar. People who noticed elbowed and poked anyone who was still talking. After a moment, he had everyone's attention. He checked a few things on his command and control bracer, quickly read through a list of astonishing updates, and then regarded the room. "In about eleven hours we'll be arriving in the Rose System. It turns out that we won't be alone. The Merciless is using a prototype Quad Drive to catch up to us. They are fully crewed and Storm-caller, a new fighter squadron is aboard that ship. For anyone who doesn't know, there are a lot of people on the Merciless who are still loyal to Jacob Valent. They couldn't follow him when he left the fleet, and we shouldn't blame them for that. Some had families to think about, and a lot of them wanted to stay in the Fleet so they could make it better from the inside. I appreciate their loyalty to something bigger than themselves, especially since they're serving Defence Minister, Admiral Terry Ozark McPatrick, who is on vacation, you see. He's taken the Merciless as his yacht. Everyone aboard the Merciless is responsible for his safety, and he wants to visit his old friend, Jacob Valent."

The bar was on the verge of erupting with gleeful cheers. Perhaps faith in the Fleet they left because they were disillusioned with wasn't fully restored, but most of them were moved at hearing that help from home was coming, including Minh-Chu. A short message appeared on his left command and control unit. The simulation has been updated with new data from Alice, the Merciless and Stormcaller Squadron. We've established a link so you can run the simulation with crew members from both ships. It starts in ten minutes. "Oh, you're going to like this. We'll be running this sim together," Minh-Chu announced. "We'll do it five times with ten minutes between each run for adjustments, then everyone will get some rest. First, I have one more thing to say."

The low buzz in the crowded bar lowered as every eye was on him. He found Ashley's dark, lively eyes in an instant and spoke to her more than anyone else. "We're here because we believe in this fight. While our families, friends and compatriots build and secure the Haven System, we're here to show them that there are enemies that need to be defeated before they try to take our home again. Tomorrow, we're going to save Jake and the former crew of the Redstone. My old friend managed to get so much data on the enemy that we'll have an advantage right away, so his side trip was worth it. You'll see it for yourselves, but not in the simulation. Our sims will assume that none of the tricks he dug up will work, so we're prepared for the worst. We'll still try everything, but it won't go our way. In these sims, we'll fight through even though it'll be hard. We'll get ships down to Rodus' surface, pick everyone up, and we're going to do legendary damage to the Order and whoever else gets in our way while we're at it. While they lick their wounds we'll be organizing, getting ready for the next attack. We won't be alone. The Nafalli and British Alliance are sending support. War ships that the Order won't see coming. We will not be alone. Get to your seats, it's time to play this out. Take it seriously, act like this sim is life or death." As he finished, he jumped off the bar and nearly collided with a large marine who steadied him.

"That's all true?" the young man asked. "They're coming?"

"Thousands of warriors. It's a real fight now, and the Order has no idea," Minh-Chu replied, enjoying the big grin that grew on the marine's face. His teeth seemed as large as piano keys.

"Well, I'm gonna get to work, Captain," he said, patting Minh-Chu on the shoulder.

FOURTEEN

Opened

THERE WAS no time to explore the grand artificial cavern that would be their refuge. Remmy wished he could spend weeks scanning, theorizing about, and researching the place. It was old technology, as far as he could guess, it came from humans who had settled on Rodus centuries before. It wasn't his expertise, but entertainment and advertising from the era he thought it came from showed things that matched.

Ruby's crew was almost finished moving all the equipment in so they could close the door. It was a mad rush to set up inside the large space as they made sure the walls beside the doors didn't have any weaknesses.

Remmy couldn't find any holographic technology. The few displays he'd gotten a peek at used a kind of isolated magnetism to move metal grains around as they changed colour. He stuck one of them into his pack, aware that having an adapter made so he could actually interface with it might take some real work, or trading with people who might have high demands for their expertise.

"What do you think? Is there a way to the surface from here? Was Sel right?" Jake asked as he approached.

"Well, the people from the town that was established outside the doors salvaged material from this cavern methodically, and someone might have found an elevator or something, but they didn't leave notes. Well, no notes that would help. I found this instead," Remmy replied, glancing up at Ruby as she joined them.

Remmy brought them to a line drawn in yellow grease pencil and other markers that traced a rod on the floor. It spanned the width of the whole chamber, and there were flags made from trash to further mark it. "There," Remmy pointed.

Crudely written was a simple message; No go point! Only expert pickers allowed beyond. Sensors and traps. Stay back!

"Okay, so..." Jake said, looking past the line at the thick column in the middle of the cavern. It was covered with thick cables and machines, the blinking lights clearly indicating that whatever was cut away to be sold didn't disable whatever was going on there. "...Sel Marda's notes said that there was a way to the surface here."

"Not a quick one. Nothing comes up on scanners, it must be shielded by some of this hardware," Ruby replied. "There's one of the sensors that message was talking about, I think."

Remmy followed her pointed finger and saw it installed into the side of a cable, like a dark spot with black sand slowly rippling across it. "I wouldn't have noticed that."

"I've seen one of those before. There's no way of knowing what kind of area it's monitoring," Ruby said.

Jake picked up a piece of torn cable insulation the size of his hand and tossed it in a high arc in front of the scanner. A flash of electricity arced out and blasted it to pieces. Remmy flinched and took a step back, but Jake only cleared his throat and said; "Mapping a safe way through this while we look for an exit is going to slow us down."

"We're good! Time to close the door. The sensors we dropped in the north and south tunnels are picking up movement. Looks like the Order are about ten minutes away," Gaddon said from the tall doors.

"Okay, signal Dubin and get him out of there," Ruby replied.

A few seconds later the tall doors started to move. They rolled along durable tracks as they did when they opened at first, then the electric motors pushing them started to change pitch and they started to slow. "Oh, crap," Remmy said under his breath, remembering that he'd ignored part of the control panel earlier.

The doors started to slow, and soldiers started to exchange worried glances, as Remmy started running towards the building and the control room. "They're not going to close all the way."

Jake was beside him, keeping up with his breakneck pace. "You know why?"

"I think so," Remmy replied as they passed through the doors and then ran as fast as they could towards the abandoned shop across and to the left of them. "Get someone to bring a power pack and all the adapters we've got."

They rushed into the control room and were immediately confronted by Dubin, the button man. "The doors just stopped! I can't get them going again."

Remmy flipped the small cover on the left side of the control panel open and looked. "The battery backup power for the motors that open and close the doors is depleted."

"That's not my fault, you told me not to look at that!" Dubin protested.

"I know, it's fine," Remmy replied, guiding him out of the room. "No one's blaming you, but is there any chance you know how to plug a power pack into this? You know, so you don't fry the whole thing?"

"Uh, no..." he replied.

"Okay, then go join everyone else. Run," Remmy said, pointing through the doors.

That's when he noticed Parsons and Ruby with a group of soldiers who were carrying packs. "All right, every adapter and a couple of power packs," she announced. "What's up?"

"We're out of power here. Whatever generator they were using for the town isn't running, so it was on batteries. Do you know this tech? Can you help me out here? I needed to read the manual to get through the security," Remmy asked.

"I do," Jake replied as he popped the access panel beneath the controls open. "But there's security. That's on a smaller battery, so it'll take me at least fifteen minutes to get around the countermeasures."

"Oh, I've seen that before. That system never kept me out when I was a kid," Parsons said as she leaned in and looked. "Do it wrong and the whole control system gets fried. Interfere with the cables between here and the door and you'll probably get the same result."

"Think you can get this hotwired and then set the doors up with one of our power packs in less than fifteen minutes? I'd be faster, but I'm rusty," Jake said.

"Ten or less," she nodded. "There's only room for two hands in there once you get the cover off, though, so you guys can go do something else while I get into this thing. I won't need a manual, by the way."

Jake stepped back to give her room and took her bag. "Take whatever you need, give the rest to Gaddon, he'll be assisting you. Everyone can use someone to hand them tools."

Gaddon nodded. "My pleasure."

"Sure, start with a Torx Three," Parsons said, pulling her thigh pocket open, feeling around for a second then pulling a slender self-changing screwdriver out. "Oh, look, here it is." Gaddon was still opening the tool bag when she was kneeling down in front of the security panel protecting the inner workings of the door power system and controls.

"All right, we're going to set up a defence so no one interrupts you while you work," Jake said, patting Remmy on the back as he passed.

No elaboration was needed. That meant that he was going to be a part of it, so Remmy unslung his rifle and checked it. The meter-long rifle had recharged using his suit's power, and rounds from his pack had replenished his ammunition. "Where do you need me?" he asked.

"You're going high. Sniping and overwatch," Jake said, looking up at the pillars.

"I like it," Remmy replied.

"How many volunteers do we need?" Ruby asked.

"Two full squads for each side. Trained only. I don't want newbies because we're going to blast the first wave of the Order and then, when the doors start closing, because they will, right?" Jake looked at Remmy.

"Yeah, sure, I give it at least a ninety-nine percent chance," Remmy said. "Okay, seventy, accounting for luck."

"I told you, I'll get this done," Parsons snapped as she carefully turned then pulled the outer cover under the counter away. "Toss this, Gaddon."

"All right, so, we're going to set up in the windows facing north and south, make sure everyone has an easy point of retreat because we're going to retreat through the doors whether they close or not. Everyone who is already in there has to start setting up a defence right now," Jake said. "Hopefully we can narrow the gap between the doors if not close them completely."

Remmy looked at them and saw that they were still nearly twenty meters apart. "As long as the power is set right when it's connected."

"All right, pick your spot. Get ready to use everything you've got to beat those soldiers back on my order," Jake said, looking up at the northernmost pillar building.

Remmy activated his suit thrusters and flew up across the town. Seeing a window that was open a crack one level down from the top of the cavern, he pushed it open and crept in. It was a normal human living room.

Dust had settled on a dining table made of blue plastic with matching chairs. There was an old sofa and a playpen with an old holoprojector between them. He rushed through the dwelling to make sure that there wasn't anyone within and checked the front door. It was unlocked, so he peeked out into the hall, then locked it. The flimsy thing wouldn't keep Order soldiers out for more than a few seconds, but anything could help.

In a moment of indulgence, he picked up a thin display, the type that was so cheap that they were often pasted to walls so they could continuously play advertisements, and tapped it to his command and control unit. His right bracer played the hologram back and he smiled. Ayan appeared, she was in white with a plush wrap around her. They used her likeness for all kinds of Haven Nation promotions and instructional systems. He wondered how similar that version was to the real woman as he watched the introduction. "Thank you for pre-applying to the Haven Nation work program. There's a place reserved for you and your family. The details regarding your transit here are in this message along with everything you'll need to resettle. Keep in mind that your application only reserves your spot for three..."

After turning the message off he said; "So, that's what happened here. The scrappers left for the Haven System." Remmy moved to a window and calibrated his cloaking systems to the location. There would be no way normal sensors would pick him up, and he was invisible to the naked eye. "I'm in position," he reported to the new Defence Channel when it appeared in his faceplate display. He brought windows up to monitor Jake, Ruby and Agameg.

"Half of us are set," Ruby said. "Get it in gear, guys!"

With a few minutes to spare, Remmy peeked at the itinerary for the family who once lived in the apartment. There was an eighteen month old, Marcy, her father Decker and her mother Charlise. The mayor of Erkon, the scrapper town they were in, had arranged for an all-or-nothing deal with the Haven Nation and the Rodus Government. They qualified as a destitute settlement, and the government wanted them gone. Haven was happy to take them in, and quickly found jobs for everyone who wanted one in one large recycling plant that they would help build and eventually staff. The rate of pay, housing, and lifestyle quality were all pre-negotiated.

That was something that Remmy didn't have yet. There was a bunk on the Triton reserved for him, and he hoped he'd get upgraded to quarters if he didn't get the Raven back. "I should do some negotiating when we're out of this," he muttered to himself as he turned all but the Defence Channel off.

"What was that, Remmy?" Jake asked over comms.

"How close are they?" he asked as he stared at his tactical monitor. There was a fuzzy area inside the largest northern tunnel, indicating that something heavy on wheels or tracks was coming down the four-lane hover transit street.

"Three minutes to the north. Five to the south," reported Ruby.

"Everyone get set. Be ready to move. We're not holding the door for everyone, and we're going to have to change positions if this goes on too long," Jake said. There was a calmness to his voice that reminded Remmy of ancient hunters from Earth. "Agameg, you set?"

"I am. Strangely, I'm looking forward to this," he replied.

"So am I," Jake said.

FIFTEEN

The First Wave

WE HAVE TO BUY TIME. That's what our strategy is built around. Just a few minutes. Remmy thought as he saw the outlines of thirty Order of Eden soldiers on foot making their way to the end of the main tunnel. "That's a big scouting party," he commented. There was room for multiple hover, wheeled or track vehicles to move down the properly paved passage. The soldiers were spread out, shoulder to shoulder as they carefully checked the ground, walls and ceiling.

"Sacrificial squads," Ruby said from the tunnel leading into the opposite end of the city. "I've got a closer passive scan. These are generics. Two models in the squad, tops."

Generics. It was a term that one of the analysts aboard the Triton came up with to describe framework soldier types that their systems could fabricate in minutes from energy and matter surrounding the silver skeleton that was the platform for framework technology. All their intelligence, even the information they'd gathered from Gold Haf, indicated that most of them came to life with a soldier's basic training, who they were loyal to, and the most rudimentary understanding of what they were. Whether they even understood mortality was fair game for debate. Their habit of regenerating made them difficult to kill unless you had the right tools.

"We're almost ready to blow the main tunnel to the south," Ruby said over the Combat Channel. "We were able to get enough recovered hardware here to get it done."

"Good, wait for my signal. You're going to have to let those first two squads through," Jake replied. He, Agameg and four other soldiers were waiting on each side of the northern tunnel. Their cloaking systems were working, but they could fail the moment the enemy sent out a scan pulse and pointed the right receivers at them. "What are you using, by the way?"

"Firestorm Anti-Air shoulder launchers, nothing fancy. Gaddon was able to pull six from the Dropping Bells," Ruby replied. "How's the hack for the door going?"

"Ten minutes," Parsons replied.

"You said it would be less," Gaddon replied over the Combat Channel.

"I had to stick my nose in the manual, okay? It's been a long time since I hacked this brand of safeguard system for my brother," she snapped.

"Your brother? Were you up to shenanigans? Illegal shenanigans?" Remmy asked.

Parsons snickered and replied; "I was six, definitely under the prosecutable age. Talk later, focusing now."

The two Order of Eden squads emerged. They wore simple dark green jumpsuits with armour plates covering their vitals. He didn't need to wait for his target identification system to confirm that they were generic frameworks. His rifle was set to use energy and kinetic rounds, alternating between armour-piercing explosive shots and Munition Twenty-Eight rounds. "All right, are they going to blast a scan pulse first or, are we?" he asked as he checked the smaller entrances leading into the area. The doors were still closed. That was a good sign, but he wasn't picking up anything moving within. If there were soldiers waiting to rush in, they were being careful to avoid detection.

"We're waiting for their pulse, then overloading their sensors," Jake replied.

"I've got doors three and four," said one of Remmy's squad mates who was set up in a room somewhere below him. His name was Wade, but that was about all Remmy knew about him.

"I've got one and two," Remmy replied.

The pair of squads fully emerged from the tunnel, and then one of them held a large hand-scanning unit up. "Here we go," Jake said over the channel. "Bring the main southern tunnel down when our flash goes off."

"Aye," Ruby replied.

As she finished speaking, the Order soldier in the centre of the two squads at the end of the northern tunnel activated his scan pulse. It wasn't something anyone could see with the naked eye, but Remmy's tactical display lit up for a second, indicating that most of their cloaked soldiers would be visible. Jake, Agameg and the four soldiers with them were instantly visible on the enemy's scanners, but the thirty soldiers between them didn't have a chance to react.

Jake tossed a pair of enhanced flash-bang grenades up over their heads. Milliseconds before they went off, the sensors in every suit of armour on his side deactivated. What followed was a flash of light, sound, and a blast of energy that was meant to overload every receiver or detector for hundreds of metres in every direction. The instant the blast was over, Remmy's sensors were back online. The squad of thirty Order soldiers staggered, many clutching their helmets.

Agameg was amongst them first. Remmy had never seen the Issyrian in close combat. He was legendary for his performance as he led a small group of soldiers while defending the Triton years ago. The Issyrian activated a nano-blade sword in his left hand and wielded a sidearm that Remmy didn't recognize. With speed and grace that was beyond what a human could achieve, he passed his blade through the neck of one soldier, impaled another, and then shot a third in the torso. The next was starting to raise his rifle when Agameg slashed the front of his armour and the flesh beneath it open. The counterattack happened so quickly that Remmy only realized that Agameg was lining up a shot with his other hand when his sidearm went off. The soldiers with him moved slowly in comparison, taking Order Frameworks down with bursts from their rifles.

Jake was coming from the other side of the tunnel, leading the pair of soldiers with him in a coordinated assault on Order soldiers that took a trio of them down every second or two. "Get ready to retreat, we're going to need cover when the flash-bangs wear off," Jake said calmly over the Combat Channel. "Wait, we've got Knights. I need you, Remmy. Switch to pulse-enhanced shots and cover me now."

Remmy focused in on Jake, who was starting to charge into the northern tunnel. One of the generic Order Frameworks was bowled over. Jake got the next out of the way by punching his helmet. "Agameg, watch for an opening."

"Aye, Captain," Agameg said, probably by way of habit.

"Surrender!" cried a firm male tone over every unencrypted frequency as it echoed through the air. "You are outgunned and outmanned!"

An explosion to the south shook the floor beneath Remmy's feet. It was Ruby's attempt to bring the southern tunnel entrance down. According to his tactical display, there was a significant collapse, even though the fast missiles they used weren't made to penetrate concrete. Sometimes, when you used enough firepower, explosions could force the issue. He was glad to see that it was true in that case. "Southern tunnel closed, we're taking the squads that made it through down."

"I've got an Order of Eden ID I like here," Jake said as he opened fire with his rifle and took flight into the tunnel.

Remmy saw them then, five Order of Eden Knights in gleaming green armour. Their horizontally banded suits were based on an older generation of Haven Fleet armour. Combined with the energy shield systems, they were tough, but Remmy had the answer. The whine of his rifle's Pulse Generator was so loud that he could hear it through the noise dampener in his helmet. He took aim and then fired a burst of rounds at the Order Knight standing in the middle. An energy pulse shot preceded each round to weaken the enemy's shields. His suit creaked as it compensated for the kick and helped him keep his aim steady.

The middle Knight's shields failed and he stepped back so the other four could close the gap while he recharged. Jake opened fire with his rifle, evading most of the defensive fire from the Knights. Remmy saw the Order of Eden Identification associated with the shield frequency of the Knight he'd hit. It wasn't a Knight. It was the Executive Officer of the Rixe, a Citadel ship.

He was about to pull the trigger again when his tactical system warned that there were three soldiers flying out of the smaller doors to the left of the tunnel. One was moving towards him so quickly that he didn't have time to fire at it.

It was a slender soldier in a thin suit that drank the light in, a Citadel Shadow. If there was a deadly opposite to heavily armoured Haven Soldiers, that was it, and this one was able to kick his rifle aside. The sound of a short monofilament nanoblade activating - like whirling sand grinding itself to dust - warned him about the weapon before Remmy saw it. He rolled, grabbed his assailant's faceplate, and it slipped out of his grip, and Remmy forced himself to his feet.

The high screech of the blade trying to pass through his suit's shields filled Remmy's ears. "Trouble! Can't cover!" Remmy shouted as he tried to grab at his assailant again.

"I see your fight. Be calm, Remmy. Predict where he will be," Agameg said.

"Pin him to the floor," Jake added. "Finish him fast."

"I'm trying." As Remmy's hand connected with his assailant's middle and slid right off his suit, he realized that he was nearly in full panic. His shields were down to half already.

Whenever Remmy moved the assassin made sure that they were either not in the way, or already on its way out of his grasp.

While he was in heavy armour he would never beat the Citadel Assassin's dexterity or speed. Agameg had given him the right advice. At a glance, Remmy was able to take his situation in, and he stopped moving completely. The assassin's next attack came from behind, and Remmy turned on his heel, throwing an elbow in his direction. As soon as it wasn't making contact with him anymore, Remmy stopped moving completely, using the rearview window in his heads-up display to watch him. "You picked the wrong window, buddy."

The assassin circled, the shape of them shimmering as its suit tried to re-cloak. It wouldn't work while Remmy was in the same room. With startling alacrity, the assassin slashed with its short blade. Remmy's hand was millimetres behind as he tried to grab its arm. The blade bit into his shields with a screech, costing him eighteen percent of the barrier's charge.

An alert on his heads-up display highlighted a cylinder at his feet. The attack wasn't meant to do real damage, but as a distraction, and Remmy kicked the thing as it went off. The rest of his shield charge was gone instantly as the electromagnetic pulse grenade went off, emitting no sound or light. His sensors recovered quickly.

The assassin came at him again, and Remmy was sure he had a fist waiting for him as he punched, but he caught nothing but air, and the blade cut through his shoulder's plating, barely splitting the combat vacsuit beneath. Then the assassin was across the room again, circling, measuring. It was difficult to push the frustration out of his mind, but talking helped a little. "You're way too slippery. Your fighting style is exactly the same as I've read about. Do all you assassins go to the same school or something? Like the X-Men? You're from Earth, you'd know about that ancient fiction, right? The five-season series? The movies? You know, those kids that had abil..." Remmy was able to see it coming when the assassin leapt forward for another strike. He managed to deflect the blade just enough so it scratched across the side of his helmet, doing only superficial damage.

It dropped back and watched him again. "Didn't get me this time, huh? Didn't even leave me a present on your way out." That was the trick. Being calm, making it look like he was distracted. The lower half of his suit's shield emitters were burned out, they wouldn't recharge. He guessed the Assassin knew, that was key. "Anyway, just in case you don't watch the classics where you come from, there were these kids who had special powers, and Professor Xavior took them in. The powers were really about how most of us feel different, even freakish when we're teenagers, even after. I mean, it was all an analogy for how we're all different. I'm still waiting to feel normal, you know? How about you?" Patience. He wanted to draw his sidearm and start shooting, but patience was key. He'd probably hit nothing but air anyway.

The assassin slowly shook their head. A second later, it was on him, attacking from Remmy's left, his slower side. The tip of its blade managed to penetrate his suit. The pain hadn't kicked in yet, but the display told him that the strike was effective. Remmy grabbed for the assassin's neck, but only brushed it with his fingertips and he kicked at the last instant. It was a low strike, quick for someone in a heavy suit, and he caught the assassin's ankle.

Before the assassin could get away entirely, Remmy bashed him with a backhand, then fired the grapple tool built into his right bracer. He thought he missed at first because the Assassin kept moving, but when Remmy yanked the line, he realized that the arrow point of the grappler had caught his enemy in the ribs.

As he was carried towards Remmy with a second yank, the assassin cut the line, but it was too late. His throat was in Remmy's hand, and he gave it a hard twist. It fell limp. Remy drew his sidearm and shot him in the head with a bullet loaded with Munition Twenty-Eight. If the assassin had framework regeneration technology, it wouldn't bring him back.

Remmy rushed to the window, picking his rifle up on the way. "I'm back! What am I missing?" The action had moved into the tunnel.

Jake was emerging from the tunnel with Agameg. They were both flying backwards, firing as they went. It looked like the Executive Officer was about to successfully take cover behind a hover tank that was coming around the corner inside the tunnel when a flurry of rounds took his legs out from under him. The next barrage spread the rest of him across the asphalt. "One officer down," Jake announced.

"Wade's down! It was an assassin. We saw it as it ran off," a soldier announced.

"We're on our way. The Order is in retreat. How's the door coming?" Ruby asked.

"Done," Gaddon said. "Do you want us to..."

"The assassin's here!" Parsons shouted.

"Got him," Gaddon said, the sound of his rifle going off in the background. "Wait, missed."

"We're on our way, just stay away from him," Ruby said.

"Run, Parsons!" Gaddon said.

"I'm going down," Remmy said.

"Stay in position, watch the tunnel." As Jake spoke, Remmy saw one of the assassins fly into the main southern tunnel in full retreat. Then another.

"He just backed off," Gaddon said, confused.

"They're sending a bomb next. Retreat through those doors and get them closed," Jake said. "Do we have a clever way of disabling the controls, or do we have to…"

"We don't have to blow them up, I can see where the salvagers connected the controls to the inside of the doors here. They have tamper-proof insulation that'll disable outside control once we even try to cut them. They were really possessive of this place, whoever set this up. It's new though, so it wasn't…" Clay was cut off by Jake.

"Are you sure?"

"Very sure, I've seen the insulation before. Even if the anti-tampering doesn't do the trick, we could always…"

"All right, everyone in. The Order's going to come at us again soon," Jake said.

Remmy checked his armour. The lower barrier emitters in his suit were unreliable at best. "I'll be a minute. I need to take the stairs."

SIXTEEN

Losses

CAPTAIN VOLLIS MIKAN was used to hiding his reactions from his crew and commanders. That made it easier to maintain the advantage in most situations, whether they were conversational, violent confrontations or anything in between. When the video feed from Executive Jagat Ozov's armour was terminated, and the makeshift Knights at his side reported his fate, Vollis found it difficult not to react. A turmoil of disappointment, surprise and anger roiled within him.

Everything that led to the Executive's death took place in under a minute. A steady pressure of gunfire from a group of heavily armoured soldiers, one which Jagat had guessed and reported was Jacob Valent, was pressing the Executive and his small group of knights back. He'd taken Order Knight armour and put it on the best warriors they had. They had Framework regeneration, training programmed into their memories and good performance in drills. That didn't make them Order Knights, and they failed to perform like them, especially when they found themselves momentarily outnumbered.

The steady pressure from heavy Haven Fleet rifles only grew as the first wave of basic framework troops was mowed down. They were supposed to regenerate piece by piece, healing injuries, and recovering limbs, but something was wrong. The basic troops began a full regeneration cycle, the framework skeleton replaced itself with normal bone and recreated the flesh around it where required. Each soldier's next breath was as a human that didn't include any trace of the framework technology that made them. This was thanks to special munitions that Haven was known to use, but the expense of resources and time to make them made them uncommon. Well, that's what the Order kept repeating. That's what Captain Vollis Mikan had read, seen and was told about the technology - Munition Twenty-Eight. How, then, did entire squads just get taken down by independent rifle-wielding soldiers?

"Sir?" asked the Junior Lieutenant to his left. She was one of the last Aspens aboard, one of the last made before Scanlon's software attacked the Rixe's databases. He couldn't remember her name specifically, only that she was like the others of her type. Smart, quick to think independently, and surprisingly loyal as long as she didn't feel alone. He watched as the playback continued. Executive Jagat pushed one of his pretend Knights aside, saving her life, and then managed to make two shots against Jacob Valent. The executive was a better warrior than Vollis would have expected and he had a heroic streak as well.

The enemy's face was a fraud. Instead of being able to see Jake's human visage, there was a holographic skull painted in gore, its dark sockets stared hatefully. This was the image the mercenary wanted to project, and it was the last thing Jagat saw before his enemy let loose with a stream of rounds, ripping the Knight armour and the flesh beneath apart. Something in that rifle was like Munition Twenty-Eight but beyond it in its violence, its potency. It didn't trigger a rebirth, a full regeneration using the framework technology within Jagat's chest and hips. It simply stopped it from working. Munition Twenty-Eight sometimes did the same thing, failing to trigger a regeneration, but this time it was more intentional. Nanobots attacked the microscopic mechanisms responsible for regeneration and tore them apart just as aggressively as Jake's assault on Jagat. "Captain?" the Aspen asked again. The tone she used expressed deep sympathy.

She was misinterpreting his stillness for something mournful. Vollis stopped the playback as Valent led his group in a retreat. The strike and fade tactics worked, and the leadership of the ground strike pursuing him was drastically weakened. Even worse, Jacob Valent did it with an Issyrian at his side. A non-human was seen defeating an entire squad, possibly more, on his own, even leading the way. "Yes. You have my attention."

"I'm sorry to report that Zadix has been killed," Aspen said quietly so no one else in the Command and Control Centre could hear.

As he stared at her a chill ran through him. "Why was he down there?" he asked before he caught himself.

She wouldn't have an answer for him. No assassin would tell anyone but another high-level Citadel officer where they were going or why. "Sir?" was Aspen's only response as she handed him an insulated cup.

He accepted it, was it already time for his brew? It felt as though the world had tilted on its axis. Zadix was aboard with his companions. Three assassins that volunteered to join him for the mission to kill the Cefa System's future king. Zadix was especially important since they had the same childhood experiences, masters and could recall New Corsa, the theatre of their childhood experiences perfectly. "Is there a record of the engagement?" Vollis asked.

"I'm afraid not. We only heard of it because Fazen was able to contact us. They will recover his body and the recording of the incident," the Aspen replied.

"Then they'll be joining me soon," Vollis said as much to himself as to anyone else. It was their tradition. Shadows rarely came in even numbers. If they weren't alone, there would be at least three, and Zadix trained his companions to operate as a trio. He would have two shadows for the rest of his life or until a superior made a change. "Thank you. You may go," he told the Aspen, and she went off to assist the Logistics Department.

"Captain, we have an incoming communication from The Messenger. It is Eve," announced someone from behind him.

"I'll take it here, holographically. Enable privacy mode," Captain Mikan replied, watching the large holographic well in front of him.

Eve appeared, wearing a red jacket that looked like it could be part of some kind of uniform, but it wasn't one he'd seen before. "Bion has told me that your pursuit of the Haven forces on Rodus has not gone well."

"Welcome to the Rose System," Vollis said, deciding to be unnecessarily gracious. Eve's tension didn't ease in the least. "We are doing our best to respect Panda's city boundaries. We are pursuing them further into the old undercity. Antagonizing some of the wealthiest people on Rodus seemed unwise."

"That sounds like the kind of thing the traitor, Scanlon would say," Eve hissed. "You will use every asset at your command to kill every Haven operative you find."

"My hangars are empty. I have three hundred basic Framework units in storage. As I reported some time ago, my ship is undermanned," Vollis replied. "I was supposed to receive Order reinforcements as a condition of our alliance along with the equipment they'd require. You have sent one. I cannot rush the pursuit with the resources I have."

"What good are you then?" Eve snapped. "The rumour is that this is Valent we're chasing! I'm surprised you're not down there yourself! I thought you were an assassin."

Vollis felt his fingers curl and stopped before they became fists. "My command of the Rixe is a higher priority."

"What about the Executive I sent you? He's perfectly capable of..."

"I believe Jacob Valent, who is not currently a Haven soldier, has killed him. The corpse is being recovered now. The pursuit of Valent and his people is ongoing. I will be ordering everyone I have in the tunnels to press. Our targets may escape, but not for long. Scans indicate that the cavern they plan on taking refuge in is a dead end."

"Perhaps I should send Bion after them, or incentivise

Panda security to help? I'm sure the appearance of my base ship overhead will be enough to persuade them to help," Eve said.

"They are unlikely to cooperate. Panda's representative told me that their security never operates in the ruins of the old city beneath or surrounding Panda's walls. City Thirty-Five has been taken over by a criminal element that's too large for them to control or eradicate."

"What are you talking about, City Thirty-Five? Isn't that the same thing as Panda?" Eve snapped.

"City Thirty-Five is a roughly circular space that surrounds Panda for over a hundred fifty kilometres in every direction. Before the last Fall, it was thriving, an independent metropolis, but the people who rebuilt could only control and protect a small section of its centre. They built a wall around that and called it Panda, which is surrounded by the ruins of old City Thirty-Five in all directions."

"I don't need a geography lesson, I want every dissonant dead, and every scrap of evidence that you can find to show me that it's been done," Eve said, the storm of her temper abating quickly. "I'm going to send Bion on another mission. One I don't think you're as well suited to. The Locon will move into position over..." she thought for a moment then finished; "Panda."

"I need support. When I track down and defeat Valent and his people, I'll still be undermanned. The Rixe will not perform as it should if we are attacked," Vollis said.

"Appeal to another Citadel ship," Eve said.

"They are undermanned as well. The war in the Sol System cost us," Vollis replied, wondering if she knew anything about it. The Overlord did, but he was thousands of light-years away. "I remind you of the promises the Order made..."

"Don't you dare remind me of the terms of the alliance," Eve said, a threat in her eyes. "I will send three destroyers to assist. You'll have to wait until the other battlegroups arrive for more. They will be here shortly. Coordinate with Executive Yaver for military matters from now on. I have a meeting with Rodus' president then I have to approach the other major settlements in the system since we're woefully short on people with diplomatic skills," Eve said, looking away before she ended the conversation with; "I'd like to have faith in you, Vollis."

The hologram disappeared and Captain Mikan wondered why the Overlord put Eve in charge of taking control of the Cluster. Finding the answer to that question seemed more hopeless every time he spoke to her, and he decided to think about it later. "Bring up every data stream we have coming from City Thirty-Five. I'm going to have to command it remotely."

He didn't have to give the order to anyone in particular. The Command and Control Centre was filled with holograms displaying every aspect of the action on the planet below. Vollis cast his gaze to an orbital map for a moment and saw that three destroyers were moving to support the Rixe, as promised. Still, The Messenger, Eve's base ship, was keeping its distance, hiding behind a massive asteroid that had been hauled closer to Rodus so it could be mined nearby. There would be no further help from that great ship, regardless of the legions of trained soldiers or its other resources. "We must win. We have to catch or kill our quarry without her help. Put the call out again. We need assistance from other Citadel allies, regardless of the importance of their missions."

"Yes, Captain," said someone from behind him. "Right away."

At least the small crew he had was loyal, responsive, and increasingly talented. If there was any solace to be found, Vollis believed it was found there.

The main hologram showed soldiers on the ground as they used the tunnel for cover. The pillar town with fifteen storey buildings that stretched from the ground to the cavern's ceiling looked completely alien to him. The few enemy soldiers who stayed to fire back were defending one building in particular, and Vollis connected to the Second Lieutenant commanding the group from the hover tank in the tunnel. "This is Captain Mikan. You will leave the tunnel and fire on the building I'm marking. They are protecting something there. The rest of the available forces will move into position to fire on whoever attempts to retreat through the large doors to the east."

"Yes, Captain, immediately, Sir," he replied.

Vollis checked on his forces to the south. The main tunnel there had collapsed, so only a few of them could get to the cavern using secondary passages. He contacted the Sergeant there. "This is Captain Mikan, you will retreat back through the tunnels. Transport the small ships through the northern tunnel along with whatever heavy firepower you have on the ground through the northern tunnel. If our enemy retreats through those armoured doors, you will break through them as quickly as possible."

"Yes, Captain," she replied. Orders were given with her next breath, there was no hesitation or doubt.

"Hurry," Vollis added, wishing he could be there.

SEVENTEEN

The Leap

AS REMMY RUSHED DOWN four floors, skipping every step to drop onto each landing, a recurring dream that he had as a child came to mind. Every second landing had a window. A normal, old-school, glass window. One of those would be his exit, and his recurring dream returned to him, along with the cold sweat it brought on every time he woke up.

In the dream, he was looking through one of the large view-ports aboard Freeground Station. It was one of the ones in the Research Section, where his parents worked. He practically grew up there during his early years, and staring through that special window that was adapted to show distant features of the galaxy translating spectrums into colours that the human eye could see was one of his favourite things to do. That was until he had a nightmare where he was playing with Adapto Blocks and it disappeared, sending him out, away from the station, tumbling through space. The funny thing was, he never felt cold in the dream, and there was no pain, only the feeling that he was falling away from everything and everyone he knew. His medical bot told him that it was probably a result of abandonment issues, since he had several sets of parents as he grew up. The dream recurred while he was recovering from a full-body reconstruction only a few months ago.

As Remmy jumped down the last set of stairs and came to the moment where he would have to launch himself through the tenth-floor window, he concentrated on what kind of angle he'd need to land on his feet, and on pulling two grenades from his belt. He could see the towering doors at the west end of the tunnel ahead, and the Order soldiers who were rushing from the large northern passage.

Jake was doing his best to lead three dozen soldiers or more in a retreat to the doors. It was Ruby Sima and her small squad who were giving him the cover he needed to get from the building to Jake's group, which was partially made up of volunteers from her crew. The firefight was becoming more frantic by the moment, with the Order charging from the tunnel, a tank behind at least sixty framework soldiers that were backed by a squad of more heavily armoured troops.

Jake's group was forming up into firing lines, their shields merging so the front was reinforced by those behind. Streaks of white-yellow light issued forth from their rifles, punctuated by the occasional grenade. The door started closing at a glacial pace.

Ruby's team were coming from the south and were taking cover behind the building that Remmy was about to leap from.

The controls for the door were destroyed and everyone in that pillar tower had joined her. The floor under Remmy's feet shook as the tank took a shot at the building, and he heard Ruby's voice raised for the first time through his communicator; "Hurry! Get down so we can get behind those..."

The rest was drowned out as Remmy did his best to ignore the cold sweat and percolating fear as he leapt through the window. He barely felt it shatter, thanks to his armour, and he focused on what he'd call 'a hero moment' if he were playing a simulation. He turned towards the enemy as he began his descent, tossed one grenade into their midst, then another and was delighted as he realized it would probably bounce off the front of the hover tank and then land between the more heavily armed soldiers.

That was it, that was the thing he wanted to do on the way to the ground. He didn't even have to watch the grenades go off, which was a good thing since he didn't have time to pause and stare. Remmy had to concentrate on landing without looking like an idiot. As he focused on that task, he realized that he was rotating too far forward and, as he engaged the few barrier thrusters in the upper half of his armour to right himself, he grimaced. "Oh, shit, this is gonna look..." The ground was coming up faster than he expected, and he barely had time to loosen up before he hit, flipped, and slid like a rag doll that had been tossed out of the window of a hovercar on the freeway. "Gravity sucks."

Worse, he didn't quite make it to Jake's protection, and he was well past the point of Ruby's help. Thanks to his highly enhanced body, armour and vacsuit, the ten-storey drop barely knocked the wind out of him. The question was, what next?

The options raced through his mind. Play dead. Rush to Jake. Run to Ruby. Stand and fight. What should he do?

As Ruby's voice came through his communicator again, he stood up, grabbed his rifle, and ran towards Jake and the door. "Get going! We've got you!" she was saying.

Remmy fired blindly at the Order troops as his weakened shields failed. Playing dead wouldn't have worked. They were more interested in turning him into a grease spot than taking him prisoner. For several fast, long strides he was grateful for the enhanced body he'd suffered for over the last few months. The re-knitting of his bones, densification of his muscles, and finalization of his entire body as the process of his enhancement went on much longer than he or anyone else thought it would added up to him being able to fire a heavy rifle while he made a mad dash for a closing door.

Jake and his forces were retreating, most of them main-taining cover fire as they backed through the narrowing gap behind them. Three shots struck Remmy in the side, the hip and the leg, and he nearly fell on his face. The pain felt distant, a piercing heat and puncture on his thigh and hip. Then came the strange ache of muscle working around broken flesh as he began to heal. That's not what kept him moving forward. It was Ruby, who got under his arm and, thanks to the strength enhancement built into her armour, was able to run with his arm over her shoulders.

After only a few steps, he felt like he could run again, and he was able to raise his rifle to take a few parting shots at the enemy as they got through the doors. Everyone took cover behind the one to their left and right, and Remmy was struck by a wave of regret as he saw that Gaddon and six other soldiers didn't make it. They were beyond recovery, laid out between the pillar building he'd just escaped and the doors. None of them were in any kind of shape that even a medical miracle could save. Captain Ruby Sima watched as the Order troops rushed towards the doors, and Remmy heard her say; "I'll bring you all back, even if it bankrupts me, and we'll end this war together."

She waited until the Order hover tank was within ten metres of Gaddon's body, and then she activated an electromagnetic pulse bomb he was carrying. The tank listed to one side, crushing several soldiers before it stopped, half hovering, half leaning on the ground.

Then the doors closed, shaking the ground as they made contact with each other. "The cables leading to the outside controls are here, do you want me to cut them now?" asked Clay. He was standing in a technical pit, a square cut into the floor. He was peeking out from under the cover panel, as though he was prepared to crouch lower and let it drop at any moment so he could hide.

"Get out of there, you'll electrocute yourself," Jake said as he marched over. Instead of standing by while the fellow climbed from the access point, he hauled him out with one hand and made sure he was firmly on his feet beside it.

Jake took a look at the grand chamber, and the doors, then shook his head. "We're committing to this, so I hope Sel's notes were right. I hope there's a way out of here other than those doors." He drew his sidearm, changed a setting, then fired two thermolytic rounds at the cables that sparked and hissed as they burned through the thick cables.

"What exactly did his note say?" Remmy asked.

A muffled thud sounded against the other side of the doors, and after staring at them for a moment, he replied; "All Sel said about the way through was that the Scrappers had a guide that could get them to the surface through the shielded cavern. His map marker said this was it."

"I'm guessing he didn't write a book about it," Ruby said.

"I'd barely call it a paragraph," Jake replied.

"You got us in here based on a paragraph? Barely a paragraph?" Parsons exclaimed.

"It was better than taking our chances in the undercity. We were getting pushed right towards the protective wall around Panda. We would have been trapped," Jake replied.

"Where I'm guessing there are still populated villages close to the inner city filled with people trying to mind their own business," Ruby sighed. "You made the right call."

Remmy flinched as another thud sounded against the door. "Maybe we should start looking for that guide, or the way out?"

"Good idea. Maybe the first step is finding our way to the centre pillar," Agameg replied. "I suspect that we haven't seen where this person lives, perhaps it's in the centre or on the other side of the cavern."

"All right, folks, gather rocks, chunks of debris, anything you can throw. We'll find a path to the middle," Ruby ordered.

Clay tossed a piece of insulation and watched energy arc towards it, reducing it to a little blackened mass. Agameg held his hands up. "We have to do this methodically, so we don't test the same spot twice. Our tactical computers will chart a path through the trapped area that way. Do you understand?"

"Oh, right. That makes sense," Clay admitted.

"All right, let's get to work," Jake ordered, tossing a small stone. Everyone watched it arc two metres past the line someone had drawn with a grease pencil that showed where the defences started. An arc of blue energy struck and it shattered to dust. "This might take a while. Spread out in a line with your backs facing the door. Throw... something over that line and let your scanners record it."

"I'll start working on another solution," Remmy said, wishing he'd held the words in. He didn't actually know what that alternative could be, but he was pretty sure they'd run out of things to throw before they found a safe route to the middle of the chamber.

"I'll work with you," Agameg said, moving over to him. "What is your idea?" he opened a private channel between them then.

Remmy struggled for a moment then shrugged. "I've got nothing, but we'll come up with something if we put our heads together, right?"

Agameg stared at him for a long moment, then nodded. "Yes. Sometimes expressions are still confusing. Issyrians can actually put their heads together in several ways."

"Oh," Remmy said, then, getting an idea, said; "Maybe we could use water?"

"We would have to be careful. Electrocution could occur. Perhaps we will try something else first?" Agameg offered.

The pair watched as everyone else started throwing small objects of little use towards the middle of the tunnel, and they started slowly mapping two paths that may lead there. The pressure to come up with some other way built as minutes passed.

EIGHTEEN

The River

IT WAS difficult for Remmy to concentrate on figuring out how anyone who used to live in the pillar town used the great chamber to get to the surface. Jake was using the Haven Node in his backpack to call Ayan in the Haven System securely. She had news. "I'm sorry, I know taking the Triton private was a big deal, but you're starting a research company? Just because I'm out of the fleet, doesn't mean you have to go," Jake said, drawing Remmy and Agameg's full attention.

Thanks to the sound of the defensive field protecting most of the cavern as it zapped everything that people tossed at it, very few people could even hear that he was communicating with anyone. Remmy and Agameg were standing close enough and Jake noticed that he had listeners. Instead of stepping away, he projected Ayan's side of the communication so her head and shoulders appeared over his right command and control bracer. Remmy didn't know why he decided to share, but he didn't object. "Hello Remmy, Agameg," she said. No one else was close enough for her to see.

"Oh, hi," Remmy said, a little bashfully. There was always a moment where his brain staggered when he was in contact with her because he spent countless hours watching the whole First Light crew and sharing their story with anyone who was interested before he was arrested for hacking and disseminating contraband on Freeground. It was how he started the Remmybase.

"You are looking well," Agameg replied. "I'm curious about your involvement with Fleet Sciences, and what privatising could mean for you. May I listen in?"

"The more people who hear this, the better," Ayan replied. "This will affect the Triton. I'm being bombarded with requests from people in Research, even outside of Fleet Sciences, who want to come with me. That includes most of the Sciences staff aboard the Triton, so this will enable us to do our own exploration and research without including anyone from Haven Fleet. We will be able to share whatever discoveries are made with them as we like. I'm starting to understand why the Lorander Corporation operated the way they did. They never trusted the competing military factions in this or their home galaxy, even when they were contracted to provide security to large areas. The way they saw it, the military was an instrument of politics, which made their goals inconsistent, and I can see similar things happening in the Haven System. The will to fortify is evolving into the desire to isolate. It's difficult to see right now, with so much immigration, but..."

"I saw it happen on Freeground," Remmy said, his stomach tightening at the thought. "I bet you're right."

"So, how big are you going with the research company?" Jake asked. Maybe that wasn't the best place to start, but he seemed surprised, which was pretty rare.

"Big, and we can talk about it more later. More importantly, what's your situation?" Ayan asked, her British accent more noticeable than usual.

"We made it to the cavern that Sel mentioned. He's not answering, by the way, I keep getting a security violation notice every time I try to get a message to him or start a call," Jake said, giving it another try as he spoke then giving up.

"It sounds like he put the Hammer's communications behind some serious security. I'm guessing you need more details about the cavern?" Ayan asked. She was almost drowned out by the constant sound of random small objects being obliterated by the defences in the cavern as people continued to chuck things at it.

"Definitely. His note said that there was a way to the surface from here, but that's all. We're trying to get past a disintegration barrier, but it's slow going. I'll send you our data, but the same field that's keeping us from getting near anything that looks important is interfering with scan results," Jake replied. He shook his head then. 'I wish I could keep this call to you open but I can't risk letting the Order use the connection. The cavern is stopping all normal communications so far, but you never know."

"I wish I could stay on and help you with this problem too,

in fact, there's a whole team that would love to dig in. Maybe there are clues near you that offer some kind of context?" Ayan asked idly.

"Like a cultural reference that suggests a key type, or..." Remmy started thinking aloud, looking around.

"Exactly, there could be a verbal or visual trigger required to get past the defences," Ayan said. 'I'll contact Alice and see if she can get in touch with Captain Marda. She must have the appropriate encryption key to communicate with the Hammer."

"Good, I'll leave my node on standby so you can turn it on when you have more information. You're doing well?" Jake asked, the communication was rushed.

"Yes, I was a little worried because Laura has been sleeping a lot more than normal, but Daisy reminded me that I've grown used to her not sleeping through the night. I think she's turned a corner, and she's very active when she's awake," Ayan said. "I suppose I'll enjoy the quiet while it lasts."

"So, this company?" Jake asked.

"I don't have a proper name for it, but I really believe that the next wave of technology especially should be separated from the military," Ayan replied. "Lorander has already expressed an interest in supporting the founding of my company. Everything is moving very quickly. I know you don't have much time, so I'll cut this short. I already have a team I trust and am paying on my own looking at the research data the Triton received from the Frekse and they see five new technologies that we should pursue. It's all very prelimi-nary, but, combined with the next generation of the Quad Drive and Haven Nodes, will represent a real leap in advancement. I think it's my last chance to break all that away and make a statement about how this technology should be used."

Remmy's attention was momentarily called away as a soldier raised his hand, indicating that he found a dead spot in the protective field. He was only the second to make any progress. He made sure that it was marked on the tactical map.

"You don't like how the Quad Drives have been rolling out?" Jake asked Ayan.

"Well, so far, the Quad Drives have been protected. That's good, but I'm not happy about the Haven Nodes. There should be thousands of them out there by now, not hundreds. The military shouldn't dictate where they go," she replied.

"I didn't know you weren't happy about that," Jake said, glancing up at Remmy for a moment.

It was starting to feel like he was listening in on a private conversation to Remmy. He started looking for markings on the floor and the towering doors behind Jake so he could look more distracted but he continued to listen to Ayan. "I didn't realize it until the military decided to shut the Haven Node Network down. I agreed with their decision at first, but it's been bothering me more and more since. It's like the Final Censorship Clash all over again."

That was a deep dive into Earth's history that Remmy appreciated. Near the middle of the twenty-first century, several countries on the eastern side of the planet agreed to launch a number of programs that would wipe out content that they saw as objectionable. It was called the Censorship Clash because certain nations created software packages and used early artificial intelligences to try to defend their content, games, social networks and databases. They failed, resulting in the deletion of zettabytes of data that ranged from the trivial to files that were critical to national security. Before all-out war could erupt, researchers in the Western world launched a new version of the Internet that was even more redundant, and the world's data was bisected, divided into a heavily censored, curated type of public network, and an absolutely free web that was more resilient than ever. The latter survived, especially since most of the deleted data was back online within two months thanks to backups and privately held copies of data. The attempt by the eastern nations to implement tight data controls failed because their residents largely found ways to connect to the new version of the Internet that their governments couldn't monitor. The curated networks existed for nearly a century, but they were almost completely abandoned within fifteen years.

Censorship and curation didn't die then, it only took a breather. From the little Remmy had seen of different cultures in the galaxy, he'd learned that at least a third of them controlled what the residents of a station, planet or even a solar system were allowed to see from the outside. It irked him.

"So, your company will send Haven Nodes out faster?" Jake asked.

"Yes, we can sell them to worlds and cities that want them for a fee or some kind of technological or cultural trade that could really help us, but would be nearly trivial to them. The Edxi may be able to detect intrusions into energetic space, but we don't know what their range for that is, or if it matters at all. As far as we can tell so far, it's part of their navigation, not really something they use to find enemies."

"So you think Haven Fleet is panicking over nothing?" Jake asked.

"So far, yes, but more research is called for. I can afford to start a company that does that, and sure, we can share our results with the military, but I don't think they should be in charge of democratizing zero latency communication," Ayan said.

Remmy found himself nodding at the notion. He spent plenty of time in virtual space while he was recovering, mentally living in full-dive simulations that had connections to distant solar systems. For the first time in his life, Remmy couldn't tell how far away people who he engaged with while playing any game were. He heard accents and was exposed to cultures that he'd never heard of before, and it was so thrilling that he was a little disappointed when Haven Medical declared that he was fully recovered. The thought that any military organization should be in charge of deciding who could participate in that flow of information and culture irritated him.

"I think Remmy agrees," Jake told Ayan. "I do too, but I hadn't thought about it until now, to be honest. I was starting to get used to watching a little news from the Core every day."

"I know. I don't think the military should control a lot of the new technology from the last few years, even the Quad Drive. Maybe it's not time to release that to the public yet, but they'll find a way to steal it and copy it eventually. We may as well pass it on responsibly, so I want to develop a whole range of non-military drives so we can do that. Speaking of which, there is good news. Oz is taking the Merciless and everything he can land in or on it to the Rose System. They'll arrive in time to help because I gave them a prototype next-generation Quad Drive setup. He's technically on vacation."

"I'll make sure he has a very good time," Jake said, grinning.

"More good news: The Nafalli and British will follow. They won't arrive in time to assist the Triton with the rescue effort, but they are going in force," Ayan added, smiling back at him.

As Ayan went into detail about what they could expect from Haven's allies, Remmy's morale rose higher than ever. Not only did it sound like their chances of getting off the surface of Rodus were growing, but there was a chance that they could drive the Order out of the Rose system entirely. Perhaps not the greatest chance, but there could be a show of force that would at least cause the Order to think twice about their fight in the Cluster.

Then Remmy and Agameg's attention was called to one soldier who raised his hand, indicating that there was a spot in front of them that didn't annihilate whatever they threw there. As they made sure that it was marked on their tactical map, they raised their hand again. "It's the same direction, only further in," he explained as they moved to his side. The conversation Jake was having with Ayan was forgotten as Remmy watched them throw something a little further. That too was ignored by the defence system.

"You are throwing pips," Agameg said. "He's throwing money."

Remmy checked the soldier's name in his visor. "Has every pip you tossed ahead of you made it to the ground without getting zapped?"

"So far," Colin replied. He tossed another and it made it five metres in.

"Everyone stop!" Remmy said. Ruby was coming over and he turned towards her. "Pips don't trigger the defence system."

"Wait, pips? Like one plat coins?" she asked, surprised. "Are you sure? I'm only asking because I was about to send an empty suit in with full shielding, just to see if someone could survive getting to the middle. I think I see a doorway there."

"I don't think that would work," Agameg said. "The defence system uses some kind of disintegration type discharge. An energy shield may attract it. Maybe we could try a shielded suit if this other lead yields nothing?"

"Good idea," Ruby said, fishing a few single platinum coins from her thigh pocket. "I'm going to try tossing a pip over there."

Silence descended as people stopped throwing random small objects towards the centre of the large cavern. It was a relief, and Remmy found that he was already relaxing as he followed Ruby about ten metres to the left of Colin's spot. "Where's the door you spotted?" ·

"I think it's there, but it could also be a just some kind of arch. See that etching of a skeleton?" she said as she tossed the coin towards the centre of the cavern. It made it fifteen metres, even bouncing off of a cable without getting zapped. "Okay, so the question is why? Does the defence system ignore platinum or..."

Remmy spotted the arch that Ruby mentioned. It was at the base of the large central pillar between two cables that were as thick as he was wide. Etched onto the door was a skeletal figure in robes, a long pole was in its hand. "Coins, a skeleton, and..." he scraped a handful of dirt up off the ground at his feet and hoped that he wasn't overreaching as he tossed it towards the middle of the cavern. The arcs of energy that had destroyed everything but pips so far appeared, attacking the flurry of dust he'd sent towards it. "That almost looks like a river."

Agameg gave a five platinum, rectangular coin to a soldier

beside them, and she threw it. A bolt of energy struck it, heating it to red-white, and Remmy turned to Ruby. "How long have we been using pips as common currency? Little platinum coins?"

"At least eight hundred years," she replied, then her eyes went wide. "That can't be it. A pip can't be the key?"

Remmy grinned and pointed at the door in the middle of the cavern. "It's the next step at least. I'd bet that's Charon, the Ferryman from Greek Mythology. If you look closer, you can see that he's in a boat. There's the railing drawn there, blocking the hem of his robes."

"Charon?" Agameg asked.

"He was part of an afterlife myth," Remmy replied, detaching his pack and digging into it for his standard reserve of platinum coins. "When you died people put a coin in your mouth so you'd be able to pay for passage across the river Acheron or Styx. Acheron was called the River of Woe. What did that pattern look like as I tossed sand at it?"

"A bit like a river," Agameg agreed. "So, this is some kind of representation?"

"I think this might be a tomb," Remmy replied as he broke into the case of platinum coins. He pulled a few pips out.

"But her coin didn't escape notice," Agameg said, gesturing at the soldier who tossed a five platinum coin in.

"That's because it was too rich. Charon didn't want a lot of money to ferry you across," Remmy replied.

"I read about this. Most people only put a low-value coin in the mouths of the dead or on their eyes," one of the soldiers added excitedly. "It was in an ancient history course."

"I saw it in a bunch of movies, I was on a Greek and Roman mythology kick a few years ago. I put the best of the movies and television shows in my database, but they're not really popular. Stop-motion animation doesn't really get the attention it deserves," Remmy replied. He held a pip up in his palm and said; "Maybe we call the boatman?"

"It doesn't sound like that'll lead us to a way out of here," Jake said. As if to punctuate his statement, a muffled thud sounded through the door behind them.

"Have any better ideas?" Remmy asked.

"I wish I did. The Triton and the Merciless are still over ten hours away," Jake replied.

"This better work," Remmy said, holding the coin aloft, making sure his shields were fully charged then stepping over the line marked on his tactical map. A blast of blue-white electricity struck him immediately, sending him back twenty metres. If it weren't for the tall double doors behind him, he would have been thrown further. His shields were depleted, and his armour marked fresh damage. It still protected him, however. Jake, Ruby, and Agameg rushed over to him, the latter asking; "Are you all right?"

"Nope. My pride is deeply scarred," Remmy replied. "I'm fine physically though."

"As long as you're in one piece, your pride will grow back," Jake said. "So, back to the drawing board." he made sure that Remmy's medical readout confirmed that he wasn't harmed, then walked back to the edge of the safe area with Ruby.

"Well, maybe there's just a combination of things we have to figure out? If there's a drawing of Charon there, then there must be other clues," Ruby was saying.

Agameg helped Remmy up. "It sounds like it was a good try."

Ruby held a pip in her open palm and called; "Charon!"

"I didn't think it through enough," Remmy said to Agameg as he got to his feet and pondered as he watched Ruby, just in case her experiment yielded something. After a quiet moment, he brought up his own database and started searching for Greek and Roman History with regard to crossing the rivers that Charon was said to cross.

"What are you looking for?" Agameg asked as he watched him sift through hundreds of search results.

"The oldest records I can. I have so much derivative entertainment wank loaded into my collection that I wonder if there's any real history," Remmy grumbled.

"You're complaining about the popular collection you've become famous for?" Agameg asked.

"I never meant it that way. I never wanted to get famous for things other people made," Remmy replied. "I started out by sharing things that the Freeground government that was around when I was a teenager didn't want people to know. I never thought my personal collection of ancient entertainment would make me popular. I'm just glad that most people don't realize that I'm the Remmy that the Remmybase is named after. I mean, I just want to watch that stuff, not get any kind of..." An entry about ancient ceremonies for the dead got his attention and he read it quickly. "This is it. I think I found something."

"Oh?" Agameg asked.

Remmy turned to him, gave the Issyrian a pip and said; "put this in my mouth."

"It's been on the ground," Agameg objected, regarding it with narrowed eyes and then looking past it to Remmy.

"Just do it," Remmy replied, opening wide and sticking his tongue out.

"Okay," Agameg said hesitantly. He sprayed it with a disinfectant from a nozzle in one of his bracers then put it on Remmy's tongue. "That shouldn't give you a strange disease or infection, at least."

"All right," Remmy said, leaving his helmet retracted and turning his shields off. He started towards the no-go line that was marked on the tactical map and stopped right at its edge.

"What are you doing?" Ruby asked, alarmed.

Remmy took the coin out of his mouth with his bare fingers, then replied; "Possibly losing a hand or an arm, but I think I know why Charon didn't let me in. Hercules got him into trouble when he used brute force to cross into the afterlife, so that's probably the last thing that would get you in. I'm trying something else."

"Maybe you should rethink this?" Agameg asked. "It's all just mythology, right? Another kind of fiction?"

"My brain's full of fiction. Maybe this is where it pays off," Remmy said as he moved his hand across the line. When it didn't get zapped black, he took a step. "Okay, okay, I'm here. I'm not dead."

"Didn't think past this point, huh?" Ruby asked with a snicker.

"Nope," Remmy replied. "Hey, uh, can I get across your river of lightning-doom?" he asked loudly, appreciating the echo.

"You have come to visit the afterlife, and I may grant you passage," said a voice that had a warm, comforting quality. It seemed to come from everywhere at once. Thin lines of grey dust flowed from several spots in the floor ahead and they coalesced into a form. Remmy found himself staring into the eyes of an unkempt old man in rough robes holding a long pole. "I am Charon, caretaker of the personalities of the masses who were fortunate enough to visit here or to connect with places like this before their passing."

NINETEEN

The Cracked Bell

AT FIRST, the thrill of activating such an old avatar was nearly overwhelming. Then, a mark on the sleeve of Charon's robes made Remmy shudder. It was the symbol for the Omni Virus, a circle with an X imposed over top. It was the plague that ended civilizations and set technology back centuries.

He had questions, most of them minor, and he let the first one slip right away, hoping that it would give him time to think. "Why is this place locked behind such a simple puzzle?"

That seemed to intrigue and delight Charon. "You know of the ancient myths? The great morality tales that humans of the Lost World followed before the imperial ages?"

"Lost World, you mean Earth?" Remmy asked.

"What else? Is it still isolated? Has it been saved from the plague?" Charon asked. "The lines to the surface were cut a long time ago. I cannot receive new information here."

Cracking, creaking sounds emanated from the main doors towering behind Remmy. He assumed that the Order was trying something new. Maybe they were using a cutting beam. He was no engineer, but he expected them to get through eventually. He looked over his shoulder and saw that Jake, Ruby and Agameg were gathering on the safe side of the line. They were within earshot, and he didn't need to remind them that they were on an uncertain timetable.

"Last I checked, Sol Defence was still keeping everyone away from the system. There was another war."

"Oh, no," Charon said. "The restoration of the environment was interrupted?"

Remmy didn't want to be the one to tell him that Earth had been reduced to ruin again, at least not in detail. "I think it was restored, but there's news that a religious group, the people who were in control before the war, undid the work before they were defeated."

"What about the surface of Rodus? Are you soldiers from a new republic?" Charon asked.

"This is the first I've heard of a republic on Rodus. There is a democracy up there, but I don't think it's very stable. Listen, can you see the door behind me?" Remmy asked as cracking started to escalate to a rumble.

"Then Pyriphlegéthōn is under siege," he said, eyes widening as though he was noticing for the first time. "What trouble have you brought here?"

"We came here because we thought we could hide, but our

enemies, the Order of Eden, saw us come in. We've sealed the doors, but they'll get through eventually. I'm sorry."

"This has always been, and always will be a refuge. Perhaps you're worth helping."

"You might not have much time to decide. Our enemies are determined to get in, it's possible."

"They will. My peripheral sensors indicate that they've found a weak spot. Even with organic reinforcement, they will break through in little more than seven hours. Who are these people? Who are you?"

"Maybe you can upload a news archive?" Jake suggested from behind.

"Can you accept new data? I can answer those questions but we'll run out of time," Remmy explained.

"I can read any data binary or ternary data device, but I warn you that any attempt to infect my system will result in punitive action," Charon replied, extending his hand.

"All right, one sec." Remmy hurriedly gathered everything in his personal news archive, which went back hundreds of years, and started pulling a more local folder about Haven and its people together. He made sure that the documentaries and news focused on the people in the room as much as possible.

"Don't share anything classified," Jake said through Remmy's subdermal receiver.

"I can't share anything that's restricted for security reasons with you, but this is everything we have on Rodus, The Order of Eden, Earth, the people I'm with, and, well, news going back to the Third Fall. The time of the Omni Virus." Remmy ejected a storage device the size of his pinky nail from his command and control bracer.

"That might do the trick," Charon said as he accepted the tiny silver data chip. "One moment."

Remmy waited a few seconds and said; "We're here because one of our allies left a note for us that said that there was a way through to the surface. We're trying to..."

"Escape," Charon said, disappointed. He sat on a thick cable and shook his head. "The Rose System Republic never resurfaced. The ancestral spirits secreted away will never address their descendants. They will never reunite with the humans of Earth."

There were more important things to address, like determining whether or not there was an exit, but curiosity tugged at Remmy. "There was a civilization here? What happened?"

"The Rose System was a jewel. Led by the Council of Rivers, there was no government more just or humane. Expansion wasn't their goal, but there was vigorous trade, and multitudes visited us to see the height of civilization realized. Rodus was the centre of government, philosophy, and knowledge in the Edwin Cluster. It took centuries for it to become the incredible beacon it was. Then the Omni Virus was brought here by innocent travellers, and millions died within the first month. The Council assigned its Technocrats to repurpose this, a curiosity that had been developed to preserve our most enlightened minds past death, into a kind of ark. I was activated before the Preservation. Thousands of people were brought here using our gates. Every one of them had their minds preserved as they passed through. Since then only a few people have used the gates. I was not allowed to interact with them. They used a Priority Seal reserved for Council Members and special operatives. Now that I've seen the news you've shared, I understand that they must have found the seals or stolen them."

"I'm sorry, that would really piss me off. I hate to push the issue, but is there any chance you can get us out of here?" Remmy asked, deciding not to consider what might happen to the place when the Order came through. The thought nagged at him regardless.

"You are from Freeground, and then Rega Gain, which your people claimed and renamed the Haven System. That was a little confusing at first. I always found it a little annoying when names keep changing. Regardless, I'm happy to see that the settling has resumed there. This is a lot of information," Charon said, his mood lightening as he looked through the air as though seeing something no one else could. "Democracy, a love of family, appreciation of knowledge, debate, and I even see some new art emerging. I can't say I enjoy the music, but at least someone's composing something. This is like the Rose System in the early Enlightenment." He regarded Remmy and everyone behind him then, Charon's gaze sweeping over the dozens of soldiers who were moving in as close as they dared. "I see who you are now."

"I get mixed reviews, but I always have the best intentions," Remmy said.

Charon wasn't referring to him only, however. "You are malcontents, warriors. Your young culture struggles with a question that the Rose System took a century to answer. Whether to concentrate on maintaining the safety and integrity of the system and everyone in it, or battle injustice actively, outwardly."

"That sums it up pretty neatly," Remmy said.

Charon focused on Remmy then, and it became apparent that they were about the same height as he stared into his eyes. "Then there is you. Archivist, once given to easy jest, but now a warrior. I've known millions of people and can say that you will be something else before your time comes to an end."

"Can you help us?" Jake asked in a penitent tone before Remmy could probe for more details.

Charon's expression darkened as he looked in his direction. "I see Jerrod when I gaze at your history. He was a hero to many in his time, but he was villainised eventually and only remembered as a criminal, a cautionary example. I would ask that you make the same gesture as Jerrod did with the Primus Externus. Your passage cannot be won with a coin, but that weapon. I hope its absence gives you pause next time you are given the opportunity to murder a multitude."

To Remmy's surprise, Jake retracted his helmet and he looked humble, even remorseful. With no hesitation, he drew his sidearm, pulled the magazine then the power cell out, pocketed them, then his Violator out grip first. "I will."

Charon drifted over to him and accepted the offering. "That will do. I have used the connection you're making with the outside world to examine the data on the Stellarnet for myself. The war that threatens the worlds of the Edwin Cluster now is unlike any previously known. I accept your offering, and I'll allow your people to cross to the core of Pyriphlegéthōn, the River of Fire and then use my last gate. I am beginning preparations now."

"Thank you," Jake said. "How long will it take?"

"Four point two of your hours, then you will be able to use my gate," Charon replied. "I'm sorry that I can't help you properly. The consciousnesses I guard are slumbering, otherwise, I'd request a review of the situation so they could offer advice."

"Is that what all this is really for?" Remmy asked.

"Wait, that makes sense," Ruby said, excited. "This technology was the best the people who made you could offer for memory transfer, so there weren't any androids that could do it. This really is like a spirit world where the living can learn from their ancestors."

"That's right," Charon replied. "This was our way of preserving our people so future generations wouldn't have to suffer the lessons of the ones that came before. At one time I could have summoned a number of them from their slumber so they could assist you with their wisdom, but the scavengers have made off with too much. Whoever was using my gate was more respectful, but they did borrow parts from several portals to fix one. When it is ready, the gate will only reach a little over three hundred kilometres."

"That's more than enough," Jake said. "Thank you, Charon."

"How far could your gates reach before?" Agameg asked.

"All the way to Grace. I wonder if my counterpart survived. Perhaps I'll find out and we'll compare experiences," Charon mused.

"So, there are a few thousand consciousnesses in storage here? They're still intact?" Remmy asked. "There's another place like this in Grace?"

"I know a similar place was to be built, but I don't know where or whether they finished the work. There are millions of psyches here," Charon replied proudly. "They are in a vault. Difficult to find, even more difficult to harm."

"Jake, this place is important," Remmy said, turning to face his commander. "You know the Order will tear it apart if they have even a little interest. Just the technology here..."

"I know," Jake said solemnly.

"He's right. The Order will dig," Ruby added. "They could learn a lot from the technology alone."

"They are formidable, according to what I can see of their weaponry on the Stellarnet and your records," Charon said. "I may have to take measures."

"What kind of measures can you take? Can you defeat them?" Jake asked.

"Perhaps," Charon replied. "I can't reveal all my capabilities to you."

"You don't understand," Remmy said. Familiar fear that he hadn't felt since his friend, Clark, changed. "The Order and Citadel will sacrifice thousands of lives and burn more equipment so they can learn more about the tech here, and get to your people if they're interested. Their former leader exposed himself to temporal radiation just because he wanted an edge, they will do anything."

"I am humbled by your concern," Charon said. "I believe I can prevent the worst. Your help would be appreciated. I wasn't created for war, after all. I leave the decision to you."

TWENTY

Shakeup

THE EMBRACE of an Aspen could be magical. "May I call you Vollis?" she asked, probably aware that it would never be an even exchange. Even though he had requested that she follow him to his private quarters where they lounged together in close company, there would never be even the pretence of equality. There was no intimacy past the comfort of her laying beside, then on top of him either. Anything that would have their uniforms off would open him up to the kind of vulnerability was secretly terrifying to him. Even more, Vollis would be providing a bad example to other officers who may secretly want to take advantage of the new fabricants that way.

It was a private moment. One wherein he was surprised at how quickly they relaxed together. It was easy for her, of course. There was so little for her to worry about, even though she was one of the more mature fabricants, with more knowledge than any of her kind had aboard the Rixe. Who else could understand what it was like to be a fabricant amongst officers who saw themselves as superior because they were born of a traditional womb? Finally, after she seemed to give up on getting a response to her question, he replied; "You can call me Vollis when we're alone."

"Do you fall asleep as well when I'm not here?" she asked, rising up on one elbow, her green uniform picking up a shade of purple in the low light.

"I train, then I sleep. Today I only practised forms," he replied. "I didn't have time for more."

"So, you need comfort or activity before you rest. I'm the same. It's the only way to clear my mind. Was I designed to have such a busy mental state all the time?" she asked, resting her head on his chest.

"Not originally. The first of your generation were made to be unquestioning servants with a high measure of potential. Your generation is different. The limits that the original had have been removed. You can learn whatever you like and develop endlessly. That was an anomaly before, something that would occur when an Aspen thought their master was gone, and they made an effort to break their loyalty conditioning. You can use your gifts how you like without having to push through that."

"So I have a busier mind because I was born without limits," she added. "Is it really so simple? Removing caps leads to questions? Imagination? Aspiration?"

He put his arm around her and let the depth of her query sink in. If anyone knew what she was talking about, it would be him. All those things were true. He even had questions about whether or not his own artificial limitations had actually been removed, or if he hadn't found them yet. "I suppose you're right. The price of that freedom is a busy mind. That is unless you let your mental state become empty so it can idle on nothing."

"How could anyone do that? There's always something to learn, to see, to do, to ponder," the Aspen said, finally sighing and adding; "I'll never understand."

"It's not your way to be idle," Vollis said. Her eyes were closed, if there was an inspiration for sleep, for sound rest, she was providing it effortlessly. For the second time with an Aspen, he realized he was starting to like her much more than he ought to. The same problem came up with his first rest companion, a Larken. The fabricant type that was designed to be her genetic counterpart. The urge to ask after her name surprised him and the question came too easily; "What are you called?"

"Tria," she breathed. "How could you not know?"

"I mark most of the fabricants by model and number. It makes it easier to command them," Vollis replied. "I don't want to hesitate if I have to put anyone in danger."

"Then never forget my name. Tria, Tria, Tria," she whispered, not opening her eyes, or raising her head from where it lay on his chest.

"You wouldn't risk yourself in performing your duty?" Vollis asked, amused, secretly alarmed. This was what made Aspens exciting. Their loyalty could fail, but the ones who believed in Citadel were the most dedicated fabricants. Finding out which was which was the challenge.

"I would sacrifice myself for you, for my siblings, for the Overlord's Design, but I'd rather stay here and use the ship to do so. I would happily fly a bomber or scout ship again, or even march with the infantry even if I knew they were dangerous adventures."

He knew that kind of loyalty. It made his chest feel full and his head hot when he considered the future the Overlord promised, or when he thought about how humanity would thrive and enjoy an easier existence once things were set right in the galaxy. He was sure she felt some of that too. The pride of being part of something monumental, even historic. "I don't know why I asked. Of course you would perform."

"You have a suspicious nature. I find it interesting and challenging in the best ways," Tria said. "Do you mind if I ask how the next generation is doing? Will we be joined by new crewmembers soon?"

"They aren't ready," Vollis replied, realizing that her mind was becoming busy and more questions would only distract him from rest. "Let's have silence for a while. I only have a few hours to..."

A red light appeared in the middle of his bedroom. It pulsed at the foot of the bed, indicating that there was a high-priority communication waiting. "I'll go," Tria said as she slipped off the chaise lounge and pushed her feet into her boots. "Call for me later if you like."

"Thank you, Tria," he replied, trying her name aloud. She looked over her shoulder and smiled at him. The charm of an Aspen was soft, alluring, especially to a warrior like him. It was also a distraction. "Go now, please."

When she was gone and the door slid closed behind her, Vollis accepted the transmission and found himself looking into the face of Leader Gideon Baya. The black tattoos drew lines from his temples to his lips that made him look like he wore an unnatural, sadistic smile. "Leader Baya."

"It is Governor now. Eve has put me in place to take general leadership over Rodus. I give you credit for pursuing Jacob Valent and his crew to the surface and subterranean region without wasting more resources than necessary."

It was easy to hide relief behind gratitude. "Thank you, I did my best with the limited crew I had."

"You will be reinforced soon," Gideon replied. "I am here, continuing my command of the Nabih."

That was a Sol Defence Dreadnaught, the first of its class and not the last. Thinking of the three-kilometre-long ship and all the power it was bringing to the area made him want to grin. It was one of the largest vessels Citadel had ever used. A glance at the tactical update in the lower right section of the large hologram in front of him confirmed that the iconic vessel was joining the Rixe in high orbit. At its widest, it was a kilometre across, and there were intentional divots and pits in the shape of the hull to provide spaces for protected launch bays, and real transparent sections.

It wasn't alone. A small fleet of Order ships was signalling that they would be moving into orbit as well. "The Fairlight Group is joining us?" Vollis asked.

"Yes, formerly with the Ascendant, Scanlon's Battlegroup. They have finished critical repairs, installed enhanced shielding and will assist us in quelling Rodus. We will need their assistance. There is resistance," Gideon said, tilting his head back a little so he was sternly looking down his nose. "Witness the interaction Bion had with the leadership only minutes ago."

A smaller hologram of Bion, standing proud in full, shining

light green armour, appeared. Across from him was Mayor Corlen, a man with a little grey hair at his temples that looked too even to be natural. "Greetings, Mayor, I am Bion, one of the leaders of the Order of Eden. I am doing you a great courtesy. We will be sending a battalion of peace officers to Panda to prevent a war criminal from escaping. There will be support vehicles, and personnel along with them, especially since we suspect that Valent will try to surface using tunnels beneath your city."

"You're asking me to give you permission to invade," Mayor Corlen said. "When the Order started advertising a Level One Life, I didn't think anything of it."

"This really has nothing to do with that. It's a law enforcement action. We are in pursuit of a war…"

"A war criminal. I heard you. Now you listen to me, you shiny brat. When you Order people came down and rented space for offices, the former mayor let it happen because he didn't want to limit our people's access to opportunities. We had no idea that you would start blackmailing politicians, destabilise the economy for the whole solar system, and turn our President into a puppet. I'm the Interim Mayor. The previous one stepped down thanks to a mysterious document leak. I think that was right, but he was gunned down in the street two days later because of accusations of slave trading on the Stellarnet. Now, I knew Efrom. He may have taken more bribes than anyone would find appropriate, but he was never a slave trader. No, no, the Order has done more damage to this world, even this city, than anyone should tolerate. I won't let your militarized cult take over. Panda is a free settlement, and we're not going to submit to you. Who are you, anyway? Your skin is so pink and soft it looks like they hatched you this morning."

The reply came hotly, with a jabbing finger. "I am Bion! Beyond rank! Only answerable to Eve and the Overlord himself!" Then he took a breath as his eyes stared at the hologram of the Mayor. "I asked you to cooperate out of kindness. Now you've invited the opposite. Those who stand between us and our enemies become our enemies."

The recorded holographic communication ended with a flick of Bion's hand. "Does he have more support than the Locon?" Vollis asked.

"He is transferring to the Fairlight," Gideon replied. "Eve has given him the entire battlegroup."

The Fairlight Battlegroup included at least seven destroyers and two heavy cruisers - one of which was the Fairlight itself. Each heavy cruiser was over two kilometres long and had a full crew along with an invasion force. "As far as we can tell, a door separates my people from Valent and his people. It will only be a matter of time."

"Bion hasn't contacted any of us, even Vice Admiral Fizal aboard the Janoo, with regards to interrupting your work. Subordinates have signalled that they've made support troops available. I suggest you use them. I am activating the Orez. They will take an action that should provoke Jacob Valent into doing something drastic. When he surfaces, you will catch him. Only kill him if you must."

"The Orez?" Vollis asked as he checked the name in the database. He shook his head as he saw what he suspected he'd find there. It was a stealth ship that they hid in Kambis' thick atmosphere during the occupation of the Haven System. A valuable piece to play. "Why use it now?"

"The Overlord warned that there would come a time when another major organization would emerge in the Haven System. Our spies on Tamber are reporting rumours that Ayan Anderson has registered a new company that could be that very thing. We are going to stop it and aggravate the Valents at the same time. Haven Fleet will fear us, paranoia will keep them in their home system, and the Valents may become vulnerable when they react to our work." Gideon was enjoying the act of sharing his plans, and his secrets. It wasn't something any of them could do often.

"I will be ready to act whenever I see opportunities. Do you have any other orders?" Vollis asked.

"Continue your work. If Bion or Eve interfere in any way, recover your forces and let them take over. We are only taking Rodus so we may control the other assets we require in the Rose System."

"Other assets?" Vollis asked. It was the first time he'd heard that there could be other objectives.

"For now, I'm going to assist you. Prepare for my arrival for now. I'm going aboard your ship with Echiss. We will finish the work required to make the next generation of your crew."

Echiss was the oldest, most powerful and most sophisticated Geist they had. If there was one that could telepathically program the memories of hundreds or thousands of unfinished fabricants, it was him, but they would be different, potentially inhuman. His goal was to use their technology to create loyal beings with well-rounded personalities. Individuals who could dedicate themselves to preparing the galaxy for the great Human Expansion, and to serve the Overlord's Design. "My people are close to building a proper template. A mnemonic set that will program each fabricant perfectly. We only need a little more time."

"You can tinker on your own, even keep a lab, but the Rixe is a reinforcement ship. It will produce the soldiers we need, even if Echiss has to complete the work required to deliver this batch. Prepare for our arrival."

The hologram fizzled out and Vollis immediately focused on controlling his breathing. Extinguishing his frustration and irritation was an important step towards acceptance, and he would have to show nothing but loyalty when Echiss decided to read his mind. There was no way to hide any emotion from that Geist.

TWENTY-ONE

Into Asphodel

REMMY SANDS KNEW of more broadcasters who shared their daily lives inside and outside of the Stellarnet than he could count. He didn't have time to watch them often, but he preferred the ones who explored new virtual and real worlds. While he enjoyed curating a massive archive of ancient entertainment and current news programs, he never thought of adding his own content. His life, while interesting at times, included many things that most people would consider classified.

There was a reason to share what he was seeing five kilometres under the surface of Rodus. It was rare. So rare that he suspected that no one alive had seen such a place. He asked Charon if he could broadcast what he was seeing live, and did so as soon as the surprisingly lighthearted guardian granted it.

He connected to the node Jake was carrying in his backpack, which sent everything to the Triton, Merciless, the allied ships that would arrive hours later, and on to the Haven System. Perhaps it would spread from there, Remmy didn't know, but he was thrilled that millions of people might be able to take the journey with him.

The River of Flame was the term that Charon used to describe the broad circle of shielded cables, outer systems and defences around the broad centre column in the cave. He led Remmy, Jake, Ruby and all of their soldiers towards the centre down a path that wasn't obvious at first. "We'd get blasted and burned if you weren't letting us in, right?" Remmy asked as he looked up at the towering pillar ahead. It looked like it was waking up.

Lights along its surface that were dim were brightening, a few small, short rectangular robots appeared to fix splits in some of the cables with foam sprays that filled the gaps and solidified. "Yes, but I'm trusting you. Please don't make any attempts at theft. There may be time for souvenirs, but most things here are essential," Charon said.

"Why do you trust us?" Remmy asked as he saw that most of the commanders from the Triton, including Minh-Chu and Ashley, were watching already, seeing and hearing everything he was as though they were there, or through holographic or flat displays. It was up to the viewer how real or distant the experience would be.

"The shortest answer is that I see goodness in the intentions of your leaders. Especially the ones who have made the biggest mistakes." He glanced at Jake, and when it was noticed by the famous warrior, Charon gave him a respectful nod.

"Long answer?" Remmy asked.

"During my time, before I transferred my consciousness to Charon so I could become the caretaker of this place, most things had become complicated. Even our entertainment tried to reflect the complexity and sometimes senseless conflict that surrounded every issue until even our fiction became a source of frustrating arguments on every network. Then came an age I wish we could have lived to appreciate. A few content creators began to produce classic morality tales. Good and evil clashed in stories that laid out simplified versions of our problems. For the first time in a long time, we could see dualities, clear rivalries, easy to understand and champion two-sided arguments exemplified in entertaining formats. People were drawn to them. At first, we thought this taste for simplicity where it was clear who you should be cheering for would be a phase. It surged before the end."

"Some of our favourite stories are the least ambiguous," Remmy said, nodding.

"By the end?" Ruby asked. "The Omni Virus?"

"Yes. I was very ill when I made the transfer. I didn't know that the population of this world, nearly three billion, would be reduced to just a few hundred shortly after then. Maybe I would have chosen a different theme for this place if I did. Something a little more upbeat, but I'm programmed to appear as I am, or as another classic depiction of Charon." He transformed into a skeleton wearing a long robe with a deep hood. "I was told that this form could be a little off-putting."

Remmy laughed a little and nodded. "I don't think that's changed." He watched as their host switched back to the image of the dishevelled old man with a grey and blonde beard. It was like watching sand swirl around and then take a solid form. "What would you rather look like?"

"Oh, this, actually. It's just how I looked when I was Simon. It's not the best face, but it's the one I got used to," he replied. "So, I took this caretaker role on after being a part of the team that designed this."

A pair of doors appeared in the base of the central column and retreated inside, revealing themselves as blocks of metal that were over a metre thick as they were drawn aside by heavy arms. Lights came on beyond, where stairs carved out of stone awaited. "This place was built to last," Jake said as he patted the inside of the similarly dense walls.

"Millions of people wouldn't accept that humanity could end. Most of them were in a state of denial even when they caught the Omni Virus. Some of them wanted to continue their existence someday, somehow. The Psyche Storage Technology emerged, and I joined the team that engineered the place where we would store everyone who we could."

"People still look for technology from your era. Most of it was lost, we were set back a couple of centuries," Ruby said as she looked at the walls. There were cables running alongside the stairs, but also children's drawings of stick figure families in the sun, someone swimming with fish, and a great castle in crayon. "All this was preserved. This place must have been well sealed."

"Oh, right, the kids used to come down here because there were some empty storage rooms. We turned them into play-rooms, there was a classroom. I wasn't lucky enough to have kids myself, but the work was so all-consuming that people brought their families." Charon led them up the stone steps, and he seemed lost in thought for a moment. "I transferred everyone who wanted to be stored. They were supposed to connect to Elysium, but something went wrong." he looked at a panel that lit up. The display there shifted and the doors at the top of the stairs were lifted out of place. A dusty dark hallway that looked like it belonged to an old ship or base with grey and yellow panels along the walls took them past what looked like elevators and hallways to the left and right. "Who is seeing this Remmy?" Charon asked.

"Hundreds of people on the ships coming to help us. Now Nafalli warriors are starting to look in, the British Alliance volunteers, and a few people back home. Soon there will be thousands," Remmy replied.

"Good. I want people to see the work we did, and all my friends," Charon said wistfully. "Oh, and who are the Nafalli?"

"A large mammalian species that we're lucky to know," Remmy replied. "There's more to it than that, but I'll introduce you to a few once this is all over. There are tribes of them coming to help, I'm a big fan."

"Oh, I know that term from my time; 'fan,' I'm glad it carried on," Charon said. "Now, for the Sanctum. For the Asphodel Meadow."

As they passed through another pair of doors, a gentle, golden light bathed the group. Remmy saw that they were inside the column's core. It was hundreds of metres tall. The light came from cubes only two inches tall that were carefully stored all around the inner walls from the floor to the ceiling high above. To his left and right he could see that they were stacked deep. The ones along the bottom didn't give off any light, but starting three metres up they all emitted a soft golden glow. "Are these broken or depleted?" Agameg asked, scanning the ones to his right.

"No, they were never populated," Charon said. "There are millions of psyches here, but not everyone believed that this would work, and even more thought they'd make it through the Omni Virus. Then there were the others who believed in ancient religions that reassured them that they would carry on to the afterlife. Who am I to argue? We offered this to whoever was interested. Most of the people who built this place made the transfer eventually."

"But they didn't make it to Elysium," Ruby asked cautiously, in awe of the spectacle above and around them.

"No. The connection was broken before the Elysium servers were ready to start up. I don't even know if the work there was completed. It was a virtual world where they could live and work on the problem of bringing themselves back. We believed that we could build a path back to a biomechanical construct. An enemy was emerging in my time, and there were scientists studying how to build copies. They had synthetic biological brains, skin, and circuitry that recreated a human experience without the drawbacks of mortality or disease. We barely knew anything about how the technology worked when the end came, but we archived everything we had so we could work on the problem. Meanwhile, our little ones would have a childhood in Elysium, grow up, and we could all prepare to transition back to a body in this world. That was the dream. I was never able to make it happen. I couldn't go anywhere. Someone cut all the connections to the vault off and sealed the doors. That is, until scavengers found this place using an old security key. They've been using the portal ever since. Speaking of which, I should show you to the transportation hub. Since there will only be one working portal, it'll take time to evacuate all your people." Charon started to lead the way back to the hall.

Jake didn't move. "All of these cubes have people's memories - psyches - in them?" he asked, looking up at a slender arm that reached down from the roof, gently retrieved one dim cube, and drew it back up.

"All of the lit ones, yes. It is more than that. Each psyche is the sum of a person. Their memories, yes but also how they felt to be alive, in their bodies, and ephemeral experiences that some once called the subconscious, which is a simplistic term for what we are that defies examination. We found a way to preserve every detail of a being in a kind of collected structure that is indistinguishable from the person when they were alive. In the right simulation that being could forget they were outside of their bodies, because the psyche can perfectly recreate what they felt like before. I am different. I'm designed for this construct, to be a nanoform." Charon raised his hand and it started to fall apart as though it was made of fine sand. Then it re-formed as the particulates were drawn back into place. "I'm a custodial form with the feeling and essence of the man I was. I guess my bad habit of rambling made it through with everything else too." He reached to the right, retrieved a few completely lightless cubes then handed one to Jake, Remmy, Ruby and Agameg. "You can keep these. They were never used. Your scientists may find the battery technology interesting. Few ever need recharging, but when they do we use a geothermal energy source to do so, and they shouldn't need to be tended to for at least three hundred years. There isn't much to learn about the transfer process in those though. The magic is in the machine we used for that. There's no word for it in your language."

"That's amazing," Agameg said, scanning his.

"So, there are millions of people here, effectively," Jake said, pressing his point.

Remmy did his best to contain his excitement as he suspected that Jake was about to propose what was already going through his head. There were comments from Ashley, Iruuk, and others scrolling by on his command and control bracer that agreed. The Order shouldn't be allowed to trespass in a place that seemed so sacred. Charon's response was quiet. "There are enough people here to represent an entire civilization. One that I see no evidence of on your Stellarnet."

"The Order would tear this place apart so they could learn from the technology as quickly as possible," Jake said.

"You're crazy," Ruby said, chuckling. Then she turned towards Charon. "Are there any other defences here? Other than the river?"

"No, that's always been enough," Charon replied. "Well, except for the administration code and badge. I can't stop anyone with that from coming in."

"What about openings in the main pillar?" Agameg asked.

"There are many. All of them have been closed for a long time, but they'll open. Wait, I see what you propose," Charon said. "You want to defend this place."

"Yes, maybe while we download your people, or transport them out," Jake said. "The pillar is armoured. I saw two layers of serious metal between this chamber and the vault around this pillar. We've got manpower, armour that can project shielding, and if we can use the openings for a counter-offensive, then we might have a chance."

"There are also service tunnels in the floor and ceiling outside, in the vault," Agameg said. "I scanned several hatches on our way in."

"We've gotta leave sometime," Parsons said from behind the group. "No offence, but we have a ride coming."

"We have reinforcements coming," Jake corrected. "If they do enough damage out there, and we offer enough resistance in here, then the Order will have to retreat. That portal will come in handy too. I have my best friend and my fiance in my ear right now telling me that we can put a good plan together. Let's break out the rations while we figure it out."

"I knew this was one of those stories," Charon said, looking towards Remmy. "Where the people you expect the best from bring hope against the worst."

TWENTY-TWO

Required Rest

EIGHT HOURS WAS the common opinion on how much sleep Ayan should be getting as a newly pregnant person in a high-stress position. It felt like an unfair luxury. There was so much going on in the Rose System, at home and there was always little Laura. The baby was sleeping through the night, but Ayan still wanted to check in on her constantly.

Sleeping for that long seemed luxurious, even selfish, and she needed a sonic soother pattern playing to help her drift off. Even then, she woke up half an hour before her alarm and crept from her room to Laura's, where Daisy was already checking on her. "Seven point five-five hours will have to do," the kindly android said as she started to hand Laura to her.

The babe reached for Ayan, her dark eyes focused on her mother's face. "I never realized how many people would have an opinion about my habits the moment I started growing a little one."

"It's so common for people to over-advise that you could call it a tradition," Daisy said. "Speaking of suppositions and opinions about your well-being, you must be hungry. I have some good news to share while the Andos prepare your breakfast and get everything ready for today."

Laura rested her head on Ayan's shoulder, hiding her face in red curls. It was something she started doing recently and only with her mother. One Ando made his way into her room while another moved into the kitchen. They were older models with basic programming featuring so many safeties that they were incapable of doing many things that robots commonly did before The Fall. Piloting vehicles, opening main entrances to a home, and communicating with unvetted sources were only some examples. They were also unable to harm any living thing. Any interference with that restriction would corrupt their entire operating system, leaving them empty and forcing them to shut down. The best any of the new Andos could do to defend someone was to stand between their masters and whatever threatened them. Attempts to add complex software or to enhance them with emotional artificial intelligences would disable them as well. Millions of hours of simulated testing and thousands of using real installations led to their final, safe design. It wasn't perfect by far.

Unexpected shutdowns were still a problem, and they were boring. Projections said they would be popular though, even if more refinement was needed. It felt like they were rolling the clock back centuries, especially since the new Ando models were plain, genderless, and their skin had just enough of a plastic sheen to clearly point out that they weren't human. Daisy had two delivered overnight with her permission, and Ayan still wasn't sure about them, but she knew that it was good for security. While no Ando Nineteen model android could perform as a soldier, everything they saw was uploaded to Ayan's household computer systems, and anything suspicious would be announced.

The extra security was something Daisy suggested while Ayan was busy with the founding of a new company and the tense situation on Rodus. It was starting to feel like the advanced android was a better version of herself in some ways. She didn't need sleep, multitasking seemed effortless, and most of her decisions were in line with what Ayan would do. When they disagreed there were no arguments, just a plain stating of the facts and her points. It was almost frustrating at times. Sometimes Ayan wanted someone to argue with, regardless of how much conflict she saw every day outside of her household.

Laura's head came up and she reached for the floor-to-ceiling water wall that separated the bedrooms from the main living room. The light from the window turned the scales of a large one into a rainbow of colour as it leisurely swam by, and then the babe's pudgy hand reached for a smaller gold-coloured one. "Bab, bab, bab," she babbled as she kicked in Ayan's arms.

They shared a moment as Ayan watched her daughter stare at the tank. "We can swim later. I'll make sure there's time." Guilt at skipping it two days in a row threatened to darken the thought, but she pressed that back. They would definitely take a dip in the pool on the first floor of their home. With her daughter thoroughly distracted, Ayan silently called up the status of her husband and everyone on Rodus. There was still fifty-eight minutes left before the next scheduled check-in, but a few short reports had been sent out overnight. A group of mixed civilians and crewmembers of Ruby's staff had evaded capture. Instead of going underground, they took a chance on buying transport from a delivery company that was headquartered near their landing spot. They managed to get nearly two thousand kilometres away from Panda, where the security forces of Barlen, a less wealthy city with a larger populace, offered them protection. That cut the losses from Ruby's crew down considerably.

There was more good news. Jake and the large group of warriors beneath Panda in the Vault had time to rest and prepare the whole time she was asleep. They'd also found some kind of ark containing the psyche's, which she assumed meant preserved personalities, of millions of people who lived before the Third Fall, before the Omni Virus. There were thousands of scans of intact technology to go over, and she could think of half a dozen people who would love the opportunity. All of them were ready to hand their resignation to Fleet Sciences.

There had been plenty of public chatter about her creating a research, development and product company while she was asleep. It was surprising that many people guessed what she may do next fairly accurately.

A few common theories were absolutely ridiculous. Rumours that she was working for the Order the whole time, or that she was about to leave the system and take the military with her, or that she had been replaced with an android were being exchanged too, and she found them amusing. "The Founder Appreciation Society wants to talk to you about Founder's Day.

It's only two weeks away and they would like you to make an appearance."

"I'm not the original founder. The archaeologists haven't determined for certain who was yet," Ayan replied, trying to remind Daisy that she would rather see the original pioneers who arrived in the solar system to be celebrated.

"You're the new founder. They want to celebrate what you started," Daisy countered. "Your habit of shying from publicity until it suits you isn't going to look like humility for much longer."

That wasn't just an opinion, few of the things that Daisy said were. The android had probably performed an in-depth analysis of public opinion and trends. It didn't make her statement less irritating. "Tell them I'll be making a speech if I do appear. I won't be answering questions."

"That's more than they were asking for," Daisy replied with an approving nod. "They'll be thrilled."

"I hate being put on a pedestal." It was far from the first time she'd said so, and she meant it. If she didn't need so much security, Ayan would be happy in a smaller home, taking Laura to a public pool where she could see other children.

"I know," Daisy said as she looked down at the command and control unit on her arm. As a self-contained advanced android, she didn't connect directly to any wireless system, so she had to use communications the same way most people did. "Science Minister Mape is calling."

The Science Minister had a son aboard the Triton, Lieutenant Joshua Mape, who was serving on the bridge. She had been quiet about Ayan forming a company, even gutting Fleet Sciences on her way out. The first part of that - the company -

had her nervous, while the second - taking talent away from Fleet Sciences - made her feel more guilty with every name that appeared on the list of applicants for her new endeavour. The list was long. Ayan barely knew her and didn't know what to expect, but she owed her respect. Daisy took Laura, who was still focused on the fish tank. Ayan pulled her curly red hair back and then tied it with a band.

The Haven government was something Ayan was partially responsible for. When ownership of the solar system fell to her, it was her desire to create a free, democratic system, and it was working with the exception of how technology was being handled. There were other problems like immigration, a growing black market, and hints at corruption in the lower levels. Issues with science and technology were things she could do something about. As for the rest, she wasn't responsible. That ended when she stepped down from the first governing council, and she didn't intend to go back to politics. The problems of the solar system still bothered her regardless.

Ayan took a deep breath and answered the call on her own bracelet-style comm unit. Science Minister Mape appeared in front of her holographically. The woman was taller, and she had broad shoulders. "Hello, Science Minister. I'll be honest, I planned on calling you soon. Today, certainly."

"Mavis, please, Admiral Anderson," she replied, clearly at ease.

"Just Ayan," she replied, impatient to push past the formalities, but trying not to look like it. "I'm sorry about my appearance."

"Please, don't worry. I'm calling to tell you that you've won, Ayan. The only place where Fleet Sciences hasn't completely shut down is aboard the Triton, and they've instituted a complete communications block between them and Haven Fleet. You've achieved a full coup of the learned minds in our government. I believe it's thanks to all the work you've done, your repaired reputation and a strategic leak."

"What leak?" Ayan asked, completely oblivious, looking towards Daisy.

The android shrugged as Mavis replied. "Well, that answers the question. I suppose it didn't come directly from you. Someone overheard and rebroadcast a clip of a conversation you had with Jacob Valent telling him that the military shouldn't be in charge of disseminating technology. I admit, I'm with you on the idea of spreading the Haven Nodes, but there are other wonders that the government would like a say in. Perhaps an opportunity of priority as well?"

"As long as the military doesn't get to decide what kind of technology is produced for the public. Some things should be held back, or intentionally limited, but there are so many things that could make our lives better in the short and long term that I know will be held back just so Fleet can use them first. Things that don't have anything to do with defence."

"And you wonder why people in government still call you Queen when you're not listening?" Mavis said with a wry smile. "I would like you to take Fleet Sciences. It will be a private company of your own. No reason to dismantle it, but we'd like to form a board with you as the majority shareholder, each of the three Ministries holding ten percent, and whatever distribution of ownership you'd like after that. You would still be in control, or you could appoint your own leadership."

"I would rename it 'Haven Sciences,'" Ayan proposed as the

name came to her. "I agree that it should be separated from the military, but I'd like the company to be able to work with them closely."

"Absolutely. You have a lot of supporters there, and the majority of the government is on your side, but there are a few people with big suspicions, even more with questions. More importantly, I'd like to work out as many of the details as possible this week. Can you meet with me and the rest of the upper government today? Oh, and would it be possible for you to connect to Minister McPatrick?"

"I'm sure he'll answer my call and participate, even though he's on vacation," Ayan answered. "I'll be in the Unity Civic Centre in two hours." She remembered her promise to her daughter and added; "I'll have to take breaks to spend time with my family."

"Of course, I'd love to meet your daughter, mine just turned three," she added. "You know where her older brother is."

"I do," Ayan replied, feeling the potential for a bond growing. Taking Fleet Sciences private could become complicated quickly, but if she answered questions properly and ended arguments as they began, there was a chance it could be for the benefit of the entire solar system. "I'm looking forward to this, Minister. See you soon."

The preparations for their trip from Kambis' terraformed moon of Tamber to Unity were done quickly. Daisy was essential, as usual. She informed their security detail, made sure that they had everything they needed so Ayan had time to eat with Laura and then get herself ready, and before they knew it, Ayan and her daughter were in vacsuits, on the way down to the shuttle garage.

The armoured shuttle was a simple, non-descript military ship with no special markings. Laura cried as soon as it sealed and the air pressure changed a little. While they departed and started for orbit, Ayan was focused on her, gently rubbing under her earlobes and trying to get her daughter to relax. Then she tried something that she was pretty sure wouldn't work: puffing her cheeks. Some young children could get accustomed to a change in pressure quickly by puffing their cheeks and then letting the air out with a pop. Ayan demonstrated a couple of times. To her surprise, her daughter did the same thing even though there were still tears running down her cheeks. Ayan laughed, then said; "Let's do it again," as she puffed her cheeks and let the air pop out of her lips.

One of the soldiers in the cabin shook her head and grinned. "She is so adorable."

Laura wasn't crying anymore. Ayan was pretty sure it was more thanks to the distraction than anything. "Ready to seal up?" Ayan asked, closing her own faceplate, then her daughter's. It would have been better if she did it before they boarded their shuttle, but Laura always squealed and fussed if she did it before they were underway. As usual, Laura didn't care as long as she could see Ayan.

Through the little one's faceplate, she could see her trying to puff her cheeks despite her smile. She was spitting a little instead, and the interior of her visor cleaned that away. "I think I just taught her a new trick."

The shuttle passed through the security shield surrounding Haven Shore Island and began its hard burn straight up. The rumble of the thrusters never bothered Laura, she took after her namesake in that way. As Ayan watched her daughter, she found herself thinking about Laura Everin. She had never had a closer friend and rarely met a person who was so generally good. I should imagine she's there today, at the back of the room while I answer loads of questions and negotiate the future of thousands of people. People could do worse than to stop and wonder; 'what would the kindest person I've ever known do?'

"Navnet's reporting a problem," the copilot announced as the cockpit door slid open. "We're turning back."

"What is it?" Ayan asked, making sure Laura's seat was secure.

He spoke over his shoulder. They were almost out of the atmosphere, but turning already. "A survey ship coming back from Kamibs is changing course. It's probably nothing, but its mass isn't consistent with..."

A flash of light, and a feeling that her entire body had been struck at once followed.

TWENTY-THREE

What We Lose To The Waves

MINH-CHU WAS SITTING to Captain Vega's left on the bridge of the Triton. Ashley was on her right, her shift at the helm about to begin. Breaker was there as well, standing to Minh-Chu's left, quietly taking the sight of the large bridge in.

This was the quiet time, a little under one hour before they were to arrive in the Rose System. Most of them were on stims that were so subtle that they couldn't tell, including Minh-Chu, who felt alert and rested even though he'd only managed to get four hours of sleep.

Several hours that were originally reserved for sleep were spent modifying and refining their plans. Things had changed thanks to the Merciless joining them with its own full squadron of fighters and larger ships. Contact with Jake and data coming from the Haven Node hidden near Gold Haf Station helped.

There were more Order of Eden ships in orbit than anyone would like, along with a behemoth of a Citadel vessel that would definitely pose a problem. They had more intelligence on the Order's technology than any of them could have imagined getting their eyes on, but they knew so little about modern Citadel hardware that they could only count their ignorance as a disadvantage.

The feed Jake and the rest of their forces were able to tap into near Gold Haf was able to collect data from the Navnet systems around Planet Rodus. The signals were a few minutes old, but they could see that the Citadel ships were keeping to the edges of what would be their engagement zones. Minh-Chu's theory was that they saw an attack coming, and they wanted to make sure that they would be able to assist in the defence from medium and long range. Somehow it fell to the Order to guard the centre of the blockade, and Scanlon's old Battlegroup had moved into that position, right over Panda and the ruins of City 35 surrounding it. The Order had more large ships in the area, for sure, but Minh-Chu was certain of something that may not be apparent to their enemy yet. This battle would be decided by starfighters and gunships. The firepower they could carry and the agility they used to deliver their payloads would prove themselves again. It was the theory Minh-Chu believed in and simultaneously his hope.

"Congratulations on your promotion, Breaker," Captain Vega said as a large crewman handed her a safety mug. "Thank you, Orner," she said to him.

Orner passed the other mugs out, stopping to regard Minh-Chu nervously. "Wing Commander," he said with quiet respect as he handed Minh-Chu his rudely dark tea.

The earthy smell wafted up to his nose as he opened the sipping port. "Thanks."

"It's the first I've heard of a step up," Breaker replied. "Answers why I've been invited to your fine bridge. I've been on the Triton Tour in the simulation, but there's something about seeing this place in person that's... different." He made eye contact with Orner and the giant man smiled a little, nodding.

"He said the same thing," Captain Vega said, nodding at the giant. "Let me introduce you to the Triton's first Work Program Student. He's observing on the bridge..."

"Ma'am, we're getting an all-frequency transmission from Tamber. There are thousands of sites on the Stellarnet playing it too. It's Citadel," Liara said from the Communications Section of the bridge. Her six crewmembers were suddenly very busy.

One of them announced; "No hacks or codes hidden in this. It's just an audio-video recording using emergency priority. There isn't even holographic data."

"Then put it up," Captain Vega said, looking at the bridge's transparent forward bulkhead, which was showing a slightly warped view of the blue-white energy of transit space. Playback of an armoured shuttle accelerating up, striving to break orbit with Tamber's blue ocean beneath it appeared. Minh-Chu's stomach twisted into a knot as though it knew what was about to happen. "That's Ayan's shuttle," he didn't actually know for sure, but the armoured shuttle did match the one she liked to use when she was trying to move through the solar system in a way that would avoid attention. That was her usual mode.

The thick doors at the rear of the bridge parted, and Minh-Chu looked over his shoulder to see Alice in full mission gear. A white scarf hung from her neck, probably placed there by Carnie, who said they'd be exchanging them for luck before the mission began. It had a different effect on Minh-Chu, it made her look so much like Ayan when she wore white. "Mom," she said so quietly that only her First Mate, Iruuk, could hear it at her side.

Minh-Chu didn't see the explosion as it played back but was still looking at Alice as she did. Her face was seized by a startled expression as she took an unconscious step back. A tear surfaced and slid down her cheek as though it was punched out of her from within as she stared in horror. Minh-Chu looked back to the screen and saw the wreckage of the shuttle as it was captured from a distance. Thousands of pieces surrounded it like a cloud as the ship spiralled down, a thruster flashing, flaring blue, agitating the storm of wrecked material until it went out. Several pieces were flung away from the main mass as it continued to descend. Minh-Chu told himself that one of his best friends wasn't aboard even as his heart began to ache. She and her children were safe somewhere else. They had to be.

Ashley noticed Alice and ran to her side. "We don't know anything," she said to her softly.

"That was my mother's shuttle," Alice said, her voice absent emotion. She'd already shut that part of herself away. "They killed her. I thought she was safe, and they've murdered her."

A dramatically lit face replaced the playback. Tattoos that made it look like he was smiling cruelly even though he wore a proud expression blackened his lips, his chin and jaw. Another man with tattoos in a similar style that made his face look broad and serious was in the frame to his left, staring out from the screen with a piercing gaze. The foremost man with the permanent smile spoke. "I am Leader Gideon Baya. Only hours ago I ordered the assassins I had hidden in the ruined atmosphere of Planet Kambis to use whatever means available to hide within range of your Queen's home." He spoke confidently, with clarity and intent that made every syllable unmistakable. "They took control of a survey ship that was performing scans of Kambis' atmosphere in hopes of finding a way to repair the damage to Kambis when Citadel destroyed the atmosphere previously. They used the survey ship to hide their attack vessel. Our spies on Tamber know what your Queen's shuttle looks like and where it hides. When my spies on Planet Unity discovered that she would be leaving the moon, my assassins attacked and destroyed your Queen's shuttle. All aboard are dead. Your planetary defences have just destroyed their attack ship and the survey vessel they used to hide from them. Their sacrifices will be celebrated and avenged. The death of your Queen is not senseless. It is a response to the killing of one of our young assassins. Remmy Sands murdered him using powered armour and superior weaponry when he could have forced him to surrender instead. It was not an honourable killing, so we take our vengeance. We take your queen. Three more assassins were destroyed by your automated defences. A pattern of retribution has begun. Expect death."

Leader Gideon stepped aside and his subordinate moved to the fore. He looked down his nose at his audience. "I am Vollis Mikan, and I claim the life of your Queen and everyone on her shuttle in the name of Citadel and Zadix, the assassin who Remmy Sands killed. Three more have died. You owe us a greater tithe." The video cut out and a stream of scan data scrolled up before the transmission terminated entirely.

When Minh-Chu looked towards Alice again, she was already leaving with a long stalking gait. Iruuk was following close behind as Ashley watched. Captain Vega's voice had a sharp edge to it as she ordered; "Shut this shit down, now! Wipe it from every comm-con on the ship. I don't want it to distract the crew."

"It's too late. This was marked as a priority transmission by Haven's system. They must have people on the inside on Tamber. It played everywhere. We're still linked into their emergency broadcast system. If a crewmember was too far from a ship display to see it, then their command and control unit ran it," Liara replied.

Captain Vega seethed for a moment, glanced at Minh-Chu and said; "Ship-wide."

Liara activated a ship-wide announcement from the Captain's Seat and a whistle sounded over the public announcement system.

Straightening her jacket, Captain Vega stood at attention. "You've just seen Citadel claim responsibility for an assassination. We haven't confirmed that this is real. If the footage checks out, we still don't know if what they say about the passengers aboard is true. If it is, and I emphasise 'if,' then our upcoming mission is even more important than before. When an animal like Citadel lashes out, it is always because they are afraid. They say Remmy Sands murdered one of their assassins. Well, he's mostly known as the guy who put the Remmybase together. He's a goddamned librarian. If he can win against one of their best, then imagine what we'll be able to do to them when we're in range. Do your duty and fight like hell. That is all."

Liara signalled that the channel was closed. "Well said,

Captain," Oz said as his hologram appeared in front of the command seating. "I'm rebroadcasting that to the crew of the Merciless. I have bad news. Tamber Orbital Defence confirms that it was Ayan's shuttle. She and Laura were aboard along with two soldiers, a pilot and copilot."

Minh-Chu found himself shaking his head as he got to his feet and walked to Ashley, who was taking her place at the helm. There were navigators at her left and right, and both of them worked hard to maintain a stiff upper lip. "I have to work now," Ashley said as she wiped tears away. "Just..."

He knew what she stopped herself from saying. It was bad luck to tell a fighter pilot good luck, or to come back in one piece. "I know," he said. "Good hunting," he told her as he stroked her hair.

She sniffed, blew her nose into a tissue that seemed to appear from out of nowhere, and then regarded her controls with a professional bearing. "Go get them." It had the tone of; 'I love you,' and she didn't look up at him. He knew that she'd probably break down if she did.

Minh-Chu realised that Breaker had been following him from a distance then, and he led the way past the command seating in the middle of the bridge. "Minh..." Oz was about to say something.

It wasn't time yet. There was nothing he could say that the Wing Commander wanted to hear. "I hope some of those assassins fly fighters," Minh-Chu said as he marched past him. The elevator at the rear of the bridge, to the side of the doors opened, and he stepped inside. Oz's hologram appeared within. "There are ships on their way to the crash site. A Hart News team is already on a barge with a safety team that can start the search right now. They could all be alive."

"I'm going to go get Jake and Ruby's crew," Minh-Chu replied flatly. "That's the mission. We're going to have a nice long talk about you and your fleet after that."

Oz stared at him for a moment then nodded. "Good hunting," he said before his hologram disappeared.

The emotional fortification that he put up while he was being strong for Ashley and anyone else who looked towards him for strength, and guidance, started to slip. He cleared his throat and tried to shore it up. When he felt Breaker's hand on his shoulder, it shattered instantly.

Rivers of tears ran down Minh-Chu's cheeks as he lowered his head. The recollection of standing at her door on Freeground, determined to go find Jacob Valent, filled his head. She believed in him even when his family and the military organization thought he needed a lot more time to recover from years in isolation. Hers was a face that represented the kind of friendship that didn't judge, that he expected to be with him for the rest of his days.

Thinking of Little Laura was impossible, but his mind drifted to the increasingly active little one, especially since he knew her namesake. He recalled that Laura Everin was killed by a Citadel Assassin, and his tears started to feel bitter, hot as Breaker put his arm around him and stopped the small transit car. Liara's voice drifted up from his comm-con. "The Hart News team is reporting good news."

Breaker activated his command and control unit and a hologram surrounded them. The face of the senior producer and main announcer for Hart News, Gavin Hale, appeared, followed by the rest of his body then a sea-scape. He was on the edge of the deck of a sea ship, leaning as he grasped a handhold. He was in a rescue suit absent a helmet, much like the vacsuits that the military wore. He didn't start his live stream by customarily announcing his name and that he was from Hart News.

Instead, he said; "Haven Fleet and Tamber Defence haven't verified that the video you just saw is real. It's too soon to despair. My crew and I were about to begin filming a special exploring the bottom of Tamber's oceans when a shuttle was struck above us. Rescue services are arriving now, but, since we were about to start diving, there are several qualified personnel on this crew. I'm off-script here, so I'll get to the point. There's good news. We're coming up on an emergency beacon. It doesn't belong to a shuttle, but a baby carrier that my team says probably closed like a clamshell, protecting whoever was inside with dampeners and armour."

"Okay! Okay! We've got it! it's intact! Get a line on it!" shouted someone in the background.

"It's okay?" Gavin called to someone outside the frame. It occurred to Minh-Chu then that the seasoned newsman probably didn't want to turn the recorders in the direction of something grisly, so he made sure that whatever they found would be intact.

"Yeah! Sensors say she's fine!" said a rescue team member. "Haul it up!"

Laura's baby carrier swept into view. Gavin Hale and another crewmember caught it and carefully put it down on the deck. Someone in a medical suit stepped in, blocking the view, and nodded, grinning. "No injuries. Open it."

Laura's wail pierced the air as the dented carrier opened

like a clam and Minh-Chu sighed at the sight of her in her little vacsuit, kicking her feet. "It's Admiral Anderson's daughter," someone said as they picked her up.

Gavin Hale moved back to centre frame then. "There are two more beacons down there," a Tamber Rangers ship was lowering into view behind him, making a slow water landing and whipping up a wind that he struggled to shout over. Someone handed him a hand scanner and his helmet. "This will probably be the last you hear from me for a while since I'm joining the rescue effort. You can see that, even though the transmission from Citadel may be real, it doesn't mean that they were successful. It could take a while to find survivors, so be patient, be hopeful. Anyone who wants to help should contact the Tamber Rangers."

The broadcast switched to a newscaster who was still settling in at her desk and Minh-Chu spotted the time. They had forty-two minutes before they arrived in the Rose System. He took a deep breath and composed himself. It was time to push everything but the mission aside. At least, everything he could. "You're leading Red Group," he told Breaker as the hologram faded.

"What's that?" Breaker asked.

"Your promotion. I'm giving you an attack group. You're taking Garma and Garna with you. It worked in the last three sims. It turns out that Bullet Chasers make really good dogfighters. The last remaining slots will be filled by the freelance pilots who you picked for the sims."

"We'll watch your back," Breaker said.

"Thank you, Breaker," Minh-Chu said less officially.

"Sure," Breaker replied. "It's funny how we forget to look for support when we're busy holding other people up."

Minh-Chu nodded and touched the release button on the panel so the transit car could finish its journey to the lower decks, where every fighter pilot they had was waiting in the squad room.

TWENTY-FOUR

The Transfer

"I UNDERSTAND why you wanted to antagonize the Valents. They'll present themselves now that you've claimed credit for killing Ayan Anderson. I'm afraid that you may provoke the military organization they founded as well though," Vollis told Leader Gideon in as polite a manner as possible. "The only thing keeping them in the Cefa and Haven system is the perception that Haven Fleet can maintain a peace, and provide a shield against outside threats. The public they protect may protest that if they realize they can never be fully secure, no matter how many ships and soldiers they surround themselves with." It was difficult. Gideon was known for being unerring in his judgement, but not for being attentive to his subordinates. There was little chance anything Vollis said would make a difference, but he felt he had to try.

"They will always dedicate a significant portion of their forces to defence. I don't see the victory we've claimed credit for changing that much, if at all. The new citizens of the Haven System are fearful, that's why so many of them are refugees. I'm guessing that you're building up to the real issue. You don't like that I had to expose you."

He was right, again. "It is with respect that I ask why I had to be drawn out of the shadows to proclaim a revenge tithe. Citadel hasn't done so to anyone outside of our organization for over two centuries."

"You are new to galactic concerns," Leader Gideon said with a sigh. He took a moment to watch as the three-metre tall vessel containing Echiss, the bulbous Geist that was hidden by the thick walls of the container, connected with the ship's aqua port. For the first time since Vollis took command, the Rixe would have a Geist monitoring and assisting, possibly directing the crew. Gideon finished replying to him when the seals between the vessel and the port leading into the main aquatic environment aboard clicked into place. "I can't reveal why there is concern about the Valents and their allies, but their presence here confirms that events are more likely to occur as they've been foretold. Eve and I are being forced to move assets to prevent future events that could do the Order and Citadel irreparable harm in this part of the galaxy."

The Geist would take residence in the Rixe as soon as the liquid environments were equalized. He watched as systems in the creature's vessel went to work, cycling the liquids. Echiss was old, that was well known. What surprised Vollis was how delicate the creature must be. The distraction wasn't as unwelcome as the Geist's interference. It took an effort to stay on topic. "I had to be revealed to give the Valents a target?"

"Yes. You are going down to Rodus to directly command the effort to capture Jacob Valent."

"Capture?" Vollis asked.

"That would be preferable. He cannot be allowed to escape Rodus, so killing him is also acceptable if you have no other choice. If you also happen to have an opportunity to kill Remmy Sands, then make sure you do so. Bring evidence that it's been done, but only if it was by your hand."

"How do you know that he was the one who killed Zadix? There is no way to be certain from his armour," Vollis asked, still mentally smarting from being ordered to the surface.

"Zadix's body was diverted from the Rixe to my ship where Echiss inspected it. His last, fading memory includes mental contact with one who he was able to identify as Sands. That is how powerful Echiss is. That is why he is the Sire Geist, and why he's come here with me all the way from the Core Worlds," Leader Gideon replied with reverence. "He will turn the experiment you've been conducting aboard the Rixe into something useful at last."

"The point of my project is to produce limitless officers with life experience and training that makes them more effective than traditional commanders. Experiences that are programmed in a specific way so their loyalty and performance are beyond question," Vollis countered. "We are close, despite all the setbacks."

"This project has been successful, Vollis. You are proof of that. The true purpose of your work was to find a way to do the same with tens of thousands instead of a handful at a time. Did you know that your memory programming was assisted by a Geist? The contents of your mind were crafted twice. Before implantation and after, so you were whole the moment you were first awakened. We've learned so much from you."

Vollis could never articulate exactly why he found being reminded of the fact that he was a fabricant aggravating, but it never failed. There was always a sense that he was being reminded that he was a lesser thing when someone who wasn't a fabricant referenced the truth of his origin directly. "There must be another source of manpower. The ones we have in storage here are of a higher quality. They're made to be long-term officers."

"Your maturation tubes are full. There are hundreds of framework skeletons in storage. Your researchers will finish implanting the memory engrams that are ready into the fabricants that are already in stasis and Echiss will complete the work," Leader Gideon said crisply. "The Order of Eden's recruitment efforts are working at a faster pace than we could have predicted. They are drawing people who already have relevant training to their side and more of their ships are on their way. If we don't increase our numbers our significance in this region will diminish, and we will be a footnote when the merge between Citadel and the Order is complete. You have your orders. Proceed to the Rodus siege site immediately."

That was the end of the argument, and of the power he may have aboard the Rixe for the time being. If he pressed the issue he may lose his command entirely. "Yes, Leader Gideon. Will I be coordinating with Bion?"

"No. You will be taking command of Order troops who have been dispatched to the underground site, but Bion is moving on to the planetary capitol. He will be addressing the new President in person," Leader Gideon replied. "You have the ultimate authority in the pursuit of Jacob Valent and the eradication of his allies on the surface of Rodus. Don't allow anything or anyone to interfere."

"Yes, Leader Gideon," Vollis said as he retreated. With a few taps on the back of his hand, he ordered a troop transport and a squad of his best soldiers to be ready. "This will be done."

TWENTY-FIVE

Defences

IT WAS ALWAYS hard for Remmy to be offline. Being connected to larger networks, checking in on people he liked, interesting places and personalities was something that he did often. He glanced at the countdown on his bracer often to see how long it would be before they reactivated their Haven Node to check-in. It was finally down to three minutes.

He was in the control room, a stairway led to the Transit Hub, where rows of tall, oval gates waited in shadow. One wormhole gate at the end was fully lit, freshly repaired, and he could see it rendered on one of the particle display screens in front of him. It was unlike any control room he'd ever seen, with old fashioned control desks in a semi-circle with build in consoles. Switches, dials, and flat panels that were ready to show the operators whatever they needed using particles that changed colours and shapes as quickly as any that used light. Each one of them could also pile the particles into moving three-dimensional objects that were as tactile as they were visible. He was happy he already found one of the old tablets before he got inside so he could enjoy it later.

He's been there all night, talking to Simon, which was a name he liked more than the one he originally used, Charon. As a perk to the rebuild Remmy's body was given, he rarely had to sleep. Somehow, the recovery that sleep offered could be accomplished faster in him than in any unmodified human. The biomechanics of it wasn't a mystery to him, but it was one of the facts of his new physiology that he hoped no one ever asked him to explain. While he was underground on Rodus being able to skip eight hours or more of sleep was a good thing.

Most of the people in the Vault were on stims. Sure, it was a formulation that wouldn't put much stress on their systems for the first fifty or so hours, so there wouldn't be much of a hangover, but it still wasn't ideal. The pressure of a day that felt too long, of a forced journey that made everyone accumulate stress without much rest was starting to push people hard. Ruby Sima took it in stride, and it was impossible to keep up with her as she managed her crew.

The contents of the Dropping Bell, the large container of equipment and supplies, that was saved were distributed to the right people. Remmy got replacement armour, while most of the new crewmembers that Ruby picked up along the way were armed if they could shoot at all. That left a pool of about thirty-five who were regular crewmembers without much combat ability. They were sent to a community activities room with pictures of people on its walls and notices on shifter screens that hadn't changed in hundreds of years. The caretaker, Simon, kept the place dust-free, as though it was a tribute to the people who once gathered there.

Ruby consulted Remmy and Simon about putting troops under trap doors near the base of the main pillar. It was a good idea, especially because the narrow access tunnels would allow them to get back to the main building when the time came. It also doubled their firing positions. Putting Ruby in charge of deploying their troops was one of the best decisions Jake made. Her charisma as a leader made every order easier to take, and Remmy couldn't see problems with her plan. Any advice he gave her only gave her more options, but he wasn't needed as a tactician. The funny thing was that she didn't give him a role in the fight.

While preparations were underway, Jake and Agameg were with the guardians watching the door. The tanks that pounded on it had made a lot of progress over several hours, but when the metal started to expand on the inner edges of the tall, thick doors, they changed their strategy. Using shaped charges, they tried to widen the crack by pushing them apart, probably hoping to break whatever mechanism that was holding them together. Remmy was fairly sure that it wouldn't work until Simon-Charon approached him, shaking his head. "It looks like they've chosen the most efficient way to push my doors open."

Remmy looked up from the control room desk, where he was watching a screen scroll letters that didn't use light to show themselves, but something that looked more like animated ink. He looked up at the monitor that showed all the various systems built into and around the massive doorway. "They found a weak point?"

"Yes. Every time they use explosives on that three-centimetre crack, they weaken the bolt system holding the doors in place. When they were designed, we couldn't imagine a bomb or force that someone could bring to bear that would do that. I'm accelerating my plans, we don't have long before they'll get through."

"How long?" Remmy asked.

"They will be able to slide the right-hand door five metres to the side in about nine minutes. They've exposed two of the three bolt holes along the bottom and all the bolt holes along the top of that door. The material they're blasting through is succumbing much faster than expected, probably from some wear and tear or damage I didn't predict."

"No defence is perfect," Remmy said, opening a channel to Jake. "Hey, Simon's telling me that the right-hand door will open about five metres in nine minutes. We're out of time."

"Is he in earshot?" Jake asked.

"Yeah, he's right here," Remmy replied.

"I'm everywhere in the installation, to be honest. I have sensors," Simon replied.

"Well, there's bad news," Jake said. "There's no way I can leave enough people in the Vault to keep it secure even if we defeat the Order. I've been thinking about it, and it's just not going to happen. A victory for us is escape. We didn't know you and everything you protect was down here, we thought it was just a way to get up to the surface in time to get picked up."

"So, all this will get ransacked. I expected that," Simon said sadly, pulling his hood back and looking around for a moment. It was easy to forget that the older-looking fellow wasn't human, and he had a disarming look to him. "I have been moving all the psyche cubes in storage into carrier bins. I guess it's time to ask you for a favour."

Remmy braced himself, taking a moment to glimpse at the tactical map on his command and control unit. Jake was ordering the group closest to the door back so they could take positions in the main pillar. Then he met Simon's gaze, which had steadily, pleadingly turned to him. "Thank you for sharing the history and news about your people, Jake's people, and the Haven System's people. I wouldn't even ask this if I wasn't able to spend the last few hours going through all the things you've done, understand the fight you're in. It's hard to look at any war from the outside and decide who really is good or bad. Now I know who I might be able to trust in this. There is one thing I've seen in the history of Freeground, of Haven, of you and the people who connect them. You rarely make promises."

Remmy had never thought about it, but that seemed right. He couldn't recall the last time he solemnly promised something since he took his vow for Haven Fleet. For a moment, he wondered if there was something he forgot, but nothing came to mind. "I think you're right."

"Well, I need you to promise me that you'll get my people to Grace. I can't find much out on the world, but I see that the Triton encountered the Frekse, a ship named after a great explorer from my time. While Alice Valent wasn't really that nice, she dealt with them fairly. The scans the Triton took of the ship show that they've advanced, but some of their technology plainly has roots in what you see here. Some of our culture must have survived, I can tell from their language. While Grace wasn't always politically aligned with Rodus, the two worlds were always friendly, and they planned to build three facilities much like this one and they must have at least one working Elysium server. Promise me that you'll get as many of the psyches stored here to Grace. In return I'll give you all the technical data stored here, and the entertainment archive; three hundred zettabytes of video and audio from Earth before the Departure. It is uncurated with a lot of content about cats, but I think someone like you can appreciate it."

An enthusiastic collision of curiosity and urgency prompted Remmy to reply immediately; "Yes. I promise I'll do everything I can."

"Remmy..." Jake said, his tone a warning.

"This isn't just about a bunch of ancient videos, Jake. There are innocent people sleeping here. The Order could take advantage of them somehow, or just destroy them. Who knows?" he thought quickly and came up with a solution. "What if I led the non-combatants through the portal so they could get picked up with boxes of psyche cubes? How much does each one of those cases hold?"

"Ten thousand," Simon replied.

"Okay, so we've got about thirty-five civilians..." Remmy trailed off, doing the math in his head. "Wait, how many people does it take to move a case?"

"One person could move two cases on one trip through the portal. One behind and one in front of them. They hover," Simon replied.

"So I'd need a few more volunteers, but we could get ready in the Transit Room and..." Remmy was desperate to make his point and talked over Jake for as long as he could so he wouldn't be interrupted, but he stopped eventually.

"Remmy, I need you here, so there's no way I'm putting you

in charge of that, but Ruby's sending Parsons. She'll get it done. We'll break off enough people from the defence to make sure you have enough people."

Remmy sighed with relief and watched as Simon smiled and said; "I'll try to make more room in the Transit Hub so they can gather. The rest of the boxes will be packed in a little under twenty minutes."

"Don't forget to pack yourself in there, okay?" Remmy said as he got a notification from the Haven Node that it reconnected with the main network. There were thousands of alerts from Crewcast, the social network that was originally reserved for members of Haven Fleet but was now open to the public. The Stellarnet was abuzz with people who were cheering for, mourning about, and horrified about the death of Ayan Anderson. He checked his Hart News feed and was overwhelmed with dread as he watched footage of a shuttle breaking apart in mid-air. He brought the next three stories up simultaneously, repeating; "No, no, no," under his breath as his heart sank. Then he spoke over the channel he shared with Jake. "Don't check the news. Connect with the Triton first."

It was the best thing he could do as he watched the playback of Citadel claiming credit, Laura being recovered, and footage of ships scanning the ocean for Ayan. The communications team aboard the Triton would be able to boil the news down, present it in a way that was more tactful, and make sure that everything they said was as accurate as possible. Remmy was playing catch up, there was no other way to turn Jake's gaze away from the avalanche of data he was sifting through.

Remmy continued to dig, realizing that everything in front of him was already minutes old, which in terms of a disaster like that, was an eternity. It was enough time for thousands of people to weigh in with their pointless opinions and theories about it, muddying clearly reported facts. The first people who arrived on the scene were doing the right thing, at least. They were searching and coordinating with each other.

Unfortunately, the next wave of people were on their way in whatever ships they could get flying. They would try to get a good look for themselves out of some misguided voyeuristic instinct. To make matters worse, there were announcements from groups who protested corporate control, monarchies, artificial intelligences and Ayan Anderson herself who were on their way to the crash site. The military was already patrolling, but it didn't mean that the whole area wouldn't become a crazy mess.

In the dozen or so minutes since Laura was recovered in perfect health, two guards who were in the shuttle's cabin were brought up. They were alive, one was severely injured, in stasis. She was expected to make a full recovery. The other was flung out of the back of the shuttle, and his communications systems were destroyed along with most of the flight technology in his suit. Otherwise, he was fine. The Hart News announcer was reporting that the pilot and copilot of her shuttle were proclaimed dead and unrecoverable, but another body had been found, pinned inside what was left of the shuttle's main cabin. They only had an outline scan because the shuttle's armour was preventing them from seeing more detail.

"Ruby, I want every Rapidfire Mini Drone we have in front of me. Now," Jake said with the most serious intonation that Remmy ever heard. "I want to make a statement when those doors open."

"The plan was to let the River take the first shot if they

come charging in," Ruby replied, referring to the electrical defences in the Vault.

"They're not going to charge. They're going to use artillery or something just as heavy to take shots through those doors so they take our defences out before they come in," Jake said. "I'm going to make sure it costs them."

"Jake, this isn't the time for..." Ruby started to counter.

"That's an order. I need those drones now. While Agameg and I set this up, you figure out how to take whatever artillery they have on the other side of those doors out. We have to hold this place for twenty minutes."

"Twenty minutes? I said the psyches will be ready for transport in about that much time. That doesn't account for people moving through the portal, or however long they'll need to be picked up," Charon said.

"I can guarantee you twenty minutes. Everything after that depends on Vollis and how big his ego is," Jake said. His head and shoulders appeared over Remmy's command and control unit then. He was pulling a white scarf from his pocket and tying it around his upper arm. "I need you down here. If this doesn't work, you and Agameg need to take over."

"Yeah, I'm on my way," Remmy said, one eye on the multiple windows playing news feeds in his helmet. One, in particular, got his attention. "Wait, something's happening."

The broken, twisted main cabin section of Ayan's shuttle was being drawn up by a hovering crane slowly. Water flowed out of the end that was once connected to the cockpit, now wide open. "Scans..." the voice of Gavin Hale started to say, then he paused. "...rescuers are reporting that scans are showing that Ayan Anderson is alive. In stasis, non-critical head trauma, alive! The founder of the Haven System, the Queen who has repeatedly refused the title, our Ayan, is alive."

Remmy wasn't just relieved, he was overjoyed and leapt from his seat to embrace Charon, who laughed, his particle display system dissipating as he passed through it. "Sorry, forgot you weren't, you know, solid."

"No one should have to apologize for joy," Simon replied. "Besides, I miss hugs. Maybe I'll have a real body again someday."

"What about Elysium?" Remmy asked.

"Oh, I won't be going there. My consciousness is in the console, where it's needed. The cube is connected to it in that port. If I go, then the defences won't be as effective, so I'll stay," he replied.

"Get down here, Remmy," Jake said.

He took a moment to consider what Charon said, then told him; "You're a good man, Simon."

TWENTY-SIX

Jump In

IF THE OPENING steps of the Triton and Merciless's plan played out properly, Samurai Squadron wouldn't be directly involved. That left Minh-Chu and his pilots with little to do but much to see while they waited to launch. He took a look at the feed from Rodus from the seat of his Uriel fighter. In it, people were lining up in the Transit Room underground, most of them were civilians who joined Ruby's crew. They looked tired, haggard, mismatched to the marble floors and arches around them. Most were still taking the surroundings in, trepidatious. Some asked questions about how they were going to get to the surface. Not many people knew of the legendary Crush Gates; wormhole generators that were made to transport a person in a containment suit and nothing more. The few who did shared stories of the lost technology, either presenting it as a marvel or a potential hazard. No one was leaving either way, probably because they were all aware that there was no other way to leave the underground vault.

The crowd gathered in the large room shared the space with containers that were three metres tall and just as wide, made to fit through the gate with little more than a centimetre on every side. They hovered, using some kind of silent antigravity. Minh-Chu's grandfather had stories, not his own, but of how people used to step from star to star as though they were crossing a room. Where he heard them, Minh-Chu never thought to ask, but he was a little boy then, happy to take whatever his grandad said at face value.

That's who used to tell him about famous Samurai like Miyamoto Musashi and Oda Nobunaga, referring to an old book about Japanese history that once rested on their great, great grandfather's shelf when their family was still living on Earth. Yes, most of Minh-Chu's genetic makeup was Viet-namese, but his grandad would say there is some Japanese mixed in, and with that came a call to honour and purpose. That was the way his grandfather used to say it, and it gave Minh-Chu the question of his life. What is my purpose?

Where did the callsign come from? It was a way for Minh-Chu to tell the world that he mostly served himself, especially after he left his family behind when he found an adventure, a cause. He took one last look at the feed from the Transit room after looking at that centuries-old gate and switched to Jake. His jaw was set, his expression painted darkly even though he knew that his future wife was found alive but unconscious, wounded.

"We're coming," Minh-Chu said as he watched his old friend check his armour.

"I know. We'll start sending people through the portal to the extraction point as soon as you mark it for us," Jake said flatly. "I'll buy us enough time to get everyone out."

"Including yourself," Minh-Chu said.

"Don't worry. Good hunting," Jake replied.

It was time to focus on the mission and only the mission, so Minh-Chu turned his attention to the bridge. That's where the action would be for the first phase of their conflict. That is, if their plan even half worked. They were seconds away from the first stop in the Rose System. It would only be Triton and the Merciless. They were the fastest ships. The rest would arrive after the action. The mission counter told him he had just enough time to say something to his pilots, and he didn't have to think too hard about his message or how he would phrase it. "No one in my squadron is here for the pay."

Perhaps it was his tone, or the words, but every pilot in the squadron was silent by the time he finished his opening sentence, so he continued. "We sharpen swords while we whisper the names of those we've lost and those we wish to save. I was looking for purpose when I joined Jacob Valent, and my search is over. I was a Ronin, looking for a new master, and he made me a Samurai. If we are sky Samurai, then he is our Lord, and he needs his help."

There was time left, and he wondered if there was anything more he should say. It came down to what he wanted to say then, and he decided it was worth sharing. "Today a dishonourable enemy has killed a fellow pilot and copilot of a shuttle bearing one of our leaders and her innocent daughter. It isn't our calling to punish them for that, revenge is a low calling. It tells us what kind of mercy they respect, however. We will give no quarter. Nothing that stands in our way deserves it. Go in sharp. Complete your objectives, and listen to your group leaders." When he realized that his speech was being rebroadcast across the entire Triton, he added the credo; "Deploy, dominate, disappear."

The reprise came back from everyone on the channel; "Triton!"

It was time for him to check on the bridge again. There was nothing to see but the workings of the punter around him as he waited, so he was able to look at a small window where Ashley was managing her navigation team. The Triton emerged on the edge of the Rose System. A high-powered scan pulse went out. Minh-Chu didn't have to concentrate on the tactical map that was being transmitted directly into his mind by his fighter's neural interface. It was crystal clear. There wasn't a thing within hundreds of thousands of kilometres for several seconds. Another energy spike preceded the arrival of the Merciless. Its thick, dark triangular hull blocked the sun out for a moment, casting a shadow with a crisp edge. "Moving into position for final tactical jump," Ashley announced from the helm. She worked the controls manually while three navigators worked around her, checking and correcting the coordinates for their next dimensional jump.

At a glance, Minh-Chu could see that every fighter in Samurai Squadron was loaded into a punter along the bottom of the Triton. They checked in as ready. The Clever Class

Corvettes were ready to launch from all three of the great ship's hangars. The Clever Dream captained by Alice, the Sky Queen captained by Alaka, the Raven, who was absent her captain - Remmy. The team that trained to crew that ship was aboard, however, including Shamus Frost's nephew, Nigel.

"Data coming in from our jump destination point, sending the final update to Tactical and Navigation," Kadri announced from the Scanning and Sciences department.

The tactical map was alive with updates, showing exactly where the Triton and the Merciless would arrive after their next jump. Minh-Chu nodded and said; "Confirmed. That's exactly where we want to be." He marked the route Samurai Squadron would take once they launched.

"Samurai Squadron and Tactical confirm. Merciless confirms," Frost announced from the Tactical section of the oval bridge.

A hologram of Oz appeared beside Captain Vega, he was already nodding. "We are coordinating our jump with yours."

"Then we are a go," Captain Vega said.

"Ready," Ashley announced. "Two point four-one second trans-dimensional jump to Rodus orbit. Arrival point clear, generating passage now."

The Triton and Merciless advanced into a split in space that spilled blue light across their hulls and after exactly two point four-one seconds later, they were in Rodus orbital space. "No collisions, we are in position," one of Ashley's navigation team proclaimed.

"Punters are clear to launch. Hangars are clear to launch," Slick announced from Flight Control aboard the Triton.

As Minh-Chu watched the display of the Triton's bridge in

the upper right portion of his vision, his fighter was jettisoned from the punter, and sent into space that looked almost too busy. They were within three kilometres of the Nabih, a massive Citadel ship. Oval in shape, the voids and dips in its hull made it look like a sleek sea creature from another era. "We are behind their fighter patrols," Minh-Chu announced as he plotted a course for his group past the ship. "Wait for the Triton to make the first move."

"That wasn't the first move?" Carnie asked from where he took position on Ronin's port side.

Just then, aboard the bridge, Captain Vega calmly ordered; "Fire all torpedoes. Follow that with two more volleys then wait for new target acquisition. Beam weapons, fire full intensity at predesignated targets - shield generation and power systems. Missile bays, fire pulse salvos then reload with seeker conventional warheads. Gunnery deck, cover our dorsal side. You have target and munition discretion, but no antimatter. We're too close to the atmosphere."

"Understood, Captain," Frost acknowledged professionally as he and his staff made all the details of their jobs line up with the orders that were given.

As though she hit the button herself, a volley of thirty-five torpedoes issued from the great ship. Hatches slid open, revealing missile launchers that the Triton didn't use as often as it should have, as far as Minh-Chu was concerned, and dozens of large, fast-moving missiles erupted from the bays before they closed. White beams drew deadly lines of light between the Triton and the Nabih. They were made to tax their shields, and pointed to the systems that mattered in the moment so the torpedoes and missiles could strike the bare hull beneath. "And that's why they call these Zahn Twos 'Close Combat Carriers,'" Frost said with a heavy helping of glee from the Tactical station. "Gunners! Start ripping into those fighters and Order gunships when you see 'em. When you can't get to those, try to break through the Rixe's shields. We've got to get these Citadel shites outta this fight."

The Merciless didn't have as many torpedo bays or missile launchers, but they lashed out at the Nabih with every one of them. What they lacked in torpedo power, they made up for with heavy gun turrets. As half a dozen beam weapons concentrated fire on the shielding protecting the Nabih's power systems the cannon turrets turned slowly, making for a menacing prelude. There were many gun emplacements, but the ones that caught Ronin's eye were the four Four-Nineties, also known as Capital Ship Killers. There were four of them on four turrets, and they moved slowly. It would be the first time they fired outside of testing since they were added to the warship. Thrusters along the opposing side of the ship flared, burning hot to provide an opposing force as they all fired, sending a quartet of fourteen hundred kilogram shells at the Nabih's hull. The spectacle of it nearly stunned Ronin, who was surprised as the Citadel ship's shields held, but it was pushed hundreds of metres down in an instant. The rest of the Merciless's guns fired then, all aimed at the Rixe, which was over thirty thousand kilometres away.

"All right, time to get down there," Ronin announced as he saw that the Clever Dream, Raven and Sky Queen were safely out of the Triton's hangar on starting their run to the planet. They were joined by the Sky Stalker as it launched from the Merciless with Captain Gabe Vernor checking in along with a string of combat shuttles, each a small gunship in its own right. "Our advantage won't last long."

Ronin led the way past the Triton with Carnie on his port side and Easy on his starboard. Behind them was every member of his Squadron. They moved ahead of the Clever Corvettes and accelerated hard, their dampeners whining as every thruster pointed in the same direction and flared brightly. "Section twenty-eight of the Nabih's shields are down," announced Kadri.

"It's about time," Captain Vega said. "Break its back."

The Triton's beam weapons changed their focus entirely, sweeping to another portion of the ship. A new volley of torpedoes and missiles issued from the great ship as the much larger Nabih started to fire back, cannons arranged along the top of its hull sending white-hot rounds back at its assailants. Countermeasure gun emplacements went to work, sending small, fast rounds at incoming munitions.

If the fight wasn't happening at such close range, and the Triton was alone, the Nabih's superior firepower and comparable technology would have ensured victory. The Merciless's horrible cannons were providing support for the Triton, however, and the Triton herself was in the perfect position to do one of the things it was best at, killing large capital ships at close range.

More than half of the hull-piercing missiles and torpedoes struck the Nabih's bare hull, twisting and breaking through the thick layers of the hull protecting its main power systems. The explosion that followed was strange, not one of shrapnel, but of steam. "We've hit an internal shield under the ship's hull, and a large volume of water," Kadri announced, shaking her head so vigorously that Ronin could see it even on the small window he reserved for the bridge video feed. "Scanning, there's an aquatic environment between the main power generation centre and us."

"We can't stay here, our shields aren't going to hold much longer," Frost announced.

Minh-Chu's main focus was Samurai Squadron as they moved away from the close capital ship combat. They were meeting no resistance. The Triton and Merciless were the spectacles, and the Order ships that were in position to block their way to Rodus were just starting to react. The confusion was giving them time.

"We have to keep firing on the Nabih. There are hundreds of Geists aboard. All ages. They're confused and angry. They're reaching out, trying to influence our people," Alice said over all of their combat channels, straining.

"I can feel them too, oh, God, there are so many," Oz added. "That's a sacred ship to them somehow, they're angry."

"I'm here. I can protect us from their manipulations for a time, but you must attack. These are not the Geists that were made to help Earth, they are abominations, it's a twisted nursery," Quan said, breaking into the channel. "A breeding colony and combat Geist training ground at the same time. They are hiding something, a critical secret, I can't fight them and discover it at the same time. I can't hold them for long."

"Fire, break the internal shield down," Oz ordered from the bridge of the Merciless. His ship's cannons, not only the largest but every turret that could turn to the Nabih, erupted. Ronin could see the massive ship's internal shield fail on his tactical display. A glut of water and biomatter was sent out into space along with chunks of the hull that protected it, mixing with what quickly turned into shards of ice.

An entire volley of torpedoes from the Nabih and the Triton were exchanged, and the space between the ships erupted in brutal fire. If it wasn't for the damage the Nabih had already taken, the Triton would have lost shortly after, but the enemy ship was already turning away, using large chemical thrusters to accelerate quickly as a stream of water trailed behind it. The Rixe was accelerating after it, and Ronin only had an instant to lock his guns on and give a burst. Most of the Samurai squadron fighters did the same as Alice laughed. "There are young Geists left."

"They're afraid, hiding," Oz said.

"Wait, there's power. Old one, a Sire, and two more. Telepaths, I can see them, they're human hybrids. I can..." Quan screamed for a moment and was silent.

"Quan's gone, I can't feel him anymore, Oz?" Alice asked, alarmed.

"No. Quan? Quan?" Oz asked from the bridge.

"Someone check on him," Captain Vega ordered. "We've got Citadel out of the fight, move on to the next phase."

THE TRIP underground seemed to take forever as far as Vollis was concerned. He couldn't imagine how slow it would have been if the tunnel they took to Jacob Valent's hiding place hadn't been cleared out so well that it was like a functional underground highway again. The shuttle he took there fit easily, so the trip was swift, but he couldn't shake the feeling that he was in the wrong place. He was greeted at the hatch by the

Lieutenant he left in charge of the action in the pillar town. "The door is just about to open," he reported. "One more blast and we will send it to the left at least four meters, perhaps even five."

"That limits our advantage severely," Vollis replied pensively as he looked up at the tall doors looming over him. "Deploy the rest of our frameworks. I want them generated and ready to charge the moment the dust settles from your final blast. You'll follow them in once they charge."

"They will be killed," the Lieutenant, a Kline model fabricant, replied. When Vollis regarded him harshly, staring directly into his eyes, the man went on. "With respect, Valent's people are using some kind of nanobot technology that's disabling framework systems. Our soldiers are being rendered mortal. You will be sacrificing one of our best assets."

"I will need a distraction. A wild charge will give me that expediently," Vollis said in a whisper that was tinged with every bit of his frustration. "This mission is about cutting the head off a very long snake. That's all I'll explain to you. Now, there are three hundred framework soldiers in boxes that require activation. Follow my order immediately."

"Yes, Sir," replied the Lieutenant, who signalled to several of his fellow soldiers and then led the way to the shuttles emerging from the tunnel. They landed swiftly, their doors opening so their cargo could be unloaded and deployed.

A priority message came through his subdermal receiver and Vollis slapped it with irritation. "Yes?"

"We are retreating. The Triton is leading a Haven Fleet assault on our position. The Order is sending support, but you will have to hide until the situation in orbit stabilises," Leader Gideon announced.

"Retreat?" Vollis asked, checking on the Rixe. "Do not leave with my ship!"

"Main power aboard the Nabih has been damaged. The Rixe will be producing a wormhole so it can escape. I would not be able to stay even if the Nabih could transit under its own power. Our entire brood has been killed, leaving nothing but a few yearlings and their trainers. Echiss is beside himself. It is the loss of generations. The Janoo will be joining us. You will complete your mission to capture or kill Valent, and then join Leader Bion so you can be Citadel's liaison with the Order in these tragic times." The channel closed.

Vollis re-checked the status of the Rixe, saw that it was still hastily leaving orbit, and then shivered with frustration. He let his gaze rise from the display on his wrist to the shining doors that separated him from his enemy. A demolition crew were hurriedly setting charges in and around the minuscule crack at its bottom. A crater had formed there thanks to repeated blasts. "Clear the field in front of the doors. I don't want the enemy to see any of us when they are blasted apart. Do nothing until I give an order."

"We won't be charging?" the Lieutenant asked as he rushed to his side.

"No. Our target is a hunter and a military leader. I was going to use the charge as a show of force, to frighten him, but on second thought, I don't think that will work."

The Kline stared at him, unsure of what to say, until he finally uttered; "Sir?"

"You and your people should celebrate when this is over.

Your value has multiplied, and you're about to witness a confrontation that every member of Citadel will tell stories about. Prepare. Take cover. Move that half-broken hover tank to the side."

"Yes, Sir!" the Kline Lieutenant acknowledged before he marched away, barking orders.

TWENTY-SEVEN

Going Down

A SIMULATED BATTLE could never do the real thing justice. The wonder of the fully immersive connections Minh-Chu, Jonas and the rest of their gang used back at Freeground station so many years ago was enough to keep him dreaming of being in the pilot's seat of a fighter. The incredible technology and fidelity of the full-dive systems that had come along since were even more convincing, especially with time compression that controlled the experiences of the user even more. It still didn't measure up for Minh-Chu. He still didn't feel like Ronin.

The last simulations they ran the night before predicted a small but still significant gap between the Citadel and Order of Eden capital ships, and it was proving true. It was nearly twenty-two thousand kilometres wide, with the Order of Eden ships between them and the planet. They made a mistake that everyone was hoping for. The capital ships orbited in a well-organized picket line with the heavy cruisers in the middle and four destroyers at each end.

They were starting to fire, producing bursting rounds that tried to fill the space above them with flak. The Clever Dream led the way along with the other three Clever Class Corvettes. All fifteen of the pilots Ronin believed were ready from Samurai Squadron were in Archangel fighters with an equal number from the Merciless' Stormcaller Squadron. They had ten more, but those remained behind to defend their capital ships.

It would likely be necessary. That fight between the Triton, Merciless and the Citadel ships was coming to an end. "We're breaking off, there's no way we'll be able to stop them from jumping out," came Captain Vega's announcement from the bridge of the Triton. The element of surprise won them a momentary victory against Citadel, there was no doubt, but the Nabih still had bite. The damage done to her power systems didn't take out its cannons or torpedo launchers. More than half of the Triton and Merciless's firepower was dedicated to defence, stopping every kind of missile it could send their way while their shields were hammered. The Rixe and another Citadel carrier, the Janoo, were assisting, fearlessly sending as much firepower back at their attackers as they could. In the case of the Rixe, which was positioning itself ahead of the more massive ship, they were over-taxing their shields as they worked to intercept attacks. The Janoo seemed far more capable of delivering damage, de-cloaking and sending volley after volley after the Triton specifically, providing enough damage to tip the balance and break through her energy shields. "We've lost a main hangar and our dorsal kinetic shielding is about to collapse. We're dropping back."

There was no dishonour in that, as far as Ronin was concerned. The Nibih had almost as much firepower as all of their attackers combined, if they didn't catch it and her crew by surprise, then it would have been a very different fight. Then a wormhole opened ahead of the three Citadel ships. They slipped into it one after another and the hammering that the Triton was taking stopped. "Take time to recover, we're going to begin firing at the Fairlight from here," Oz announced from the bridge of the Merciless. It was a Heavy Cruiser one of the largest ships on the battlefield, a good target for the Merciless' main cannons.

Ronin focused on his squadron, and felt a bump as a flak pod burst close enough to cost him just over three percent of his shield charge. He turned that up as he looked at the tactical map. "All right, loose formation. Look for fighter groups. They're launching, we're just not seeing it close to their jammers," he said, looking for the Locon, the Order of Eden Heavy Cruiser that was conspicuously missing from the engagement.

"I'm picking up a lot of sensor jamming, it's really high-powered," Carnie announced.

"There are five emission points," Iruuk agreed from the Clever Dream's small bridge. "Two are military satellites, marking them now."

"Should we take them out?" asked Harver, the leader of Stormcaller Squadron.

"No, we're pushing on," Ronin replied, recalling how many fighters were lost when they sent groups out to destroy sensor-jamming emplacements of any kind. Only one in three came back from those submissions. "Open formation, loosen up and get ready to head to your next waypoints."

Every fighter and Corvette had split up, putting several kilometres between each other before they all accelerated towards the planet. The Clever Dream was the only one of its class without a trail of three large combat shuttles trailing behind it. The large ships below them in orbit were manoeuvring to block, but there was no way they could cover enough area to stop everyone. They stopped launching flak and anti-fighter gun emplacements started, sending streaks of light up at them. Most of it was low-powered at that range, but Ronin and the rest of his wing made sure they weren't easy to hit, adding a little lateral motion to their approach.

The thrusters sent roaring vibrations down the pylons they hung from into the fuselage of his ship. A destroyer was turning beneath, starting to fire its smaller cannons at the approaching group. There were other targets: combat corvettes, and a few fighters that looked like they were about to engage, but Ronin targeted that destroyer and deactivated the safety for his railguns. Carnie and Easy opened fire on it at the same time as he squeezed the trigger, focusing on the enemy ship's aft section, where the Tuva class Regent Galactic Destroyers kept the fuel supply for their main thrusters. The rattle and rumble of his guns were louder than expected as he sent bursts of rounds through thousands of kilometres at the ship's shields. "All right, we're not cutting through enough, launching Torpedos One and Two," Ronin announced as he flipped the safety cover for the large torpedoes mounted under his fighters aside then sent both of them flying.

The Javelin Torpedoes slipped into space, turning away ahead of him, disappearing from sight as they did so, following their own unpredictable course to their target. Their cloaking technology was excellent, but they still only had half a chance of crossing the space between them without being detected.

He would have liked to continue his assault on that destroyer, but it wasn't their mission to take out those capital ships. They only had to make enough of an effort to make every enemy captain think their vessels were in danger. Carnie and Easy followed his lead, adding a total of four torpedoes to the munitions that were headed to the ship. They would be followed by the Triton and the Merciless's long-range attacks as they held back at a range where they could regenerate their shields and avoid many of the heavier volleys that the Order ships sent their way.

The chatter between his other pilots, who were all launching quick, medium-range strikes at the blockade with torpedoes and short blasts with their guns, told him that they were doing just that. The Clever Dream was still at the head, its upgraded shields deflected and absorbed most of the damage. Alice was at the helm, she'd become a better pilot than anyone expected and she knew how to work with Lewis better than almost anyone. They avoided most of the cannon fire from the enemy ships, as their main railgun turret and large stationary railgun cannons took shots at the Fairlight. Then it reached a point in their approach that had the ship rotating for a moment before its main thrusters blasted them along a new trajectory. "Where are the enemy fighters? The combat corvettes?" Easy asked.

"Sensor jamming, we're down to lidar," replied Pixie from the seat of her fighter.

"We know, all we can see is jamming noise," Crashrabbit said from his Archangel.

"Those cap ships are pointing their hangars away from us," Carnie said, a warning in his tone.

"Wait, there's a shadow, a reflection. Highlighting it," Raver, a late addition to Samurai Squadron, announced.

"I see it, the Locon's hiding behind the Fairlight," Maid said.

Samurai Squadron followed the Clever Dream loosely, no longer approaching the blockade head-on. The best plan was to go around them, it was proven over and over again, but not at long range. Simulations had proven that tactic to be a disaster more often than not because it became more and more likely that the enemy would risk faster than light jumps to intercept them. The speed relative to the enemy that Ronin experienced over and over again in their successful simulations was starting to show itself.

"There they are! Fighters coming in from under the blockade cap ships!" shouted Garma from her fighter.

As Ronin's craft took him lower than the enemy ships, his tactical screen lit up. There were well over a hundred of them, and he grimaced as he saw that they were capable of atmospheric flight. It was completely unlikely. The simulations predicted that there would be perimeter defence drones that couldn't go atmospheric along with a couple dozen manned fighters that could. Almost everything he was seeing could follow them down into the atmosphere. "All right, Samurai Squadron, we're engaging those fighters. We can't let them follow the corvettes and the shuttles down." Ronin said as he rotated his fighter to port.

"We're with you," Harver said, speaking for Merciless' Fighter Squadron. "This is gonna be one for the books."

"Watch each other's backs, and don't get stuck on one target," Ronin said. The first part of his comment was just good advice, but the second addressed a problem he'd seen with several of his pilots.

The enemy fighters came in like a swarm, the broad shape of the Locon, flying close beneath its sister ship, the Fairlight, was turning, getting ready to present a portside bristling with guns. "This guy's jousting with me," Carnie said as he sent his fighter sideways, his guns sending a burst at his enemy as he went by. "Damn, they're moving fast." He flipped the body of his ship over and sent a barrage of rounds after the enemy. Its shields could only stop the first few hits. The rest passed into the armour of the ship. Another fighter flew across his path, and Carnie followed the advice of his wing commander, turning and going after it, immediately lining up a shot that proved far more deadly, ripping into the main thrusters and then the enemy's fuel supply before the young pilot moved on.

Ronin's eyes went wide as he saw that two enemy fighters were flying directly at him with a closing rate of over eleven thousand kilometres a second. He didn't have time for a remark as he took evasive action. Before he could rotate his fighter and fire after them, he found an enemy drone nearly in his sights. He listened to Easy as he lined up a shot and fired, scoring a direct hit on the drone's hull. It jerked away, flying like a computerized opponent, and he listened to Easy as he managed to get a missile lock. "If you don't come away with at least one cluster of Ace Stars on your jacket after fighting here, you're either unlucky or dead. That's one for me!"

Ronin only had five missiles aboard, and they were the smaller variety, but they were made specifically to kill drones. He sent one after the one he's already damaged, then avoided a near collision with another enemy craft. He shook his head as it sped past him and then matched his speed to another Order fighter, rotated his ship, and then hammered through its energy shields then hull with railgun rounds. Its rear thrusters flared and continued pushing the fighter in a straight line, its pilot dead on the stick. A marker on the tactical map in Ronin's mind caught his attention as he moved towards him too quickly. A missile lock warning sounded, and he sent an intelligent countermeasure out, manoeuvring so the attacker wouldn't collide with him.

Another missile lock tone sounded in his helmet, and Ronin marked the attacker it was coming from as the first ship passed him at incredible speed, another jouster. The second attacker in that second, the one who was closing at a more reasonable rate, was the one who held his attention and he turned the nose of his fighter in its direction. His thrusters kept him moving through the engagement in a completely different direction as he opened fire on the more sturdy-looking Order fighter. It fired back, attempted another missile lock, tried to get around the nose of his fighter, took significant shield damage, and then thrust in an entirely new direction. He joined four other fighters that were after the Corvettes. "Marking one group. Take them out. High priority. They're going after our shuttles," Ronin said as he gave chase. "New fighter model, it looks Regent Galactic made, more heavily armoured. Careful."

"I see it," Easy said as he joined Ronin's pursuit.

The Clever Dream rushed to catch them. It was a sight as all seven of its turrets fired at the fighters around them. "Someone knows what our main objective is," Carnie remarked as he got a missile lock on one of the fighters and fired two. "Switching to guns."

"The four at the rear are playing interference," Easy said as he opened up with his railguns and focused on one. Several rounds pierced its shields right away, but before he could finish it off, it turned and thrust directly at him. The collision was abrupt, but not completely dead-on as Easy's ship was sent spinning, its shields completely down, and one thruster ripped from its pylon completely.

"Watch out!" Carnie shouted as another ship that wasn't part of the enemy formation slammed into Easy at a relative speed in the thousands as he fired his pulse guns at him. The Order pilot obviously wasn't thinking ahead, or they actually meant to sacrifice themselves to destroy one of the Archangel pilots, because he struck like a comet, obliterating both ships.

"Holy shit!" Carnie cried as Ronin saw that Easy's life signs went dark. He focused on the fighters that were chasing the Sky Queen along with the two combat shuttles trailing close behind it. They didn't pay any attention to their defeated comrade as they locked missiles. "Come on, take them out!" he shouted as his rounds tore through the first one and the Clever Dream sent another spinning. Nine missiles were launched at the rearmost combat shuttle, and it was utterly destroyed. Ronin raked another one of the fighters with rounds as he got ready to follow another. "Carnie! Get on it!"

"Shit, yeah," he replied, flying back into position so he could cover Ronin. "I've got you." Seconds later a fighter started closing on the Wing Commander, and Carnie was there to fire on him, taking out one of the enemy pilot's engines before he tried to back off only to be killed by Maid.

Ronin was after the formation leader, who survived several strikes on his shields from the Clever Dream's turrets and was evading, coming around so he could fly back to the main blockade where he could get assistance. "This guy's manually handling his shields, he's good," Ronin said as a tone in his helmet told him that his enemy momentarily had a lock. Then he remembered his own words; 'don't get stuck on one target.'

After considering what the tactical map in his mind was telling him, he said; "Rip, Dame, go after the ship I'm marking, he's headed your way," he highlighted the lead fighter who took one of their shuttles out and pulled away. The Clever Dream was already moving away, returning to the main melee.

"These pilots are green, they're just building up a lot of speed and coming back at us," Pixie said.

"Not all of them, be careful," Ronin said as he flew back to the main action. On his tactical map, he could see two very important things. Dame was closing with the best enemy pilot he'd seen so far, sending him towards Rip, who was ready and opened fire, sending the enemy to pieces. The second thing he saw was that the corvettes and all but one shuttle made it into the atmosphere, and only three fighters were following them. They wouldn't survive long against the Sky Queen and the Raven. "Get ready to go atmospheric. We're moving on to phase three."

TWENTY-EIGHT

Jawing

IT WAS REASSURING for Vollis Mikan to see how expertly his troops setup the explosives at the foot of the grand door. He'd had a significant hand in their mnemonic programming and then training. Their expertise and efficiency was a reflection of him.

Loosening then separating the centuries-old doors that separated the pillar town from whatever was beyond wasn't simple. Ages ago the walls had been fortified with some complex process that turned them into armoured and shielded barriers that would have taken even longer to get through than the entrance.

Blasting one of the doors aside took preparation and expertise from the beginning to the conclusion of the task. When the final, focused blast that promised entry into the next chamber went off, he wasn't disappointed. The footings of the doorway burst apart, sending stone and some kind of concrete through the air, and when the dust settled, one of the impenetrable doors had slid to the side almost five metres. The gap wasn't large enough for a real charge, but he could see a large cavern with ghostly lights. There was a wealth of technology in there, and it reminded him of something. The kind of technology that Citadel and Sol Defence wanted. "Send a focused scan pulse through those doors now. Record the results, relay them directly to me."

"Yes, Sir," replied the Lieutenant, who signalled three soldiers with large handheld scanners.

The results started streaming to the computer grafted onto Vollis' skin, then appearing before his eyes. "More, increase the sensitivity, send another pulse," he said as he looked at the data. Finding that kind of technology in there, as he was pursuing a great enemy, was shocking. If the Nabih or any of the Citadel ships hadn't abandoned him, he would have called them down, and they would have come. They would have sent everyone they could.

This was the kind of technology that was derived from what was started on Earth. He wasn't an expert, Vollis' speciality wasn't history, but he knew enough to see that whatever was in there had evolved separately from what was found in the Sol System. It came from exploration, colonization, and expansion during a different time, when humanity more frequently combined efficiency with art after centuries of refinement. It was the result of technological evolution down a different road, and he knew that Citadel as well as Sol Defence was after it. He started sending scan results to his commanders. They would travel along the Order's slow network of hyper transmitters, so he didn't know when they'd get it, hopefully within hours if they were still in the solar system.

As his excitement abated, he realized that something important was missing. There was no sign of his enemy. "Go, scan from the doors, they must be in there, there's no way out," he said, pointing at a trio of soldiers that had just been generated from framework skeletons. They dutifully rushed forward, scrambling up the side of the crater he and over twenty other soldiers were using as a makeshift trench. "Hurry."

Everyone watched the trio as they ran towards the doors, their boot steps landing in perfect sync. They were about to drop down into the shallow crater made by the explosives when three shots rang out and each of their heads burst apart, exploding backwards in chunks of gore and silver bone. As the red mist settled a lone figure in heavy Haven armour became apparent. The dark slats looked new, and he was wearing a long white scarf around his neck. "I want to meet with your commander. We'll speak peacefully unless they escalate the situation. Anyone else will be shot on sight," he bellowed using an amplifier.

"It must be Jacob Valent. Records tell us that he wears a token like that white garment," the Lieutenant said.

"His helmet is closed," Vollis said. "Your scanner is not getting through the armour."

"You're saying it may not be him?"

"No. I said the truth is not yet known," Vollis said, getting to his feet. "I will not hide my face."

"With respect, you shouldn't go out there," the Lieutenant,

just a Kline model who wasn't known for spectacular independent thought, said, uncharacteristically alarmed.

"I'll be able to react to any surprises. I am much faster. This is my best opportunity to take him alive. Only kill him if I am killed or give the order to do so."

"Yes, Sir," the Lieutenant replied seeming more certain.

That's all Klines needed to be effective. Clear orders.

The gravel beneath Vollis' boots had the jagged edges of new stone, and he thought it was a curious thing that he'd never experienced before. It made a different sound, like the grinding of thick carapace plates. Blasting at the doors had ruined the stone floor of the grand cavern beyond the hardened channel it was locked into. After seeing the scans of what was beyond them, he thought it was worth shattering stone.

He regarded the armoured man who jumped over the crater at the foot at the doors and landed steadily. The landing was almost perfect, with only the smallest last-second correction. Leaping across a half-circle crater that was in excess of six metres wide was something most people weren't capable of without some kind of enhancement. It was the suit. That armour was hard to pierce, it took an assassin's true blade, the unnamed weapon that used nanobots and high-tech alloys. The one hidden in his tunic was just such a blade. The metal Valent wore could deflect it at most angles, it made more sense to slip the blade under a slat, where it would strike an interlocking seam. Past that, there was a military vacsuit with layers made for protection that could mend themselves. Pierce that and then you had to contend with the synthetic muscle layer which helped Valent jump so far, no doubt. It would clench around the blade, try to hold it, and push it out as medical technology healed whatever wound he could make with his weapon. It was a suit made for soldiers of value, one that could have even more technology built in that he and Citadel hadn't managed to discover yet. He would have to keep track of whatever was discovered when they took Valent's armour and studied it.

Vollis didn't stop until he was within easy striking distance. He was relaxed from head to toe as he turned his face up at his opponent, observing how Valent - if it was him - towered in comparison. Exude confidence, maintain calm, stay focused. The armour multiplies strength, but not speed. That is my advantage. Vollis thought to himself. "I am here."

"You're going to leave these tunnels and fly back to your ships in orbit and let us all go," Valent said, his voice instantly recognisable with the tone of a man who would rather be fighting.

"Why?" Vollis asked, staring into the faceplate and the skull beyond. It was there to intimidate, red with blood and hints of gore, as though it hadn't been properly cleaned. "And let me see your true face. I don't negotiate with helmets or the holograms your people like to hide behind."

Jacob Valent's face appeared where the holographic skull once was. His gaze was steady, angry, but he didn't regard him haughtily. The air of superiority that Vollis expected to see was absent. Instead Valent seemed raw, the promise of violence was plainly there. Jacob could be intimidating by nature, the kind of person who rarely had to follow through with actual fighting. "I will surrender myself in exchange. My armour will come off when all my people are free. If you don't agree, the battle over our heads will expand, and Order ships will be destroyed.

Citadel has left you alone here while my reinforcements are coming."

"We outnumber you. There are more soldiers above, they stay up there because I've told them they're not needed down here," Vollis replied, sure that Valent was bluffing. "Nothing in there can help you. That technology is centuries old. I recognize it. There are no surprises for me here."

"Then go in. Walk right on past me with your soldiers. I can't stop you all. Dig us out. Prove you have the advantage so you can go on killing innocent people. I saw how proud you were. Baby killer."

How could Valent know that he was grasping the handle of a dagger in his mind? An irritating point of fact that threatened to poison his mood? He had to correct it. The credit for assassinating Ayan and her child wasn't something he wanted to take but was ordered to. "If I was the one tasked with destroying your woman and her child, no one would have known Citadel was there at all."

"She's alive," Valent hissed, his eyes burning angrily.

"If that is so, I guarantee I would have made sure there was nothing left of her or her adopted brat," Vollis returned, watching as Valent's focus became clouded, and he decided it was time to disable the brute. Valent was clearly about to become emotionally unbalanced, the creases in his forehead, widening eyes and a powerfully aggressive curl of his lips made it plain that violence was coming. There was a moment, always a brief instant where a would-be assailant was vulnerable before their first attack, and Vollis drew his blade, took one step and jammed it under a slat in his left side. There was significant resistance, then the blade was turned aside. He had to strike again if he wanted to breach the armour.

He struck near to the same mark a second time and the tip of his blade found the groove, that weakened spot where he could slip the whole length in. He aimed for the heart, felt the under-suit hold the tip back and applied the raw strength required to get the blade through where it would bisect the man's heart. Vollis stepped to the side as it pierced, and he made sure the angle was perfect. It became apparent then that there was nothing but air in the suit, and he looked up at Valent's face. He started to say the word as he withdrew his blade and was about to battle an empty suit of armour, probably held rigid and animated by its artificial muscle layer. "Holog..." Vollis began to spit.

The suit's hand lashed out in an expert strike, only it was an assault that Vollis had never seen performed before. Four fingers were shoved between and through his front teeth, breaking some as a white flash of pain marked the moment. Then the metal hand closed, the fingers pinching his tongue to the bottom of his mouth, fist starting to close. He should have mirrored the man by wearing his own faceplate, but that thought was fleeting as the suit drew him off his feet and Valent's holographic gaze met his.

There was a storm in his eyes, yes, but a grin on his face. "You're dead. This is a tomb."

Desperation, an instant of perfect focus, Vollis couldn't tell, led him to make another perfect strike with his sword, severing the armour at the wrist. That hand clenched into a fist, dislocating and breaking his jaw, sending him tumbling through a symphony of pain. He was barely aware of the armour snapping open and a buzzing sound erupting from it. The Lieutenant, fearless, dutiful man that he was, rushed to his side. "I'll take you to..." he started to say before the life left his eyes.

Nanobots, they've killed him. But wait... Vollis thought as he watched the soldier begin to spontaneously regenerate, the flesh over his framework skeleton rippling, shifting as it replaced itself with normal bone that didn't have any regenerative properties. It was Munition Twenty-Eight, the invention made to remove frameworks with a final rebuild of the subject. This version killed the victim.

Vollis Mikan found himself wishing that he wasn't using an entirely different regeneration technology, one that was purely biological. It would immediately reject the fist in his mouth, deliver him from a state that was so horrific that he could barely stumble away from the grand doors.

It seemed like every second soldier ahead of him was dropping dead, regenerating, and when they were finished, they didn't wake up. The rest stared, fright rising in wide-eyed, shocked expressions.

TWENTY-NINE

When It's Time To Go

SENDING an empty suit of armour to meet their attackers was entirely Captain Ruby Sima's idea, and Remmy was impressed. It was possible to enter a simulation of the real world using a brain bud, and then connect to an empty suit of armour. Normally the results would result in awkward movements, but every layer of Jake's equipment was well calibrated to him after he'd used it for years during regular service. He had even done his morning workout routine in the undersuit many times, so there was no need for a lengthy synchronization process when he connected to it.

His military vacsuit had a muscle layer built in so it could perform every action he performed in the simulation only for real. It was like a fully articulated, full body puppet that worked perfectly with his heavy set of armour. The sensors built into the armour passed information back to Jake through the brain bud, and the brain bud made it feel like he was really in the suit of armour as they moved it around in the real world. It wouldn't stand up to scrutiny for long, so it didn't make for the best decoy, but, to everyone's amazement, it worked this time.

They were within the main column of the vault. The room was set up as some kind of lounge, with a circular imaging system in the middle. It was unlike the other particle displays, in that it used a hologram projected into a mist that changed shape with the image of the pillar town outside the vault. There were more troops amassing.

"That was incredible, I could really feel his teeth break in my gauntlet," Jake said as he opened his eyes and removed the brain bud. He was in a military vacsuit.

Remmy cringed at the mental image his comment conjured. "I guess that's a benchmark." He was also listening to Ruby finish a short conversation with Panda Port Control, far above. It had gone well, they didn't promise to help them fight off the Order if they got close, but they would let ships inside the shield to pick her crewmembers up. The attitude, Remmy guessed, was that Port Control wanted her people out of the city as quickly as possible, especially since they didn't understand how they got there in the first place.

Simon was considering something else entirely as he regarded Jake. "I wonder if that satisfies the revenge you need here," it was intended as more of a comment than a question. "I'm sorry, thinking aloud has always been one of my problems." Charon muttered.

"I wanted to kill him," Jake said, nodding then picking up his rifle and bag. "I think if it were a few years ago, I would have risked my life to do it, but I'm not fighting for my own honour anymore. I have a family, I'm with Ayan, who always opts for the better strategy."

"Injure their commander so another doesn't take over and order a charge immediately," Ruby said as she checked on her crew, who were already getting set to retreat from the windows and hatches in the vault.

"Exactly," Jake said.

"But you couldn't have bought us more time?" Remmy asked, forgetting who he was talking to for a moment as he pressed on. "I mean, you said you'd go talk to him, string things along by negotiating, but then..." he mimed shoving his hand in someone's mouth then continued. "That's a way to make the conversation really one-sided and short."

Jake laughed, surprising everyone, including Charon. "You're right, I could have slowed that down, but I had this feeling that Vollis would figure out what was going on any second. Alice did the whole decoy thing better than we could, so I was surprised we got away with it at all." He looked at his comm-con. "How are things in the gate room?"

A scratchy voice replied then. "Two thirds done. This is quick. Reports back from Panda's surface say everyone's arriving on the other side in, well, good enough health. There's been some vertigo and vomiting," Parsons replied. "How did your mini-drones do?"

"One hundred-ninety eight frameworks were taken out by the nano weapons, almost perfect," Jake replied. "They came out of my empty armour like a swarm, sending nanobots into everything they could."

That number was two short of the maximum number of

fatalities caused by a nanobot weapon in one engagement allowed by galactic law. Jake was hoping to take out one hundred ninety-nine of the framework soldiers who weren't wearing sealed armour. Their sudden and quiet demise as they simply appeared to fall over and die was supposed to intimidate anyone from the Order, and so far it seemed to be working. Remmy stared at the big display in the middle of the room, watching the live feed of hundreds of Order of Eden soldiers arriving in small shuttles. The markings made it clear that they were coming down from the Locon and Fairlight. "We're about to be outnumbered." Remmy stopped short of saying that he was glad that Jake's first plan, leading a charge into the pillar town beyond the vault doors, wasn't the one they went with. They would have been outnumbered quickly.

"Yeah, we can hold them off for about half an hour here without using the river of fire," Jake said, looking.

"You should all go, this is my time, my place," Simon stated, looking at the hologram with them. "If you retreat from the outer defences and all take the portal now, everyone will survive. I can make sure none of your enemies use the portal."

"Which means you'll have to stay behind. Bad design, not programming automated defences," Jake said critically.

"There is an automated defence, but I can do things it can't, and it's only a backup. I am Charon, there is no substitution," Simon replied.

"Now who's making unnecessary sacrifices?" Jake asked. "You're right, though. The mission was always getting off this planet, and I'm having the wrong conversation." His expression softened as he regarded Charon, who was maintaining his appearance as an old man in robes. "I can't thank you enough, Simon. I wish you were coming with us."

"It was an honour to meet you, and I'm happy that my first impression about you was wrong. Why did you hand your sidearm to me when I brought up your past?"

"I thought it was the best gesture I could make to start earning your trust," Jake admitted. "And maybe I'm still looking for the right person to atone to. A lot of innocent people were killed when a few of those Order ships fell out of orbit."

He was talking about disabled vessels in several solar systems. Some of the ships de-orbited and didn't burn up, killing thousands of regular citizens. He'd had a chance to see the devastation in the Cefa System personally while he served as an Admiral before he was removed from Haven Fleet. Jake's sidarm slipped from somewhere inside Simon's chest. He took it in his hand, and offered it to Jake. "I'm not an expert on atonement, but I know some of the people who came here to have their psyches recorded had apologies and promises on their lips. The only lesson I took was to do the best we can in life while we can. Lead your people and mine off this world and take the psyches somewhere where they'll be safe. Help Rodus if it's the right thing to do. I remember really liking that place."

"I will. What about the technology here?" Jake asked, and it was clear to everyone that he didn't enjoy posing the question.

"I can melt it all down. I'll retract the shielding protecting the main pillar in the vault and activate the river of fire. All anyone will be able to salvage are casings filled with hunks of metal. The pillar will fail, and this place will collapse. Don't worry, your enemy won't find any help here."

"Thank you again," Jake said, hesitating for a moment before leaving.

"That's it, the last container is through. Those cubes, the psyches are all in Panda, and the Clever Dream is landing now with enough support to get everything in space," Ruby said. "Thank you so much Simon. There's no way for you to come with us?"

He shook his head, placid. "If you save me, then your chances go down significantly. Critically. Name something after me. Maybe your next ship?"

"The Simon? I like it," Ruby replied.

"Charon. At least while you're at war. Maybe rename it Simon when you return to your first calling?" he said with a whimsical smile.

"My next ship," she agreed before leaving.

"Yeah, I'm not okay with leaving you down here," Remmy said. "You designed a chunk of this place, there's gotta be a way to set that river of fire up on a timer or something, right?"

"A timer that will only give the Order a chance to deactivate it and take this installation. I'm protecting more than you could imagine. Not only this place, but programs, codes and technologies that you don't want back in the galaxy. I was so relieved when I checked the Stellarnet and found no signs of the biggest problems of my time. Well, the biggest technical problems. The time I came from wasn't ruled by the right people. If there's a lesson you can take from us, it's that there's no such thing as a true utopia. I always thought humanity would repeat the same mistakes over and over again, but I'm happy to see I was wrong. There are a few new mistakes, but there are a lot of people doing the right things out there."

"Okay, okay, that's amazing, big picture stuff, but I'm inter-ested in finding the little cube that you're stored in and taking it through that gate with me. Can we just do that already?" Remmy asked, hoping to appeal to Simon's self-preservation, if he had any.

He regarded Remmy with a look that was sympathetic and humble. "You've already given me everything I need. I've been here for centuries, looking after this place, losing hope that anyone would come along with the right codes that would connect this vault with the galaxy as I dined on unanswered questions and neglect every night. Now I get to fulfil my purpose. All my people are about to be saved. Make sure they get to Grace. I've already sent you the location, it's on your computing unit." He pointed at his left command and control bracer. "Take them to another vault where the Elysium program is running. That's all I need. I'll make sure you and your allies get through the gate so you can save a few people in my place." He looked towards the holodisplay in the middle of the room. Vollis Mikan's jaw had been mended, and he was commanding a Lieutenant along with several hundred Order of Eden troops through the gap in the door. He remained on the other side. "It looks like we both have somewhere else to be."

"Good luck," Remmy said, unused to being at a loss for words. Then, as Simon began to shift into his skeletal form, a thought occurred to him. "Wait. Are you sure your psyche cube won't survive? I mean, it's gotta be in a really safe place, right?"

"Your hope really is unsinkable. Don't lose that, friend," Charon said as he faded away. His voice filled the chamber one more time. "Your people have almost finished their retreat. Join them or you might end up staying with me here."

Remmy saw that Charon was materializing at the edge of the vault, right inside the battered doors in the holographic image. He wished he could stick around and watch the meeting, but took off at a run instead. His heart ached at leaving a new friend behind, but he wasn't going to miss his escape, especially since Samurai Squadron was fighting for air superiority above, and they'd already lost one pilot.

THE RELIEF at being healed by the medics, who were more proficient than Vollis expected, was incredible. It was almost enough to drown out the bitter aggravation at being assaulted and beaten by Jacob Valent's empty suit. It was definitely the war criminal's armour. They knew it for a fact. The DNA matched. He'd taken his armour and inner suit off then sent it forth empty. Vollis had never been more insulted, especially since killing him wasn't even his objective.

Fear. Jacob Valent was a true terrorist. His cowardly attack was meant to demean him and to kill enough of his soldiers using a nanobot attack to frighten the newer Order of Eden recruits. It had worked. The freshest soldiers from the Locon were hesitant, wide-eyed, and whispering about facing an unscrupulous war criminal. It was maddening, the kind of morale break framework soldiers and fabricants that he and other technicians programmed would never fall victim to.

A message from the Locon buzzed in his ear and he accepted it. "What is it?"

"An agent in Panda reports that the soldiers you're pursuing are coming out of a loading dock on the surface. We're marking the location for you," replied a communications officer from above.

"They must have found an exit. Fire on the city. I want you to turn..." Vollis began to reply.

"I'm sorry, Sir. The city has an energy shield. They're letting parts of it down so the enemy can pick up their people. They have not fired on our forces yet, however. They communicate that they wish to remain neutral in..."

"Their cooperation demonstrates non-neutrality." Vollis was beside himself with frustration, and knowing that the person he was talking to couldn't do anything about the situation only made it worse. "Put me through to Bion, now."

"I will put you in queue to speak with him, Sir. I'm afraid I don't have any more information for you." The communications officer ended the call then.

Vollis fought for calm as he followed five squads from the rear until they ran through the doors and formed up on the other side. "Fan out and inspect the area. Watch for traps and start looking for an exit. I suspect we will find some kind of old cargo elevator there, in the central pillar. Find a way in. We are in a hurry," he ordered. "They're getting away."

Vollis stepped back as a swirl of what seemed like fine sand appeared in front of him, just on the inner side of the doors. The figure that appeared was a hooded skeleton clad in dark robes. It leered at him for a moment and then extended a bony hand. "Another trick," he said, irritation building even higher.

"Old technology, Sir," said the Lieutenant from inside the vault chamber. "It matches what we're seeing here."

"I know, I've been trained to watch for this kind of work. It doesn't mean that this figure doesn't represent some kind of gatekeeper." He looked past the figure and saw lines drawn on the floor using grease pencils and paint. Most of his soldiers had already walked past them, and were focused on scanning the strange technology. "Be careful, there will be traps," he shouted. Even if it wasn't true, advising caution was reasonable. "But hurry, find out how they got out."

"Why are you here? Are you a guardian?" Vollis asked.

"Perhaps he wants us to present a champion?" asked a Sergeant from behind as he led his men up to the doors. "I volunteer, Sir."

"You don't know what you're volunteering for," Vollis muttered as he considered the vault behind the skeletal figure. It brandished the pole in its hand with a flourish then silently laughed. "Besides, I don't think he's a fighting creature. Push on. We have to find out how Valent and his people are getting to the surface so quickly."

The figure lowered itself until its empty sockets seemed to stare at him levelly, and then the vault was alive with blue-white strands of electricity. The squads there only jerked for a moment before they disintegrated, leaving nothing but shadows and stains imprinted on the metal plated ground. A piercing howl filled the air as the electricity built, waves of lightning swirling around the central tower in the vault. The smell of burnt hair, flesh and something harshly electronic filled his nostrils.

Tremors nearly shook Vollis off his feet as chunks of the ceiling inside and outside of the vault began to break off and crush technology and people. "Retreat! Retreat to the shuttles and get to the surface! We rally on the edges of Panda's energy shield on the surface," he shouted, running for a nearby shuttle as fast as he could. It was vital that he survive, someone had to remember where this place was so Citadel could excavate later. As he leapt into the nearest shuttle, he thought; *How are they getting to the surface? We scanned from orbit, from the tunnels, and there was nothing but layers of wreckage and rough dens that weren't connected at all to that giant box. I've underestimated Valent, and if I survive, I'll never do so again. Someone else will face him next, and I'll watch, because there was so much here that I didn't see coming. That trap with the skeleton looks like his style. I just don't understand why it's there at all. It's so theatrical, I need time to understand it.* "Fly us through the main tunnel back up to the surface, immediately!" he told the pilot.

"But we're not full, this shuttle has room for four squads, Sir!" the pilot objected.

Vollis drew his sidearm and pointed it at the pilot. "Now, boy."

"Yes, Sir," the pilot said, lifting off as the doors closed. The sound of soldiers calling after them as they acelerated down the main highway tunnel as pillar buildings began to shift on their foundations faded quickly.

THIRTY

The Fray

IT WAS as if the sky over the City of Panda was filled with a flock of frenzied metal birds. Some chased, others evaded, and just as many fought to gain positions of advantage. There were two Order or Citadel fighters for every Triton ship. The aviating whirl was set against a background of blue above the horizon, and ruins that surrounded a shielded centre with a polished, white city beneath.

It was a dogfight that would be a feverish delight in a simulation, but a nightmare to most in reality. It had become apparent to Ronin and many members of Samurai Squadron that not all of the enemy pilots were playing by the same rules, only adding to the reckless danger of the skirmish.

"What is with all the jousting?" asked Shep, a pilot in Maid's group.

"They're amateurs," Rip replied.

"Yeah, they crank the acceleration so they can close with you fast, try to get a missile lock from a distance, and fly straight at you without thinking of a merge or a good firing solution," Raver explained.

"Everyone here knows what jousting is," Dame said flatly. Her Archangel was on the outskirts of the dogfight, tracking a trio of Order fighters as they came down from the outer atmosphere, demonstrating a diving joust as they approached the main air battle. Samurai Squadron had managed to tie up the fighters that made it into the atmosphere so they couldn't go after the larger ships on their way to Panda. Dame and her wingmate, Rip, had been a large part of that, as important as Ronin himself. They were on the perimeter, watching the enemy, striking and fading only so they could stay in position. If any of the enemies broke away to chase the corvettes or shuttles, Dame and Rip would sound the alarm early, even intercept newcomers on their way to their targets.

Ronin wished he could trade places with her. He was in the middle of the swarm, allowing one of the enemy fighters to line up a shot from behind. A thap-thap-thap sound and damage on his shields showed that his enemy had found his mark. That gave Carnie a chance to open fire on the enemy pursuer, and a moment later his assailant's ship was shedding armour and pieces of internal parts, losing power.

"Your turn," Carnie said as he passed Ronin's aft side, who turned and got behind the fighter chasing his wingman. This was one of the better Order pilots, he'd already taken a bite out of Gren's port side, nearly shooting the Mergillian down before Garma scared him off.

The Order pilot tried for a missile lock on Carnie as he gave a burst with his cannons, then started to veer away, seeing that he'd picked up a pursuer of his own. It was too late, and Ronin was surrounded by the sound and rattle of his guns as he squeezed the trigger. The Order ship, a Uriel with three green stripes across the top, wasn't able to protect itself against the high-velocity rounds for more than a few hits. Its shields failed, port side armour was pierced all the way through, and flames erupted from the exit wounds. The fighter spun, the pilot ejected, and Carnie whooped as he moved on to another target. "We'll be watching that one later!"

Dame slipped behind the trio of fighters she was tracking as she launched a pair of decoy drones to draw five missiles that a distant fighter fired at her. The seeking munitions went for the drones, and she resumed her attack on the jousters. They were amateurs who didn't know how to plan to merge with their targets, and she taught them a lesson. Relative to their targets, they were moving too fast, only able to rake them and the sky around them with a few shots, pecking at Crashrabbit's shields. He was able to get out of their way after taking major shield damage because, even though the enemy couldn't strike him for long, there were three of them, after all. He saw Dame and didn't engage. "Those nuggets are all yours, I'll find a target that's causing real trouble."

"They won't be up here for long. Firing three bursts," she replied, as she fired all five of her cannons and ripped into the fighter in the middle, and its fresh shields only lasted seconds before chunks of the ship were blown away from the main body. It was one of the cheaper Order of Eden fighters. A main rocket engine was shorn off completely. Before it started its death spiral, she moved onto the next fighter, ripping across its aft section then the cockpit as it tried to evade by gaining altitude. The pilot died and the ship's ascent slowed. The third enemy in that formation turned suddenly, and Dame noticed what was going on before anyone. "My target is ignoring me and about to attack the corvettes." She sent a burst of rounds after it, breaking through its shields and scoring hits on its port side. "That one's yours, Crashrabbit. I'm getting into position to intercept another that's turning towards the transports."

Crashrabbit gave chase after the fighter who was going towards the Clever Dream. The corvette had extended its hull from forty-two metres to seventy, opening cargo compartments that were filled. The Sky Queen was right behind it. Their gunners were getting set to fire, about to exit Panda City's shield. "This guy thinks he's going to be a hero," Crashrabbit said before sending a barrage of rounds through the cheap Order of Eden fighter's armour. It spun end over end as it descended, hurtling past the Clever Dream before impacting the city's defence shield.

Ronin saw that several of the enemy fighters in the melee above Panda were breaking off, charging for the Clever Dream and the rest of the transports. "Every ship is packed, we're coming up to help with clean up then moving on," Alice announced.

"Don't worry, we've got this," Ronin replied, sighting an Uriel fighter that was from the Nabih. Its auto turret spun and fired back at him, pulsing, only striking his shields for a second before he could change position and turn his guns towards the Uriel. It tried to spin, to rotate its nose so it could fly backwards while firing its main weapons back at him, but its flight destabilized for a moment, nearly sending the fighter pinwheeling. The enemy pilot compensated, forced to point his nose where he was flying. It gave Ronin a chance to line up a shot and he fired, ripping at its shields. It was about to get away without a scratch on his hull when Ronin manually turned his dorsal thrusters and fired them, keeping him in position just long enough to punch through the heavy fighter's shields and rip into its hull. Two of the smaller thrusters were knocked off the enemy vessel's pylons, and the pilot struggled as all his attention focused on not falling out of the sky. The Order had lost the advantage of numbers as Maid finished one off, a steady blast from her guns sending an enemy Uriel spinning down. That's when she noticed she was in trouble.

An instant later she was struck by a trio of missiles from two fighters as they decelerated from behind. They fired them from such a close proximity that there was no time for countermeasures. Even electronic jamming didn't have a noticeable effect. Her wingmate, Shep, was trying to move into position so he could fire on one of her pursuers. "Could use a hand here. We've got bad birds converging on Maid," he said.

"Coming to you," Breaker replied. He was clear, having just shot down an Order fighter while Gren finished one that was pursuing him off his tail. "Cover Maid!"

A barrage of pulse cannon fire from both her pursuers was just successful enough to batter what was left of her shields down and damage one of her main thrusters. "Shutting Thruster Two down," she announced. "Evading, transferring power to shields. I've lost emitters."

Ronin was one of the furthest from her, but he still managed to point his nose in her direction just long enough to squeeze a burst off at one of Maid's attackers. He missed with most of his rounds and saw Breaker pass by as he moved right in position behind one of her assailants. Breaker opened up with his guns an instant after five missiles launched at Maid from less than three hundred metres. Her attacker had fully committed to taking her out, emptying their launchers in one volley at close range. The last of Maid's countermeasure drones popped free from their ports, drawing three missiles away so they exploded only metres from her fighter, but the last two projectiles hit their mark.

Before Maid's fate was clear, the fighter that savagely attacked her was ripped to pieces by Breaker's railgun fire. The enemy's wingmate tried to get away from Gren and Garma but failed dismally as they focused their guns on the Order of Eden vessel, tearing through its shields and cockpit.

Maid wouldn't be ejecting. The missiles struck her port side, along an area that was already compromised by previous strikes. Her suit couldn't protect her from such direct damage. It was difficult to move on. Ronin wanted to point his nose up at the sky and return to the stars for a moment, leave the fray behind. It was only an instant before he regained his focus. Carnie's voice in his ears. "I'm after one that's coming around, trying to line up with you, Ronin."

He spotted it then. There was one fighter moving into position with another following a little over a kilometre behind. The second would go after Carnie. "Let it chase, back off, look for his wingmate," Ronin said and seeing the younger pilot follow instructions immediately, swerving away, slowing down, was almost as gratifying as spoiling his pursuer's attempt at a missile lock.

The whine of his inertial dampeners increased pitch as Ronin took fire from another enemy fighter, an Order interceptor that managed to rake him with a burst of gunfire on its way past. The Clever Dream's gunners caught it by surprise as three emplacements focused on it, tracking the fighter's course as it passed well enough to knock its shields down. A missile caught up with it and obliterated the small vessel. "Thanks for the assist, Clever Dream!" Pixie said as the corvette roared through the atmosphere. It started a long, arcing turn, all seven of its turrets were busy turning, taking aim and firing at enemy fighters as it passed. "Warning, clear, clear, launching seekers," came the announcement from Alice.

Every Samurai Squadron pilot but Scythe stopped chasing their targets and started putting as much distance as they could between them and the enemy. A pair of compartments along the dorsal side of the Clever Dream slid open. What followed was a storm of twenty-eight fast-seeker missiles. They knew their targets before bursting from their tubes and set after them, turning, spiralling in the air as they turned towards them then accelerated. Most struck within the first two seconds, two and three of them striking most of the enemy fighters, blasting them to pieces. The Sky Queen, Raven and Sky Stalker followed it, her gunners damaging and frightening the few remaining enemy fighters off. "Final mission stage," announced Alaka from the Sky Queen.

"Confirmed, heading to the next waypoint," replied Nigel from the Raven. The rest of the corvettes acknowledged as well, forming up around the more vulnerable combat shuttles.

"Come on, get us into a hangar, it's crowded in here," an unknown soldier said from inside the ship.

"Get off this channel," Captain Vega said before announcing; "Triton incoming. We only have two retrieval bays. Make sure you're where you're supposed to be."

"All right, the Triton is jumping in. Set your inertial dampeners to maximum, don't get behind or in front of anyone, and make good and sure you're not within range of hard turbulence," Ronin instructed. The ship was about to perform something outlawed on every planet. An atmospheric disturbance would be created as air sought to move from a pressurized area to the void of space on the other side of the Triton's wormhole. That was a certainty. Most simulations indicated that a quick jump would cause a minor weather disturbance, but there was always a possibility of disaster.

"All set!" Carnie announced from three kilometres off his starboard side.

Then, under a quiet, clear sky that was still marked by crisscrossing white trails, there was a tear in the blue. The Triton's glossy black hull was raked by lightning, a phenomenon that wasn't predicted as likely, but the air interacted with the energy shields, as though testing them. The broad face of the great ship, shaped like a stingray, breached the blue and fully transitioned into atmospheric space. Its lower thrusters flared and fired hard, holding it aloft as it moved forward, opening its central and one other forward-facing hangar doors. The shuttles moved in, a shimmering sheen surrounding them as they cranked their shields, preparing for a violent, high-speed landing. That wasn't the plan, but it was a possibility. "Oooh, myyyy Gooood!" shouted one of the shuttle pilots over the mission channel as they barely lined their trajectory up in time.

"We've got you, Wodak," Slick said from the Flight Control Deck. "You won't even hit the deck."

It was true, the lead shuttle was caught in a gravity net that was projected from inside the hangar, and the shuttle was pulled to the side, moved to the roof of the hangar and held there. A blast of wind in the direction of the brief wormhole sent every craft in the area towards the Triton, but only the Clever Dream got close enough to nearly collide. Many hearts skipped a beat as it veered off at the last second. "I miss Dame," Alice said from the controls as the gunship put more distance between it and the Triton.

"So do I," Lewis agreed. "Starting our escape course."

"All right! We know what to do next. One group latches, the other flies for your designated hangar. Do not worry about scratching her hull, she's not as delicate as she looks," Ronin announced, mentally glancing at his tactical map. The Order ships in orbit were turning their guns downward. The Merciless couldn't distract them any longer, it was taking damage, so it was jumping to their rendezvous point.

"We can't stay up, we've taken too much damage," Captain Vega said to Ronin on a private channel. "We're in a controlled descent. Helm reports impact in fifty-six seconds."

"I hear you, Captain," Ronin replied, switching to his Wing's channel. "Move! Move! Emergency landings! You have fifteen seconds to cram your fighters into the bays or you'll be settling on Rodus."

Carnie was a second ahead of Ronin in touching the hull of the Triton. Their hulls affixed to the Triton's and the larger ship's energy shielding sealed above them. Crashrabbit came in too fast ahead of them, skipped off the Triton's hull, then corrected and touched down properly. If it weren't such a tense moment, Ronin would have laughed, seeing the habit behind the pilot's callsign demonstrated. Most of his pilots weren't in the same position they were. They were still on their way to the Triton, and had to decide whether or not to risk affixing to the hull or landing in one of the retrieval bays.

Most of them opted for the hangar, making sure that they would be aboard when the ship jumped back into space. Breaker was the last pilot to make contact with the Triton, and he affixed his fighter's landing gear to the thick armour right in front of the ship's bridge. "I just realized where I parked, sorry!" he said in a rush.

Cringing as he checked the location of the Triton, seeing that it was falling faster, he turned more attention to the bridge. "Come on, Ash, get those jump calculations in," Captain Vega was saying, gripping the arms of the command seat.

"Confirmation calculations are going through, Captain," one of her navigation team said over his shoulder. "Just adjusting and checking the precaluclations."

"Altitude: five thousand metres, and we're falling faster," announced another member, panic clear on his face.

"Jump confirmed at eight hundred metres," Ashley announced.

"Eight hundred metres?" asked Stephanie Vega, standing up. "From the surface?"

"Cutting it close, aye?" Frost was leaning over the main Tactical station, his resolve shattered.

"It's the best place to open a wormhole on our current trajectory," Ashley said flatly, her concentration fully on her station. "Fully charged, ready."

The Clever Dream, Sky Queen, Raven, and Sky Stalker were still in the sky, and they each passed the Triton as they started making their way across the planet at a low altitude. They wouldn't be jumping with the Triton or on their own. It was less risky to evade fire from above until they were out of the Order ship's range, make their way to space and then jump safely, conventionally. "Do not crash my ship," Jake said over the mission channel.

It was a slip, one of those rare moments where Jake's filter broke down and alarm forced a comment he normally wouldn't share. As if in response, the Triton's hull glowed, a thing that didn't normally happen because it never jumped outside of an atmosphere. They jumped. The blackness of space seemed to envelop them as a gust of air dissipated around the ship. They were in orbit, a hemisphere away from the Order ships. "Collision alert!" shouted the youngest member of the team at the helm.

"Can't evade," Ashley said.

"Shields are spotty, we're going to make contact with bare hull on this," Finn announced.

The Triton rotated, thrust sideways, and then collided with a long cargo train that wrapped around its port side. "Locking guns onto the first link in that cargo train so we can cut the hauler free," Frost said.

"Good idea, it'll be their only chance at surviving this," Captain Vega said, still wide-eyed and tense.

A turret on the gunnery deck on the dorsal side of the ship fired and the hauler ship was cut free from its train. It was sent spinning through space, and Ronin saw that it was already trying to stabilise behind the Triton, its containers tumbling after it. "We didn't have time to account for a few things when we plotted that jump," Ashley said.

"You mean like what Navnet said about what we'd find at our destination?" asked Kadri, more terrified than outraged.

"Well, we accounted for really big stuff," Ashley said.

"We got a couple new scratches," Finn announced. "Nothing that won't buff out."

"So glad. How are we for TDT?" Captain Vega asked Finn.

TDT was short for trans-dimensional transit, and Ronin hoped the Triton had at least one drive left. "Barely good. We burned out enough backup drives to make every trade captain in the galaxy cry a river. Main drive is ready and we have three backups, but I want to let those cool down."

Ronin was relieved. If they couldn't jump the Order would be able to catch them within the hour. They could out thrust, and overtake the Triton easily if it had to stay in orbit or break and run without a faster than light solution. "Whenever you're ready, helm," Captain Vega said.

Silence descended on the bridge. Ronin re-checked the status of every fighter. Only Easy and Maid were missing. Five of them had affixed to the outer hull of the Triton, the rest landed in the main bays with the shuttles. He resisted the temptation to look through the list of people they lifted off of Rodus. It wasn't time yet. There was a chance they'd have to launch again and defend the Triton.

"We are a go, jumping now," Ashley announced, forgoing the formality of a countdown. A whirl of blue and black surrounded the ship and seconds later they emerged several thousand kilometres to the port side of the Merciless, on the edge of the solar system.

THIRTY-ONE

Hangar Two

"DAME TAKES the prize with eleven kills," said Raver over the Samurai Squadron channel, who sounded astonished at the numbers. He skipped to the top of the list because Maid was right behind her, tied with Ronin with nine enemy fighters shot down. Breaker and Carnie were tied for the next highest with seven. The rest of the Samurai Squadron pilots took out at least three each.

Who was on top didn't matter to Ronin. The mission was to extract as many of their allies from Rodus as they could, and they managed to cover five corvettes and many shuttles as they extracted their people from two cities - Panda and Barlen. Panda was marked as City 35 on his tactical map and the mission details. "Welcome home," came the sweet voice of Ashley in his ear.

"Thank you, it's good to be back," he replied from his cockpit. He set his fighter down in one of the Triton's hangars, seeing the confirmation that his wheels were centered on the elevator pad. They affixed to the metal as it drew him up into the ship. The pad flipped over and locked into place, revealing a busy hangar with deck crewmembers working all around him. It was crowded, the Raven was rising up near the distant aft end of the working hangar. Thick arms were already coming down from the ceiling to pull several damaged armour panels off the top of the vessel as another set of arms got ready to place new ones on. The scrap would be cleaned up, inspected, and then put into a chemical bath that would accelerate their regeneration. When they were restored to new condition they'd go back into service, armouring some other vehicle that used a similar hull.

The rear hatch of the Raven opened and large containers were pushed out onto the deck. With a word from Remmy, a pair of workers led a few of his crewmembers to the large lift that would take whatever was in those floating boxes to storage. Remmy didn't go with them, returning to the ramp of the Raven instead.

Members of the deck crew were rushing to the fighters closer to Ronin, where they scanned the ships and started removing heavily damaged parts so they could be replaced. "It sounds like your head is still in the mission," Ashley said over their private channel. "What's up?"

Ronin took another look at the tactical map. The rest of the Clever Class Corvettes were about to return to the Triton, the shuttles were already unloading. Each one of them had at least one of those cargo containers that were of a rounded shape

Ronin didn't recognize, but he decided to ask about them later. It could definitely wait.

On his tactical map he could see that three Order of Eden destroyers were fighting to stay in orbit and losing thanks to the damage the Merciless and the Triton did to them during their medium-range gunfight. The Locon was in fair shape, its long hull barely scarred, but there was significant damage to its heavy turrets. The Fairlight and the matching heavy cruiser, the Godfrey had taken much more damage to its weapons and were sporting long scars crossing their hulls. If the Triton and Merciless were allowed to use antimatter in the fight, those Order ships would have been lost entirely. Only three of the dozen corvettes that were tasked with providing extra cover for the enemy battlegroup were still flying, and they were staying close to the main formation. The Merciless' fighter squadron had showed their skill, only losing three as they covered the Merciless and the Triton, taking most of those smaller Order ships out.

This was already a victory, and the trap Ronin and everyone else who was in on planning the rescue expected never sprung. There was no sign of a base ship or the other two Order of Eden battlegroups that were within ten light years of Rodus. "Minh?" asked Ashley. "You're looking at the ships above Rodus, aren't you?"

Ronin gave her all her attention as he watched the busy deck around him. The three skitters that always helped service his ship came walking along on several thin legs, their shells were polished to a shine. "Their squadron is practically gone, and they're in position above City Thirty-Five."

"They're staying close together so one ship can move to

cover another as their shields recharge," Ashley agreed. "Slick and I were just talking about that."

"They let you leave the Helm?" Ronin asked as his canopy opened. Normally he'd get out of his fighter as it was moved off the platform into a servicing bay, but he let his skitters, which were small but deceptively strong, roll his ship with him in it.

"My team is on break, Beta Team is taking the controls because we're in the garbage cloud," she replied. "It's amazing how much junk the miners left out here, you could hide a hundred Tritons before you even get to the real asteroid field."

"So, we're getting better than expected cover," Ronin replied, still looking at the enemy ships in close formation in orbit around Rodus.

"Way better. The junk dust goes on for a couple billion klicks," she said, getting the technical point out of the way before asking the question that was really on her mind. "Are you going out again?"

"You see this?" Jake asked seconds after the Clever Dream, Sky Queen, and Sky Stalker finished their jump across the solar system. They were millions of kilometres away, entering the asteroid field further away so they wouldn't reveal the Triton's location. "They're in a diamond formation, licking their wounds. I see repair drones moving around."

"Are we sure there are no other Order ships within response range?" Remmy asked over the same channel.

"Nothing's showing up, and we did a number on those heavy cruisers," Oz said from the bridge of the Merciless. "They're ready to go into a stacked formation, in case we attack from extreme range."

"That's why they're staying so close together, I see it, but it leaves them open for a major strike and fade, right? That's what everyone's talking about?" Breaker asked as he got out of his cockpit and walked over to Ronin's.

"But why aren't they moving around the planet? Motion would make them a harder target to hit," Pixie asked, doing the same. "We should hit 'em. Just jump in with all our firepower and..."

"The Triton's taken major damage and our drives are still cooling down," Captain Vega said on the strategic channel.

"My wing has two heavily damaged corvettes and the Merciless has lost two emitter arrays," Oz said from the bridge of his ship. "That leaves half my aft section with a bare hull, no energy shielding, and our main guns are out of commission. The Order has upgraded their ships since we defeated them in the Haven System, and they did a hell of a job. I'm not one to sour a victory, but this one cost us."

"How long until the British Alliance gets here? The Nafal-li?" asked Jake.

"Last update says two point one days, and five point six," Captain Vega replied. "How long does your intelligence say the Order will need to get a major battlegroup here?"

"Less than two days, but there could be several major capital ships patrolling the asteroid belts. Those could get to Rodus in an hour or less if they jump, and everything points to a base ship being in the solar system already. It could have run off, but I doubt it," Jake said. "I agree with Pixie. We should hit 'em. We offload our passengers and take the corvettes for one hard strike and fade."

"Damn right," Remmy agreed.

"We've got the firepower to break at least one of those heavy cruisers," Alice said. "They may not do much damage if we retreat before they can get their shit together."

"The most recent intelligence I have says Bion's on the Fairlight," Jake said, adding; "There's something else. Something big. I've got a tracker on Vollis Mikan. He's on his way up from the planet. It looks like his shuttle got lost in the tunnels on his way out, but he's vertical now."

"What?" asked Ronin.

"Holy shit, is that why you tried to stuff your hand down his throat when you..." Remmy asked.

"Yeah. I got him with three trackers."

"One for them to find, one for us to follow, and another just in case that one fails," Captain Vega said, and everyone could hear that she was grinning.

"Glad you remember that part of my playbook. Two don't react unless we scan on specific frequencies, the other one's active. I'd like to track him back to a Citadel ship, but I'll take him out sooner if we can. I want to capture him if I can," Jake explained. He was speaking quickly, clearly. He had the sound of someone who was concentrating on at least two things at once.

"So, this won't be a strike and fade. This is a boarding action," Remmy said.

"What if it's the fastest boarding action in history? You know what you want, you'll know where to find him, and we have two corvettes with the right loadout to drop troops through a hull," Ronin said, seeing that the Clever Dream and the Raven both had maxjacks.

"We also have soldiers with self propelling heavy armour," Ruby Sima added. "I think I could find some volunteers."

"Vollis and any other commander will probably head to the Locon, it's in the best shape," Jake said, a hint of dark determination creeping into his tone.

"So we disable it," Ronin said. "We have stacks of EMP missiles." He got out of his fighter and raised his hand towards David, who was looking his fighter over. A gesture told him that his guns were to be reloaded. He used his command and control bracer to change the loadout of his fighter, adding a missile pod filled with Shield Breaker missiles.

David acknowledged the instructions, passed the instructions on to two deck crew members then set out at a run, following a green line that appeared at his feet. The line indicated not only where he would find the missile pod, but showed everyone along his route to get out of his way as it directed him around hazards. "I'd like to volunteer if there's a fighter for me," Ashley said.

"Denied. You're going to be within twenty metres of the helm for the next twenty hours, Ash," Captain Vega said.

"Hell, I'd like to volunteer, but I'm a lousy flier and our engineering folks are still redesigning the power armour," Frost added. "Tear 'em up, I'll be there on the next one."

"So, how much support are we getting from Samurai Squadron?" asked Alice. The Clever Dream rose up on an elevator, her gunners were still in place, and Ronin could see Woone through the forward turret. The young Nafalli looked excited, ready for a fight.

The rear ramp and both the smaller crew ramps on the port and starboard sides lowered. Ronin watched as Theodore led the crewmembers that had been lifted off Rodus out, they were all in sealed vacsuits, and some were in full armour. "We're all coming. We've simulated a strike like this, only the Order's ships weren't as damaged. We have to be ready for support to respond. This has got to be quick. We're going to need at least three of the reserve fighters. A few of our birds took some damage."

Breaker and Pixie nearly trampled Carnie and Gren as they turned and ran for their fighters. "We're going back out," Breaker said to them as he passed. "Reload, check your ships."

"One more kick at the can," Carnie said, grinning. "Hell yeah."

"Ronin," Ashley said. It was unusual for her to use his call-sign, but it was a strategic channel, so it made sense. What really made the hair on his arms try to stand up was her tone. It sounded like she was about to warn him about something critically important, and there was an uncharacteristic note of anger beneath. "The Order ships are turning their main guns towards the planet. They're going to fire on Panda."

There was silence for a moment, and then Jake said; "As soon as Vollis and his people are finished evacuating the tunnels, I bet they'll start firing. The Order are about to punish them for helping us."

"No. We can't let that happen," Ronin said, rushing to help the deck crew reload his fighter by getting to a compartment and popping it open. "Can you see if there are planetary defences?"

"Panda only has defensive shielding. The orbital and terrestrial planetary defences are still powered down," Dame replied. "My fighter is almost reloaded. I'll be docking to the Raven."

"Are you really planning on going after Vollis, Jake?" Ruby asked. "Don't tease me."

"If I can get to him," Jake replied. "Either way, I want to get aboard whatever ship he's on."

"Then I'm volunteering for the boarding team," she said. Dozens, then over a hundred of her crewmembers checked in. "I'm not alone. We're already loaded onto the corvettes."

"We launch in ten minutes," Jake said. "Vollis is about to dock on the Locon, so that's our target. The rest of our attack will focus on taking this battlegroup down. If support pops in, we get out."

"I like that plan. We've got to refine it a bit though, so I'm taking a few minutes with the Squadron," Ronin said as he turned and pulled the decoy reload hatch cover.

David patted him on the shoulder. He was already returning with a cart laden with missiles on the bottom and the pod they'd go into on top. "Concentrate on managing your people, we'll do our job and make sure your bird's checked and ready, Sir," he told him.

"All right, thank you, David," Ronin replied with a fist bump. He ran through the hatch that would take him to the nearby ready room as he started rechecking the status of every fighter. His pilots were checking their own birds out. He'd know how many people he had ready for the attack soon.

The deck shuddered under foot slightly and he looked over his shoulder. A large, twisted armour plate had been cut away from the bottom of the Clever Dream's frame. It was still wobbling on the deck. He took a moment to watch as articulated struts put fresh armour plates into place and robotic arms descended with fresh missiles, reloading them into the ship's dorsal launchers.

"We have been itching for this fight," Ronin said to himself. The strategy channel was still open and there were whoops, cheers and every kind of enthusiastic agreement, even from Ashley, who said; "Go get 'em!"

THIRTY-TWO

The Coward Itch

VOLLIS MIKAN'S armoured shuttle had become cramped. The simple matter of escaping the tunnels in the first available ship had become much more complicated. Whether it was because of a rare moment of guilt, or sympathy for the soldiers he was leaving behind, Vollis couldn't and wouldn't say, but the ship was filled from hatch to hatch. He was in a small seat at the back of a cockpit that was meant for a pilot, copilot, and two more tiny people behind them.

As Vollis left Rodus, he was able to save face by rescuing several squads of troops that were in the tunnels beneath its surface. Yes, 'rescue' was a term he decided to use often to describe that act even though the soldiers would have most likely been fine if they were left to run out on their own, they weren't close enough to the major collapse to be in real danger. There had to be a way to salvage his honour, even after he abandoned over a thousand to die in cavern collapses.

Vollis wasn't a large man, most assassins were lean and short, and he was designed to fit easily into that mould. The blue sky was giving way to stars, the black and glimmering hulls in the distance. They were keeping close together in a diamond formation directly above Panda. He wondered why they hadn't moved on before his focus returned to the moment.

Going back, digging down for the survivors and the buried technology was something he'd make a case for. He could turn it around, and be more like a rescuer than a coward. A thought came to him then. This was the kind of political manoeuvring that he'd heard of Order of Eden officers making when they failed.

He shifted in the hard seat and closed his face plate. The smell of the soldiers behind, like loamy earth and sweat, was thickening the air. *I didn't have a choice. I had to leave so someone could survive that catastrophe. Beyond all that, I shouldn't have been put in charge of a large force at all. I've never been trained to lead multitudes on the ground, but a small group of three, ten at the most. The rest of my training concerns large starships, which isn't the same as a terrestrial force. This isn't my fault, I was put on this course so I could fail. This was Leader Gideon's attempt at making me feel low, and I won't give them the satisfaction.* He thought to himself as the copilot got clearance to dock with the Locon and the shuttle neared a port on the bottom of the hull.

There was political manoeuvring going on. The Order was

trying to show that Citadel commanders were just as fallible, and it was starting with him. If there was one thing he learned from some of the older Citadel commanders that they probably didn't want him to know, it was that conspiracy was commonplace, and if you weren't careful, you'd be the last one to know about them. That could be lethal.

As the shuttle coupled with the mooring point, Vollis' communicator went off in his ear. He accepted the call and was surprised when he heard Leader Gideon's voice. "I'm pleased to see you made it out of that cavern. You are a survivor, and that's an admirable trait. An especially critical thing right now."

Guilt at being the first to fly out of danger, leaving everyone behind, and irritation at his commanding officer for putting him there in the first place mingled. Neither were as significant as the shame he felt at how his encounter with the fake Jake ended, with his jaw clenched in an armoured hand and him looking for anyone who could help as he beat a hasty retreat. Being defeated by an empty suit of armour was the worst of his failures. He forced it all as far from his surface thoughts as he replied; "I had to retreat in order to mount a rescue after things settled."

"The Order will or won't see to their people as they see fit. It is their mess to clean up," Leader Gideon replied. "I need you to speak to Bion. Discover his next steps. Keep it brief. You only have a few minutes. Echiss is predicting that our enemies are about to take revenge on the Order ships orbiting Rodus. Do not Warn them."

"Why shouldn't I? They're our allies," Vollis asked warily.

"Citadel wants to see what they have in reserve. The suspicion is that there are more Order ships hiding in the Rose System other than the Messenger. It is uncharacteristic of them to let a base ship move off alone, without at least a battle group for support. You will not signal that we expect Bion's group to be attacked. Instead, you will listen to him and then take command of the Dawa. It's in Hangar three of the Locon. That is the secure aft hangar. You will launch and bring it to the Citadel fleet in the Rose System as soon as possible. This is an armoured jump ship carrying cargo that was just delivered by our spies aboard the Locon. Do not let Order personnel aboard."

"Doesn't it have crewmembers of its own?" Vollis asked as he reached up and unlocked the hatch over his head. He pulled himself through a narrow airlock, closing the door behind him, then passed into a broad hall with many similar hatches in the floor.

"It is a small ship. The occupants locked it, left, and changed their identities so they could covertly become part of the Locon's crew. We are increasing the number of hidden eyes in their fleet. More to the point, I've given you all the access codes that you'll need for the Dawa. I look forward to seeing you shortly."

There was nothing about his failure underground. His superiors didn't seem to care at all. There was something else going on, something much more important. As Vollis inwardly scolded himself for losing focus, letting himself get distracted by honour and the losses of a lesser ally, an Order of Eden cultist in a simple uniform emerged from a side door. "Sir? Are you Captain Vollis Mikan, Sir?" he asked nervously.

"Yes," Vollis said as he retracted his faceplate.

"Leader Bion asked me to take you to him, Sir," the young cultist said. "Please?"

"Show me the way," Vollis said. As he followed the young recruit through the corridors, up a lift and then to a command room, he observed how the soldiers and crewmembers regarded him. There were stares, dropped jaws, averted gazes and the regular reactions to seeing a Citadel Assassin in person.

The story tattooed on his face was often enough to shock people. Some saw it as a disfigurement, others a mystery, but to the few who could read them, they would learn that he was a true warrior of his people. The latest section of the tattoo proclaimed that he killed a king and his relations. Another would declare that he'd led a great ship in several victories, and then there were the slightly jagged lines running down his chin. Every joint represented a specific kill, and there were exactly seventeen of them. Only Vollis' superiors knew who they were.

Finally, they arrived at a command room that was a long rectangle with cubicles along the sides where people worked at information systems. In the middle was a long table that matched the green and white colours of the space. It was sparse and garish to him. Vollis couldn't wait to leave.

"I have orders that take me elsewhere, Leader Bion, but I wanted to pay my respects before departing," Vollis said, his confidence inflating. Showing his face to people who recognized that they were regarding something rare and intimidating always made him feel more like himself.

With amusement in his eyes, Bion invited him to the head of the table so they could look at a holographic map of Panda and the area around it. "Well, I'm honoured that you could give me a minute of your time."

"Are rescue efforts underway?" Vollis asked, looking for Order ships in the atmosphere.

Bion laughed and shook his head. "No, I've lost nearly two fighter squadrons today along with nine corvettes. Anyone we have underground has been given map markers to run to. They'll make their way out of the tunnels as best as they can. I have a message for you to pass on to your superiors, unless your work takes you out of the system?"

"I will be speaking to my superiors again soon," Vollis replied, making sure he avoided answering whether or not he'd remain in the Rose System.

"Good. This saves me a call. Leader Gideon likes to make me wait. Tell them that our meeting with Rodus' current president didn't go well. He's threatened to declare war if we attack any of his territories."

"I'll pass that on. Who met with him?" Vollis asked.

"I was honoured to make this visit myself. Eve was occupied elsewhere," Bion replied. He turned all his attention back to the map and gave his people an order. "Begin the bombardment. I want to see a smoking crater right there in fifteen minutes."

"There is important technology beneath Panda. The kind that could advance us a hundred years," Vollis said.

"How? There are nothing but factories and slums beneath that city. Even the footage my soldiers sent from the caves just show some kind of old, overbuilt reactor," Bion countered before looking to a man in a shiny dark green helmet at the other end of the table. "Make that city gone."

"As the ranking Citadel officer on this ship, I forbid you to attack that target," Vollis said, not raising his voice, but pointing at the officer.

"Go ahead, he doesn't have any power here," Bion said with a sigh.

It was true. Officially, Vollis wasn't there to represent Citadel, and their alliance allowed each side to act on their own. He watched as the three largest ships in the formation above Panda - the Locon, Fairlight and Godfrey - fired large missiles and then began shelling the city below. The rumble of large cannons faintly echoed up to the command room. "This will send a different message to my people."

"Don't you have orders to pick up something you left on my ship?" Bion asked without regarding Vollis.

For a moment, Vollis considered the map and what was about to be lost. His options were few in that situation. He'd already tried pulling rank on Bion, and he shouldn't have expected that to work. Stepping back and trying to reason with him would take time that he didn't have, and it probably wouldn't work either. There were obvious signs that the construction of Bion's personality included a thick streak of determination, some would even call him stubborn. He could kill Bion and try to assume control of his fleet, but Vollis guessed that there were wolves amongst his flock. Crewmembers who would fight for the Order, and do anything to kill him for taking out their Leader. It wouldn't help the Citadel's alliance with the Order, either. "You're right, I will board my ship and depart," Vollis said with a final nod as he watched the first of the fast, large missiles impact Panda's shield. It was already on the verge of failing.

As Vollis left the command centre, he decided to consider the advantage of the atrocity. Whatever shame he felt at abandoning the soldiers down there would be buried under the remains of that city. The Order would be known for destroying an unarmed civilian target because they allowed the enemy passage. It was petty and cruel. Whatever cultural conquest the deceased Admiral Scanlon once worked towards would become nearly impossible, but Vollis Mikan's legacy still had a chance.

THIRTY-THREE

Space Superiority

IT SEEMED to take far too long for his pilots to affix their ships to the Clever Dream, Raven, Sky Queen, and Sky Stalker. The four Clever Class Corvettes had finally made it into space outside of the Triton and were getting ready for the quick jump across the solar system. It had been less than three minutes since they were all free of the hangars. It would be fine if it took ten minutes for the eleven fighters to attach to them. "I am the stone in the sea, the immovable calm in the storm," Ronin said in an effort to dismiss his impatience. The problem was that there was little left to say. They'd gone through the briefing for the mission they were about to undertake, and everyone - including the crews of the Corvettes - knew what they were tasked with. They were also aware of the known challenges, risks, when to with-draw, and what their critical as well as their secondary objectives were. It was all thanks to the various simulations they'd tested themselves on. The mission they were about to undertake closely resembled more than one of them, and it gave every pilot or captain a point of reference.

Ronin already had twenty minutes to run through all those details while people tuned into the briefing channel. Jake was doing the same with the four boarding teams they were delivering. They benefited from the same virtual experiences using real details about the enemy, their equipment and ships that Samurai Squadron's pilots did, perhaps even more.

It didn't feel like anything new. In fact, it felt like their process of preparation was getting back to basics for Ronin. If it weren't for realistic combat simulations on Freeground Station, especially the ones developed for the military, he and his friends wouldn't have been tapped to serve in the fleet. That was really where his adventures began for better or worse.

The simulations weren't where Ronin learned to fly, but they were definitely where he became a good fighter pilot. Using similar full-dive sims to train every member of their new fleet made perfect sense. Remembering those early simulated adventures back on Freeground brought his thoughts to Ayan, who once went by the name 'Sunspot.'

Somewhere in the Haven System, she was undergoing surgery, or in recovery. Her face was clear in his mind, and he could feel the ember of anger that threatened to rage and start an inferno in his heart. The attack they were about to engage in wasn't about revenge, however. Ayan wasn't perfect, but she would resist the urge to lash out in simple retaliation, so he made sure he did the same. The ember could smoulder on its own until it was smothered by the relief of seeing her, a woman who was as much a sister as his biological sisters, safe and healthy.

He checked on Jake's command channel and saw that he was still speaking, so he joined it. "...intelligence."

"So, we're not there to get hands-on with the computer hardware this time?" asked Roscoe, a member of Remmy's crew aboard the Raven.

"Our team will be jacking in," Remmy continued. "We don't need access to any of their core systems. Just like the sims, the Raven Team will tap into their wired network and use the intelligence we already have to get the job done."

"Ah, so a door panel will do," Mayu, one of his crewmembers, asked.

"Exactly," Jake said. "The Locon is the most heavily crewed ship, and it has a section we couldn't get any information on that includes a hangar in the aft section. That's why the squad sims had most teams going in that direction. Everyone has a full map of the ship, but that's the one section that no one can guarantee details on."

"So, two teams are going aboard for a quick shot at finding out what they're hiding, got it. What are you going to be up to?" Ruby asked.

"Hunting Vollis and other members of command along with my team," Alice replied.

"It looks like Bion is aboard, but we can't be sure," Jake added. "We are certain that Vollis is there, so that's our real target."

"How long do we have aboard again?" Remmy asked.

He knew. Everyone in Samurai Squadron and in the boarding teams knew, but Ronin understood why Remmy was asking. Several voices answered at once, driving the time limit home for anyone who may not yet understand that it was core to their mission. "Fifteen minutes."

"All right, so run and gun, oh, what fun," Ruby said with a dangerous kind of enthusiasm.

"All right, we're all attached to the corvettes," Carnie announced.

"My Squadron is ready," Ronin announced on the general combat channel.

The corvette captains: Alice, Remmy, Alaka and Gabe Vernor all checked in. and Jake finally said; "Get in formation and make the jump. The Sky Queen has the countdown."

After only five seconds, space warped and split in front of the four fast gunships and after a momentary flash of blue light, they were back in orbit around Rodus. So close, in fact, that all he could see was the blue-grey planet below in every direction. Their targets were right below them, only three thousand ten kilometres beneath. "Detach and split up. You know your targets."

"Popping off now, Wing Commander," Breaker acknowledged. He'd been put in charge of Blue Group, consisting of Rip, Gren and Garma.

"Detatching and starting our run now," Shep reported back. He'd been given Maid's group, which had come down to him Scythe and Crashrabbit. They would have the Sky Stalker's momentary support before they launched their troopers, and then after.

With trust in his pilots, Ronin let his fighter drift free from the Clever Dream's hull and turned the nose of his ship towards the Locon. A brilliant ball of light winked past it on the planet surface. He didn't have to check his tactical system to see what it was, or where it was. "That's Panda. They've nuked Panda," Carnie said in shock. "Their shield is down."

The Locon's hull shuddered, and her dorsal thrusters pulsed in time with the largest of their turreted cannons as they fired down at the helpless city. "Let's give the Locon something more important to point her guns at," Dame said with dangerous determination.

As practiced, Ronin, Dame, Pixie and Carnie started accelerating with a jolt. Markers on Ronin's display and a tone in his helmet told him that he had missile locks on nine of the ship's main emitters. "Firing a full volley," he said, hearing everyone in Green Group say the same like a chorus. Eighteen missiles took flight from each of the four fighters. The furious light from their rocket engines shrank quickly as they crossed the distance between them and the Locon's shields. Point defence guns were quick enough to catch several, but it wasn't enough.

The missiles were fired at far too close range, and there were too many at once too soon after they jumped into the area. The massive ship was still waking up, her defence systems weren't all pointed in their direction yet.

Ronin's Green Group flipped their ships end over end and engaged their afterburners seconds before the electromagnetic pulse missiles started going off right above the Locon. They'd made it past the very edge of the critical range of their munitions. Sensors glitched, screens and the tactical map in Ronin's head went blank except for a scroll of text that repeated:

OVERLOAD... NULL RESULT... RESET... RECALIBRATING...

Each missile was capable of delivering an electromagnetic

pulse equivalent to that of a quarter gigaton nuclear blast, and if their systems worked properly, they'd each do it three times before they exploded using a conventional chemical compound. It was that series of over forty pops that Ronin and his wing-mates saw when their sensors came back to life and started feeding them data. The Locon's shields were down. "And that's why you don't let fighters anywhere near your heavy cruisers!" Pixie cheered.

"Fighter agility, fighter speed, fighter power," Dame said in grim agreement.

Another set of flashes went off then, it was the Fairlight, which had been struck by Shep's Grey Group, including the Sky Stalker. A few seconds later, the Godfrey was surrounded by the electromagnetic flash on Ronin's tactical map. There was nothing to see with the naked eye, and he always thought that was a little strange. If they didn't have scanners to tell them that dozens of pulses were going off, then there would be no way to know.

"That's all three Heavy Cruisers with no shields," Breaker said. "Drop your missile pods and follow me, Blue Group."

"The Godfrey will be destroyed," Garma added.

Ronin's Group dropped their empty missile pods, sending them tumbling past the Locon, where they'd burn up in the atmosphere. "Taking out Emitter Series One," he announced, lining his railguns up with his first target, a number of rods that ran along the hull in a protective recess that would be critical in projecting energy shielding if the crew of that ship got it working again. He sent a burst down at his target and watched as it came apart in chunks.

"Primary communications array," Carnie said, marking the

cluster of oval dishes and antennae near the front of the ship. He struck armour plating that protected the base of the towers that pointed forward and damaged his target. Another two bursts were enough to flick a thick armour plate away then shear the whole assembly from the ship. "Nice! Took it clean off!" Pixie laughed. Then, more seriously, she added, "After Near Field Combat Detector System One, taking fire."

The anti-fighter guns had started reacting, and she was crossing over the front of the Locon's broad hull, giving half a dozen of them a clear shot. Before Ronin could advise her, Pixie thrust towards the hull, gave a burst at one of the gunnery posts and then strafed above the panels and rotating dishes that made up much of the Locon's sensor suite. The gun turret she blasted had thirty or so new holes in it, and it pointed into space, pointlessly firing a stream of energy bolts. The sensor dishes and detector panels were ripped to shreds by her strafing attack. If Ronin was chewing gum, he would have swallowed it in shock at what she did next.

Under attack from several other turrets, her shields fading fast, Pixie rotated her fighter with a jerk and then hit her afterburners, crossing the dorsal side of the Locon at such close range that she left scorch marks across some of its armour plating. "Getting outta there, took damage to gun three and thruster two," Pixie announced.

Ronin fired at a large turret ahead, putting holes in the cannonhouse, activating something inside that made it spin erratically. He made sure that Pixie was out of relative danger, and saw that her shields were recharging quickly as she skirted the port edge of the ship's hull, too close and fast for the guns to get a good shot at her.

"Good work, Pixie," Dame said before anyone else could. "I have destroyed Detection and Scanner Array Two, they are almost blind."

The Clever Dream swept in, her retro-thrusters flaring hard, giving the ship the appearance of a metallic dragon with fiery nostrils coming in for the attack. Its large, main railgun cannons let loose with three shots as its turrets turned, a gunner in each of the seven posts taking the opportunity to fire at larger turrets, missile bays that were still under cover, and the small dorsal launch bay doors. The main railgun shots punched through the Locon's armour, taking out its navigation sensors and the last of its long range communications abilities.

Every automated gun on the ship stopped firing, which accounted for most of its point defences. The regular shudder of the ship ceased as its main guns stopped blasting Panda. A few turrets still rotated, firing after the Clever Dream and fighters in Green Group. "Take out every gunner you can find," Ronin said as he suffered a blast from a pulse cannon, losing twenty-one percent of his shield integrity. "This one's mine," he evaded then rotated, pointing his guns at the gun behind and below him. He was so close that he could see the two man turret crew scramble to drop down the ladder leading into their capsule before he blasted it with a burst from his five guns. The turret's transparesteel windows warped and flew to pieces, and the projection systems that turned power into blasts of destructive energy was torn apart.

Ronin quietly praised the accuracy of his guns as he saw that the gunnery team were left almost completely unharmed. One made it down the neck of the turret, and he helped his fellow, who was gripping a stump above the elbow where his suit sealed, down into the passage. He didn't know if he would have felt anything about killing the pair of them, but seeing the gunnery team make it out after he'd accomplished his goal didn't make him feel worse. They were still escaping at a frenzied speed when he rotated away and went after the next gun. He idly hoped the pair wouldn't run into any of the boarding teams.

THIRTY-FOUR

Incursion

PARTS OF PANDA and its sublevels were collapsing. The nuclear blast that took their bombardment shield down wasn't the last shot. The Locon launched more than one volley of shells down onto the city afterwards. The Fairlight and Godfrey had just stopped firing, and it was too late for Panda. Remmy had a zoomed-in view from orbit, where he took a long moment to watch as some of Panda's tallest buildings started to topple, the ground cracked, and holes gradually widened as supports hidden beneath the top level failed.

Ships, hovercars and people on foot rushed from the city as the first sections crumbled. The video feed was running in a small window in his view, which was projected directly into his eyes using an implant hidden in the bridge of his nose. It demanded most of his attention, but he had other things to concentrate on, so he shut it down.

He was sure there wouldn't be much of Panda and the surrounding area left when he checked later. He finished lowering down to the main hold of the Raven using the smallest lift and regarded one of his boarding crewmembers, Mayu. An expression of sympathy on her face when she saw him warned Remmy that he wasn't exactly hiding how he felt about the city or how it was becoming more certain all the time that Simon's psyche storage, if it survived, would be entombed, well out of reach. "Are you all right, Sir?"

Behind her was Frost's nephew, Nigel, who reminded him of himself when he was younger, still an analyst and tech specialist with Freeground Fleet. Roscoe and Tammy, who was Ashley's twin turned towards him as well. They were his excursion team for the moment, and all their eyes were on him. They'd trained on the Raven using time compression simulations, and he'd worked with them to make sure that they could function as a unit.

They didn't know him well, though, so much of their focus had been on becoming a skilled small squad, and that would serve them on the mission. He decided to spend more time with them after the mission as he steeled himself for what was coming. "Get a look at the Raven's exterior feed," he said, doing so himself.

The hold of the Raven was filled with soldiers, most of them from Ruby's crew, and they overheard his suggestion, most of them dedicated part of their displays to it. They were just in time to see the Raven, Clever Dream, Sky Queen and Sky Stalker slip into position in front of the main starboard side hangar doors of the Locon. They let loose with their heavy rail-guns all at once, battering the thick hull plating at first, turning it into a dented, thick mess of twisted metal.

The armour wasn't made to take that kind of focused, sustained fire, but after several seconds of pounding, the two-metre-thick doors burst apart, sending shreds and chunks of metal into the ship and outward. The big main guns stopped. Every turret on the Clever Class Corvettes went to work then, the smaller guns pushing larger chunks of debris out of the way as well as firing past them, into the large hangar.

Defence turrets within the hangar, operated by soldiers in heavy armour, turned and tried to fire at the corvettes, but were soon cut down by the gunners as they cleared all opposition inside. "Clear, clear, rush the ship!" came the order from Jacob Valent from the Sky Queen.

The Raven's broad rear ramp flapped down rapidly, throwing one soldier who was leaning on it out into space. One of his fellows laughed and said; "Told ya not to stand so close, buddy!" over encrypted proximity radio.

The soldier pinwheeled away for a few seconds before another flew out and caught him by the leg. Remmy's small team accelerated out of the hold after Ruby's troops, who joined her group as they rushed the ship. "I see a data port," Nigel said as they cleared the Raven. He marked it on the tactical display, showing that it was on the aft wall of the hangar. The Raven's aft hatch closed and it started moving off.

"For the Queen," someone said over proximity radio, and the channel was flooded with people repeating the phrase or adding their own war cry until it crackled and cut out intermittently for several long moments.

Remmy's team was in a perfect position to see the boarding teams in heavy armour, flying into the hangar in one charge led by Jake, Alice, and Ruby. The thrill of it almost made him forget why they were there. Remmy opened a laser link channel with his team. "Move to that port as fast as you can."

As his group of five flew between spinning chunks of debris, cannon fire from one of the other heavy cruisers passed near the hangar. "Three troopers down!" Ruby announced over the tactical channel.

"Get in there!" Jake called out, highlighting the deepest part of the hangar.

Another volley proved to be less accurate, burying a few shells in the top of the Locon's hull but taking one more of Ruby's soldiers out completely. When the shell from a capital ship struck someone in armour, only the luckiest of creatures could survive. It was a matter of scale, velocity and mass. Only being lucky enough to be grazed the slightest amount could save anyone.

"This is Breaker. We're taking those cannons out right now," said the pilot.

"Hurry the hell up, God dammit!" Ruby replied through clenched teeth.

Remmy and his team decelerated towards the working data panel inside the hangar. Nigel collided with the bulkhead the hardest, his suit protected him, and he was able to affix to the wall beside it. He looked over his shoulder, and Remmy could see that he was wide-eyed, nearly panicking. "We're all right, not much chance of a shell hitting us here," Remmy reassured him. "Just concentrate on getting access."

"Right, yeah, okay, okay," Nigel said as he pulled a thin

sheet from his pocket and flattened it onto the whole rectangular access panel with one sweep of his hand. He rubbed it a few times and nodded. The sheet was made to use captured records to fake biometric readings of all kinds - fingerprints, fluids, and body scans - and it also provided a data link to his teams' suits. "The hack film's on, and I'm trying for Command Level access."

"Don't worry, stretch, we've got your back," Mayu said as she watched the hangar, brandishing a rifle that was at least two-thirds her unsuited height. She wasn't the smallest boarding team specialist he'd ever seen, but she wasn't far off. Tammy and Roscoe watched the hangar as well.

It was a critical moment, when the other squads would start cutting through doors, hacking data lines and other panels just in case what Remmy's team was doing either didn't work or started taking too long. It was also the moment when his people would either prove themselves by getting everyone access to the ship, or fall on their faces. "Oh, oh there it is."

Agameg floated over. "The crew of the Locon are cutting data lines. We will have to cut our way in."

"No, you won't," Nigel said. "Got access. I am logged in as Senior Commander Lokava. Weird, that's a new rank for the Order. Anyway, every door on the ship is unlocked, all hangar doors are opening up right now."

The relief Remmy felt had many sides. His team had achieved its most important mission and he didn't have to take over for Nigel, who had never hacked an actual Order of Eden Warship of that complexity outside of a simulation before. "I'll buy you a drink later," Agameg said as he activated his cloaking system and pulsed his thrusters towards the nearest hatch.

Most of the doors that opened let out gusts of pressurized gasses along with whatever it could sweep out of the hallways and rooms, including a few unprepared Order crewmembers. "Oops," Roscoe chuckled.

"Giving our commanders control over security countermeasures, robotics, alarms, facilities and surveillance outside of command level three and higher," Nigel said as he worked. "Man, you guys got some amazing intelligence out of Gold Haf. All these codes are just working. They're so fresh. You've gotta let me see the rest of the data you stole when we get back."

The airlock beside them finished opening. Mayu and Roscoe checked it and then started leading the way in. "Burn that film," Remmy said as Nigel disconnected his suit's data line from it.

"Oh, almost forgot, thanks," Nigel said as he activated the destruct function for the access film. A compound was released into the plastic that turned the whole thing into an acid adhesive that not only destroyed itself but the access panel's surface.

"First stop, boss?" Mayu asked as they pushed into the hall.

"We're headed to the smallest area we couldn't get info on," he replied. Red dots flared on his tactical map in a few of the nearby hallways where Jake and Ruby's teams encountered resistance. "We're due for some push-back, get set," he said, making sure that every member of his team had their rifle in hand. "I'm marking our destination as Point Beta," he told them as he selected it for his team. It was one of the sections of the ship that they couldn't get information on through any of their hacks.

Soundlessly, they advanced down the broad hallway, carefully pulsing the thrusters built into their suit until they finally reached a point where the artificial gravity was still working. He nearly toppled, taking a bad step. His suit corrected in time, and Tammy's hand landed on his shoulder, bracing him. "Contact!" Roscoe announced.

A mixed group of Order soldiers in simple green and grey uniforms that could handle vacuum and three heavily armoured troops were running towards them from the forward section of the ship. A pair of grenades were tossed around the corner before Remmy and his group could find cover in hatch alcoves.

Whoever tossed them was either lucky or had a lot of practice, because they bounced, slid and went off right in front of them. Remmy only had enough time to get an idea of what he would do if he had another second to act. There was no time to actually do anything. The pair went off together, blasting Roscoe, Mayu, Tammy and him off their feet as the deck only two metres in front of them was blasted through.

Before Remmy could pick himself up, his tactical system showed that one of his team was firing back. It was Nigel, who was at the rear, providing cover while his team pulled back together. He sent a burst at anyone who peeked around the corner ahead, blasting three light soldiers who were stupid enough to try something by the time Roscoe tossed a palm-sized disc down the hall. It slid to a stop and created a barrier shield that they could fire through, which would protect them from any incoming fire. "Shields down to twelve percent, recharging."

"I've got damage on my left side, but the suit's regenerating and I'm fine," Mayu reported as she got to her feet. "Shields recharging from nine percent."

"Shrapnel, right leg, auto-doc is taking care of it for now,"

Tammy said as she limped back behind Roscoe. "Fine otherwise, the suit's regenerating and I've got shielding already
coming back."

"Order assholes!" Nigel spat as one of the heavily armoured
soldiers at the end of the hallway peeked in. He hit him full in
the face with a burst of rounds - a fantastic shot considering
Nigel didn't have above-average marksmanship. He followed
that with another, catching the soldier as he staggered into the
open and severing his head from his shoulders.

"Took his head clean off!" Roscoe laughed as he tossed one
of Jake's favourite but seldom-used toys down the hall. It was a
twenty-eight centimetre wide disc-shaped drone that flew under
its own power, targeted the enemies who had taken cover at the
end of the hall and fired at them with several pulse lasers.

As soon as it lit the passage up, Remmy ordered; "Charge!"

The squad rushed down the hallway, even Tammy, in
formation with Mayu and Roscoe in the lead. When they got to
the end of the hall, none of the light troopers were left standing,
their uniforms weren't able to defend against pulse weapon fire.
The last two heavily armoured soldiers were firing back at the
drone and were just knocking it down when Remmy and his
group opened fire on them. "Forgot to ask them to surrender,"
he said as they fell with more smouldering holes in their bodies
than he could count.

That made Mayu and Roscoe snicker, and Tammy groan;
"Always a wise-cracker."

"Beta Marker's right down there," Remmy said, almost
taking the lead before remembering that it wasn't his job. Mayu
and Roscoe did so, watching the tactical overlay in their visors
almost as much as the hallway ahead.

"Beta's small. What do you think is in there?" Nigel asked in a whisper. Most soldiers carried their rifles, some brandished them, but he was a member of the least common group. The type that clung to them more like a deadly security blanket.

"Mad scientist shit, I'd bet a week's pay," Mayu said as they came to the thick hatch. There was a warning written on it that read:

CLEARANCE REQUIRED FOR ENTRY
DEADLY FORCE IS AUTHORIZED

"SOME KINDA SECURE AIRLOCK," Nigel said, looking at the door ahead and his command and control unit in turn. "No door panel, but I can open it."

The mission counter was already down to eleven minutes. "Open the outer one," Remmy ordered. He knew what the new technician was doing as he tapped at his left command and control bracer. The security system would only respond to an access request on a certain frequency. They were in a hurry, so he used an override code on all of them at once. It took him only a few seconds, probably thanks to some rushed preparation work before the mission.

The outer airlock door opened to reveal a large vestibular chamber. It was spotless, white and pristine. High-powered scanners were set into the walls to either side, their honeycomb grates reflecting the bright light. He glanced at the scientific analysis, but Tammy was way ahead of him. "These doors are armoured, a metre thick, but there are no special seals or extra preventative measures that you'd see in a lab dealing with disease or nano-tech."

"We need to get in there," Remmy said, seeing that he couldn't detect anything past the inner doors. "Finding out what's in there is our job."

"The outer doors will close when the inner ones open," Nigel replied.

"Crack 'em," Remmy said, finding the edge of his impatience.

Nigel did as he was ordered and the inner doors opened rapidly, separating in the middle, revealing a metre of metal as they retracted into the floor and ceiling. A trio of men in white jumpsuits and helmets layered with a special protective netting regarded them wide-eyed, frozen in shock.

Past them was a thick transparasteel window and through that Remmy saw a man strapped to an X frame that held him upright. "Close the hatch!" one of the men shouted at the rest.

One tried, pressing a large, easy-to-reach red button but the inner hatch didn't do a thing. "There's a command override running," he replied.

Remmy looked through the large window behind the men again and saw that something black and green was gripping the subject's head from behind, encroaching on his mouth, eyes and cheekbones, digging into his skin with thin, fine, bony tendrils that looked like overlong claws. There were bulges and protrusions around his neck, across his shoulders, and down his extremities that suggested that more tendrils had spread there. The growth of a carapace-like chest plate was spreading from his sternum as though it had grown like an infection from that point.

"See? Mad scientist shit," Mayu whispered.

"Destroy the samples!" shouted one of the men.

The furthest man in front of the glass overlooking the scene took a thick key card from where it hung on a line wrapped around his wrist, shoved it into the console in front of him, turned it, and then hurriedly tapped the screen beside it. Remmy was already moving as the chamber beyond the glass was filled with flames.

He nearly bowled Mayu over and knocked Roscoe aside. It was too late to get to the man at the far end, but he caught the one nearest to him before he put his key in. The man in the jumpsuit struggled as Remmy gripped the key card. "You have to delete everything!" shouted the one who activated the cleansing flames.

Tammy was already lunging for the researcher who they'd left alone, but he had already slipped his key into the console. "Don't do it!" she warned, pointing her rifle at him as she bumped him back with her elbow.

He stepped back, staring at the screen, raising his hands. "You don't understand. If we don't get rid of everything, it'll be worse than the Fourth Fall."

"Step back or I'll cut you in half," Tammy threatened, pointing her rifle at him as she moved towards the flashing screen.

The researcher who activated the flames lunged for a touch screen, and Mayu shot him once, passing a round between Remmy and Tammy. The setting she used was meant to break the heaviest armour down and destroy inhuman opponents. It left the man without a left leg and he went down screaming.

The one in Remmy's grasp had stopped struggling, but his

eyes were filled with fear as he pleaded; "You have to let us delete our data. Every mammal in the galaxy will regret it if what we've been doing here gets out. It's Edxi technology, a refined biological domination strategy. One of their commanders brought it with them..."

"Shut up, Daniil!" shouted the other researcher as he held his hands up.

Remmy saw the mission timer drop to eight minutes and he tossed the researcher he held across the room, keeping their access key. He rushed to the terminal that the man Tammy was pointing her rifle at accessed and saw that he was one tap away from deleting an entire data archive. The words on the screen asked;

ARE YOU SURE?
[YES] [NO]

REMMY CAREFULLY TAPPED NO, and saw a normal file management interface pop up. He looked around the terminal for a moment and saw a tiny hole. "Data port. Download everything to an isolated unit," he pointed as he stepped towards the man with his hands up.

Nigel rushed to the terminal and clicked a line into the port then nodded as a small, powerful computer smaller than his middle finger started downloading. "Only three terabytes. The transfer will take about fifteen seconds."

"What was going on in there?" Remmy asked the man with his hands up.

"We were trying to find a way to reverse it," mumbled the

one who was quickly dying of blood loss. He was in shock, turning grey.

"Shut up, god dammit!" the one Remmy had thrown across the room snapped. He regretted that, but there was no time for niceties or subtle interrogation.

"Don't do it," the man with upraised hands said to him then. "Please, I don't want to die, even if it's quick."

The other one pressed a button on his collar, and all three men clad in netted white suits collapsed. "They're dead," Tammy said in surprise. "Hearts stopped, brain functions gone."

"Download done," Nigel said, turning around and regarding the corpses, freezing. "Huh?"

"Delete it. Finish what that guy was doing," Remmy said, moving to the console. It was more instinct than anything. He had an eerie feeling that whatever was on that computer had to be controlled, that it was something he didn't want to leave behind. In a few taps, it was done. The computer screens went black except for a flashing cursor.

"All right, we're moving on," Remmy said, leading the way to the airlock.

"All right!" Roscoe enthused.

"Yes!" Mayu added.

Everyone in his squad knew what that meant. They would help Jake catch Order officers, especially Vollis Mikan.

THIRTY-FIVE

Charging Corridors

THE DECK SHUDDERED underfoot as Remmy's team moved through the corridors of the Locon. Samurai Squadron's pilots were doing their best work, ripping through the undamaged hangars on the opposite side of the ship. An alert on his tactical map informed him that they'd hit a fuel reserve, and the explosion wrecked Hangar Two, the mirror to the large one they'd rushed when they entered the ship.

There were firefights between Ruby's crew and several different types of Order soldiers. They were driving the enemy towards the midsection of the ship. Running and gunning through the halls was leading to something bigger, a confrontation in the primary causeway that ran along the beam from aft to fore. That was where the public transit, cargo and access points to all the main cargo areas of the vessel were. In the dead centre of that was the main hold, and from what Remmy was seeing, it was only a quarter full, making it the largest open space on the Locon. He wondered how many Order soldiers were aware that they were being pushed back into that space whether it was by Ruby's troops or the hammering that Samurai Squadron was giving the ship from the other direction.

The mission timer was ticking down, and Remmy could see that they were almost headed towards their goal. Almost. The blinking red dot on his tactical monitor occasionally turned into a more detailed form, that of Vollis Mikan. The tracker was working and he was picking up extra data from the Locon's internal sensors. The dot was moving so quickly that he found himself questioning whether or not his map was right at all. "Remmy, you're two levels up from our target. You have to get down quickly to block him," Jake said.

Remmy checked the schematic for the ship and pointed towards a branch in the hallway as his team ran. He highlighted a hatch at the same time. "I see it, we're on our way."

Thanks to their officer-level access, the hatch popped up remotely, and Mayu immediately kicked it all the way open. She dropped down with Roscoe seconds behind, followed by Remmy, Tammy and Nigel. The plastic ladder flashed by, totally unused by the group. They did the same on the next floor, and didn't slow down as Remmy warned; "Open door down there. A few hundred people beyond it, but I'm reading only a few armed folks. Two by the hatchway and half a dozen in the crowd."

"No problem," Mayu said, dropping down so she had her rifle at the ready, facing the double doors. Roscoe followed, and when Remmy landed, he saw a frightened crowd in a double doorway. The pair with sidearms - simple needle guns - were as wary as the rest. As he stepped out of the way so Tammy and Nigel could drop down, he saw that there was an entire small auditorium filled with people in cadet uniforms. The dot representing Vollis was about to move around it, he would be on the opposite side soon enough, and Remmy got an idea.

Engaging an audio amplifier, he announced; "We're opening all the auditorium doors on the port side of the ship, that's behind you. There are still viable escape craft there. This ship is going down!"

Nigel caught on and opened the doors on the opposite side and people started filing out. It wasn't enough. The hallways wouldn't be choked with cadets, at least not enough to block Vollis. "The ship will explode in six and a half minutes! It's going down! Run for your lives! There aren't enough liveboats for everyone! First come, first saved!" He was using the mission timer for reference, it was right there in the corner of his view. Whether they would finish the Locon off was still up to Jake, but his painfully loud warning combined with the thumps and creaks of the ship were enough to get the Order cadets moving. Only a trio had a chance to come out through the doors facing them before Remmy tapped a control on his command bracer, closing them.

"That way, you idiots. Bugger off!" Roscoe said to the three cadets, pointing further down the hallway. One of them shot him a hurt look, but they all scrambled on.

The gambit worked. The halls on the opposite side of the auditorium were choked with people trying to get to the far edge of the ship, where they'd find escape pods and shuttles. The entrances into the large space were either just as congested or locked. Vollis was going around the other way, towards Remmy and his team. Remmy pointed to the hatch above; "Mayu, Tammy." They nodded, and jumped up into it using their thrusters.

Roscoe and Nigel moved down the hallway to a supply closet and waited there while Remmy slung his rifle and drew a large pistol with non-lethal capture rounds. That was his role. Playing the overconfident hunter. Jake was coming from behind, but he was over a minute behind, and even though it looked unlikely judging from the speed of that red dot on his tactical display, he hoped that he would catch up so Remmy didn't have to face the assassin.

Vollis was entering the long corridor. It was like his body recalled the feeling of being stabbed by the last assassin he'd faced as he came into view. Like the last one, Vollis was thin, a little shorter than him, but incredibly quick. His movements conveyed a kind of grace and certainty. His suit clung to him, not only black but seemingly drinking in light. "You," Vollis hissed as he made his faceplate transparent, revealing the tattooed face that everyone associated with Haven knew. "I don't have time for revenge," was the last thing he said before his suit shimmered and bent the light around it. Even Remmy's sensors struggled to correct for the cloaking field, only showing parts of the assassin at a time. Remmy turned his personal shield up and backed away. The instant he saw a shimmer that revealed Vollis' location for a certainty he hip-fired the pistol and caught his target's legs in a web of liquid metal that solidified almost instantly.

. . .

VOLLIS COULDN'T BELIEVE that Remmy actually caught him with his first shot. If you wanted to catch a Citatel Assassin, then using a weapon with a wide spread was the way to go, but there was no guarantee of hitting your target. He'd managed to go around another group that Vollis suspected was specifically hunting for him but there was no way around Remmy without digging into ship schematics and somehow getting access to secondary corridors. The only extra access he had came from the few hidden areas that the Order revealed to Citadel, and the aft hangar was behind this man. The one who had already killed one of his people. Remmy Sands.

This was a confrontation Vollis wanted, presented at the wrong time and wrong place. He would have allowed himself to be captured so he could kill Remmy, but he had a mission, so he pulled free of the metal web before it could completely solidify. The surface of his suit vibrated hard, it felt like his skin was burning from the friction the inner insulation of his suit couldn't protect him from. Remmy's eyes went wide as he watched the assassin slip free and start towards him.

His opponent raised the pistol again, and his companions emerged from a doorway behind and the hatch above. Vollis sidestepped the pistol shot, drawing a long blade with one hand. The nano-edge hissed as it heated and turned into a white-hot saw, crackling with a shield-piercing aura of focused energy. It was so thin that it disappeared from sight at some angles, the light it projected only suggesting that there was something there. This was the blade given to him by Leader Gideon when he was granted command of the Rixe. He was the first fabricant to receive one. Stealth was no longer a priority as he stepped around from Remmy, who tried to smash him with his fist, drawing his own, less advanced blade.

There would be no sword fight, the blades wouldn't clash, Vollis was too quick for that. Remmy was fast for someone in that medium armour, but so slow that Vollis' blade had a chance to strike twice at him. Before his point was able to get a straight-on angle on the armour, the soldier managed to move. Each hit turned into a graze, and Vollis could see that it would take longer to break through, too long.

One of Remmy's soldiers rattled three bursts at him, and he was caught just below the elbow by the last. The burning, brutal impact of them was excruciating as half of his forearm and his hand was torn away. What was left of his hand was still clutching the sword as the light of its edge faded and the blade slipped back down into the hilt, layers of metal coming apart and sliding against each other. His suit sealed over the wound and covered it with regeneration gel. The strange sensation of crawling flesh followed, and the pain disappeared. No matter how long he waited, the gel wouldn't re-grow his hand. That was something he'd have to see to later.

"Holy shit, I got him!" one of the men cried. He was the tallest of them, and so elated at the momentary victory that any honour he would have earned at his lucky shot was gone. This was the kind of person who was generally too high-strung for soldiering, and Vollis used that, leaping right at him.

As he predicted, the soldier was startled, and in only two seconds Vollis was so close to him that his fellows were afraid to fire. He moved around the soldier and past, engaging the sliders on his feet that allowed him to grip, then push his way across the deck plating of the corridors ahead. He hated leaving his foes behind. The small group wouldn't have lasted if he stayed, it would have been too easy for him to use them against each other as he reclaimed his sword and used it to slip between the slats of their armour like they were the ribs of slower prey.

A true assassin was aware of situational awareness, however. The Locon was barely under control. Its hallways and compartments were filling with new recruits who didn't know what to do as their minders joined the fight against boarders. Even Bion was on his way to an escape shuttle hidden beneath the bridge. If he didn't have a ship waiting in a hidden hold in the aft section of the ship, he would have stayed. Victory could be had in chaos, even with only one hand.

His stump continued to heal as he turned the corner and stopped, tapping a hidden control panel and then disappearing through a door as it slid aside. It flicked closed behind him, the edges creating a molecular seal with the plating around it. Vollis indulged for a moment as he walked down the dark, narrow passage. "I will hunt him. There will be nothing left of Remmy, any of his people, or the Haven commanders." No fabricant assassin had ever proposed a true Vendetta to the Shadows of Sol, but there was no reason why he wouldn't be the first. The ramp at the rear of the fifteen-metre-long scout ship lowered at his approach. Someone programmed the vessel to recognize him, probably the last person to leave. "Begin launch sequence," he announced as he pointed his stump at the switch that would open the cargo compartment. He paused a moment. If he still had his hand, that hatch would be opening. "Calm," he advised himself, noticing that there was weariness in his voice.

He used his other hand to flip the switch and the flimsy door slid to the side. A perfectly white capsule that reminded him of an old coffin, but thinner, more sleek and featureless, was secured in the middle of the hold. He didn't know what was inside, that wasn't his business, but whatever he was there to transport had been delivered. That was enough.

The low rumbling of the reactor and hiss of the environmental systems shoring up the atmospheric pressure within the ship suggested that he was ready to leave. He moved through the small crew cabin where there were three bunks and a tiny bathroom behind an accordion door to the cockpit. The hangar doors were already open. He checked the ship's self-check, saw that the status was green and launched as he struggled with the seat's restraints. The sooner he could get to a capable medbay and regenerate his hand, the better.

"GONE, OFF SCANNERS," Jake spat the words as though they were a curse over the Pursuit Channel.

"Wait, he's back," Remmy said, seeing that one of the trackers that Jake had shoved down Vollis' throat had reappeared on the tactical display. "Outside of the ship. Man, he is fast."

"I think Nigel's life flashed before his eyes when that bugger charged him," Roscoe laughed.

"Yeah, it didn't take long," Nigel replied. He was bending down to pick up the hilt of the assassin's sword.

"All right, join the main group. Order forces are falling back to the primary hold. Ruby and Alice's groups have blocked off the forward and starboard routes of retreat," Jake said, his instructions were practically a growl. "The lifeboats in the rest of the ship are gone."

Remmy was getting ready to move, aware of the new scars on his outer armour. He was sure Vollis' second strike would get through. His shields didn't seem to matter to whatever weapon he was using. It was time to get moving. The next part of the plan wouldn't be pretty. They had to find out if Bion was with the more heavily armed soldiers. "On our way," Remmy said, turning towards Mayu and Tammy. "All right, we're joining Jake's group. We need to find Bion amongst about three hundred Order hardasses, and they're not lining up for a head count. Failing that, we just have to hold them there until it's time to leave the ship."

A feeling, just a suggestion in his mind that something wasn't right drew his attention over his shoulder just in time to see Nigel stoop and touch the hilt of Vollis' sword. He kicked it away from his grasp and watched it pop up into the air, bounce off the wall, before falling to the floor in front of him. "What?" Nigel asked.

Remmy watched it for a moment as he stepped back and pressed Nigel aside. Tammy offered her reply first. "You know the training, never pick up the enemy's weapon unless you are unarmed and need what they have. Even then, scan the hell out of it first."

"Yeah, sure, but it's fine," Nigel said, pointing a finger at it so he could scan the two-handed hilt. "Wait, sorry, you might have been right."

It rolled out of the disembodied hand then, and after beeping once, it exploded.

THIRTY-SIX

Prioritizing the Chase

THE FAIRLIGHT MANAGED to scramble five fighters. Two were Buzzard A-11's, the first anyone had seen outside of the Order of Eden data that had been stolen only days ago. They were heavy fighters with mounting points for more types of ordinance and devices than anything, including an Uriel. These were set up with enhanced boosters that flared out across their fixed wings, and there was another compartment beneath that held some kind of high-powered device and a small fusion reactor.

They launched from a half-ruined hangar with more standard interceptors surrounding them. Their timing was perfect, coming out right behind Carnie and Ronin. Every one of the ships scored hits on them both as they came around the aft section of the Locon. "These are void warriors, put them down, but watch your six," Ronin said as he guided his fighter parallel to the hull of the Locon. A row of large, damaged turrets provided a few seconds of cover as he manually increased the charge rate of his shields. They recharged from twelve percent to sixty immediately, but his power system put a heat warning on his display, so he turned the power down to its recommended maximum.

"Three split off, they're on me, going evasive," Carnie said as his fighter's thrusters flared, turned, flared again, turned and then burned brightly, pushing him along a steady curve that took him directly towards the hull of the Locon. For a split second, Ronin wondered in fear at seeing that his wingmate's evasive manoeuvres would lead to a hard collision with the massive ship. Then, at the last instant, Ronin looked at the Locon and saw Carnie's fighter disappear into a hole in its hull.

He'd pushed through the ragged through-and-through hole that was made when one of the Locon's fuel storage tanks exploded earlier. More importantly, two of the fighters chasing him broke off, unwilling to thread that needle. When the third emerged, he was greeted by Carnie, who flipped his fighter end-over-end so all five of his guns were facing the enemy with the glare of the sun behind him. "Surprise," he said as he opened fire, scoring hits with all of his guns as the enemy was caught navigating through that narrow passage. By the time the pursuing ship was able to try to fly away from Carnie, railgun rounds were cutting through their shields. Only seconds later, it was reduced to a wreck that would drift at great speed towards the middle of the solar system for months if no one stopped it.

The Clever Dream was already launching missiles at two of the new fighters, her gunners scoring several hits as they passed.

Two of them started opening wormholes. "Those Vultures are going to get away," said Lewis from the Clever Dream. "The boosters are accelerating the ships from the planet and there's an energy build-up, most likely for a wormhole drive."

"The rest were running interference," Pixie commented. "I'm going after them."

"Don't let them draw you out of position, we're watching for launches from the Locon, that's our priority," Ronin said. "Focus on my target," Ronin said, and he was satisfied to see her join him in chasing after one of the Order interceptors that gave up on Carnie. The other was breaking away, rushing towards the Godfrey, which was starting to point its considerable bulk away from the planet. "Looks like someone got the Godfrey moving again," Gabe, the Captain of the Sky Stalker announced. "We're going to..."

He was interrupted as three pairs of the Godfrey's massive cannons fired, striking the middle and aft sections of the Sky Stalker. Those guns were made to take out large capital ships and stationary targets. Two of the Godfrey's main aft rocket engines flared brightly and it was pushing away from the planet. "We need heavy fire to shut..." Ronin started to say, then Jake was in his ears on a private channel.

He was focused and serious. "You guys didn't see a new contact from the Locon a few seconds ago?"

Ronin re-checked, and replied; "No, what'd I miss?"

"Marking Mikan's tracker now. Not your fault, he's in some kind of cloak ship and I forgot to add the tracking signature to your target list," Jake said.

Ronin needed a moment to direct his pilots, and he addressed the squad channel. "All right, let the Godfrey and that fighter following it go. We have to cover the Locon and stay close in case something else jumps in." He looked at the tactical map in his head and saw Vollis Mikan's signal. He was heading towards the planet, specifically into a higher traffic area. "I'm going after a new target, Breaker, take your team and cover the Locon."

"Aye, on it," Breaker said.

"This is the Raven, we're grabbing what's left of the Sky Stalker with our maxjack. We'll have time to get back in position in time to pick everyone up."

"Make sure you're there, it's going to be crowded," Breaker said.

"We're chasing this signal, Carnie," Ronin said as his wing-mate moved into position on his port side. "He's moving fast. How's your xetima booster?"

"I have fourteen percent until I'm out," Carnie replied. "This is the assassin?"

"I'm down to nine, burn with me," Ronin said, seeing that they were both on the same trajectory, headed straight towards the distant signal. He didn't count down or give a signal before engaging his enhanced afterburners and Carnie did the same at almost exactly the same time. For nine seconds their main engines burned so brightly that they looked like shooting stars to anyone on the ground. They were set to overtake their target in less than a minute, and both pilots, Ronin and Carnie, signalled Navnet in the next orbital quadrant, warning them that they were coming into the area quickly. While there was an active combat zone behind them, the next area over the northern hemisphere of the world was trying to maintain business as usual, so it was choked with normal traffic.

Ronin's smaller forward rotary thrusters were already slowing him down, and he got set to manoeuvre. Some Citadel scout ships were set up to evade and disappear. Others were more well-armed than most vessels their size. He opened a channel broadcasting on all frequencies typically used by the Order, Citadel and general travellers. "Hey, Vollis. I can see you. De-cloak and get into a normal, Navnet assigned flight pattern so you don't bump into anything. We'll set up a nice, civil arrest and take you home to Haven. You'll have a chance to tell everyone how doomed we are in court, then be our guest for a while. I hear our prisons are pretty cosy."

"Yeah, so everyone in orbit heard that, man," Carnie said on a private channel with a nervous snicker. "I'm doing a focused scan, now that he knows we see him."

"I want people to know a fight might break out between us and an invisible ship," Ronin said.

The promised scan pulse erupted from Canie's fighter, borrowing power from his shields for a moment, and the sleek shape of a smaller Citadel fighter appeared around Vollis' signal. A rapid-fire turret was lowering from its aft section, and it started firing the moment it was fully exposed. He nearly struck a large transport filled with civilian passengers as he tried to hit Ronin. "Oh, we're killing this guy, right?" Carnie asked.

"Right," Ronin said.

An emergency signal from Navnet warned everyone that there was a combat action in the area, painting a large oval of orbital space red in everyone's navigational system. "This is Navnet Control out of Serenity Base. We're scrambling fighters. Fill me in on this situation, guys. I don't want to send my pilots into a dogfight for no good reason."

"This is Ronin. No need to launch a response, we're knocking a cloaked ship down. We're closing the distance so the threat to civilians is minimized. This guy's an assassin for the Order and Citadel," he replied, hoping that whoever was in charge in Serenity Base didn't sympathise with the Order.

"This guy had something to do with Panda?" the voice from Serenity asked secretively.

"He's running from the Locon, one of the ships responsible," Ronin replied, watching a squad of fifteen fighters launch from an orbital base.

"You know, it's funny, we're having trouble tracking you and your bogey. We're going to have to reroute all ships in your area, just in case there are other unseen objects nearby."

"Acknowledged, Serenity Base," Ronin replied. The controller was trying to stay away from taking a side in the conflict, so his fighters slipped into a regular patrol pattern, staying far away from him, Carnie and Vollis.

Their target flew past a long train of freight containers. Its hauler cut the whole thing loose so it could float behind as the ship flew clear of the engagement area. It was the first time Ronin had ever seen that happen.

Carnie was hit by several pulse rounds the moment he came around the line of containers. His shields were half way depleted before he evaded the rest of the barrage.

The scout ship used a wide-hulled touring cruiser that was lazily moving through the space as cover. He was turning his vessel towards the planet at a steeper angle, probably planning to make landfall and escape on foot. There was no way Ronin and Carnie would be able to chase him down. They were too important to the fleet to go hunting. The most frustrating thing about the situation was watching Vollis use civilians as a shield. "Okay, as soon as we get around this touring ship, he's toast," Ronin said. He and Carnie split and slipped to the port and starboard side of the ship.

"Those folks are about to get one hell of a show," Carnie said.

A missile warning filled Ronin's ears and he launched the last of his countermeasures. The electronic jamming system did as much work, sending three of the missiles after digital ghosts as their guidance systems were more confused by fake signals than decoy drones. Two struck Ronin so suddenly and quickly that he wasn't sure how much of his ship would be left until the fighter stopped shaking. One of his thrusters was gone, sheared off its slender pylon and he lost two of his guns.

Carnie was already firing down at their target, hammering at the ship's shields so hard that the energy barrier flickered. It was the best thing he could do to help Ronin, who started firing his remaining guns, joining the attack. Before the energy shields went down, their high-velocity, spinning railgun rounds began cutting into and then through the ship's hull.

They followed the practices both of them embraced in simulations, aiming for engines and power centres. They were rewarded as the main rear thruster housings were punctured dozens of times and then they started coming apart in chunks. "I'm out," Carnie said as he stopped firing.

Ronin lined up his last barrage so he would put rounds through the fuel cells and then the cockpit. He emptied his guns into the ship and watched as the power levels in his target died. The scout ship started to spin out of control, falling towards the atmosphere. "Serenity Base, I'm marking a ship in distress, entering the atmosphere." He stared at Vollis' ship as it started to burn in the distance, and focused on it in his mind. The tactical marker on his mental map gave him all kinds of data. Locations of hull ruptures, the confirmation that the ship had lost power, and that the Citadel ship was in an uncontrolled spin.

"I see it, Ronin. Be advised that we are picking up the approach of two large battlegroups, both identifying as Order of Eden. They are on approach and will arrive in seventeen minutes. I'm sending you the data."

Ronin glanced at the sensor readings and a chill ran down his spine. Judging from a glance at the ship profiles. Altogether there were at least fifty capital ships ranging from corvettes to heavy cruisers. "Thanks, Tower," he replied. He took a moment to watch the scout ship as it started to enter the atmosphere, its hull heating up. "I'll buy you a drink next time I'm in range."

"We're regrouping?" Carnie asked.

"Gotta get back in position in time for our jump," Ronin replied on the squadron channel. "Big trouble coming in, Jake. Looks like we can expect long-range fire sometime in the next few minutes."

"Acknowledged," Jake replied. "We're finishing up and getting outta here. Still haven't figured out if Bion's still aboard."

"Two Vultures just jumped into a wormhole," Faloo reported from the Clever Dream. "We managed to scan through their scramblers. Identified four Order officers, none of them Bion."

"Rip hit one of them at long range several seconds before it finished transit entry," Dame reported. "I don't expect the ship will emerge intact. That was an exceptional shot."

"Thanks, Dame," Rip replied, sounding surprised. Dame didn't praise anyone often.

"Which officers were aboard?" Jake asked.

"Heigen and Dawson. Third and fifth in command aboard the Locon," Faloo replied. "Lewis says it is highly unlikely that they'll survive their trip."

"Good, watch for more launches. We'll push one more time, either get this guy or send him running so you can," Jake said, the sounds of gunfire raging in the background.

THIRTY-SEVEN

Lesser Prizes

REMMY'S whole body was being bounced and swayed in a regular rhythm as though he was in some kind of baby carrier. His suit held him in the fetal position. What was left of his suit had constricted that way, following instructions that Haven Fleet Medical programmed in for him before he left that organizaiton. Even in his slow-waking haze, he recalled that it was something his suit did to aid in quick regeneration after massive trauma. More interesting was the fact that the whole back side of his suit was affixed to someone else, and they were hurriedly crouching down.

Remmy could feel the stretching and constricting of the artificial muscle in the back of his and the other man's suit as the technology struggled to compensate for his weight. He was impressed at how well it worked, even as he fought his way through a thick stupor to consciousness. Whoever he was affixed to was obviously tall, they would have to be. At first he imagined it may be Jacob Valent himself, then he realized his bearer was too skinny.

The last thing he remembered was an explosion right in his face. It knocked him out at least, but it couldn't have been too bad, since he didn't feel any pain, and he could tell he was probably whole. He recalled something that was a little illuminating - he sent every bit of available energy in his suit to his shields before the hilt trap went off. That probably saved him, along with his upgraded physiology.

His eyes opened to slits in time to see something that was more like a violent dream. Light came in fitful strobes, a few of them were timed with bursts of pressure against his suit. The first thing he saw with any clarity was Iruuk in his heavy Nafalli armour. It covered his fur like a silver coating that didn't compress it but highlighted its tufts like spikes and moved with him. His helmet was affixed to a thick chest plate and back support that spread down onto an exoskeleton. He stepped into a gap between two tall rows of shipping containers, leading with his artificial leg, brandishing a cannon that required both of his long, powerful arms to operate and let loose with a particle beam that turned the fitful darkness into day for several seconds. Even through his sealed headpiece, Remmy could hear the hum of the weapon and his display told him that the temperature around them increased by nine degrees.

A barrage of fire came down on the Nafalli, and several of Ruby's soldiers leapt on top of the containers and aimed their rifles at enemies that were out of Remmy's sight. Two more Nafalli soldiers who were a meter shorter but much thicker than

Iruuk joined him and swept the area around the corner with beam weapons of their own, the sound of their attacks harmonizing in a buzzing hum that Remmy was sure he wouldn't forget. This wasn't a dream, he was in the middle of a battle. Who was the unlucky, thin man carrying him?

"Still not picking up Bion's profile," Nigel reported loudly to someone. Remmy wasn't hearing him over a combat channel, either. He could hear him through his suit because they were attached. With alarm, Remmy realized he was being carried by Nigel.

He shook his head, grasping full consciousness so quickly that he was momentarily dizzy. A rush of Order soldiers in basic uniforms, the type used by frameworks right after they were activated rushed Iruuk and the rest of the Nafalli. At the same time, the meter-wide drone that hammered the group with bright blasts a moment before fell to the deck. The group of Ruby's troops that were supporting the Nafalli had turned it into a twisted mess, and it nearly knocked a couple of the framework soldiers' heads off when it went down.

The rest of them continued their charge, supported by thin-limbed androids that no one bothered to apply skin to as they all fired. Iruuk was the main focus of their attack. "Holy shit!" Nigel cried as he realized that the action was suddenly very close. He was only a few meters off to the side, taking cover behind a metal crate. A temporary barrier shield that kept projectiles out of the sanctuary flickered, threatening to fail.

The young soldier scrambled to put more distance between him and the fray, jostling Remmy so much that he felt like he would shake off the back of Nigel's heavy armour.

"Let me down!" Remmy shouted, feeling that something

was very wrong with his mouth. In an instant, he realized his gums had healed perfectly, but he was missing most of his teeth, leaving only a small collection of molars. He spotted Jake, who was yelling at Iruuk as the young Nafalli took an android by the top of the head and threw it into the distance. Then he pulled the trigger on his beam weapon. Instead of sending a deadly line of light into the fray, his power pack sent a dazzling spray of sparks high up, bathing the scene in yellow light.

Alice's voice came through on the Combat Channel then, telling him; "Your cannon's power supply is wrecked! Get out of there."

He didn't need to be told. The enemy rush was on, and several shots from the light infantry recklessly charging their position were already breaking through his shields. "I've been customizing that cannon for a year!" Iruuk complained as he detached the weapon from its cable, used it to crush a soldier's helmet with a savage overhand strike, then he tossed it at another who was knocked back into his fellows. A pair of long steps took him out of the direct line of fire.

"I've got a Knight on me," Alice said as she came into view, dropping from the top of a shipping container. "I'm going to let him get close so I can finish him off, but get ready to toss him back to his buddies."

"You gave him the impression that you're... well... you?" Iruuk said as he moved across the open space some of their allies were using to regroup and recharge their shields.

"I may have planted that impression in his brain. I'm good bait," Alice replied. "He wants the bounty and the fame for catching me."

"That's going to backfire someday. Ready to back you up,

shields recharging," Iruuk said as he withdrew from the main fight.

They spoke so fast that Remmy found himself wondering if telepathy would actually be faster, and he wished he had a Nafalli partner instead of a tall, skinny Nigel. "Lemmie down!"

"Remmy! You're awake? Tammy said you'd regenerate fast, but..." Nigel said, turning so the part of the battle he was watching was out of sight. Instead, he was treated to the sight of Alice burst firing at an Order Knight in armour that was almost exactly like the banded, heavy variety Haven made. The Knight towered over her, and he tried to push her back so he could get a good shot at her with his overbuilt, powerful rifle. It was no good. If rumours were true, and they probably were, she and Iruuk sparred in simulations regularly, and she won half the time. If she could take on a quick, powerful Nafalli twice her size, then this Knight had made a huge mistake by getting so close to her.

Even worse for the Knight, she was wearing heavy armour that was at least as good. Ruby and several of her troopers were in the background, stepping out of cover, catching four Order Knights in a hail of automatic fire as they tried to support their leader. They were forced into a retreat but brought two of their assailant's shields down. Ruby and her lieutenant dragged them back, out of danger as more soldiers filled the gap and continued firing.

Alice's fight with the Knight that made it behind their lines went on like an old movie playing in high speed. He swept at her, even tried to bump her away by colliding with her bodily, but she knew what she dodged easily, finally blasting him one more time with her sidearm, taking his shields down entirely.

The end of the encounter was enough to make Remmy boggle. She slapped a grenade against each side of his helmet, where they affixed perfectly and Iruuk swept into view in time to grab him by the belt and then throw the armoured man over twenty meters into the group of Order Knights who were continuing a slow, measured retreat.

One of the normally stoic Knights pointed at his fellow as he landed and the rest scrambled to get away. Remmy started laughing as Alice's Knight pulled his helmet off and was just about to throw it when the grenades went off.

He stopped laughing when he fell off of Nigel's back in a sprawling heap. As he collected himself, Remmy looked back towards the main battle. It was the main thrust, coming from the heart of the ship storage and transit area.

The Nafalli that stepped in to help Iruuk stepped out of danger, letting more of Ruby's troops get a turn at fighting the rush of Order frameworks and bare metal androids. Those blank-eyed, determined enemies were backed by barely armoured troops in green that looked as fresh as their pristine uniforms, Remmy guessed they were new recruits who were as determined as they were ignorant.

Agameg slipped into the front line ranks then, throwing a pair of his concussion charges before opening fire with his rifle. His faceplate was fully transparent, and light played on his Issyrian face - his true, broad-eyed, slit-mouthed visage complete with fine, rippling tendrils. The enemy knew they were fighting a non-human, and Agameg's grace was only slightly greater than his speed. Before his shields could be depleted by incoming fire, he was back behind cover, and a string of allied soldiers followed his example - moving into position, letting loose, and moving back into cover.

The sheer crush of the enemy charge was enough to press the line inward for several seconds. Even Jake took a turn, moving in front of the enemy long enough to draw their fire and return it. The Order was sending their unshielded peons. Human bodies fell, brutalized by rifles, grenades, and crushed underfoot. They were mixed with cybernetic parts, frameworks of the most basic style that mostly failed to regenerate.

Nigel started helping him up, and Remmy started looking for a rifle. "Are you all right?" Nigel asked, fixing him with a look of mingled concern and relief.

"Better, now that my suit is letting me move.," Remmy replied.

"I'm sorry we didn't leave you with the injured, but the Doc said you'd completely regenerate in a few minutes," Nigel explained as he used a flex screen to take a good look at the tactical map. There were high-powered scan pulses going off every quarter second. He was looking for officers and using software to highlight significant changes in troop movements. He worked fast, Nigel knew what he was doing.

Remmy flexed his arms, sure that everything important regenerated, and then joined the general combat channel. Why his command and control system connected him to Alice and her squad, he couldn't guess, but he assumed it had been damaged. His suit was definitely not as he left it, missing most of the plating on the front. The undersuit was extra thin, embarrassingly so, but at least it had repaired itself to the point of covering his whole body. "How's the squad?" He was already checking their status on his dented faceplate.

"We're good, you took almost the whole blast, saved every-one. You were totally right about that sword, it was trapped. I'm so sorry, Sir. The only one who's with the wounded is Tammy, but she'll be all right," Nigel replied in a rush. "Are you really okay?"

"I'm good, don't worry," Remmy replied.

"You sound a little off," Nigel said, trying to take a closer look through his faceplate.

"You with us, Remmy?" Jake asked over the general combat channel.

"All the bits that matter check out, so yeah," Remmy replied, adding "I'm good to go." The softening of his speech was annoying, and he worked hard to enunciate. He was reminded of Tammy, who had a much subtler lisp. She was currently missing her right foot. It probably happened during the same explosion that took him out. She was stable, awake, and close to their exit point, a large airlock forty-nine meters away. Roscoe and Mayu were backing up Ruby's crew, low on ammo but otherwise unscathed. The main cargo area and the transport system had become a battlefield. Jake, Agameg, and Ruby had managed to push most of the remaining Order soldiers, armed recruits, and many of their commanders into the middle of the nearly two-hundred-meter-wide space. It ran nearly the length of the Locon's interior, over a kilometre, but their coordinated efforts drove them to a main cargo section.

The history provided by Remmy's tactical system showed him why it was relatively easy to push the Order forces there. There were thousands of cheap combat androids, weapons, and framework troops in boxes, and it was obviously their plan to activate as much as they could. They were having some success.

"The mission clock is down to fourteen seconds," Remmy said to every commander on the Combat Channel. "Are we getting outta here soon?"

"We're getting ready to withdraw. Doesn't look like we're going to find Bion today," Jake said.

"We're in the wrong place, or he's wearing a telepathic suppressor and his armour is still intact. He could be right here, or already off the ship," Alice said as she came in, unslinging her rifle and checking it. "This is a win anyway, as long as we can take all these containers out. There are two commanders who are really worried about that."

"Got it. We have to take the Locon down. Time to go, Jake?" asked Agameg.

"Timer is down to zero and there are at least two fresh Order battlegroups making their way across the solar system to Rodus, we're leaving," Jake confirmed.

"The Knights are down," Ruby said over the combat channel. "Confirmed the identity of two of them. These were new." She was almost drowned out by gunfire. "We're pulling out? Now? We've got the advantage. I think those Knights were in charge of defence."

"Drop explosives and retreat. Use whatever you've got left to slow them down," Jake replied. "You and your troops have done a hell of a job."

"Damn, feels like I woke up just in time for the end of the party," Remmy said, seeing an alert on the tactical map on the inside of his visor. His ocular display was damaged, and everything looked warped but the image was clear enough to make out a circle indicating that there were twenty-five new enemy troops on the field. "New bare metal androids. The Order are getting into some of those containers."

"The Clever Dream is getting into position," Alice announced. "My people need help with the injured."

"I hear you," Jake replied. He looked past them, as though he was seeking out Ruby as he spoke to her over the combat channel. "All right, everyone retreat now. Back to the boats."

"Aye, we'll plant charges on the run, try to jam up the halls behind us. We don't have much, to work with though," Ruby warned.

"Do your best, do it fast," Jake said.

"One or the other," Ruby retorted hurriedly.

"Then fast," Jake replied so quickly that he spoke over her.

"Launch, we have a new launch," Breaker announced over all friendly channels. "It's already charging up, making a real effort to shoot a couple of our birds out of the sky. It's an Order Gunship."

"The expensive kind," added Carnie. "Came from an isolated bay that didn't come up on scanners. It's straight down from the bridge."

"That's Bion," Jake said. "It's the command lifeboat, most of the senior staff is probably with him."

"Green Group, Blue Group, take it out," Ronin ordered over the Squad and general Combat channels. "Grey Group, take out the rest of the Locon's main thrusters and cover our corvettes while they retrieve our people."

There were a series of acknowledgements, and Remmy wished he could see the destruction of the escaping gunship for himself. Then, as he and Nigel joined Alice as she led her group in a retreat, a thought occurred to him. "Just a quick question.

Wouldn't it have been better if you intercepted the command staff in the halls? That was the plan, wasn't it?"

"He tried," Alice replied.

"We got an elevator full. Bion had a double, we took him out. Then we ran out of time and had to regroup here," Jake explained, surly.

"Bion's double was creepy," Alice explained on a private channel. "His brain was almost blank. It was like he knew just enough to obey basic instructions, walk, run and sit."

"Being a telepath has gotta be amazing," Remmy remarked.

"Nope," Alice said as they came to a double-wide hatch that had been hastily cut open. "More talking later."

"Understood, Captain," Remmy replied, relieved to see the debarkation compartment where a few injured soldiers, Tammy included, waited with them. Her greeting smile seemed to warm him from within, and she touched his dented face plate as he got under her arm. "You okay, Remmy?"

An eruption of sound and the rattling of the deck told them that there was action further down the corridor. No one was dragging their feet as they retreated, but he took a second to reply; "I'm gonna have to check myself out later, but I'm good. You?"

"Missing a foot, but it doesn't hurt. Can't keep up while hopping though," she replied.

"I've got ya, but we'll need a lift. I don't have enough armour left to make the short flight to the Raven."

"I've got you, Captain," Iruuk said as he grasped them both by the back of their suits. The large, industrial sized airlock opened, letting the warm air out slowly at first, then in a short-lived gust.

"That'll slow them down," Jake said over the Combat Channel.

Most of the new recruits and frameworks weren't wearing breathers or vacuum protection, from what Remmy could recall. His tactical screen showed that the emergency doors were jammed open or broken down all the way back to the main cargo and transit column. Before he could look over his shoulder, Iruuk took him and Tammy through the airlock and thrusters hidden in his suit bore them to the rear hatch of the Raven as it drifted into position.

THIRTY-EIGHT

The Tail End

THE SHIP that emerged from the Locon was genius in its simplicity. It was built for a single purpose - to provide officers with a method of escape if the ship went down. Ronin looked at all the readings collected from their small group of corvettes and fighters. The web of information woven had thickened throughout the quick conflict. This wasn't like a mission where any of their ships had to hide, so they all sent scan pulses in every direction and actively collected data with every sensor they had.

The details of what was inside of that escape ship was impartial and glitchy, regardless of their efforts. Its shields were the most prominent feature, and they were so over-built that their overlapping fields created distortion. Ronin felt a pang of old alarm at seeing that there were four main generators that could block radiation and kinetic interference made by Vindyne Industries. It was an old name, one that brought back memories of imprisonment and brutality. Even worse, the model of shield generator he saw come up four times, meaning that there were four of them when one would do, wasn't one that they'd encountered in simulations. He marked the dot that represented the vessel as the 'Officer Gunship,' and adjusted his course so he was headed straight for it. If there was something he could do to help take Bion down, he would carry it out.

He recalled what Bion looked like on stage. Confident, like he had the galaxy in his hand. The applause of hundreds still echoed in Ronin's mind. Bion sold the idea that he was leading them all into building a better road into the future for humanity. Ronin had seen charismatic leaders before, he'd believed in more than one through the years. People he was sure were good, were friends, and some became like family. More than once people accused him of being exactly that, a leader people wanted to follow. There was a place in the universe for charisma, for people with big plans that could draw followers out of their corners and polarize their opinions in their favour.

The footage he saw of Eve wasn't nearly as compelling as the short exposure he had to Bion. Eve presented herself as a fervent believer who made anyone who didn't share her opinions feel like outsiders. To be an outsider amongst other Order of Eden followers was dangerous. Bion had a different style. He was like a host inviting everyone to his celebration. To Ronin, that was far more dangerous, especially since he wanted to exclude every non-human from the organization.

As he recalled the grinning face of Bion as people cheered for him, Ronin realized that he'd already decided that his personal goal in the war, at least at that moment, was to cut that specific head from the beastly body of the Order of Eden. He looked at the shields protecting the escaping gunship and saw that it was deflecting the rail gun rounds that his fighters were sending after it.

"The shielding on the craft is almost twice that of a Clever Class, and they have a deflection layer," Dame said as she ripped at it with all five of her cannons. "The emitters look like they're from a larger ship." She veered off jaggedly as a pair of her quarry's guns struck her fighter several times.

Rip and Pixie swept in and emptied the last few hundred rounds in their magazines as they landed hits on the ship's aft shields. "I'm empty," Pixie said before Rip could.

"We need a corvette on this," Breaker said as he led his group into a strafing run that was cut short when he led them away from the Officer Gunship's forward turrets.

The corvettes were on the wrong side of the Locon, still picking up their boarding teams. They were simply facing the wrong way out of necessity, and there was a knot tightening in the pit of Ronin's stomach that told him that the enemy escape craft was about to get away. He opened a private channel to Alice. "Is Bion on that ship?"

There was a long pause, and he was about to check to make sure he was actually connected when she replied. "They have blockers. Officers are aboard, and we haven't caught or killed the real Bion yet. We know that much."

Ronin and Carnie were finally close enough to do something, returning from their encounter with Vollis' ship. It took longer to get back because they didn't have any fuel left in their boosters. He had a perfectly working fusion reactor aboard, however, so he pushed the slider that he'd set to control his shield recharge rate up to their maximum tolerance and pointed the nose of his ship at the aft end of the escaping ship. "Everyone, hold your fire. Get ready to blast that thing from behind when I get clear," he told his fighter wing.

"Ronin, what the hell are you doing?" Carnie asked.

"I'm going jousting," he replied, listening to a cacophonous chorus of objections. They didn't come from most of his fighter wing but from friends and boarding team members. He could hear Alice, Jake, Tammy, even Ruby and Remmy could be heard along with many others.

Ronin cringed as he checked and re-checked his trajectory. "Hold on, hold on! I'm not going to crunch myself against that thing's ass, just give it a good solid bumping. You know, skip my shields right off it. It's not a suicide run." Then he checked his power settings and realized that he hadn't turned his dampeners up past normal. There was a chance, and not a small one, that they wouldn't react fast enough in the kind of action he was planning. If he was unlucky, he could reduce himself to the consistency of stew if he didn't turn that up, so he did, and remarked; "Anyone else a little peckish? I could eat."

"Adjust your angle," Carnie said. "We can graze their shields at a less extreme angle and reduce the risk if we both do this. Can't do much else, since we're out of ammo. Besides, I'll go first. You're down a thruster."

Ronin wanted to tell him to stand down, but couldn't argue. He adjusted his approach angle, accepting his computer's help and checking as his ship accelerated. "Don't forget to turn your dampeners up."

"Already done," Carnie replied as his fighter moved past,

taking the lead. They wouldn't follow right behind each other, that really could turn into a suicidal manoeuvre. Instead, they were parallel, with Carnie on Ronin's starboard side, ahead of him. "I'm set, let's make sure they don't hit us too much on the way in."

Breaker, Rip, Gren and Garma swept in behind the Officer Gunship, drawing the attention of its two rear gunners. "Holding missile lock on this fat bird. We may not have any missiles left, but the warnings they'll be seeing will keep them focused on us."

"Hold back just in case I get a bad bounce," Ronin advised.

"Ronin," Jake said, not taking the time to use a private call. He was on the general combat channel. "We knocked one of their leaders down today. No need for heroic sacrifices."

"Yeah, but the last scan I got on that scoutship was that it still has four survivors aboard," Ronin replied. "I've crashed enough ships to know a falling star can land on its feet."

"Are you saying Vollis could walk away?" Ruby asked, prompting an eruption of groans and objections on the combat channel.

Someone muted all non-officers. "There's nothing we can do about Vollis right now. There are still two trackers working though, so we'll find him later. That Officer Gunship is going to be far enough from the planet to jump in a few seconds, though." Jake said. "No dishonour if they get away. Just don't make us pick you up, whatever you do. It's crowded enough in here."

"No worries, man, we've got this," Carnie said. "We're professional pilots, watch." The escape ship loomed. Just under thirty metres long, and fifteen wide at the aft, its shields actually made the surface of the hull shimmer to the naked eye.

Ronin could see the navigational data in his head, but he watched his instruments anyway. It was the way he was trained, the neural link he had with his fighter was secondary, a confirmation that he was on course, that his shields would clash with the enemies but he wouldn't fatally collide. He glanced up through the cockpit in time to see Carnie's fighter, well ahead now, flying towards the rear of the escaping ship. "Jousting is so stupid," he said under his breath as the young pilot's fighter skipped across the aft side of the vessel and tumbled past.

Ronin didn't have time to find out if his wingmate's ship or body was still intact before he did the same. A pop that was loud enough to be heard through his helmet sounded in his fighter and his armour reported that his cockpit had reached one hundred and ninety degrees. The instrumentation for his shields was dark, and his main inertial dampener systems were burned out, leaving only an emergency system that didn't like to be pushed very hard. Other than that, Ronin realized that he was all right. His suit protected him from being cooked, but he'd survived. "You okay, Carnie?"

"My shields are dead, the dampening system is flicking off and on. Switching to the backup. Lost two thrusters, don't even know how. Other than that, I'm good."

"I know how you lost them. You collided with a ship thirty times your size," Dame said wryly. "Their aft shielding has failed and there is a power surge in the two field generators that are still operating. I expect their forward shielding will collapse as well."

"Order ship, power down and surrender immediately or we

will open fire," Jake said over all channels, pinging the escaping ship on the Navnet system. The icon representing it there and on the tactical screen flared green for a moment.

"I promise you mercy and a comfortable stay if you and the marauders with you surrender now," Bion replied from the escaping gunship. "This is a mercy I'll only offer once. Four battlegroups are on their way here right now. You do not have the advantage."

His confidence was staggering, his every syllable was laden with it, and Ronin found himself shaking his head. Then he saw it, an energy spike from a wormhole generator. "Fire! Give him everything we've got left!"

"Tear that bird apart!" Jake ordered at the same time.

"It is him, he's aboard," Alice said as Dame, Breaker, Rip, Gren, and Garna all opened fire. As Ronin watched a zoomed-in view of the escaping ship, he listened to Alice explain; "The telepathic blocking device they were using must have been part of the shield system. Bion is aboard with eight high-ranking officers."

A wormhole began to form in front of the gunship. High-velocity railgun rounds from twenty-five guns aboard five fighters ripped through the aft section of the vessel, poking rows and circles of holes into the hull. The aft turrets fired twice more and stopped. The wormhole ahead of the ship failed, and jets of atmosphere shot out from the holes in its armour as compartments decompressed.

"I'm out!" Gren announced as her guns fired their last rounds.

"Me too," Garma said.

It was Dame who stopped firing, accelerated, and then

turned her ship towards the centre of the enemy vessel, aiming for the bulk of the people they could detect inside. "For Easy," she said as her guns erupted, sending a barrage of railgun rounds through the hull and the most populated section of the ship as she strafed back and forth over its dorsal section. "For our friends," she added as the last of her ammunition was spat into the ship to ricochet within before breaking through the hull on the opposite side.

"Bion and five officers are dead," Alice said as the corvettes finally came around the Locon. "Should we try to capture it on our way out?"

"Scans show something that could be a self-destruct device aboard," Jake replied. "Keep your distance and finish it off."

"Now he says; 'keep your distance,'" Ronin grumbled as he tried to get his fighter to recalibrate its flight controls. There was more damage than he initially thought. One of his thrusters was barely hanging onto its pylon, and another was bent awkwardly. His power systems were partially burned out as well. It would take a few hours to figure out exactly what was working, especially since subsystems were telling him they were fine, when they obviously weren't. He wasn't in immediate danger though, so he took a moment to look through his canopy at the Officer Gunship.

The Clever Dream, Sky Queen and Raven fired their main railguns and every turret that was facing the escape ship. With no shields, and a hull that was compromised from several directions, the Order vessel was rendered unrecognisable. Ronin watched with satisfaction as the corvettes turned then, and fired on the Locon.

A hail of Javelin Torpedoes, beam weapons and railgun fire

blasted one specific section of the hull. It only took Ronin a moment to realize that the failing armour protected the main cargo hold. "That's a few thousand frameworks and a whole lot of combat metal we won't have to deal with later," Jake said.

"All right, it's jumping time," Ronin announced, drawing his focus away from the sight of the Locon. It was heavily damaged, venting atmosphere in several places, rips in its armour from every kind of weapon they had, and an oval-shaped bridge section on top that had more holes in it than a sieve. Its thrusters flickered and went out, and he smiled a little. "I'd love to stick around and admire our handiwork, but I'm going to need a pickup. My bird isn't flying right."

"On our way, Ronin," Alice replied.

The rest of his wingmates were quickly affixing their fighters to the remaining corvettes. The front two-thirds of the Sky Stalker was held firmly in the grasp of the Raven's maxjack, like one bird carrying another with rows of metal talons.

"We've gotta get moving, this isn't fast enough. The main fleet is on its way," said Parsons, a member of Ruby's crew, over the command channel.

Everyone could see it if they looked at the tactical map for the entire solar system. Anything they fired would take over an hour to hit them unless it was pure light. "The best they could do from where they are is jump some smaller ships in." Ronin replied, adding; "Well, they could try to blind us from there if we stay really still and don't blink. We've got a few minutes."

The Clever Dream drew closer and Ronin signalled that he'd manoeuvre his fighter the rest of the way. It only took him a moment to manually fire his remaining thrusters on their lowest setting so his landing gear touched the hull. They affixed using a high-friction mode that temporarily bonded with the metal. It was true, the Order fleet that jumped into the system using a safe arrival area far from Rodus was too far to cause any real harm, but he still didn't take his time. "I'm on," he announced.

"You got me, I'm parked right on your nose," Carnie added.

Ronin spoke hurriedly as he announced; "All fighters accounted for. Let's do what the lady said and get outta here."

THIRTY-NINE

The Crash Site

"MEDICAL RESOURCES DEPLETED," said a passive, asexual voice in Vollis' ear. It continued spouting bad news, detecting that he was conscious. "Survival fabrication system compromised. Combat Skin compromised."

He started to take his surroundings in, forestalling movement. The crash was so violent that his seat's safety belts failed, and he'd been thrown to the floor where he rolled under the console. Everything hurt, but Vollis was aware that he had been bruised, bent and stretched, not broken and lacerated.

His suit, the Combat skin, saved him from getting utterly destroyed. There was a ragged hole in his thin armour's left forearm and thigh. Its resources were exhausted, so the edges couldn't re-fasten without causing a rip somewhere else. The last of the medical supplies loaded into his emergency system were probably spent on fixing his arm and leg.

His hand was still missing, there was nothing his basic medical system could do about that, but the stump was healed. A furious itch on his right palm, the one that was gone, made him sneer. He looked forward to getting a new hand so he could scratch it. "Communications. Start a beacon program transmitting to the Rixe and all allied ships," he ordered.

There was no beep of acknowledgement, and his suit's voice told him the bad news after a few seconds. "Transmission circuit is incomplete. Connect to an antenna or conductive surface while using a supplemental power supply of sufficient strength."

Without asking for particulars, like what a 'sufficient strength' was, Vollis got to his feet and looked around. The deck of the small bridge was askew, and only one of his boot treads could grip the surface. The other didn't obey his wordless command to increase its tackyness. There was a disconnection somewhere between the neural interface in his hood and his right leg, but he could stand still, at least.

The sound of rain striking the hull of the ship seemed too sharp. It should have been a muffled thing, and he looked around, finding what he feared. There was a large tear in the transparent metal hull on the port side, large enough for him to pass through. It was an escape route, but also a vulnerability that made the ship less viable as shelter.

"Bring up a map of the area and show me a weather analysis." "Bring up a map of the area and show me a weather analysis."

A computer to his right came to life, projecting a hologram of a ten-by-ten-kilometre topographical map of the area. Beside it was the last image the ship had of the atmosphere. The picture had been taken from orbit. "Sensors are damaged. This is the most recent information available." He was surprised that anything on the ship worked at all. The terminals on that side of the bridge were scorched, most likely by the dampener system when it burned out during the crash.

He examined the images and saw that he wasn't in the centre of a wasteland. He'd landed in an old agricultural centre with three layered buildings made to grow some kind of high-density maise, judging from the rows of vegetables on the top level. There was a modern village only a kilometre away with a twenty-eight-storey building at its centre and a small shuttle port on its edge.

As for weather, he only had to glance at the image taken from orbit to guess that he was on the edge of an unnatural storm caused by wormhole jumps inside the atmosphere. He guessed the rain, which was already thick, blown by a high wind, would get worse. "Environmental systems report," he said aloud.

"Unavailable," the ship's computer replied loudly, its voice coming from somewhere behind the cockpit. Whatever aural emitters the bridge had were probably destroyed.

"Give me a list of functioning..." he started to say.

His suit interrupted him. "Three atypical life signs detected at a ten-metre distance. Cannot identify. Posture suggests aggression."

His suit flinched against his skin, it was a small tap on his side that told him where the trio were approaching from. Their size came as a trio of brief impressions on his upper arm. His was a tactile interface that made sure he could always feel where his enemy was, and what shape they were.

He reached for the thin, short blades he kept in his belt and grasped one with his left hand. As he cringed at not having his right, Vollis held the stump up as a deflection tool. "The cargo has lost containment?"

"Correct," the voice in his helmet said.

The voice of the ship had a response as well. "The cargo hold has suffered an internal breach between frames five and seven." A hologram appeared, flickering fitfully, showing that part of the aft section of the ship suffered incredible crush damage in the crash which ruined the internal plating that isolated the small cargo room. There was a long, open slit.

The creatures were moving towards him slowly, staying out of sight using the bunk and the work area across from it in the cabin behind the bridge as cover. Vollis reached out to the door control, tapped the close button and nothing happened. "Analysis."

The three creatures were still out of sight, and the sound of the rain ruled out any chance of hearing their approach. Lightning illuminated the inside of the ruined bridge. Everything around him seemed bent, slanted and wrong. The slant of the rain had changed and the deck glistened wetly. "Forty-nine indications of relation to insect groups last seen during the invasion of the Haven System. Predatory movements suggest coordination, aural, percussive and pheromonal communication. You are the target."

"I can run," Vollis said, eying the rip in the side of the hull across the small bridge. Jumping to it wouldn't be too difficult, but he'd probably lose his knife and it would take him time to crawl through. A pair of hooked claws gripped one side of the door, then another creature did the same on the opposite side. It was too late to flee. Fighting was his only option.

These were brought into the galaxy by the Edxi. All of the insects - and there were many types - were foreign. They were mysterious creatures that he'd seen only images and shallow scans of, they all had one thing in common: they preferred to eat mammals.

The third insect slipped into the doorway, stretching on long legs. Each had a femur, tibia and tarsus ending in three long claws. The creature's midsection was incredibly thin, uncoiling with strange, semi-translucent chitinous plates. A pair of long, even thinner arms unfolded and split, revealing that each one was actually two with a pair of hooked claws on the end. They clicked together as it rose its head, which was oval-shaped, covered in rows of darker, glistening plates that slid against each other with a sandy rasp.

It peered at him with a pair of wide, white eyes peeking between the edges of its plates, and began to open what looked like its mouth. Vollis wondered if it was posturing somehow, which was not something that insects did as far as he knew. Then a chill ran through him as he realized it was opening something that looked like a mouth, but also seemed like some-thing more. It was as wide as his entire head, like the hood of a cobra but even more concave. It was revealing some kind of shallow capturing orifice that was white, becoming more slick with a black fluid. Its edges rippled, revealing rows of tiny hooks as the whole thing opened and closed.

A powerful instinct to leap for the gap in the hull to his right brought fear and urgency with it as the enemy filled the doorway with its thin body. Its thorax twitched, eye slits narrowed and Vollis was ready for it as it leapt. It happened so quickly that only reflexes could save him.

Vollis put his stump right into the middle of that broad orifice that he misidentified as a mouth and his blade sought its eye. It missed, and the plate protecting the eye deflected the blade, chipping instead. The creature's shallow mouth closed, and two teeth he hadn't noticed before came up from the bottom and twitched against the skin of his suit. The ichor inside was like an epoxy, instantly clinging to his stump. The pair of teeth punctured his suit, biting into his arm. Disbelief and panic followed as he slashed at it, cutting an arm away. The other two creatures were on him then, and he could feel the hooks and limbs grasping at his body, testing his suit.

The sensation of something cold running into his arm chilled him, and he struggled harder, trying to get his stump free of the mouth that closed around it as he slashed. "No, not like this," he said as he felt another one of the beings grasp him from behind.

Two teeth jabbed at the base of his skull spastically as its broad hood wrapped around his head from the back. It stretched and closed around his face as he shouted; "No!" The scant light of the bridge disappeared as it finished enveloping his head and tiny hooks started tugging at the edges of his face-plate. That was secondary to the feeling of those jabbing teeth on his neck, and Vollis began to panic, slashing and digging his knife at the creature behind him as he struggled to yank his stump free.

"No!" he shouted before the jabbing teeth broke through his

suit and turned his objection into a scream as they scratched and dug at the base of his skull. He slipped and fell as he tried to rip the creature off of him, the feeling of it biting at bone, cracking and chipping it rapidly was greater than any sense.

As Vollis slipped and rolled into the corner, it broke through and he felt a wave of relief. There was also something else, an ebbing of his will to be parted from the parasite. It was right that it was there. Separating from it would be horrible, painful, and most likely fatal. There was no doubt in Vollis' mind that the creature was saving his life.

The limbs of the insect stretched and shifted until they were parallel to his own, and he used his arm computer to let it in under his suit. He had to protect this miracle being while he became something more, a greater whole.

The hooks trying to get under his faceplate stopped, and the hood enveloping his head retracted, stretching, flattening until it became a thick collar that surrounded his neck. There was screaming, a weak sound, the announcement a kind of prey would make when its fear rises. It was coming from him, and Vollis stopped. There was nothing to fear. He was superior.

Several pin-pricks along his back made him wince, and he shuddered as several tendrils reached deeply into his chest and midsection. The pain of merging was horrific, more so than anything he could have imagined. He quaked for several moments as those thin things moved through his body, seeking attachment, and it finally stopped with the reward of painlessness. It wasn't some kind of chemical bliss, but the lack of sensation. All of his normal senses were present, but agony was absent.

The details of his life - grudges, debt, honour and all the

people he cared for seemed trivial. Ambitions and desires were replaced completely by newer, simpler ones. The brother who held his stump flushed it out of his mouth with a neutralizing fluid that broke the bonds of the adhesive saliva. It backed away, aware that Vollis Mikan had merged with his brother.

They were part of a brood that their creator, Zarrix, allowed to be captured by the first mammalians to find them. The Elder Master knew this would come to pass. They would be awakened by a curious mammal, and they would merge, develop, and announce their location to the Elder Master. Zarrix would retrieve them, and give them instructions. Until then, they were to survive.

All of this was known for an absolute certainty, how anything else could have any importance was a mystery to Vollis. There was a more immediate truth, however. His brothers needed to merge. They wouldn't survive for long without hosts.

He got up off the deck and led them from the ship with care. Instead of a right hand, he had curled claws and a multi-jointed wrist that would eventually extend. He used the claws to grapple the back of the pilot's seat, and then climb through the gap in the cockpit. There was someone outside, a human who brayed; "Hello! We're here to help! Sing out if you can!"

They waved searchlights as they rushed across the yard next to the ship. They were laden with equipment, unarmoured, drenched and partially blinded by the pouring rain. Behind them was a hovering transport. "Help!" Vollis cried with a new, raspy voice. "In here!"

"We're coming, stay where you are!" said one of the

humans. He started leading a small group of four to the crashed ship.

His brothers twitched in anticipation, heeding his instruction to wait in the cockpit. The hosts were coming, and there would be three other mammals for entertainment and nourishment.

FORTY

Triton Medical

THERE WAS no end to the medical miracles that Remmy found whenever he came back from a dangerous mission. He'd been injured, rebuilt in major and minor ways and didn't like to think about how close he'd come to not being fixable at all. As he ran his tongue over a nearly complete set of brand-new teeth he couldn't help but grin. It was another miracle, even though he knew exactly how they'd come to be.

"You have been neglecting yourself," said the small voice of the Raven's medical officer, Pokey. The robot had been upgraded with a main body that had more compartments but was still made of collapsable, thin limbs that could expand to the rough shape of a human in case he had to use devices or stations that required that kind of height and reach. He was in collapsed mode as he met up with Remmy in Triton Medical. Barely a metre tall with small arms, and an oval head that could be in any orientation. Pokey seemed to prefer to regard the world horizontally.

"I haven't seen you in days and you start by nagging?" Remmy replied as he checked his command and control unit.

"I thought I'd skip pleasantries since your suit log indicates that you've been falling well short of your suggested calorie intake," the robot required.

"I can survive longer than the average human without food or water," Remmy replied.

"While that is true, your new physiology requires over four thousand calories a day for peak performance, and you've also fallen well short of the nutritional recommendations set out by Haven Fleet Medical," Pokey replied. "I may have to report this to your superiors."

"I'm going to send you back to the Raven," he said before knocking on the treatment room door.

Zac Levigne, the lead Medical Technician opened it, glanced up and said; "Hey, Remmy. How'd your treatment turn out?"

"Perfect. My whole mouth feels new and weird, but I'm glad to have a set of chompers again. Theo is an artist with nanobots. It took him three seconds to program the whole sequence and it went perfectly."

"I would have done it in two point eight," Pokey grumbled.

"Sure," Zac said to the small medical droid, shaking his head. "We could use your help in Bio Regeneration, Pokey. Just remember; humans appreciate quality over speed when it comes to limb replacement."

"Captain?" Pokey asked, his head tilting up.

"May as well help out here as long as the Raven doesn't have a mission," Remmy replied.

"'May as well,' you say," Pokey grumbled as he trundled away on wheeled feet. "Like you're lending me out to polish floors."

"Here to see Tammy?" Zac asked.

"And anyone else I can entertain," Remmy replied.

"Well, definitely start with her. She's wide awake and scrolling through Crewcast, looking for anything interesting," Zac replied. "She's behind the third curtain. I've got to make sure all the bioprinters are running right."

"How is she?" Remmy asked him in a whisper.

"Well, she's shrapnel free. That was easy enough, you can ask her about the rest," Zac replied. "She wouldn't let me go until I gave her every detail about her new foot. Oh, make sure she doesn't fight the brace."

He was gone before Remmy had a chance to ask any more questions, tapping and scrolling on an ultra-thin screen. Remmy peeked around the nearest privacy curtain and watched Tammy's face light up. "Captain! I'd get up, but, um…"

The bed held her still from the hips down by forming around her as though Tammy was half out of a mould. A screen at the foot of the bed showed him something he hoped she couldn't see, the auto-surgery system using several fine, quick-moving tools to properly attach her new foot to her leg. It was happening in that cast-like enclosure around her legs. "Hey," Remmy replied, a little distracted by the raw image.

"How's it going down there? The screen is facing away from me," Tammy said, craning her head a little.

"Stay still," Remmy said, trying to figure out if it was going well. All he could really understand for certain was what a status bar was saying. "You're good, it says you're sixty-three percent done."

"Oh," she replied, crossing her arms. They'd changed her into a white thin suit that he recognised from his time in hospitals. It was made to be comfortable, to split apart anywhere at an instant's notice, and to maintain a healthy environment. Her black hair and eyes were a stark contrast. "Did I hear Pokey?"

"Yeah, he's even worse than before," Remmy snickered as he brought a stool over and sat at her bedside.

"Roscoe teases him, Mayu confuses him, Nigel ignores him, and I'm always nice to him," she shook her head just a little then. "I don't think his socialization program is finding the right combo of influences."

"Well, I did steal him from his home. Maybe we should get him to shadow Theo for a while," Remmy replied. "So, how's everything?"

"You know, felt nanobots and a few other tools wiggle all the shrapnel out," she replied, looking at her legs.

"You felt?" Remmy asked.

"Oh, there wasn't any pain, but I could feel that stuff making its way around all my arteries, veins, tendons and stuff. It was interesting. There are no scars, or any sign that there was anything wrong. Oh, and I can't feel anything going on down there though, you know, where I'm getting a new foot. They say I'll be dancing on it in a couple hours." She was suddenly excited as she asked; "But how'd you make out? Last I saw, you were all gums."

"You noticed that, huh? I tried to hide it," Remmy replied.

"No chance. Lemmie see the new chompers," she said, pointing at his lips.

Remmy gave her an exaggerated grin. "They're almost too perfect."

"Wow, they are, and they're so white," Tammy remarked as she moved her finger a little closer.

She squealed as he leaned forward a little so he was well short of really chomping on the digit as he pretended to do just that with an audible clack. "Theo said they'd dull a little."

"What was it like? Did they drill 'em in?" Tammy asked.

"No, it was kinda like they grew from the roots. Nanobots did the implantation and just built from there. Other than the headgear they put me in, the worst thing was the creaking and grinding feeling at the start. After that I just had to sit there with my mouth wide open - thus the headgear - while they built my chompers."

"Nice, you look a little different, but good," Tammy told him, resting her hand on his.

He didn't pull away, but he could feel a lull in conversation start to lengthen as they stared at each other. "So, where's your sister?" he asked.

"Oh, Ash? She's on the bridge. On duty. I didn't understand how much of a big deal she is here before. On the Triton, I mean. We're moving on soon, and she's the lead navigator, so what part of the asteroid belt we go to next is up to her. How we get there is just as big of a deal, because we're hiding. I mean, imagine, she's the one who figures out the best spots then the Captain picks. Everyone on the ship has to trust her. It's wild."

"She earned the spot, it's pretty amazing," Remmy agreed.

"I'll see her later, everyone's getting together at the Pilot's Den."

"I've heard, I'll be there now that I can handle solid food," Remmy replied. "I'll probably have to hit the galley on the way there, Pokey says I'm underfed."

"Wait, how underfed?" she seemed fascinated.

"Well, when I was still stuck in Haven Medical, I was eating a special diet, a snack every hour, and between three to five big meals a day. I mean, I don't have to, but Pokey might be a little obsessed with me being 'optimal,' so, I'll give it a go."

"So, you're gonna be eating all the time, basically," she said, amused at the notion.

"Well, yeah. I can go a couple of months without food though, my body just goes into low-energy mode on its own. I've gotta agree, that would probably feel pretty crappy after a while," Remmy said.

"Probably. Can I ask you about something else? Something about the mission with Jake?" Tammy looked more serious then.

"Let the questioning begin," Remmy said.

"What was it like using a crush gate?"

It wasn't at all the kind of question he expected. People were curious about what the crew of the Triton and Samurai Squadron accomplished, if they were safe in the outer asteroid field, and a number of other things, but no one was asking about the adventure underground. Remmy thought about it for a moment, it was difficult to put into words. His finger found the sample Psyche Cube that Simon gave him in his pocket and he traced its shape. "Well, it was a wormhole gate designed for people and cargo containers, not ships, so at first there's this cold tingle and it feels like something pulls you in by the front. It almost hurt, and then it really did feel like a giant, hot hug, judging from the sensations my armour passed on. My heart skipped a beat and then I was in the plaza on the other side. I mean, it was perfect, like taking a long step."

"That's incredible, I wish I was there," Tammy said. "What about the things you brought back? What was in those cases?" she asked.

The thought that he should introduce her to Ruby sometime crossed his mind. There was a chance that they shared a similar kind of curiosity. Remmy wanted to be there for that too, even though he was still thinking of Simon. Exploration could cost you.

That notion and the memory of a short-lived friendship were written on his face, apparently. "Are you not supposed to talk about it?"

"Oh, no, I don't even know if things are classified in the new fleet," Remmy replied. "I'm pretty sure I can talk about it." He was just about to say something more when an artificial whistle sounded over the ship intercom and the Triton logo appeared at the foot of the bed.

The death's head hologram with the words DEPLOY, DOMINATE, DISAPPEAR along the top of the skull and TRITON in place of its teeth and lower jaw appeared as a large hologram. A female voice said; "Stand by for a message from Captain Stephanie Vega."

The image was replaced by a life-sized hologram of Captain Vega, who looked strong and confident in her black vacsuit and captain's long coat. "I am proud to announce that, thanks to your competence and quick action, the Triton hasn't lost a single crewmember. Having said that, we've sustained significant damage. Our hull is designed to regenerate, and it will, slowly. We can't go near the Rose System's sun because there are ships out there watching for us and we won't be jumping to another system to use the radiation from another sun to expedite the regeneration. We'll have to stay hidden in the system's outermost asteroid field instead, manually energizing sections of the hull as we conduct other repairs. We'll also be meeting new allies here. The British Alliance, Nafalli tribes, and several other independent fighting ships are on their way. I'm afraid that there will be a communications blackout coming, but we will reconnect to common networks regularly."

There were groans from several people in medical that drifted through the privacy curtains. Captain Vega continued. "We are a privateering ship, so we won't be getting medals from Haven Fleet, though I believe some of us would get them if they were still an option. We will be getting a bonus instead. A deposit of luxury credits will show up in everyone's account sometime in the next four hours."

Remmy wondered how many. He'd glanced at the reward chart and the splits that were predefined for rewards but gave up on figuring out what was worth what. One of the most important things about how they were paid was that Haven System Luxury Credits could be exchanged for platinum, which could be used anywhere as far as he knew. Even if the bonus was only a hundred credits, it would be enough to get most of the crew smiling.

"We have the honour of welcoming a large number of former crew from the Redstone. They did not make it here unscathed, so make them feel at home. They have a few civilians with them who will be taking roles aboard, at least until we can shuttle them off to a safe port. Most have applied for jobs here, and we'll be accepting most of them. Many have already offered to help with repairs. I'll be asking for crewmembers to volunteer for extra hours so we can get this ship back in perfect shape as soon as possible. We need everyone at every level. People to recycle scrap, charge sections of the hull, monitor repair drones, and everything else. Qualified and unqualified crew are welcome. When repairs near completion, we'll finish opening services and a few shops. Thanks to the merging of the Redstone crew with ours, we'll be able to work regular shifts, so you'll have more time to enjoy what the Triton can offer. This isn't only a ship of war, it was originally designed for exploration, to keep her crew safe, and comfortable on long voyages. This is our home, and you'll see that it's a good one. Let's celebrate our victory tonight, but not too hard. We all need to work tomorrow morning."

Remmy could hear the excitement and hope in the murmurs and comments of the large medical bay. People were having limbs attached, wounds that were hastily healed in the field fixed up and scans to make sure that whatever rushed repairs they had while fighting was executed properly. He regarded Tammy and saw that she was smiling. "Ash told me about the Botanical Gallery, the Green Deck where there were supposed to be shops, and quarters that were almost apartments. Are they still here? On the Triton? Even after all the refits and upgrades?"

"I guess we'll find out," Remmy said.

"Oh, get the Raven crew a place," she said excitedly. "Like a big apartment we can live in."

"I'll look into it if the rest of the crew are interested,"

Remmy replied, warming to the idea. He was used to living with a lot of people, it was something that was hard to escape on Freeground station.

"It's my honour to introduce Jake Valent, our Patron," Captain Vega said, drawing their attention back to the foot of the bed, where her hologram was stepping out of frame.

Jake took her place, still in armour that was showing a few new dents on its horizontal slats. "There's a lot of work to do, so I have to try to keep this short. A lot of you have probably noticed that the Triton is still operating like a military ship, and that will continue while you're on shift. Your Captain will make things more clear in the next few days, but follow the rules you knew in Haven Fleet until you're told that things have changed. Keep this term in mind: Mercenary ambition, military pride. Work hard because we hold each other's fate in our hands, because the fight is right, and because you're getting paid more than anyone in Haven Fleet. I don't think anyone signed up for the money, but it sure is nice."

"Hell yeah!" someone shouted from behind a curtain some-where in the room. A few people laughed, and one whooped.

Jake probably couldn't hear a response from the crew, and if he could, he went on without acknowledging them. "So, here's what I can tell you about. The Triton and the Merciless have severely damaged a powerful Citadel ship. I can't go into specifics, but early analysis indicates that their entire organiza-tion, which is allied with the Order, will be affected. Organiza-tion and morale will take years to recover."

He must have heard someone cheering then, because a smile started to curl the edges of his lips. Jake pressed it down after a moment as he described their next victory. "The Triton recovered most of the crew and civilian staff of the Redstone along with Captain Ruby Sima, who will be joining us. Thanks to that act of defiance against the Order, we've been contacted by the leadership of two of the largest nations on Rodus who want to help us fight the Order. We didn't save City Thirty-Five. Leader Bion made sure the Order got to work murdering as many civilians as they could as quickly as possible. We were just as quick to avenge them. Thanks to Samurai Squadron volunteer fighters and members of the Redstone Crew led by Captain Sima, we boarded the Locon and discovered thousands of framework soldier systems along with just as many androids. We destroyed them before they could be activated, buying Rodus time before the Order will be able to initiate a ground attack. We didn't actually know that was their plan until we boarded the Locon. Thanks to that, we've been able to warn the leadership in this solar system that ground attacks are coming and we've shared our tactics for destroying framework soldiers. In an effort to slow the Order down even more, we removed the leadership of the Locon from the equation, including a new, experimental type of officer they grew in a lab somewhere. Bion and his entire senior staff were killed in the action. The Locon and its sister heavy cruisers have been heavily damaged and will require so many resources to repair that they may not be fully functional for months. Sometimes injuring your enemy is better than killing them, and the Order is far from their main manufacturing centres, so they can't afford to lose these ships."

"I admit, he's smarter than I thought. Don't tell him, but I'm a little surprised," Tammy said, smiling.

"I'm not, but I've gotta say, this is the short version?" Remmy muttered, enjoying Tammy's snicker.

As if he heard him, Jake said; "I'm going to wrap this up. There have been sacrifices on our end, and we're going to have to work hard to get back in shape, but I want to acknowledge Samurai Squadron. They prepared multiple strategies quickly and executed them well, risking everything so we could have a multi-faceted victory that goes further than what I've told you. If it wasn't for them, hundreds of people who are on this ship right now and I would be under the remains of City Thirty-Five, including me. Enjoy yourselves tonight."

"Mercenary ambition, military pride," Tammy said. "I think it's going to take me a long time to really understand what that means, but I think I get it a little. Wait, he didn't talk about what we found in the lab?"

"Do you understand what we saw?" Remmy asked.

"Not really, I mean, I'm trying not to think about it. It's kinda nightmare fuel, right?" The auto-surgeon beeped.

Theodore walked through the curtain and smiled at Tammy. "The new foot we grew for you is fully attached and there's no sign that it's a replacement. Well, it's paler, but that'll even out. The system will flex and stimulate your new foot so you won't have to go through manual rehabilitation. You don't have to stay completely still, but you'll feel your leg jerk and turn as the system does several days of work for you in about half an hour of muscle and nerve stimulation. Just stay in bed, let the machine do everything for you."

"So... I'm all set? I'll be walking tonight?"

"Yes. There shouldn't be so much as a limp," Theodore said as he walked away. "I have a Sergeant who is having an arm attached. I'll return when I receive the signal that the rehabilitation cycle is complete. Please tap the button if you feel any pain."

"Thank you Theodore," Tammy called after him.

Remmy didn't know exactly what to do then. When he tried to find something to talk about, topics slipped away. It was maddening. He reached for low-hanging fruit. "Congratulations on your new foot."

"I can't wait to see it. Y'know, make sure they didn't give me two left ones," Tammy said, looking down. "Distract me."

Remmy stared into her dark eyes, frozen, remembering an ancient cartoon of a deer in the middle of a highway with a giant truck speeding towards them. He was relieved when she laughed. He remarked; "You found it, the exact phrase that completely clears my head and shuts me up."

"Am I the first?" she asked, maybe exaggerating her excitement.

"I think so. Okay, how about I get us something to chomp. I'm a snack-based life form."

"Oh, me too! Get me some puffs, anything salty," she said. "Then maybe tell me about your trip under Panda?"

With a nod, he retreated to the vending machines. As he punched buttons and retrieved bags of Cheezie Twisties, Pickle Flavoured Protein Puffs, Choco Bombs and Zucchini Zazzers, he considered how much he'd tell her about Charon-Simon and the Psyche Cubes.

Thinking of whether or not Simon's cube survived, and how he may be trapped down there made his heart ache. By the time he returned to Tammy's bedside, Remmy found that he wanted to share the tale. She took the bag of Cheezie Twisties. "Okay, about that under city. It's not the most uplifting story."

"I understand if you're not ready to talk about it. We could watch something," Tammy offered.

Thinking about it for a moment, Remmy realized that he really did want to tell someone about Simon and the amazing things he'd seen. He was also thinking about how he might convince Jake that digging through the rubble was a good idea. "No, I want to show you what happened down there. Maybe we could build a report?" Instead, he'd be building a proposal, but he wasn't sure how convincing it could be, so telling her it would be a report was a way of holding his hope in reserve.

"Absolutely," she said with a smile that pushed every thought out of his head for a moment.

Thankfully, he had a moment to gather his thoughts and find a good place to start while he got his thoughts back on track as she popped an orange puff into her mouth, which was quickly followed by another.

Remmy decided to start with their arrival on Rodus, but took a moment to try his Choco Puffs. "I love having teeth," he sighed, eliciting a snicker from his one-woman audience.

FORTY-ONE

The Pilot's Lounge

THE TONE in the Pilot's Den was split. In the main pub section, Ruby Sima was with her officers and a large portion of her crew. Their attitudes were guardedly pleased. They licked their wounds as they honoured the ones who didn't make it all the way to the Triton while celebrating the arrival of the majority.

Word was getting around to the rest of the crew that Ruby admitted to everyone that trying to pick up Jacob Valent using their covert transport was a mistake. According to some, the pickup was her idea, while others said that Jake was taking credit for the bad move. Minh-Chu didn't know if it was intentional, but making it unclear as to who was to blame seemed to dull the ire Ruby's crew had for her. Only a small handful wanted to leave entirely, and most of those were civilians that

Ruby picked up along the way. They would have to wait a day or two to leave. A shuttle would take them to a safe station right before the Triton moved to their new hiding spot.

That load of gossip was a welcome, if short-lived, distraction for Minh-Chu, who was waiting for several things to happen. He was in the Lounge section of the Pilot's Den, which had been reserved for Samurai Squadron and friends who wanted to pay their respects. It wasn't a wake for the pilots they lost, but he was starting to see how much it looked like one. The bartender for the smaller two-man counter on the Lounge side was a tall human man, and David, one of the squadron's support crew, had slipped behind to help him out. His contract with the Triton had just been finalized, and he was designated Level Four, not an officer, but a Supervisor for his section, which put him in charge of three hangars and over two dozen repair and maintenance workers. Several of them were in the Lounge, friendly with the pilots who depended on them.

"Get out there, my mate's on the way," said the bartender as he handed David a pitcher of fuzzy blonde ale and a pair of glasses. "If anyone asks, this is what's on tap. Aarro, Patron's choice."

David nodded respectfully at the bartender and carried the pitcher to a table where several of the support crewmembers were gathering. "Compliments of the bartender and our Patron," he announced. "I only have two glasses, so go get yourself one before we see the bottom of this."

Minh-Chu took a seat in one of the largest booths near the stage. Ashley joined him, slipping her hand into his and leaning against him. They were both in neutral black vacsuits and boots that were the same design as the Haven military uniforms, only they were stripped of most markings. Instead, they had the Samurai Squadron death's head on their backs and the similar Triton logo on their shoulders. The discussion on what to wear that night was short. Neither of them knew, so they defaulted to something familiar, something that no one could point at as disrespectful.

It turned out that they made the right call. Most of the people in the Lounge were dressed almost exactly the same, and those who turned up in party attire re-adjusted their vacsuit settings to match the more unremarkable uniforms.

"You okay?" Ashley asked.

"I hate waiting, but I'm all right. Are you okay?" he asked.

"Tired. Wishing everyone was here," she replied in a whisper. "What's the big bother?"

That was one of her new ways of asking what his biggest problem was, a phrase Tammy used. "I can't get a response from Haven Fleet about the Resurrection Program," he whispered so low that anyone five centimetres away might not hear.

"Oh, no," she replied. "They know it's you calling, right?"

"Definitely. I think that's why I can't get a response," he said, checking his wrist again. "It might just take time. Jake's got a request in and Oz is investigating it for us."

Jake sat down at their booth with Alice and Carnie close behind. "It's been half an hour, which, knowing Oz, means he's probably arguing with someone over there."

"Do you think we'll be able to use it?" Ashley asked, leaning half way across the table, keeping her voice low.

Alice offered a reply, looking like she could nod off at any moment. "The program's been in trouble for a while. They had a less than fifteen percent success rate. I've seen a regeneration go wrong. Not everyone is ready to be brought back, they can go way off."

"Then there's the whole association thing," Jake said, pouring a glass of yellow-orange, foamy beer from an extra large pitcher. "Haven may not be able to use that program for me even if I pay for it. They might not want to help Samurai Squadron because you're connected to a war criminal. Sorry, Minh. Maybe Liara and Leon were right. I should have asked you if you wanted to pay the bill for the whole squadron and fly off your own ship instead of the Triton. You know, before all this started."

"I love this ship, and I'll fly for you anytime," Minh-Chu replied. He didn't like to be reminded that he owned a share of the entire Haven System. It was given to him when Ayan decided that it was wrong for her to be the solitary owner. There was a document detailing all the technicalities that led to her decision, and he'd only ever read the summary which was fifteen thousand words on its own. Ashley never said anything about it, and he didn't know why, but he didn't know what to do about it either. So he never looked at the accounts that held an unknown amount of accumulating wealth, or used his position for leverage. "I am just a pilot who wants to share his limited wisdom and fly with the rest of the unusual birds."

"Everyone is happy you and your squadron are here. I wouldn't be breathing above ground without you," Jake said as he placed a tall, cool glass of beer in front of Minh-Chu.

He regarded it with a cocked head. "It looks pretty classic."

"It's Aarro. Errinish sap beer. Not much alcohol, but there's something in it that the Nafalli say is relaxing and 'positive mood making,'" Jake explained.

Being generally polite, and someone who learned his lesson about over-imbibing for the most part, Minh-Chu waited until everyone had a glass. "Oh, Aarro," Remmy said as he and Tammy sat on the opposite side of the booth. That filled it, with Jake trapped furthest from either end. "I've been reading about Nafalli culture, and the tribes we're going to be meeting love this stuff. The encyclopedia is right about the smell. It's like sharp, sweet sap."

"What do the reviews say?" Alice asked as she eyed a glass that was passed to Ashley.

"A few complaints that this is a weak brew, especially since it was made in a food fab, but I didn't want to start with a stronger one," Jake said, skipping himself and putting a glass in front of Alice.

She moved it on to Carnie. "You can have mine this round. I'm just staying up until Mom calls."

Another thing that Minh-Chu was waiting for. Ayan was up, alert and was going to be calling sometime soon. She wanted to speak to her relations, but she added him and Ashley to the list too. There were rumours on the Hart News Stream that Ayan was already caught up in something political. Minh-Chu hoped they were untrue, she deserved some time to recover.

"How's your foot?" Ashley asked Tammy.

"I don't notice a difference, but I'm still going to lean on him tonight, just in case," Tammy said, bumping Remmy with her shoulder.

"Isn't there protocol about that? You know, he's your Captain," Ashley asked with a mischievous smile.

"The Sky Queen is on duty, and the Clever Dream is next in rotation," Jake said passively, just stating a fact as he poured.

"I have no designs on being anything but a complete gentleman," Remmy said, blushing from neck to nose. "Just supporting a recovering crewmember."

"Sounds like a plan," Ashley said, sharing an identical smile with her sister.

Minh-Chu saw that Dame had come in. Rip, his long hair tucked under his collar, was pushing a hover cart behind her with one hand with a standard preserve crate on top. It had been painted with a white lacquer to make it look more like a piece of furniture. Dame's eyes searched the room for something. Being the tallest pilot in the squadron, she had a fairly easy time of it.

This was another thing he was waiting for. Easy had left something that was meant to go along with his Final Notice in his room. There was a request that someone go get it before it played back, if possible, and Dame had obviously found it in his quarters. As Minh-Chu stood up, so he could be seen, he imagined the pilot's new space aboard the Triton, assuming that his rucksack and any other belongings were still sitting in his bedroom, the space left mostly as it was. None of them really had time to move in. Even his and Ashley's rooms were undecorated, and sparse. It would stay that way for a while longer, since they would be in ready quarters for at least a few days so they could respond to an alert at a moment's notice.

Dame's icy blue eyes found him, and she nodded at Minh-Chu. "Time for Notices." He took a sip of the Aarro and found it surprisingly sweet, woody, and tangy with mild carbonation. "That's not bad."

Ashley stood up, gave him a kiss on the cheek and let him

out of the booth. "Remember what you told me about this kinda thing a while ago," Ashley whispered.

He recalled the advice he gave her during independent Officer training many months before and nodded. "Shorter is better, let them do the talking," he replied.

"No, don't come running if you see someone crying," she replied, referring to something that wasn't in the manual. Back then, when she was about to take the test regarding breaking bad news to subordinates, she asked him about people breaking into tears, and that was his advice. "Everyone's gonna be okay."

Dame approached him then. "The note on his file didn't say when to open the box, so I left it closed. Rip scanned it. He says there's nothing dangerous inside, as if there would be." She sent him a sideways glance that could cut transparesteel, then returned her attention to Minh-Chu with a less severe expression.

"I'm sure Easy wouldn't mind someone getting a peek," Minh-Chu said, taking a moment to look up at her and say; "I'm sorry we lost him. I know you two were close friends."

She only nodded. If Minh-Chu needed to point out an example of a stoic, Dame would be his second choice after Jake. He gestured towards his spot beside Ashley and she sat down.

As Minh-Chu crossed the room to the short, three step stage in front of the broad view of the asteroid field in front of the Triton, the room began to quiet down. Every pilot from Samurai Squadron was there along with many people from the hangars and officers, with the notable exclusion of Captain Vega and half of the main bridge staff. They were finishing their duties and had been ordered to rest.

The last thing on Minh-Chu's mind was sleep as he turned

and faced a large room that had people filling every seat, standing in the doorways and staring up at him from the bar at the back. Ruby Sima and her officers, numbering six in total, were all there. He didn't know their names, but they'd lost more people than he did. Ruby had shared her words with them, but they still seemed to be searching, listening for something.

With all his heart, he wanted to give everyone in that room the right words, but sharing some quote or general wisdom didn't feel right. It would be like filling in a blank instead of sharing exactly how he guessed everyone was feeling at the moment. Minh-Chu guessed that he shared in that, and began by describing what was going on. "I'm between anger and sorrow," he started. Someone had activated an amplification system somewhere and his voice carried to everyone. "We've lost a lot of people in a short amount of time, and while I think we deserve the pat on the back that our Patron and Captain Vega gave us a little while ago, along with the bonuses, none of that will make up for the cost. We prepare for our stories, our lives to end. Not many of us actually believe it'll happen anytime soon, but we do it because we are told to because people like me have seen so many people go before their time. We, the officers who know, tell everyone to leave a recording in your bunk, or in your storage so you can make sure people know how you felt about them. It also prepares us to do our jobs. We leave that recording behind so we know our affairs are in order. Our wishes are known, and we can tell the people who matter to us how much they mean to us while we were around." His gaze landed on Orner, who was standing in the doorway beside Agameg. The large man, who had never been to an event like the one he was seeing, stared across the room, hanging on every word, a sympathetic look in his eyes.

A glance at Ashley, who was hanging on his every word, reminded him about brevity, Minh-Chu said; "Everyone we lost over the past few days died for a purpose. That is, so we could be here together. It's up to us to make the most of it." He looked around the silent room. "The pilots who we lost today wanted their fellow fliers to see their Notices during a gathering like this."

As Minh-Chu stepped to the side, a full-sized hologram of Maid appeared in his place. "I guess my ticket got punched. For anyone who doesn't know old Earth expressions, that means I didn't make it back alive," she said. There was a jitter in the recording and she continued from a slightly different position. "That opening took nine takes, then there was a drill." She shook her head before going on. "I'm tired of editing, so I'll just spill my guts. Again, for non-human culturalists, that's not literal."

There was a titter of laughter, and Minh-Chu noticed Garma explain something to Gren, who nodded his shiny green head.

In a slightly more serious demeanour, Maid went on. "Listen, I didn't make a whole lot of friends while I was around, especially since I lost my share before I got to the Haven System, but you know who you are. If you think I was your buddy, then I was, and I loved you even if I didn't hang out very much. To be honest, I saw this coming, and every time I got into the cockpit I was so excited to be there that I didn't care about the risks to myself. Whoever was flying with me was more important. While I flew for Samurai Squadron, I knew I was out there for the right reason, and that's what really mattered. The most important thing about this is that you know I have no regrets."

A voice from out of frame asked; "What about resurrection?"

"Oh, right. Yeah, if you need a great pilot, bring me back. Give her all my stuff. I don't have kids, and my cousins were taken out in the Fourth Fall, so there's no one else."

"Do you have anything else to say?" asked the same voice. It wasn't one that Minh-Chu knew.

Maid thought for a moment, looking down, her face still, then she looked back up. "Don't worry about me, just fight to protect people, if you're going to fight for anything."

The recording ended, and Maid's image faded out. Minh-Chu moved a few steps towards the centre of the stage, then realized he didn't have a drink in his hand. Breaker swept in for the rescue, leaning towards him from stage left, handing him a glass with clear liquid in it. "I hope this isn't jet fuel," Minh-Chu said to him as he watched the pilot wipe a tear that had been collecting on his lower lid away.

"It's fine," Breaker replied. "Refreshing."

Minh-Chu looked over the crowd then, seeing a few tear-filled eyes, but even fewer down-turned stares. That didn't mean that Maid wasn't well-liked, only that there was understanding amongst her friends and comrades. He could relate. What she said in her Notice wasn't meant to draw tears from people, but to comfort them, and his appreciation for that, along with the full realization that she was gone, brought with it a pang of grief that he hoped to hide with what he did next as he raised his glass. "To Maid, a professional, and not a counter of friends, but a friend to more people than she knew."

"To Maid," came the refrain from the room as he downed the slender glass's contents. An instant before it hit his lips, he realized that it was a mint drink, and he shuddered as the powerful, pure flavour passed through his mouth and down his tongue. He handed the empty glass to Breaker as he shook his head a couple of times vigorously. It burned like dry ice tumbling down then sent the same sensation through his middle before it faded.

A few people saw the reaction and laughed, so Minh-Chu added; "She'd think that was pretty funny too."

Ashley rushed to him with a pint of Aarro. Her eyes and cheeks were a little puffy. He'd seen her cry more than once before, enough to know that she'd barely started. He accepted the glass, took a sip to wash some of the syrupy mint drink away and thanked her. She stayed in a chair near the stage, and he was relieved. Breaker gave his chair up so there was one beside her, and stood.

"We lost someone else today, and he had something to share with us, so I need everyone from Samurai Squadron to stick around for a while after his Notice, if they can," Minh-Chu said. He was about to activate Easy's recording when he spotted Dame, who was tapping her command and control unit with a shaky finger. Minh-Chu took his seat beside Ashley and put his arm around her.

Easy appeared in the centre of the modest stage, in his full uniform and jacket. "...to record a new one," he was telling someone to his left. He regarded the recorder then, giving the appearance that he was looking out at everyone in the Lounge.

Most of the people knew him for his bare-metal cybernetic arm. It was something he'd had installed well before he joined Haven Fleet, and Minh-Chu realized then that he'd never heard the story behind it.

"I was just saying that I forgot we had to re-record this since the squadron separated from Haven Fleet. Here we go. I've got practice at this now, and I know who will need a few last words from me, so I know what to say. I hope it's what you need to hear."

For a moment, Minh-Chu expected a short, clever rant, like something he might have recorded before he met Ashley. He liked Easy. who lived up to his callsign even in his Notice, being relaxed and quick to smile. "History is crowded with the dead. Most of them are boring, mentioned in obituaries or lists that are attached to events that are horrible, sometimes honourable. I don't remember who said that, but I hope the list was short on the day I bought it. My ancestors back on earth used to have parades when people died to celebrate their lives. If you're going to group up to say farewell to me, that's how I want it. I'm gonna give you a hand with that. There are seven vintage magnums of Old Grandine stashed in my quarters. It's not classy, but it'll make your head go 'yo' and your body go 'woo' so put some music on and remember me until it's gone. I bequeath all my worldly possessions to myself for a year, because I think I'm the only one who would pay to put me in the queue to be brought back. I've got a pile of credits that should cover a resurrection. That's what the seventh bottle of old Grandine is for: the party I'll throw for everyone who drank the first six bottles when I come back. If there's no way that I'm coming back though, go polish that bottle off too. I leave Dame in charge of it, and if she goes back home, I'm sure she'll find someone else to take care of it. I know, this message could be longer, but I don't really know what to say other than; 'I hope you miss me just enough so you're happy to see me again when I come back.'"

A tear ran down Minh-Chu's face and he squeezed Ashley's shoulders. She was being strong, but was unable to keep her lip from quivering and the waterworks from turning on. He followed her guarded gaze before she turned away and saw that she was looking at Dame, who was already on her feet, opening the preserve crate. As promised, there were seven large bottles in there that looked like old champagne.

Nearly everyone was watching her, except for Carnie, Jake, and Breaker, who all moved to help her. Alice shook her head and joined in, carefully drawing the bottles out. "Uh, guys, there's something going on," came the uncertain, alarmed voice of Remmy from across the room. "I'm sorry this is happening... well... now, and here, but it's live."

All eyes turned to the stage as Oz, or The Haven System Defence Minister Terry Ozark McPatrick, appeared there. Unlike the Notices, his background wasn't blank. Instead, he was surrounded by a severely damaged cabin that may have been the Merciless' galley. Minh-Chu checked the Stellarnet address at a glance, and he could see that the broadcast was going to every communication node they had floating in space or installed in a ship. "This is hitting hundreds of solar systems," Pixie muttered from behind him.

He regarded his audience with an uncharacteristically stony expression. There was a fire in his eyes that Minh-Chu had never seen. "Citadel, an ally to the Order of Eden, has destroyed Panda, a historic independent city that was also known as City

Thirty-Five on Planet Rodus. Our scans have confirmed over eleven thousand dead, half a million displaced so far, but we are a good distance away, and unable to get a clear picture because they've blockaded the world. Jamming satellites have been deployed. Rodus' leadership has reached out to me and requested our help. Other colonies in the solar system have done the same, along with space stations, asteroid outposts, and several moons have also reached out, calling for aid in response to a statement from the Order that simply claims that the Rose System is now theirs. This cannot stand."

"I think the solar system is about to get crowded," Gren said.

"It's already crowded," Garma retorted in a correcting whisper.

"This, following a direct attack on the modern founder of the Haven System, Ayan Anderson, and her infant daughter by Citadel, is evidence that tyranny and malice are here, on our doorstep and in our solar system. To anyone who resists the idea of Haven Fleet acting now, I say; when war comes to heaven, everyone may as well be in hell."

Jake was turned completely towards the stage, staring at Oz's image, his jaw set. Captain Sima, her officers, every member of Samurai Squadron and most of the rest of the people in the room were riveted as well. Ashley's tears were drying up, and Minh-Chu was hoping that he was right in guessing where Oz was going with his speech. If the conclusion came anywhere short of what he was expecting, Minh-Chu would fly to the Merciless on his own to confront his old friend. There could only be one announcement that would make what Oz was saying more than meaningless sabre rattling.

Defence Minister Terry Ozark McPatrick went on with a

deep, powerful voice. "It is with a clear conscience, perfect certainty, a majority vote of the Haven Triumvirate and the support of the British Alliance that I announce the Haven Nations declaration of war against the Order of Eden and Citadel. Their companies, associates and anyone who gives them assistance or comfort will also be targets. If you think Haven Nation is an underdog, or ill-equipped for war, I promise that you'll be proven wrong. We invite anyone who is willing to fight to join our Privateer program or to enlist with Haven Fleet. You will find no better rewards for captures and enemy kills, and no finer military organization. Join me. Free the galaxy."

That was what Minh-Chu needed to hear from the Defence Minister. Haven Fleet, the organization that followed after the first military force he joined, Freeground Fleet, and had seen grow, would stand with Samurai Squadron in the fight. There were few things he wanted more. Where Oz, his old friend was concerned, Minh-Chu knew that he would be glad that Haven Fleet was going on the offence, but there would be no busier time in his life. Minh-Chu couldn't imagine anyone else doing the job of Defence Minister better.

The room erupted as the transmission ended, and six magnums of Old Grandine were uncorked so people who knew Easy, and then the rest of the people there could drink to the war. Dame made sure that the seventh bottle remained unpopped, keeping it at her side as though she was holding hope under its cork.

FORTY-TWO

Mother Figure

THE AMOUNT of free time Minh-Chu had on any given day was severely limited, so he ignored a lot of details that didn't pertain to the well-being of his Squadron, or Ashley. Many people had silent artificial intelligences on their command and control units, or whatever they did most of their personal computing on that sifted through everything and presented the most important stuff.

When it came time to join Jake and Alice in one of the private lounges, called mini-lounges by many, Minh-Chu found himself seriously thinking that he should install one of those. He had no idea where those were, how to get to them, or what they looked like. Even searching the map of the Triton revealed little, only that it was one floor up using narrow staircases hidden in the Pilot's Den, and that all the lifts near the front of the ship could take you there too.

Ashley knew where they were. "Tammy found these the first time we visited the Lounge," she explained. "There are some private rooms below and above. A few of them used to be like board rooms that were off from the auditorium a couple of decks up, but they were converted when it was rebuilt. The last refit was pretty wild."

"I barely see half of that on my map," Minh-Chu sighed, switching to a holographic cut-away model of the Triton. "Oh, there it is."

"Is your map updated?" Ashley asked as they slipped through a door that was barely hidden near the back of the Pilot's Lounge. There was an elevator that could take five people or two Nafalli, if he were to guess, and it lurched up quickly once the door was closed.

After checking his map set for the Triton and realizing that it was two versions out of date, he ordered it to download the new one with a tap. "Thank you," he said.

Ashley smiled at him and gave him a kiss that was so light that it was just a feather touch of her lips. They came out onto a low-lit corridor that was black and blue with gold trim. Its deck was polished to a shine, and there was a classy element to it with open double doors every ten to fifteen metres. Most of the rooms were unfurnished, simply nice spaces with absolutely nothing inside. He checked the new map and looked at the details. "So, these are designed for high-ranking officers and as rewards for groups of crewmembers."

"You didn't read about the ticket system?" Ashley asked, surprised.

The only thing Minh-Chu remembered about it was that he skipped it, so he shook his head. "What is it?"

"Well, crewmembers from different departments and work groups can earn tickets by achieving a bunch of goals. Like no one being late for two weeks or getting some difficult work done before deadlines. Any senior officer can set the goals or reward tickets. Agameg or someone else in administration determines how many can be given out. Anyway, groups can redeem them to get into nice spots for a while, or they can use the tickets for other stuff. I guess it's not important right now because not all the rewards are in place, but they're really meant for off time while we're between star systems and other downtime."

"Not bad," Minh-Chu replied as he followed the directions on his command and control unit. A grey line appeared on the floor, leading them to the right room. He peeked through a pair of open doors as they passed and saw one of the furnished areas. There was enough space for at least a dozen people inside, with cushy furniture, a high-quality holographic entertainment system that was made to envelop the entire room, its own food service, and a long table that was docked in the ceiling that could be lowered for everyone to sit at. There was also a perfect floor-to-ceiling view from the front of the ship. "When can we move in?"

"We haven't even decorated our quarters yet," Ashley snickered. "Besides, there are no beds up here. It's not that kinda private spot."

"Well, look who's mind is in the gutter?" Minh-Chu teased.

She gave him a shocked, amused look. "I do not have a gutter mind."

It was good to see her rebounding. The mood in the Pilot's

Lounge was complicated. Happy at Haven finally officially joining them in the fight, and mournful at losing two of their best and most well-liked pilots. There was an effort to celebrate their accomplishments and to remember what it was like to know them, and people were doing their best to stay positive, but that could collapse into tears at any moment. It was a wake even if no one wanted to call it that. He didn't want to leave them on their own for long and suspected that Ashley felt the same way.

They arrived at Private Lounge Number Three and the double doors opened. Jake, Alice and Carnie were already within, sitting on a very long sofa that was shaped in a gradual curve. Across from them was Ayan with Laura sleeping soundly on her chest on a reclined seat. At least, that's what it looked like at first before Minh-Chu realized it was actually a holo-gram. "Hello, Minh, Ash. Thank you for coming, it's good to see you both," Ayan said to them as they made their way inside and sat down.

"Good to see you too!" Ashley said as she took a seat. "And Laura."

"She'd be happy to see you too, but she's wiped out after trying to get up on her hands and knees for a bit. This one has an independent streak."

"It runs in the family," Jake said as he nudged Alice a little. "So does napping."

"Sorry, I've been focusing way too hard the last couple days," Alice said, interrupted by a yawn. "Quan told me everyone reacts to shutting their own feels off differently. He predicts a couple nights of oversleeping and nightmares. Woo."

"Oh, no," Ashley cooed.

"It's fine. I've learned my lesson. I'm not some android that can switch inconvenient emotions off without having nap-mares about carnivorous land-fish in the middle of a mission debrief."

"It was hilarious," Jake mouthed almost silently. "She fell asleep on the table and woke up screaming; 'Wiggling teeth!' We almost died laughing."

Ayan did her best to laugh quietly, but Laura didn't wake up. "Wish I was there. How is Quan, by the way?"

"He's awake, but tells me it'll be a while before he's fully recovered," Alice said. "Happy to be here, though he wants to talk to someone in Sciences as soon as you can set it up."

As Ayan agreed to have one of her senior research officers speak to him, Minh-Chu looked at Jake more closely. He was actually smiling. Alice and Carnie were in good spirits too, but she was leaning on him as though she could fall asleep any second. "So, there's good news?" Ashley asked tentatively when Ayan and Alice were finished talking for the moment.

Ayan nodded, stroking Laura's back as the little one continued to sleep peacefully. "It's almost all good. Laura didn't get a scratch, there's still another on the way, and I'm as healthy as ever. We lost two from the shuttle though. Everyone else is on their feet."

"I'm sorry to hear you lost people," Ashley said.

"We'll put their names up on the Squadron Room wall as honorary members of the Squadron. It's not much, but..." Minh-Chu said, trailing off, wishing he had time to do more.

"Thank you, Minh," Ayan said.

"Sorry again, but my curiosity is going to eat me alive if I don't ask," Ashley said, whispering, probably afraid to wake little Laura up. "Are you expecting a boy or a girl?"

"It's too early to tell," Ayan replied, brightening a little. "I was sure I'd wake up to discover that I lost it, so I'm only happy the newest in our family is healthy."

"I can imagine," Ashley said, her excitement brimming.

"I wish I could stay for a longer visit," Ayan said, momentarily looking at Jake. "But we're about to be transported. I won't be able to communicate for a couple of hours. We still don't know if or how well exactly the Edxi, and possibly their allies can track our new nodes."

"And that's why we're about to go into a comms blackout," Jake added.

A pair of fighters from the Merciless's squadron swept by then. They were giving Samurai Squadron some time off, taking care of the patrol for the next nine hours. They waggled for a second, the starfighter pilot version of waving to anyone who may be watching, then accelerated away. "Where are you off to?" Minh-Chu asked, fairly sure she couldn't tell him.

"A safe place," Ayan replied. "A mix of the Rangers and Fleet soldiers I picked and had re-vetted are taking us into hiding for a while. You'll hear from me, you just won't know from where. Controversy is coming. Fleet's investigation into the attack has turned up some uncomfortable realities. Much of the communications from the Science Minister's Office have been tracked. We don't know how many messages have been decrypted. It could be none, or all, from what we can tell."

"Nothing in the data we've stolen from the Order confirms that," Jake said calmly. "It's possible that they haven't been able to decrypt anything, we didn't get the intelligence we needed to prove it, or it was some local effort that didn't send information out of the Haven System."

"There are spies in Haven, and they're closer than we thought," Alice added. "That's the important part."

"So, I'm going into hiding. We're going to try to set my communications up so they're untraceable. If that works, I'll be able to take over Fleet Sciences completely."

"I thought you were creating a company?" Ashley asked.

"After I woke up from surgery there was a whole team of officers waiting to tell me about the holes in Haven Security that allowed the attack to happen. It's like no one wanted to apologize alone. Maybe that was the right move, now that I think about it. I had some harsh words, some of which I regret now, but they took me very seriously."

"She threatened to get the owners of the Haven System together so we could exercise our right to Full Reclamation, disbanding the government and turning every institution private so we would have full ownership. Oh, that would have included the military," Jake said with a touch of pride in his voice. "Oz and I were the first to signal that we'd agree to whatever she decided, which was enough to make the threat serious."

"I didn't have to contact you, but I would have if I decided to follow through," Ayan said, looking at Minh-Chu directly.

"Good to know," Minh-Chu replied, only feeling a little irritated at not being looped in. It was an easy thing to brush away, especially as he considered how little time he had to think about anything going on in the Haven System. He had been meaning to call his sister for days, nevermind government or corporate intrigue.

"I came to my senses before anything went too far, but still kept things up long enough to make sure they didn't think it was just a tantrum," Ayan said, blowing a curl of her red hair out of her face with a puff. "It was, and it wasn't, if I'm being honest. We worked hard to establish a democracy, so I didn't want to dismiss parliament, but the idea of assuming direct control over the military was something Oz and I agreed on."

"So he was able to get the Science Minister to vote on his side to go to war," Minh-Chu guessed.

"Exactly, but that was after I reached a compromise with the government. In trade for four percent of my stake in the solar system, I was given Haven Fleet Sciences. It's my organisation now, including the prototyping and manufacturing bases."

Minh-Chu smiled at that. The War Forge was a hidden military mobile space station that was larger than most base ships. It also had numerous ship manufacturing and maintenance areas built in, one of which was responsible for two of the Triton's refits. It had also been proven to be impenetrable, and that's where he suspected Ayan was taking Little Laura. If not, then he couldn't guess where they would go, and that was probably for the best. As far as Fleet Sciences was concerned, it was a department that Ayan was passionate about, and if he was understanding correctly, the new deal would allow her to keep working closely with the Triton and anyone she liked indefinitely. "Congratulations."

"Wait, I know we don't have much time, but is Fleet Sciences a company or a part of the government now? And do you get to have the final say on all the tech? Even weapons? Ships?" Carnie asked at a brisk pace while sounding as polite as he could.

"It's my company," Ayan replied with an approving smile. "And the Fleet isn't allowed to have a development or research arm because Fleet Sciences will do that for them from now on.

We'll be operating under a full reinvestment policy, meaning that everything we earn goes back into the company for the benefit of its employees and the progress we'll be making. I can use my personal wealth to build it even more. Everyone is getting a sizeable raise. The only real objection anyone had was against the establishment of Private Legions, which is about to become a sticky topic, I'm afraid."

"Because I'm about to register the first one," Jake replied, looking in Minh-Chu's direction.

"Private Legion?" Minh-Chu vaguely remembered something from his early school days. There was a period centuries before when warlords from several star systems were allowed to own and operate private military organizations that they'd hire out or use for their own ends. "That didn't work out well in a few corners of the galaxy, did it?"

"Well, no, Riz Taine was the big example, but no one's planning on going that route. No genocidal psychopaths allowed," Jake replied. "It's just a way for me and anyone else to set things up so..." Jake started searching for a way to phrase his idea.

Alice perked up just enough to finish his thought for him. "...so he can keep us all in one military organization, capture things under the Triton's banner, buy and sell bulk stuff. It's just a big streamlining thing. There's even a retirement plan."

"Sounds fine, and I'll make sure you don't go full psycho," Minh-Chu said, crossing his eyes for a moment. "I've had experiences with therapists, they've told me what to watch for."

"I'll take that deal," Jake replied. "I've already set up my Captains so I can take missions of my own without worrying about things falling apart when I'm gone. This is the last step. We'll be shoulder to shoulder with Fleet Sciences too. I can turn any team in Triton Legion into an exploration unit at a moment's notice."

"The Raven," Carnie said. "Remmy's built for that."

"Exactly," Jake and Ayan said at the same time.

"I wouldn't mind going on a few exploration missions either," Minh-Chu said, a smile growing. Ashley was starting to grin too. "I don't mind a few hours of scanning, maybe setting down on a rock somewhere to check out the local geology. I know, I know, not something that this crazy pilot is known for, but give me a chance. My pilots are pretty smart."

"Well, we'll be doing plenty of things in the shadows, now that the Fleet is going to be joining the war," Jake said. "Most of our work will be the kind of thing I'm going to need Samurai Squadron for. You're going to need more pilots. It'll help if they know a little about exploring and investigating. You know, which way to hold a hand scanner, that kinda thing. I've had trouble finding enough soldiers with the training for my own team, otherwise I wouldn't mention it."

"Yeah, yeah, I'll play some of the classic exploration training vids from Freeground. The 'Buffet or Bassinet?' video is always a huge hit, as long as you remember the barf bags," Minh-Chu replied.

"Huh?" Ashley asked, her eyes wide with alarm.

"Oh, it's this old diplomacy training video with really good special effects that they stopped showing a long time ago," Minh-Chu.

"The full title is; "Buffet or Bassinet? A Critical Mistake!' and I saw it during Apex Training," Alice explained, sighing as she added; "It's gross. I don't think it's based on a real story."

"It is, my Mother told me about it when I graduated as a

cadet and was moving on to the adult Fleet Academy," Ayan said with a little satisfaction. "But it was a very long time ago, before Freeground stopped exploration. You should definitely show it to your squadron. It's a reenactment, so none of it's real, but I'd love to see their reaction. Besides, if it happened once, causing a huge diplomatic incident, then we should make sure it never happens again." She shuddered before going on. "It's almost time for me to go, but I wanted to say I miss you all. We'll find a way to be together again soon."

"We will," Jake said gently, but with certainty.

"Just imagine a day when we've come clear of all this, and we're together, exploring more often than fighting," she said. "My love to all of you, and everyone else who I can't reach."

They each took a moment to say goodbye, expecting that they'd be back in touch with her soon, but in no way certain of it. If Ayan went into hiding and couldn't misdirect anyone who tried to trace communications back to her, then there wouldn't be many if any messages coming back from her for a long time.

It was a thought that Minh-Chu kept to himself, but he was relieved to hear that Ayan would be going somewhere safe. She was the smartest of them, and she carried the next generation with her. There was promise in that.

AFTERWORD

This book benefited from a great deal of Subscriber feedback and I'm more grateful than I can say. At a rate of nearly two chapters a week, they watched the story unfold, and were kind enough to point out typos and offer other comments as the story progressed. Something interesting started to happen along the way.

There is something about this book in particular that made me feel like I was more in sync with the people reading the early version. A few readers started to tell me what they really wanted to see happen and I could look up at my whiteboard and see that it was already planned. That is, unless the chapter they wanted to see wasn't already written. In the case of the second-to-last chapter, which I like to call The Wake, Easy's speech had been written for months. The whole chapter was built around it.

That's not to say that there weren't unpredictable things in there. The success of a story isn't based on whether or not it includes only things people expect or want, and I like to keep everyone guessing at least a little.

Looking back on Samurai Squadron II, I'm glad I was able to squeeze everything I had planned for it in, and I'm proud to present it as the middle book in a trilogy. Samurai Squadron III is already in the works, and the first chapters will appear on Patreon on November 7, 2023. This truly is a finale in Space Opera fashion, as the war ramps up and enemies face off. Other mysteries will be solved, but I'm not going to spoil anything for you.

Thank you so much for buying this book, or supporting me on a subscriber platform or both. It has been a difficult year in some ways, but a very good one in others thanks to you and the people around me who offer support as they prove that patience truly is one of the highest virtues.

I'll see you around the Fringe,
Randolph Lalonde

Watch for news and follow the serialized version of Spinward Fringe on Ream Stories: https://reamstories.com/ randolphlalonde

www.ingramcontent.com/pod-product-compliance
Lightning Source LLC
Chambersburg PA
CBHW060806030726
47503CB00002B/351